WHAT A MAN NEEDS

Stuart grabbed her hand and led her toward the stairs. Charlotte picked up her skirt and ran after him, flushed and giddy. She felt young and reckless, having a clandestine rendezvous in the middle of the afternoon.

At the top of the stairs, he stopped suddenly, catching her shoulders and pushing her back against the wall. His mouth came down on hers, hot and demanding, and Charlotte melted.

"I have wanted you for so long," he whispered, his breath flowing over her skin. "Tell me you want me. I have to hear it . . ."

"I want you," she gasped as his fingers flew down the buttons at her back, then gathered the edge of her bodice and pulled it down . . .

Books by Caroline Linden

WHAT A WOMAN NEEDS*

WHAT A GENTLEMAN WANTS*

WHAT A ROGUE DESIRES*

A RAKE'S GUIDE TO SEDUCTION*

A VIEW TO A KISS

FOR YOUR ARMS ONLY

YOU ONLY LOVE ONCE

ONE NIGHT IN LONDON

BLAME IT ON BATH

THE WAY TO A DUKE'S HEART

LOVE AND OTHER SCANDALS

IT TAKES A SCANDAL

LOVE IN THE TIME OF SCANDAL

*Published by Kensington Publishing Corporation

What A Woman Needs

CAROLINE LINDEN

ZEBRA BOOKS
Kensington Publishing Corp.
http://www.kensingtonbooks.com

ZEBRA BOOKS are published by

Kensington Publishing Corp.
119 West 40th Street
New York, NY 10018

All Kensington titles, imprints, and distributed lines are available at special quantity discounts for bulk purchases for sales promotion, premiums, fund-raising, educational, or institutional use.

Special book excerpts or customized printings can also be created to fit specific needs. For details, write or phone the office of the Kensington Sales Manager: Attn.: Sales Department. Kensington Publishing Corp., 119 West 40th Street, New York, NY 10018. Phone: 1-800-221-2647.

First Printing: August 2005
ISBN-13: 978-1-4201-3751-4
ISBN-10: 1-4201-3751-4

eISBN-13: 978-1-4201-3752-1
eISBN-10: 1-4201-3752-2

10 9 8 7 6 5 4 3 2

Printed in the United States of America

To Eric,
for being just what this woman needs—
sometimes more, but never less.

Chapter One

Stuart Drake wasn't opposed to a plain bride, but he didn't want an ugly one. He didn't require a witty girl, but he couldn't bear a stupid one. Her disposition was negotiable, depending on her dowry, but he couldn't see himself tolerating a shrew. His single inflexible condition was wealth; tall or short, plain or pretty, sweet or sour, she must be rich, exceedingly rich if at all possible. If he had to marry for money, then by God, he meant to marry a lot of it.

He didn't think it would be difficult. What he had to offer a wife was not inconsequential: one of the oldest and most distinguished viscountcies in England, as soon as his grandfather and father shuffled off their mortal coils. Granted, it might be years before his wife lived as Viscountess Belmaine in the fine house at Barrowfield, but barring his own death it was an absolute certainty, and when the title came, it would bring enough wealth and status to satisfy any female.

Fortunately he had come across a fine girl at what passed for a ball here in the wilds of Kent. Miss Susan Tratter, and her fortune of twenty thousand pounds, was everything he was looking for in a bride. She was pretty, in the rather pale tradition of English girls; clever, at least enough to sneak away from her chaperone for private strolls on the terrace; and more than wealthy enough. She was quite simply perfect, as well as completely infatuated with him almost from the moment they met.

The only obstacle to his courtship was her guardian. Susan was convinced her guardian, who was also her aunt, didn't want any joy in her life. Aunt Charlotte had traveled all around the Continent in her youth, but refused to take Susan even to London. Aunt Charlotte had kept company with any number of men when she was young—scandalous men, even—but refused to allow Susan to take so much as an afternoon drive with a gentleman. And, most damningly of all, Aunt Charlotte wore anything she wanted, much of it highly inappropriate for a woman of her age and widowed status, yet forced Susan to dress like a child in plain, girlish frocks that weren't at all fashionable. Aunt Charlotte, in fact, did Stuart's cause a world of good, all the more so by being out of town and leaving only a hired companion to chaperone her niece. In her absence, Stuart was free to console and sympathize until he found himself on the brink of a marriage proposal he knew would be accepted.

That was perhaps part of the problem, he reflected one evening. There had been nothing challenging about his pursuit, and Stuart could never believe it when anything fell into his lap so easily. He was always certain the benefits would be offset by some hidden deficiency. Now that he had Susan Tratter, he was beginning to doubt he wanted her. On the surface he did, no question. His father had cut off his funds and told him not to come back, an action Stuart still thought way out of proportion even to his supposed offense, let alone to the truth. There was no way he could possibly earn enough in time to satisfy his banker, even had he had a profession. Marrying an heiress was the quickest, easiest way out of his financial problems—or so he had thought.

He sighed and resumed pacing the Kildairs' library. This was supposed to be his triumphant hour. Aunt Charlotte had returned to town, and tonight he would meet her, charm her, and ask for her niece's hand in marriage. Susan would accept his formal offer tomorrow, and within a month he would be a wealthily married man, no longer subject to his father's rigid dictates and an object of amusement to the gossips. He would be financially secure for the first time in his adult life, and should be reasonably content; Susan was a nice girl, and he was sure they would get on well enough. But even though Stuart couldn't quite put his finger on it, there was just something . . . wrong.

He reminded himself that he was mad to reconsider now. He ought to be happy the plan had gone so well instead of questioning the plan itself. If only it were done already, and he didn't have the luxury of wondering whether it was the right thing and not simply the least objectionable thing. He forced aside his doubts as the door clicked open behind him.

Susan hurried forward, wringing her hands. "Oh, Drake!" she said with a little sob. "What are we going to do?"

"Come, my dear," he said in surprise, taking her hand. "What's the trouble?"

"It's Aunt Charlotte," she wailed, gazing up at him

with wet eyes. "She'll never let us marry, never! She's a spiteful, dried-up old witch!"

Stuart's eyebrows shot up. "I've not even asked for your hand yet. How can you know she'll refuse?"

"Because I hinted you were going to ask, and she told me she wouldn't allow it. She said terrible things about you—as if she would have the slightest idea, when she's never even met you. Please, Drake, please, say we shall run away together! I'll go with you tonight, I will!"

"That would ruin your reputation," he reminded her. "I don't want to do that to you."

"I don't care!" She flung herself on his neck, sobbing loudly now. Stuart patted her back for a moment, suppressing another sigh. Everything would be fine if only she'd let him handle things instead of rushing off to bungle them by herself. What had she accomplished by telling her dragon of an aunt they wanted to marry? Nothing good; now the woman had made up her mind against him without even the courtesy of meeting him. While he still had every confidence he could persuade her—elderly ladies were always impressed by a title, even a future one, and Stuart did move in the most elegant circles in London—it would have been far easier had he taken her by surprise.

"Come, calm yourself," he said when the sobs seemed to be dying down. He extricated her arms from around his neck. "You must put on a cheerful face and go back to the party."

She sniffed and rubbed her face with the handkerchief he offered. "A sad face is the least of my problems, thanks to her. I can't imagine what my papa was thinking, to make her my guardian."

"None of that is within our control, so we must

simply try to make the best of it. You promised to introduce me this evening; let me meet her, and see if I can charm away her doubts."

"Oh, Drake." She hiccupped. "If anyone could do it, you could, but I think even you will find her as receptive as a stone."

"Are you implying my charm can't touch a stone?" he demanded lightly. She smiled up at him, starry-eyed.

"Well, perhaps. Come, I'll introduce you, and if she doesn't consent tonight, we can run away tomorrow."

Not bloody likely, Stuart thought as he chuckled for her benefit. He couldn't afford to marry her without her dowry, and it would serve neither of them to elope into poverty. She hesitated, then leaned forward slightly, her lips pursing in his direction. He almost recoiled in alarm, then recovered enough to kiss her lightly on the forehead. Her mouth turned down in disappointment. "Not until you are my wife," he whispered. "It would be improper."

She brightened. Stuart felt another pang of misgiving. It was frankly embarrassing how quickly she had fallen for him, how open she was about her infatuation. It only served to remind him how young and innocent she was.

He couldn't do it. He hadn't committed himself yet, he could still walk away. She would feel hurt and misled, as she had been, but he would still be free . . . free to watch everything he had slip away. Stuart gave himself a mental shake. Oakwood Park needed only another year or two to become profitable, and Stuart refused to let it go now without exhausting every possible salvation.

He had discovered the modest estate last spring.

The house was a wreck, with a leaky roof and a crumbling east wing, but it still had a certain charm, and Stuart could see renovating it into a very comfortable manor—for a sizable sum of money, of course. The real draw, though, was the land itself: gently rolling hills, prime forest, and the richest soil he had ever seen. Though not large, the property would more than support itself, if properly managed. Stuart had borrowed the entire purchase price from a friend and bought it four days later. Then he had turned around and mortgaged it to pay back his friend, and borrowed some more to get the estate running again. For over a year he had been pouring everything he had into Oakwood Park, growing more and more attached to it and to what it meant for his life. Stuart was tired of being dangled on a string by his father; with his own estate he would be a landed, respectable, independent gentleman. Unfortunately, he needed money to pay the mortgage until the farms were profitable, and his father had suspended his only income without warning. If he didn't marry Susan, he would marry another heiress, and nothing would be different except that he would have wasted this time courting her. He couldn't back out now.

Stuart reached into his pocket. If he gave her the ring, he would be as good as engaged. "I cannot bear to see you sad. Perhaps this . . ." He unfolded his hand to show her. "Perhaps this will bring a smile to your face," he whispered. "It will be yours tomorrow. I have great confidence in my persuasive ability."

Her blue eyes opened wide, and her lips parted in a soundless gasp. "Oh, Drake," she breathed. "Really?" Stuart nodded. She took the ring reverently, cradling it in her cupped hands. "It's beautiful." She looked up, her eyes swimming with tears again. Stuart touched one finger to her lips.

"Now go back to the ballroom, my dear. Your aunt will be missing you."

She smiled, holding the ring close to her bosom. "I am sure she'll consent. And if she doesn't, we shall run away at once. I would do anything to be with you."

"Go on," he said gently. "But it must be a secret until tomorrow. Your aunt might not appreciate it, and we must do what we can to secure her blessing."

She nodded, looking as if she would throw herself into his arms again, but then turned and slipped out the door. He smiled until she was gone, then dropped into a nearby chair the instant the door closed.

The whole thing made him feel vaguely pathetic. Here he was, a grown man, strong in body and sound in mind, reduced to charming a young miss barely out of the schoolroom. He told himself that if he had already inherited his title, young misses would be lining up to be charmed, heiresses and otherwise, and society would applaud the one who caught *him.* There was absolutely nothing exceptional about his actions. Stuart told himself this even as he knew it was different, to him at least. It was one thing to marry well, and another to marry well because the alternative was ruination. Stuart had never liked being cornered.

But the die was cast now. He had declared himself, and given her his mother's ring, the one thing he wouldn't sell to support himself or Oakwood Park. Although, in a way, it felt as if he had just sold something dearer than a ring.

He leaned forward, reaching for the decanter on the table close at hand. He needed a drink before going out to charm grumpy old Aunt Charlotte. Perhaps two drinks.

"Has she gone? Goodness, the child belongs on the stage." Stuart nearly choked on his brandy at the husky voice, tinged with amusement. He swung around and peered into the shadows.

"Eavesdropping, madam?"

"I didn't plan to," she said with a low laugh, coming forward. "I only sought a quiet moment alone with my thoughts. Libraries are usually quiet, are they not?" She stepped into the light, and Stuart's interest came to full alert in an instant.

Dark curls gleamed mahogany in the candlelight, diamonds glittering in their midst. Her skin was as golden as her gown, giving the material the appearance of being transparent. In fact, it almost was transparent, as he could clearly see when she crossed in front of the lamp, revealing the curves underneath the silk. A long, narrow shawl draped over and around her shoulders, drawing attention to the swell of her breasts, full, enticing breasts that swelled above a tiny waist and made her rounded hips all the more voluptuous. She strolled into the light, stopping in front of the lamp and leaning back against the table. She braced her hands on either side of her hips, and tilted her face up to his. Stuart realized he had come to his feet without thinking.

A smile lit her face. It was a beautiful face, even without the smile, but that mischievous look made her entrancing.

"I don't believe we've met," he said, his senses sharpening. This sort of woman was much more to his liking.

Another mysterious smile. "No, we have not, Mr.

Drake." He considered her a moment longer, then put down his glass.

"How flattering that you know who I am. How I wish I could return the favor."

"Oh, I daresay we would have met eventually. The society in Kent at this time of year is rather limited." There was a suggestive lilt in her voice. Stuart could hardly believe his ears.

"That is not altogether a bad thing. Often I find myself wishing to limit my society to one person entirely."

She arched her brow, dipping her head in a thoroughly seductive way. "Do you? How very decadent."

His blood thrumming with excitement, he moved a little closer. She didn't retreat at all. "Do you like decadence?"

Her laugh was throaty. "I've known a bit in my day," she admitted. "But what would your betrothed think?"

He paused, disconcerted, then remembered Susan Tratter. "She's not my betrothed."

"But you do plan to marry her?" The mystery woman twined one finger in the lone curl lying across her shoulder.

"That's surely a private matter, isn't it?" Stuart leaned against the table beside her, not wanting to discuss his marriage plans. Her pose emphasized her bosom, and Stuart couldn't stop himself from admiring it.

She tilted her head toward him, with another coquettish smile. "I just wondered. She seems to think you do, although I admire your forbearance in refusing to run off with her."

He smiled, no longer caring what they talked about. He wasn't accustomed to flirting so aggressively with someone he didn't know at all, but if she was willing, so was he. Being seduced by a mysterious beauty would do a great deal to restore his humor this evening. His country exile looked suddenly brighter; even wooing old Madame Dragon wouldn't be half as dreadful with this lovely piece on the side. He wondered if she was widow or matron, and why the hell he hadn't met her before. "What is your name?"

Her smile faded. "Does it really matter?"

He met her smoldering glance with one of his own. "I would like to know it."

"Sometimes, don't you think things like names and station are irrelevant? Sometimes, isn't it only important what we desire deep in our hearts?" she whispered, her dark eyes glowing with intensity.

For a moment neither moved; Stuart could not recall when he had been so aware of a woman, so hot with desire for someone he hadn't even met ten minutes ago. He wanted her, as much as he had ever wanted any woman, and unless he read every sign wrong, she wanted him, too. "No," he whispered back, leaning closer. "Sometimes it really doesn't matter at all."

Just before his lips met hers, she turned away, trailing her fingers along the polished surface of the table as she walked. "I find myself wondering what you see in the girl. She seems far too . . . innocent?" Her shawl slipped from one shoulder, artlessly. Entranced, Stuart followed, toward the darker end of the library. "I never understand what men see in children. I find it quite off-putting."

He stopped her by catching the edge of the shawl, his fingers brushing her bare shoulder. She smelled of something foreign and exotic, not the usual rosewater English girls drenched themselves in. Did she taste as warm and spicy as she smelled? He was suddenly wild to find out. "You are not a child."

She laughed softly. "Certainly not." She took another step forward without turning around. Stuart kept his hold on the shawl, and it slid over her shoulder with a whisper.

"What a lovely gown." She took another step. The shawl tightened across her body, leading his eyes over very pleasing contours. Stuart let it drop to the floor as the end slid free. She glanced over her shoulder, her eyes gleaming.

"Thank you. You didn't like my shawl, I take it."

"Indeed," he murmured. He touched one finger to the nape of her neck and let it drift down the furrow of her spine, bumping over the buttons he was already thinking of unfastening. "I could hardly bear the sight of it." A slight tremor shook her shoulders, and white-hot desire roared through his veins. He slid his palms up her arms, easing her back until she was almost against his chest.

With one movement, she ducked her shoulder out from under his hand and stepped away, taking three short steps to the sofa. "Isn't your fiancée waiting for you?" she asked teasingly.

Stuart shrugged, not at all upset by the progress she was leading him on. "We are not formally betrothed."

She studied him, an odd little smile playing around her lips. "You'll break her heart."

He stopped, took a deep breath. "Not by design."

"Ah." She nodded sagely, and sank down on the sofa in a flowing motion, reclining against the side and casting one arm above her head to toy with the dark curls. "But you don't love her. Is it only desire that drives you into her arms, then?"

It was desire hammering away at his gut right now, screaming inside his head to spread himself on top of her and accept the invitation in her eyes. "No, not at all."

She crossed her legs with a flick of one ankle that belled out her skirt for a moment. That foot continued to swing, drawing his attention to her legs. Legs explicitly outlined by thin silk. Was this woman wearing any undergarments at all? Stuart lowered himself to the sofa beside her. "What did you intend, when you spoke to me a moment ago?"

Her smile was arch. "To meet you."

Better and better. He braced one hand beside her head, and when his face was merely an inch from hers, whispered, "Let us become acquainted, then."

"Oh, I am already acquainted with you," she purred. He tried to capture her lips, but got her cheek instead. "You have already proved yourself everything I thought you to be."

He laughed against her hair, nuzzling her ear. "And the night is only beginning." He brushed the loose curl back over her shoulder, letting his fingers linger on the slope of her shoulder, tracing the neckline of her gown. She stopped his hand there.

"And are the things you've heard about me true, Stuart?"

He paused. Her chest was rising and falling rapidly under his hand, but the teasing note was gone from her voice. "I do not know who you are," he said in a cooler tone. "And I begin to wonder what you've heard of me."

"You do not know my name, and yet I think you

would make love to me if I released your hand. Am I right?" He said nothing, and she moved, rubbing her hip against his erection. "Your silence speaks louder than words."

"Who are you?" he demanded, rolling completely on top of her. Her eyes widened for a fraction of a second, then became hard and opaque again. She didn't move, and even though the feel of her body under his sharpened the desire coursing through him, he ignored it in a belated burst of suspicion. Who was this woman, and why was she here in the library, waiting to lead him on like this? "What exactly do you believe you know about me?"

"Why, Stuart," she said softly, "I've heard as much about you as you've heard about me. Do you want to make love to me? Would you be curious to learn my name after? Or would you go back to the party in search of still another woman to seduce?"

"If anyone seduced, you did," he growled. "What game are you playing?"

"I told you." She smiled again, sly and triumphant. "I was curious about you. I came to the library to think, before meeting you. Because we were destined to meet this evening, you know; Susan told you so herself."

He stared at her, unmoving. Her smile widened.

"I am Charlotte Griffolino," she whispered. "Spiteful, withered, stone-hearted old witch. As well as Susan Tratter's guardian."

He released her hands. "You can't be. Her aunt is old."

She lifted one shoulder. "In Susan's eyes, I am, having celebrated my thirtieth birthday this spring."

Stuart said nothing; she was only two years younger

than he was. A terrible fury knotted in his chest. Susan had deceived him about her aunt—frightful old crone, indeed—and her aunt had deceived him about her true identity. And now he had lost all chance of Susan Tratter—and her fortune. He sprang to his feet.

"You must be quite pleased with yourself."

"In what way? To have learned beyond a shadow of a doubt that my niece has fallen prey to an adventurer? That the man who nearly ruined two other young heiresses in London nearly ruined my own brother's daughter, while she was in my care? No, I am far from pleased."

"You deceived me!" He thrust his finger in her face.

She lifted one eyebrow. "Mr. Drake, I never said anything to encourage you."

Stuart shook with the force of his anger. She damned well had led him on, knowing exactly who he was when she invited him to make an advance, deliberately entrapping him. "You knew who I was!"

She laughed at him. "And I told you so, didn't I?" In a flash, he caught her arm. He wanted to shake her and punish her, and he still wanted to make love to her. He settled for the shake, but ended up dragging her against him.

Her eyes searched his, superior and disdainful. "Stooping to forcing yourself upon a woman?"

He released her in a heartbeat. "I have never forced myself on a woman. You invited me."

Her eyebrow arched mockingly. "Did I? The way Miss Eliza Pennyworth invited you to take her driving from London to Dover? The way Miss Anne Hale invited you to molest her in her own grandmother's garden?"

Stuart swore. "You know nothing about what happened to either of those two young ladies. I never ruined them."

"No, not at all. Tales of their disgrace reached the wilds of Kent purely by chance."

Stuart seethed. The gossips had seized hold of two incidents that were only unfortunate in their timing—mere days apart—and convicted Stuart of worse sins than he had ever committed. That gossip in turn had sent his father into a fury, and led to his banishment. But this woman made it sound as though he deliberately debauched innocent maidens for sport. "I have nothing more to say to you." He turned toward the door.

"I am very glad to hear it," she said behind him. "Do show some trace of decency and leave without speaking to Susan again."

Stuart stopped, one hand on the doorknob. He should do it, turn the knob and leave without a word to anyone, especially Susan. But he had never been able to leave without the last word, had never had the discipline to keep his mouth shut when all reason dictated it was best, particularly when his temper was raised. There was nothing to be gained by taunting this woman . . . and yet . . . "She pleaded with me to run off with her."

There was a rustle behind him, a shrug, no doubt. "You won't agree." Damn, but he hated that faintly patronizing tone, from his father and now from her. Especially from her, especially now.

Still holding the knob, he turned slowly. In the dim firelight, she looked warm and golden, just the slightest bit rumpled, as if recently from a lover's embrace.

Thwarted lust mixed with anger in a dangerous combination. "You're very sure of yourself."

She tilted her head, studying him thoughtfully. "Yes. Or rather, I am very sure of men like you."

"Oh?" Stuart hated few things more than being taken lightly, dismissed out of hand and relegated to some category beginning with "men like you."

"Why is that?" he asked.

She smiled, her full mouth pulled down in scorn. "Because you haven't the slightest interest in Susan, even though you've seduced her into thinking she loves you. It's all about her money, and if you run away with her, you'll not have a single shilling. I can and will assure it."

"You would deny your own niece the comforts she's accustomed to, just to spite me? How loving, Aunt Charlotte."

She shrugged at his sarcasm. "What would you have me do, admit to soft-heartedness when it will give you license to do as you wish? Do you think me simple? Don't ever mistake me that way again, sir; my heart is as cold and as unmoving as marble. The day you take Susan for your wife, I'll invest her every pound in long-term ventures in places you'll never track down if you spend the rest of your days looking."

"It is her inheritance," he reminded her.

She collected her shawl from the floor and draped it lightly over one shoulder, catching the other end around her elbow. "Left in my care, by her father. George would agree wholeheartedly with my decision. He abhorred fortune hunters as the lowest creatures on earth. They care nothing for stealing a young girl's hopes and dreams, crushing her heart and leaving her reputation in tatters. Her life means nothing to them. It's all a grand illusion, and when it ends they are in possession of a fortune they did nothing to earn and a wife they cannot abide."

Stuart closed his fists. "You judge me quite harshly. Is your niece allowed no say in the matter of her own heart?"

"If her heart has chosen you, it's made a grave mistake, one she'll thank me some day for preventing." She picked up a fan from a nearby table and flicked it open, waving it once before closing it with a snap. "You were on your way, I believe."

He let out his breath in a gust. She was right; he should be on his way. He had only come tonight to meet and woo Susan's aunt, which was obviously out of the question now. The bitterness of how close he had come to his goal struck him then, and Stuart cursed himself for letting a woman cloud his mind. Whatever doubts he might have had about marrying Susan, she was by far the nicest, most suitable girl he had met so far.

"Yes, I am," he said at last. "But don't think our paths won't cross again."

Straightening her shawl, she barely glanced at him. "I hardly care whether they do or not, Mr. Drake."

"But I do," he murmured. "Very keenly."

Charlotte ignored his last veiled threat. The door closed behind him, and she calmly finished untangling her shawl.

"That was not a nice trick to play on him," said a voice from the shadows.

Charlotte shrugged. "It was no more than he deserved. A man of honor wouldn't have rushed to the assumptions he did."

"Cara, only a man with no blood in his veins would not have made his assumption."

Charlotte fussed some more with her shawl, ignoring Lucia's dry comment. It was not Lucia's niece hovering on the brink of calamity, and therefore it was not Lucia's place to criticize Charlotte's actions. "Nevertheless, it only confirms my suspicions about him. He doesn't care a fig for Susan or her feelings if he would make love to another woman the moment her back is turned."

A thin plume of smoke wafted through the drapes that screened the terrace doors. "I do not think it was a good idea. That one will not take well to being fooled."

"I don't think it's a good idea for you to smoke, Lucia," she replied testily. "It's not good for your voice. I must see to Susan. Shall you come with me?"

"No, I think not." She blew more smoke. Charlotte waved one hand in protest, starting toward the door. "He is not as you told me he would be," Lucia said just as Charlotte put her hand on the knob. "I hope you do not underestimate him."

Charlotte paused. Stuart Drake was more dashing than she had expected, it was true; there was a feeling of pent-up energy and recklessness that made his charming smile and manner all the more tantalizing. What really lay beneath the gentlemanly veneer? It was a veneer, Charlotte was sure. She had known more devils in angels' garb than she could count, and Stuart Drake's halo radiated falseness. The way he had rolled on top of her, simultaneously exciting and alarming . . . Some women—and some girls—might find that attractive, but Charlotte knew better.

"No, he is just like every other man," she said, only adding very quietly, almost to herself, "fortunately."

She walked down the hall to the large drawing room where the rest of the guests were, summoning a gracious smile for her hostess. Lady Kildair beamed in reply; Charlotte knew it was craven delight at getting someone as scandalous as Charlotte and someone as rich as Susan in her drawing room. Those qualities tended to bring out the eligible gentlemen, something Lady Kildair would sell her left arm to do with three unmarried daughters of her own in the house.

Charlotte paused in the doorway, searching openly for Susan and covertly for Mr. Drake. She found him first; odd, since he was almost completely behind another gentleman. He looked younger than she had first thought, but undeniably handsome, with dark hair and eyes and a tall, athletic body that even now sent a strange shiver up her spine. *Because the man would have assaulted you on a library sofa,* she reminded herself, just as he glanced over his companion's shoulder and met her gaze.

She didn't move, just stood there, without a smile or a sniff or a melodramatic toss of her head. No sign that she feared him, just that she saw him. His gaze was dark, displeased but not defiant. Neither looked away, until the air between them seemed to sizzle with the ferocity of feeling on both ends.

"Aunt Charlotte?" She turned away immediately.

Susan was beside her, plucking at the fringe of her shawl.

"Yes, dear?" She smiled at her niece. "Are you enjoying the ball? I went out to get a breath of air."

"Yes, I noticed you were gone." Susan looked a touch guilty, as she should, having sneaked off to meet a scoundrel. "Did Lucia leave?"

Charlotte laughed. "No, heavens, she's trying to assassinate Lady Kildair's garden with those cigarettes."

Susan wrinkled her nose. "They are quite vile." A giggle burst out of her, and she stifled it with a nervous glance. "I'm sorry, that was rude."

"Well, the truth often is." Charlotte tucked her hand around Susan's arm. "Come, shall we have some champagne?"

"Really? May I?" Her niece brightened. "Papa never let me have champagne except on very special occasions."

Charlotte felt tonight qualified as such. "Let's treat ourselves, shall we?" Susan nodded eagerly, and they headed for the refreshments.

Charlotte, fond aunt that she was, thought Susan quite pretty. She had hair the color of ripe wheat, without any of the curl that plagued Charlotte's own hair, and clear blue eyes. But Charlotte was also objective enough to realize that Susan wasn't, and probably never would be, considered beautiful, at least by the world in general. Still, she was determined to see Susan wed to someone who cared for her happiness, as well as for his own.

It wasn't until they were sipping their champagne, watching the floor clear for dancing, that Susan brought up the topic Charlotte knew had been on her mind all evening. She knew not only from the bits of conversation she had overheard earlier, but from all the clumsy intimations Susan had made over the last few days about a wonderful gentleman she'd met, and wouldn't Charlotte be so happy for her when she married? In many ways Susan was still a stranger to her, but in this she had been completely transparent.

"Aunt Charlotte, you always said I could speak to you about anything," Susan began, her voice a little higher pitched than usual. "There—there is something I would like to tell you."

"Of course, dear, what is it?" Charlotte saw him approaching from the corner of her eye. Oh dear, he wouldn't go quietly. Susan gulped some more champagne, her eyes flitting toward him on every other word.

"I'm not a child anymore," she said in a rush. "I am almost eighteen, old enough to know my own heart, and I have met the man I intend to marry."

"Ah."

Susan looked momentarily surprised by her meek reply. "Please don't stand in my way. I love him and I want to marry him. Papa wanted me to be happy, and Mr. Drake will make me happy."

"Susan, I don't think this is the proper time or place," said Charlotte gently. Why couldn't the wretched man simply leave? Susan would be hurt, but at least it would spare them all a public scene. A confrontation in Lady Kildair's ballroom would only humiliate Susan as well as break her heart.

"Please meet him, Aunt Charlotte." Susan faced her with wide, intent eyes, her spine straight and her hands clenched. "Please listen to his suit."

Charlotte hid her sinking heart behind a serene face. "If you wish, dear." And then he was before her again, just as tall, just as devastating, just as wicked as before. Charlotte looked up, somewhat unsettled by the realization that he seemed even bigger and darker here than in the library. She had thought it all a trick of the light.

"May I present Mr. Stuart Drake," Susan was saying. "Mr. Drake, my aunt, the Contessa de Griffolino."

"Good evening." Charlotte inclined her head, and he bowed.

"Drake, I've told my aunt of how much we've come to care for each other," said Susan, becoming more nervous. "And that we wish to marry."

The man smiled at her, so warmly Charlotte could almost believe he meant it. "Indeed, you've stolen my best line."

Susan giggled, looking very, very young and vulnerable next to him. Charlotte's resolve firmed; over her dead body would this scoundrel marry her innocent niece. She adopted the cool, remote smile any Italian would recognize as a rebuff, wanting to tear a strip off his hide after all, scandal be damned.

"Perhaps you would honor me with a dance," Mr. Drake said, holding out his hand. "That I might argue my fitness for the honor of your niece's hand."

Charlotte looked at his hand, then at his face. The charming smile was still in place, but it didn't reach his eyes. She wasn't sure she wanted to put herself in his grasp again. Susan waited by his side, hands clasped in supplication. "Perhaps you would prefer to call," Charlotte said. "We will be at home tomorrow."

Susan caught her breath and turned anxiously to Mr. Drake, but his eyes never wavered from Charlotte's.

"No, I would prefer to dance. In truth, I cannot

wait until tomorrow. I would have my answer as soon as possible."

"Please, Aunt Charlotte?"

Charlotte hated him even more for the hope in Susan's voice. *You have already had your answer*, she promised him silently. Giving in, she handed her glass to Susan. "If you wish. Susan, will you wait for me?"

"Oh, yes!" Her niece beamed at both of them as Charlotte took his hand. Instantly his fingers closed over hers in a firm grip, and he led her to the center of the floor where couples were just gathering for the next dance.

"You are wasting your time." She adjusted her shawl to a more secure position and waited for the dance to start. He said nothing, but caught her hand and pulled her close, right into his arms. Charlotte barely managed to restrain her gasp. "What—?"

"The next dance will be a waltz," he said, refusing to let her back away. Around them, she saw other people eyeing them in surprise. The musicians hadn't started yet, and the waltz was still rare in the country. Very rare.

"It will not. This is Kent, not London." His arm was like iron around her. She pushed as inconspicuously as she could, with no effect. Everyone was staring at them still, and even though it made her wildly uneasy to be this close to him, she didn't want to cause a scene by struggling with him on the dance floor. She settled for pinching the inside of his thumb.

His smile was wolfish, and he simply squeezed her hand until she had to relent. "And Lady Kildair has just learned no hostess in London does not include at least one waltz. I gather our hostess doesn't wish to be countrified, even if she lives in the country."

"Persuading Lady Kildair to play a waltz does not improve your standing with me." The musicians were, in fact, beginning a waltz. She hadn't danced it in over a year, but soon found it hardly mattered. He was a dominant partner, leading her through the steps with a forceful control Charlotte disliked. Even allowing for the fact that they were moving completely as one, she hated being steered along almost without any effort or will on her part. "You needn't turn so hard," she snapped. "I know the steps."

He quirked an eyebrow. "My apologies. Perhaps you would like to lead as well?"

"Mr. Drake," she said coldly, "I did not wish to dance at all. You have already had your answer to your suit. Leading Susan on in this manner will only make it harder on her when you leave."

"You're very sure I'm going to turn tail and run at the first black look from you."

Charlotte was surprised into a short laugh. "Black look? Goodness, I thought it was so much more! Have I mistaken the matter? Are you in love with Susan after all?"

"No. I have never professed such a thing, not even to her." He was still smiling, the wretch. "Not everyone willfully misrepresents themselves."

"I did nothing of the sort. You assumed a great deal." Something changed in his face, slight but significant, and Charlotte felt suddenly even less in control. Her hand was still tight in his, his arm was around her waist, and he was moving her around the ballroom so effortlessly Charlotte was sure they would continue waltzing even if she stopped participating altogether.

"I assumed what a normal man would assume.

Surely you know that. Or perhaps you've never seduced a man before?"

"I didn't seduce you," she hissed, trying to wriggle her hand free. He refused to let go, and that unsettling light in his eyes burned brighter.

"Then you should learn not to tease a man. He might get the wrong idea."

"Oh, of course!" She pulled a face. "I might have known you would fail to comprehend what any sensible person would see at once. Let me make it clear, then: you shall never, under any circumstances, marry Susan. I hold fortune hunters in the lowest possible esteem. I will not change my mind."

"Every woman changes her mind, even, I daresay, withered old witches."

Charlotte jerked, but his grip tightened again. "You understand nothing of women if you think that."

He laughed under his breath. "I know a great deal about women."

"All men think that. Fools, every one."

"A fool for a woman? Why, yes, I believe most people would agree with that. I've been a fool for more than one woman, after all. I just can't help myself; I like them too much."

"Particularly those of good fortune."

Another wicked smile gleamed down at her. He was devilishly handsome with that smile. "Of course. Often it is a woman's finest attribute."

Charlotte gave him a condescending smile of her own. "Naturally. When that's all you want in a woman, it would of course be most important."

"Ah, but think of all it can atone for: a sour disposition, a shrewish temper, or looks fading with age." His hand shifted, as if he were testing her figure, and he cast an appraising glance downward. Charlotte went rigid.

"Release me at once," she said between clenched teeth.

"You," he said, his voice dangerously soft and calm, "are a hypocrite. You flaunt yourself to show how depraved *I* am, yet freeze up like an outraged virgin when someone else plays that same game. And yet, you're nothing like a virgin, are you?" Charlotte gasped in shock. He lowered his head to murmur the rest in her ear. "Don't think I consider this contest over. It's only begun."

Without regard for the social consequences, Charlotte drove the heel of her shoe into his toes, and whipped out of his grasp as he choked on a curse. The musicians were still playing, and although there were other couples on the floor, most of the guests were watching. In full view of eighty members of the best society Kent had to offer, Charlotte turned her back and walked away from a furiously angry Stuart Drake.

Chapter Two

They left the ball almost immediately. Susan was shocked speechless. The other guests had whispered in glee at the delicious scene unfolding before their eyes; it was Kent, after all, and there was precious little in the way of gossip. Aware of every glance of bewildered longing Susan cast at Stuart Drake, Charlotte wasted no time in marching her niece from the ballroom, feeling his eyes on her all the while. Lady Kildair came scurrying out to bid them farewell, blatantly prying for information. Charlotte put their hostess off, promising to call the next day and hoping she would have a story by then that would avert a scandal. Thankfully their carriage arrived quickly, and they even made it home before the argument started.

The instant they reached home, however, it quickly became a screaming row. "How could you do that to me? To him?" Susan cried. "You humiliated both of us!"

"Susan, dearest," said Charlotte, "he's not a respectable sort of man. You'll understand when you're older."

"Oh, oh!" Susan waved her hands. Her face was

blotchy pink, her voice high and shrill. "When I'm older! Because I'm so naïve now? I must be, if I don't see how *you* can be rude to anyone you choose and yet expect me to follow every silly rule about the color of my dress and the number of times I may dance with a gentleman!"

"He was insulting," Charlotte said evenly. "And rude."

"He wouldn't be!" Susan gulped back a sob, and pressed one hand to her stomach. "He's charming and polite to everyone, not just to me, and you must have said something to make him rude, if he was rude at all!"

"Do you think I'm lying?" Charlotte was indignant. "He's a rake. A rogue. He's not decent enough for you."

"He is, he is," wailed Susan, the very picture of misery. "I love him!"

"Susan, I only want—"

"I know what you want! You only want to ruin my happiness, so I'll end up as miserable as you are!"

Susan was hysterical, but it still stung. Charlotte lifted her chin and repressed a cutting reply.

"I won't, you know! I'm not going to wind up alone and bitter, too. I'm going to marry someone who will know how to be happy and have fun and enjoy life!"

"And I want to make certain you *will* be happy. He's a fortune hunter. What do you think life will hold for you, when he's spent your inheritance and you're both destitute?"

"You're just jealous!" Susan lashed out, tears quivering in her eyes. "He's handsome and charming and you're jealous because he's not paying attention to you! Does it hurt you so much that he might want to marry me instead? Why do you think the worst of every man who isn't cow-eyed at you?"

"Now, Susan," Charlotte began.

"I don't care, I don't care! I won't give him up, just because you don't like him. I love him and if you won't give him your consent, we'll wait until we don't need it!"

And pigs will fly, thought Charlotte. "If he waits three years to marry you, and his devotion never wavers, I'll withdraw my every complaint. But he won't wait," she said harshly, as disbelieving joy radiated from Susan. "He'll be gone before the end of the week, no doubt, now that he knows he won't be marrying an heiress any time soon."

"He does not want my money!" Susan looked appalled. "Just because you married for money doesn't mean everyone else does!"

Charlotte felt the blow very keenly, but she tried to hide it. Susan was not responsible for what she said in the heat of anger. "I think you should go to bed, and we can discuss this in the morning."

Susan's face crumpled. Charlotte, still battling her own temper, crossed her arms. "I'm sorry if I hurt you, but it's best that you face the truth about him." Susan covered her face with her hands, and her shoulders heaved. Charlotte felt a wave of sympathy, and laid a hand on her shoulder. "There, now, it will all end well," she said gently, but Susan shook her off.

"It will all end well for you, maybe," she choked. "Your life is over, so you've gone and ruined mine!"

"Oh, really!" Charlotte snapped. "That's quite enough."

"I hate you," sobbed Susan. "And I will never speak to you again!"

She didn't wait for a reply, but turned and ran from the room, leaving Charlotte to stare after her in mingled frustration and worry. What was wrong with the child? Susan was ignoring what anyone of sense could see. Stuart Drake was a fortune hunter; he had as good as admitted it. He didn't love Susan, only her money, and yet Susan clung to her irrational belief that he could make her happy. *Oh, Susan* . . . Charlotte sank into a chair, her anger melting away. How could she make Susan see reason before the scoundrel broke her heart?

She could tell Susan her beloved Mr. Drake had attempted to seduce her aunt. But he, no doubt, would manage to turn the tale to his own advantage and have Susan believe the worst of Charlotte instead. He had obviously taken the poor girl in quite thoroughly, and Charlotte sensed her best course was to say nothing more of him. Perhaps if Susan met a more suitable gentleman? Charlotte still shied away from London, but they might go to Bath, or to Brighton . . .

No. That would never do. God alone knew how determinedly he would pursue Susan and her inheritance, and Susan would focus all her resentment on Charlotte for taking her away from the man she foolishly loved. Charlotte would do anything to protect her niece, but she couldn't bear to have Susan hate her forever.

The front door opened, then closed, and a moment later Lucia came in, smelling of roses and Turkish tobacco. "What a night," she said breezily, settling into one of the large overstuffed chairs and kicking off her shoes. "Goodness, these parties are so dull, but the people here, they do have their charm."

Charlotte smiled half-heartedly. Lucia, who had

once been one of the brightest stars in Milan, renowned for her clear, light soprano, had become something of a minor celebrity in their short time in town, even though she could no longer sing in the manner that had made her famous all over Europe. Now that the war with Napoleon was over, there was a great demand in England for all things continental, even fading opera singers who had lost half their range.

"But you! You, *cara*, what a scene you left!" Lucia fished one of her small cigarettes from her bag. "I have yet to see such excitement in the English as you caused."

Charlotte rose with a swish of silk, pacing from the windows to the fireplace. "Susan says she will never speak to me again."

"Bah." Lucia lit her cigarette from a nearby candle, inhaling deeply. "Let her pout. It is good for a woman to know how to pout. Now it will not help her, but later, with a man . . ." Lucia nodded, gesturing with her cigarette. "So. What did he say?"

Charlotte frowned, and handed Lucia an ashtray. "Your voice will never recover as long as you smoke those."

Lucia blew a thin stream of smoke. "I haven't lost my voice, only my muse. When I find him, my voice will return."

Charlotte let it go. Lucia had always done just as she pleased, when she pleased. It was hardly Charlotte's place to badger her about either her voice or her belief that sexual satisfaction would bring it back. "He made no attempt to deny he's after Susan's money. He said a large fortune was often a woman's best asset."

"And a man's, as well," interjected Lucia with another nod. "One can hardly fault him for speaking truth. What else?"

Charlotte stopped at the window and pulled back the drape. "I told him I would never consent to the marriage, and he made the most insulting remarks about my fitness as Susan's guardian."

"Ahhh," said Lucia with increased interest. "What did he say?"

"He called me a hypocrite, and said I was no virgin."

"Well, this is true, is it not?" Charlotte glared at her. Lucia shrugged. "What man has any use for a virgin, anyway?"

Charlotte snorted. "Englishmen do. So long as they've money, at least." Then she sighed. "Perhaps I am a hypocrite—I did marry Piero for his money, in part—but I've learned from my mistakes. I'm just trying to keep Susan from making those same mistakes."

"You married Piero for his protection. And his money, of course, but think why he married you. Let us not even pretend he was man enough for a woman who could have been his granddaughter. He wanted a beautiful woman on his arm, and he got one. What would this Stuart Drake give Susan, besides his lovely self?"

"His grandfather is a viscount," muttered Charlotte, staring blindly out the window. Stripped to the bone like that, it didn't sound like a bad match: the handsome heir to a respectable title would be a fine catch for a girl whose father had been merely a gentleman. Only the details revealed the ugly truth.

"So she would be a lady someday, and he would be

rich now. What other sound reason do people have to marry?" Lucia took a long drag on her cigarette, waxing enthusiastic. "Such a pity it is the English feel compelled to marry to enjoy each other. It is much better to leave marriage out of the picture. Why tie yourself to one man when there are so many in the world?"

"Naturally I won't tell Susan your opinion," said Charlotte dryly. "She sees only one man right now."

Lucia laughed. It was the one time the glory of her lost voice shone through, and always made Charlotte a little bit sorry for introducing Lucia to the Turkish prince who had in turn introduced her to his tiny, addictive cigarettes. What a waste, for Lucia to smoke herself hoarse. "Well," said Lucia with a meaningful glance, "at least he is a delight for the eyes to see."

Charlotte refused to discuss that. No matter what Lucia thought, Stuart Drake was dangerous; Susan was an innocent, naive girl with romantic dreams of love, not a worldly woman who knew what men were really like. "Her infatuation wouldn't last a week if they were separated."

"What love affair would?" Lucia sat up, her face brightening. "If you do not wish to seduce him, perhaps I shall. Do you think that would help? I offer for Susan's sake, of course."

"No!" Charlotte didn't want to think about his hot mouth on Lucia's throat, his long fingers caressing Lucia's body. She stirred uncomfortably at the memory of his mouth on her throat, and his hands on her body. Then she forced herself to remember he had almost made love to her minutes after assuring Susan of his desire to marry her. Stuart Drake did not deserve to be seduced, he deserved to be shot.

"No, Lucia, I don't think that would help. Besides, he's too old for you."

"Oh? How old is—?"

"Older than I am," said Charlotte sharply. She was reasonably sure that was true, from his expression when she told him Susan considered thirty to be the brink of death. Lucia sat back, mildly disappointed, and Charlotte began pacing again, thinking furiously. Contrary to what Susan thought, Charlotte *did* remember what it was like to be seventeen and in love. Of course she also knew a great deal more about the world, and men, now, and couldn't possibly allow Susan to throw her heart away on a mercenary cad like Stuart Drake. She knew all too well the heartache and ruin that followed.

But she also knew Susan would resent any interference, particularly from her. Mr. Drake needed to go, and preferably on his own. If only some outside force would act on him and let him know he was no longer welcome in Tunbridge Wells. Surely there were others in town who would appreciate Charlotte's reasons for wanting rid of him, someone who could take actions Charlotte didn't dare try herself, for Susan's sake.

And then Charlotte stopped pacing, with a faint breath of relief. "No matter, Lucia; I have an excellent plan to deal with the charming Mr. Drake."

Stuart's morning was turning out to be almost as wretched as his previous evening had been. First, it was rent day, and his landlord had proven distressingly prompt in asking for his money; today, he required it before breakfast. Stuart counted it out with a pained sigh, trying not to think how depleted his funds were becoming. He had expected to have a wealthy bride, or at least a wealthy fiancée, by now, which would be enough to get credit from the suspicious merchant populace of Tunbridge Wells. If word got out that he was even further from solvency than he had been yesterday, they might start requiring payment in advance.

Second, the post brought another letter from his mother. Even though Stuart loved his mother dearly, he dreaded her letters. She never wrote a word of reproach, which only deepened his guilt at being such a disappointment to her. He had long since realized it was impossible to please his father, and had given up trying, but that had hurt his mother. Stuart no longer worried about his father's good opinion, but he did regret losing his mother's. He read her letter quickly, allowed himself a pang of remorse at leaving London for the two months a year she lived there, and then put the letter and its guilt aside.

Third, he discovered his fascination with Charlotte Griffolino hadn't died the sudden death it should have after she publicly cut him during the waltz. He had spent the rest of the evening thinking about her, mostly how he would like to paddle some manners into her perfectly rounded bottom. He had tried not to think too much about other perfectly rounded parts of her, with limited success, but the moment he saw her while out on his morning ride, that battle was lost.

He reined in his horse and watched her climb out of her open carriage and up the steps of the Kildair house. Even though she moved with the same sensual grace that had taken him in last night, today she was dressed more like a prim governess than a siren. Her dove-gray gown had a high neckline, long fitted sleeves, and an unadorned skirt, and she was most definitely wearing a petticoat. Her modest bonnet of pale blue framed her face almost angelically, and Stuart half-expected to see a prayer book clasped in her gloved hands. She was almost unrecognizable as the woman who had flirted with him in the darkened library last night.

Stuart frowned. There was something odd about that. He would bet his last borrowed farthing this wasn't her natural style. He watched as she was admitted to the house, more and more certain she was up to no good. Why he knew this, he couldn't say, but Stuart suddenly had to know what she was plotting. He ought to avoid the woman like the plague, and yet somehow, he just couldn't. He loosened the reins and touched his horse's flank before he could think better of it.

He tied the horse to a shady tree in the park just across from the Kildair house. Setting his hat at a jaunty angle, he strolled over to her carriage. The driver was drowsing on the seat, but snapped awake at Stuart's question. "I say, is this Madame Griffolino's carriage?"

"Aye," said the man without a trace of curiosity.

"I was just on my way to see that very lady; what a pity she shan't be at home to receive me." Stuart affected dismay. "Is she planning to pay several calls?"

"Don't know, guv." Stuart was sure the driver had been hired only for the season. He had employed many temporary servants himself, and knew the signs. The temptation was too much; he gave in to the urging of the devil on his shoulder.

"Aye, just the one." The driver caught Stuart's coin with practiced ease. "Told me to wait here, she did."

Stuart looked up and down the street, which was

growing more crowded as the fashionable hour for paying calls approached. "Bad for the horses to stand in the sun, don't you think?"

"Aye, but I've got my orders." Stuart flipped him another coin. The man slipped it into his pocket in the blink of an eye, and straightened in his seat. "'Course, can't have them standing too long. Blocking traffic and all."

"I quite agree," said Stuart. "A turn about the park should serve."

"G'day to you, guv." The man tipped his hat before snapping the reins. Stuart watched him drive away, a faint smile spreading across his face. Hopefully her expression would be worth the two shillings, for he really couldn't afford to waste them. He took up a position near the steps, and waited.

"Lady Kildair." Charlotte smiled tremulously at her hostess as she was shown into the drawing room. "I feared, after last night, you wouldn't receive me."

"Not at all, not at all," Lady Kildair said, hurrying forward. Her eager eyes took in Charlotte's subdued air. "Are you unwell? Do sit down and have some tea." She led Charlotte to a place on the sofa and took a seat nearby, pouring a cup. Charlotte took it, blinking rapidly.

"You are too kind. I . . . I must apologize to you for my actions last night. I never meant to cause a scene—" Charlotte broke off, pressing a handkerchief to her lips in mock distress. She drew a deep breath and turned back to her hostess, who was balanced precariously on the very edge of her seat, her curiosity almost tangible.

"My dear Contessa!" Lady Kildair reached out for her hand. "Whatever has upset you so? I declare, it was a trifle last night, not worthy of note." A bald-faced lie, but Charlotte simply nodded, pressing Lady Kildair's hand.

"You are too kind to say so. I expect it caused some comment, perhaps even outrage. Mr. Drake . . . Oh, I know he's been received as a most eligible gentleman. Naturally, no one had any idea he was not! But Lady Kildair, if you knew what I have heard of him—! And then to find my own dear Susan had fallen under his spell and was in danger of being compromised . . . It was too much for me, too much, and I lost my head. Do forgive me, please." She turned a pleading gaze on a severely disconcerted Louise Kildair.

"Why, Contessa." Lady Kildair cleared her throat. "Whatever can you mean? Do you mean to say that Mr. Drake is a . . . ?"

Charlotte closed her eyes and inhaled sharply, as if the mention of the word would be painful, and Lady Kildair obligingly stopped. Charlotte waited a heartbeat, then nodded heavily.

"Yes. I have been in London this past fortnight settling affairs in Italy for myself and Madame da Ponte. I did not go out much in society, for there was a great deal to be done regarding my late husband's estate, but even in my limited circle of acquaintance I heard of Mr. Drake."

She paused again, and Lady Kildair clucked in sympathy and urged her to take some tea. Charlotte sipped, letting her hostess wait in suspense. So far it was going beautifully.

"And what I heard was terrible. He is reputed to be

a rogue of the basest nature: always in debt, notorious for his gambling, associating with the most scandalous people. And the worst . . . Oh dear, I can scarcely bring myself to say." Charlotte shook her head again, biting her lip as if tears threatened.

Lady Kildair sprang forward. "But his family! So well-connected and respected!"

"His family," interrupted Charlotte, "has cast him out. His father has banished him from London and revoked his income. Everyone was speaking of it in town. He is quite penniless and without support until he inherits. And that may be years from now—both his grandfather and father are in excellent health."

"No," breathed Lady Kildair, eyes wide. "But we all thought him so . . . so . . ."

"Eligible?" Charlotte nodded. "He meant everyone to think so. He meant to catch a wealthy bride. But the reason his father cast him out renders him beyond the pale for any decent girl."

"Indeed?" Lady Kildair hadn't blinked in minutes, it seemed.

Charlotte picked up her tea again. "Yes. And when I think of how near to disaster my niece strayed, because I was not here to advise and guard her, it is almost more than I can bear."

"Naturally." Lady Kildair cleared her throat delicately. "But what, precisely . . . ?"

Charlotte hesitated. She opened her mouth to reply, then closed it and looked away. Just as Lady Kildair drew breath to speak again, Charlotte leaned forward, lowering her voice to a confidential whisper.

"There were two young ladies—heiresses—who suffered from Mr. Drake's attentions. One was ruined when he was caught removing her stockings in her grandmother's garden. Her family hurried her off to the country in disgrace. The other young lady agreed to take a drive with him, no doubt unaware of his true nature—how vigilant a parent must be, Lady Kildair!—and when they did not return in a reasonable time, her brother pursued them. They were already on the Dover road, and heaven only knows how far he might have carried her! She was fortunate in having a suitor who was not turned off by the scandal, and she was married at once. But Mr. Drake went on his merry way, until his father called his bluff and sent him away."

Lady Kildair's mouth formed a perfect O, but no sound emerged. Charlotte sat back, shaking her head sadly. "I had no idea it was the same gentleman Susan had mentioned in her letters. Of course she only saw him as he presented himself, not as he really is."

"And you really think he would have . . . That is, is he truly so dishonorable?"

Charlotte swallowed, reaching for her handkerchief again. "Lady Kildair, I believe he would have ruined her beyond redemption! And it would have been . . ." She drew in a shuddering breath and clutched the handkerchief to her breast. "It would have been all my fault. It was only by chance I was fortunate enough to learn the truth in time. Oh, it is too horrible to contemplate!" By the end of her speech, Charlotte was sobbing quietly into her handkerchief. It was mostly for effect, but Charlotte was very keenly aware of how nearly Susan had missed complete disaster; she had heard her niece offer to run off with the cad herself, after all. If she had remained in

London even a day or two longer, who knew what might have befallen Susan?

Lady Kildair sat stunned for a moment, then rushed to Charlotte's side. "There, my dear! But you could not have known. As you said, you are only just returned to England, and had no way of knowing. Why, those of us who have been here had no idea." Lady Kildair fell abruptly silent as the ramifications of her words sank in. Charlotte sniffled into her handkerchief, letting her think about it. So far this had gone as well as she could have hoped. Lady Kildair was following exactly where Charlotte was trying oh-so-subtly to lead her.

"Yes, we were all of us taken in," said Lady Kildair a moment later, her voice growing shrill. "He seemed so charming and genuine! He was received by the best families in Tunbridge Wells, particularly those with marriageable daughters. And all this time, he was nothing but a common fortune hunter! My dear Madame Griffolino, we owe you a great debt for exposing him."

"Yes." Charlotte dabbed at her eyes and sat up straighter. "Why, I never thought of that—but of course, now that I have refused to allow him to see Susan again, who knows where he may turn his attentions? He must be quite desperate for funds, and will likely not scruple to seduce his next target."

Louise Kildair swelled with outrage, rising to her feet. "Never fear, Contessa; we shall make known his perfidy. I wager he'll not find a friendly reception in this town again."

"But he will say I am blackening his name because I did not approve his suit of Susan. And my poor niece is still upset over the whole affair," Charlotte protested. "I would rather have nothing more to do with that man."

She watched with immense relief as her hostess smiled. Smugly. "Why, of course I understand. I would be only too happy to relate what you have told me." *No doubt*, thought Charlotte, *you ceaseless gossip*. Lady Kildair's left hand would tattle on her right, if it could.

And thank goodness for it. Charlotte rose and let Lady Kildair take her hands again. "I cannot thank you enough. It has been a great relief to unburden myself to a sympathetic ear, and you will do a service to every female in town if you warn them of Mr. Drake's intentions."

"Now, now." Lady Kildair patted her hand as she led Charlotte to the door. "It is all thanks to you."

Charlotte smiled back. "You are too kind."

Lady Kildair pressed her hand; Charlotte interpreted it as thanks for depositing the season's most delicious scandal right in her lap. With another effusive thanks, Charlotte left, confident Stuart Drake would be rumored a liar, a rogue, and even worse before the end of the week. And all Charlotte would be guilty of was repeating gossip, somewhat dramatically, but she had indeed heard everything just as she had told Lady Kildair. Stuart Drake could blame no one but himself for his own behavior, which was reprehensible if the gossips were even half right. With no one willing to receive him, he would have no choice but to leave, and then Susan would realize how shallow his affections had been.

Poor Susan. Charlotte wished there were any way to prevent her inevitable hurt at that discovery. She would take Susan shopping, she decided, and even allow her to choose the colors. A few new gowns wouldn't ease the ache, but they would at least give her something else to think about, and perhaps it would signal a new beginning to the relationship Charlotte was trying to build with her niece. They would begin anew, Charlotte decided, and this time she would stay close enough to nip any more unfortunate attachments in the bud before they had the chance to blossom into trouble.

Lost in plans to win Susan's trust and friendship, Charlotte didn't notice her carriage was no longer in front of the Kildair house until she reached the walk. She stopped short with a frown, glancing up and down the street.

"Lost something?" She started violently at the low voice behind her. She whirled around to see Stuart Drake standing less than a foot away, so close she had to tip her head back to look him in the face.

And what a face it was. Last night, she had been focused on crushing his designs on Susan, and while she had noticed he was a handsome man, she hadn't really recognized how handsome. Dark blue eyes looked out from under arching brows the same midnight black as his hair. His cheekbones were wide and flat, and though his nose was a bit long, his sensual mouth more than made up for it. He was impeccably dressed in clothing that fit perfectly, with no evidence of padding or cinching anywhere. There were no signs of the dissipation Charlotte associated with rogues like him; either he had the best tailor in England, or he really was as hard and muscular as he had felt, lying on top of her the night before.

That memory made her flush, and she turned her back on him, scanning the street again for her carriage. She had explicitly told the driver to wait here, and the man had gone off somewhere. "Good day, sir," she said coldly, without looking back.

"Thank you," he said, his voice tinged with amusement. "I half expected you to scratch my eyes out." He moved to stand beside her.

Charlotte glared at him from the corner of her eye. "Only half? How terribly I failed."

"Well, I can't say I half expected you to throw yourself at me again, can I?"

Charlotte clenched her teeth together in fury. "I did no such thing."

He waved one hand negligently. "No matter. I came to extend the olive branch. Heal the breach. Mend the rift. We began badly last night—or rather, we began well, but then our relationship took a turn for the worse. I apologize for any offense you inferred, for I never meant any."

She sniffed. "We have no relationship, sir, nor shall we. I know very well what you meant, and no apology would suffice."

He was smiling, the wretch. "And I thought you'd had a change of heart. An enchanting siren at night, a virtuous saint by day, willing to forgive her fellow man his transgressions."

"Mr. Drake. Surely you have something better to do."

He made a show of looking up and down the street. Charlotte was nearly shaking with anger at her coachman for deserting her and subjecting her to this. She would have started walking, but she didn't want to walk all the way home with him following her. "And leave a lady in distress? Never."

"You are the cause of my distress," she pointed out.

Stuart laughed, admiring her profile. Up close, her attire was every bit as severe as he had thought when he first saw it from across the street, but perversely, he found it enthralling. Her drab gown couldn't hide the swell of her bosom or the curve of her hips. He imagined peeling it away, inch by inch . . . He reminded himself how she had tricked him, no matter that she had the body of a goddess, and that he had other concerns with her.

"I would like an end to the hostilities," he said. "I'm disappointed you won't consent to my request for your niece's hand—"

"I'm sure you are," came her acid retort.

"And you, no doubt, acted impulsively when we were dancing—"

"You shall wait a long time if you hope to hear an apology."

"And so I propose we call it even," Stuart continued, ignoring her interruptions. "Tunbridge Wells is a small place to wage a war, and—"

"I agree." She turned toward him at last and smiled. It was a close-lipped, coy smile that made him catch his breath in a mixture of desire and suspicion. "Much too small. I'm delighted you agree, and hope you find the hunting better somewhere else."

"Pardon?" Stuart was still distracted by that smile, and the light on her face. Even buttoned up like a vicar's wife, she was breathtaking.

"That is what you're doing, isn't it? Hunting for a fortune?" Her carriage rumbled to a halt beside them.

"I doubt you'll find the prey so susceptible from now on," she added. Stuart stared at her, eyes narrowed. Her smile turned gloating as her driver jumped down to assist her into the carriage. "Good bye, Mr. Drake."

Stuart said nothing as she drove away. He stood on the side of the street, filled with a growing sense of apprehension. What had she done, calling on Lady Kildair dressed like a she-wolf in lamb's wool? What did she mean, he might find the hunting better somewhere else? He had no plans to leave Kent. Tunbridge Wells was still a moderately fashionable spa; there were several families of good fortune spending the season there. Susan Tratter was by no means the only heiress in town. With his name and expectations, he was still an eligible match.

Unless someone managed to ruin his reputation.

His fears were swiftly confirmed. By the end of the day, he had been given the cut direct by no fewer than five of the haughtiest matrons in town. By the next morning, he was openly snubbed in the park, and young ladies who had once all but thrown themselves at him scurried behind their mothers with horrified, accusatory glares. Stuart didn't need the confirmation from a sympathetic widow with whom he had shared a brief flirtation to know what had happened to transform him into an outcast.

Stuart could stomach being refused Susan Tratter's hand—in some small way, he was almost relieved—and had sincerely meant his attempt at peace with Charlotte Griffolino. He could accept that she didn't like him, and that she had played him for a fool. It had been his own fault for falling for her ruse, after all. But Stuart also had no doubt that she was behind his ostracism, and that he could not forgive. It made his precarious finances desperate, and left him with little hope of restoring them soon. She could only have done it to spite him, and somehow, in some way, Stuart meant to pay her back.

After all, anything was fair in love . . . and war.

Chapter Three

It was a modest townhouse on a quiet side street in the fashionable section of town. For a woman in control of the enormous Tratter fortune, it seemed rather dull of her to rent such an ordinary place. Somehow a woman with such lush, exotic looks seemed out of place in this very English house. Still, given what he had come to do, Stuart ought to be grateful it wasn't a well-staffed fortress.

From his position ignominiously crouched in the bushes, Stuart watched his nemesis leave. She wore blue, the color of the sapphires around her neck. At her side, Susan also wore blue, but a paler shade, and she kept her head down. Stuart made a mental apology to her as he watched her climb into the carriage; he was certain this wasn't her fault. If it hadn't been his mother's ring, Stuart would have let the matter go, but sadly, it *was* his mother's ring he had given Susan. His mother had meant for it to go to his bride, and Stuart found, somewhat to his surprise, that he felt the same. Since he clearly wouldn't be marrying Susan Tratter, Stuart would like that ring back.

He knew this wasn't entirely defensible. He had freely given Susan the ring, and it seemed rather churlish to ask for it back. To salve both her feelings and his conscience, Stuart had scraped together enough money to buy a small token to replace the ring, something he could ill afford to do, and sent a note asking to call. If Charlotte Griffolino had been a reasonable woman, Stuart would have simply explained matters and hoped for the best. Instead, his polite request had been returned unopened, and when he rang the bell he had been turned away by the footman and told not to come back. After failing at means fair, already goaded beyond endurance and his pride still smarting, Stuart had resorted to means foul: he was going to steal back his ring.

When the carriage drove off with all three ladies aboard—Susan, her aunt, and the Italian singer who lived with them—Stuart took one last fortifying swallow of whiskey from his flask, pushed aside the branches, and sidled around the corner, where he could slip into the garden behind the house.

Once inside, he made his way to a row of darkened windows. With the ladies out for the evening, he expected the servants would retreat to either the attic quarters or the kitchen, and the main floors would be empty. He found an unlatched window without much effort and hoisted himself over the sill. Dropping to his hands and knees, he listened for a moment until satisfied all was still quiet. Slowly, cautiously, he got to his feet and peered around, his eyes gradually adjusting to the dark room.

It was a library, but not a well-used one. The room reeked of neglect and dust, and Stuart swallowed a curse as he realized his every footprint would be clearly marked on the floor. Leaving the window open, he walked on tiptoe to the carpet, only to come smack up to a large box.

"Damn!" he said soundlessly, grabbing his knee. What the hell was that doing in the middle of the room? Cautiously, he began groping his way forward, only to discover that there were a great many boxes and trunks in the room. Dozens, it seemed, all precisely located in his path. He reached out to feel for them, and tripped over something low and round; a rolled up rug, he learned, going over it onto his already aching knee. Crawling forward, he hit his head on a metal-strapped trunk, and cursed out loud as something heavy and oddly furry slid off the trunk and covered his head.

"Blast!" he exclaimed in a moment of panic. Had he been noticed? Was he caught? The covering came off as he flailed about, and Stuart rolled to his feet, heart thumping and every hair standing up on his head. Was the house filled with traps for hapless burglars?

It took several moments, but he finally convinced himself there was no reason for alarm. He considered going back out the window; it seemed he had been in the house an hour already, and he hadn't even found the door out of this room. Was the ring worth this? Stuart thought of how many times he had disappointed his mother, and crept back to the window. Forcibly controlling his breathing, he lifted the drape a little, letting in enough moonlight to reveal the room. The thing that had fallen on him appeared to be a tiger skin. Stuart stared at it in revulsion and curiosity. What sort of woman kept such a thing in her house?

He shook his head. This was not the time to

ponder Charlotte Griffolino's character. He was here to retrieve what was his and leave with all possible speed. He let the drape fall and, with more confidence, made his way through the room and slipped into the hall.

Only one lamp burned near the door. The hall was empty, as expected. Stuart stole up the stairs, crossing his fingers that he could find Susan's room quickly and easily. At the top of the stairs he paused to listen. The maids might still be about, tidying their mistresses' rooms. All was quiet, though, and he began trying doors.

He was just reaching for the third knob when he heard voices—giggling female voices coming up the stairs. In a flash Stuart was through the door, easing it closed behind him. He flattened himself against the wall right behind the door, holding his breath and straining to hear. The voices came nearer, pausing right outside the room he was in. Above the pounding of his own heart, he could dimly hear one relating something about her beau to the other; he was the tailor's assistant, and *so* well-dressed, she confided. Ooh, he sounds just lovely, came her companion's reply. They continued to chat, their voices gradually growing fainter though never fading completely. But it seemed they weren't coming into this room.

Slowly Stuart rested his forehead against the wall and let out his breath. He was stuck, though not caught, and this clearly wasn't the right room. In fact, looking more closely, Stuart realized exactly whose room it was. The warm, exotic scent he remembered too well, the riot of bold color in rich fabrics . . . It could only be Charlotte Griffolino's bedroom he was trapped in, and for a moment the precariousness of his situation escaped Stuart's mind.

The fire had burned low, but gave off enough light to see. The room itself was ordinary, but the personal things blazed and glowed even in the firelight. The bed was hung with blue and green—very fine linen, Stuart noted, running his hand over the duvet. There was a writing desk in the corner, and a chaise nearer the fire. Both held a variety of clothing, and it gave Stuart an odd sort of pleasure to know she was a bit slovenly. He paused, listening, but the murmur of voices continued out in the hall. Still trapped. In that case, Stuart decided, he might as well make himself comfortable.

He eyed the heap of clothing on the chaise, and something caught his eye. Well, now . . . Gently he teased a fine lawn chemise out of the tangle. He certainly wouldn't mind seeing her in this. *Or this*, Stuart thought, spying a blue silk negligee that appeared to have no sides. Thoroughly intrigued, Stuart looked closer at silk stockings and lacy dressing gowns and— my, oh my—a red satin corset. It looked as though she had tried everything on and then flung it aside. That probably meant the maid would come in soon to set all to rights. Stuart ventured a quick look out the window, to see if that offered any hope of escape, but it was a straight, exposed drop to the front steps.

Only half disappointed, he took a more leisurely turn about the room. There was no place to sit but on the bed, so Stuart seated himself, sinking into the luxury of a feather mattress. Her scent was strongest here; it rose out of the linens and filled the air he breathed. He leaned back and inhaled fully, enjoying some small taste—or rather, scent—of vengeance.

Of course it was impossible to sit on her bed and smell her perfume without thinking of having her in the bed with him, and Stuart frowned as his body stirred in unauthorized arousal at the thought. He had learned his lesson on that score, and was not going to be distracted by such urges again. He sat up and listened; the maids still chatted in the hall. What the devil were they doing, he wondered impatiently. No matter how much fiendish delight it gave him to see Charlotte Griffolino's undergarments, he wanted to accomplish his mission and leave. The longer he was in the house, the greater the chance he would be caught.

He drummed his fingers on his thigh, scanning the room again. A small chest on the bedside table caught his eye, and he idly flipped it open, momentarily taken aback by the blaze of jewels within. *Good Lord.* Stuart picked up the box and poked through it, amazed. An absolute fortune in precious gems just sitting on the table, and the house was all but wide open.

The sound of a door closing very nearby startled him out of his thoughts, so badly he jumped. Several pieces skittered out of the jewel case in his hand, slipping across his lap and into the plush folds of the duvet. Stuart swiftly scooped them back into the case and replaced it on the table before sprinting back across the room to the door. The voices had gone quiet, and he could faintly hear one person, humming. Footsteps went up and down the hall, up and down. Stuart tensed, expecting to be discovered at any moment, but finally the footsteps faded completely.

He turned the knob soundlessly, and opened the door a bare inch. After a long moment of listening, he slipped into the hall. It was quiet and deserted. He glanced longingly down the hall, at the doors he hadn't tried, but decided it was too great a risk. Better to admit defeat and come up with another, safer, plan. He clearly wasn't cut out to be a successful thief.

He made his way back down the stairs, quietly and quickly, and back to the library, where he had left the window open. Only when he had closed the door behind him did he realize he had made a mistake; this was not the library, even though it was also filled with crates and trunks, all the way to the ceiling in some places. Was she packing to leave, or just lazy about unpacking to stay? And why hadn't she rented a bigger house if the latter? Curious, Stuart tried the lid of a nearby crate. It opened to reveal straw, packed around . . . a vase, he discovered, feeling inside. A large vase.

A faint sound made Stuart freeze as he was replacing the lid. Tensed for flight, or fight if the need arose, he circled the crate, straining to see in the dark room. A scrape, a rustle, then silence until a low whisper; something being dragged, perhaps? Stuart moved forward stealthily. Whoever it was hadn't brought a lamp. He closed his fist around a broken slat from one of the crates and lifted it over his head, just in case, and edged forward.

A dark shape was bent over another crate. Now Stuart could see the lamp, a tiny thing with a cover almost completely covering it. A weak glow barely illuminated the open crate, and cast the figure in front of it into a blurry shadow. He hesitated. Another burglar? What was this one after? And what the hell should he do?

Stuart was struck by the absurdity of it. Here he was, breaking into a house for the express purpose of taking something, and yet the sight of another intruder brought out the English gentleman in him. How hypocritical, to want to defend the house he himself had broken into. He shook his head at his own lunacy, a moment of self-examination that was nearly fatal.

The figure crouching over the crate whirled with no warning, one arm swinging upward. Stuart flung the broken slat by instinct, dodging to the side. The intruder—the other one—clipped him in the waist, and Stuart lost his breath in a whoosh as they toppled backward into another stack of crates.

The fellow was small, but wiry and strong. He also had a knife, which Stuart barely managed to keep from his own throat. Grunting, they rolled back and forth, neither gaining the upper hand, until the sound of running footsteps reached them. His opponent froze, then leapt up and fled with the speed of a deer, stepping squarely in the middle of Stuart's stomach on his way.

Breathless again, Stuart staggered to his feet. The thief had vanished, and he was about to be discovered in the wreckage. Realizing that he had no possible explanation for being here, Stuart limped to the window he glimpsed behind some more crates, and pulled on the sash.

It stuck.

The door was opening, the light of a candle seeping into the room. Stuart wrenched at the window as the nervous face of the butler appeared around the door. He refused to get caught trying to break *out* of the house. The butler stepped in, lifting his lamp. "Who is there?" he called in a quavering voice.

With one last yank, the window flew up with an

ear-splitting squeal, and Stuart dove headfirst out of it, landing in the honeysuckle. Ripping the vines from his legs, he hurtled across the dark garden, away from the shouts and screams coming from the house behind him, and didn't stop until he was several streets away.

Panting and sweating, shaking with delayed panic, he leaned against a wall to catch his breath. Christ, that had been close. Just his luck, to break into the only house in Kent already being burgled. He dragged one hand over his face and realized his fingers were sticky with more than sweat. He swore as he saw the long slice across his palm from the fellow's knife. He dug in his pocket for a handkerchief, and felt something unfamiliar. With a feeling of growing dread, Stuart carefully pulled out—*Holy Christ*—an emerald necklace. It must have slipped into his pocket when he dropped the jewel case.

Stuart crammed it back into his pocket and concentrated on wrapping his bleeding hand, feeling as though a thousand eyes glared down on him. Just bloody lovely; now he was a jewel thief. How the devil could he return it without incriminating himself? He certainly wasn't going back now. Squeezing his cut hand in a fist, he made his way home, cursing the day he had met Charlotte Griffolino.

"But is anything missing?" Charlotte asked for the fifth time, standing in the middle of her destroyed music room. Dunstan, the butler, could do little but wring his hands and beg her pardon. Charlotte sighed as he began again, stammering through another apology.

"Don't worry, Dunstan. I don't expect you to have stopped him. I just want to know what he took."

The butler looked around unhappily. "I've no idea, madam."

The two footmen came back then, finished searching the house. "There's no one, ma'am. We checked all the rooms, all the cupboards, every hiding place."

"Thank you." She dismissed them all, and told Dunstan to have a glass of port. She went back down the hall to where Susan still huddled with Lucia and the maids. "The house is safe. Whoever was here has gone."

"Oh, Aunt Charlotte," Susan sobbed, running forward to fling her arms around Charlotte. "I never dreamed! In Kent, of all places! What if we had been home?"

"We weren't, and that's what's important." Charlotte sent a speaking quick glance over Susan's head at Lucia, who was on at least her second cigarette. Charlotte didn't have the heart to remind her not to smoke around Susan, since Lucia was dragging on it rather hard, as she always did when upset. "Go up to bed, dearest. I will take care of it."

"But what if he comes back?" Susan wailed. "We're not safe in our own beds!"

Charlotte tipped up her chin, her heart constricting at the sight of Susan's red-rimmed, fearful eyes. "Don't worry," she said gently. "If Dunstan can scare him off, Tom and Henry should terrify him. They'll both sleep here in the front hall tonight. We shall be quite safe."

"All right." Susan's eyes filled with tears again. Charlotte hugged her, murmuring reassurances. She walked Susan to her room, where they both checked it thoroughly and made certain the window was locked. Charlotte sent a maid for a cup of warm milk, and tucked her niece into bed as if she were a child. All their differences were forgotten, and Susan even smiled at her as Charlotte bade her good night.

She went back downstairs to the music room, followed by Lucia, whose nerves seemed to have been steadied by the tobacco. The servants had been too frightened to sweep up, and Charlotte was content to let them do it in the morning. She wanted to examine the scene herself, on the slim chance the thief might have left a clue behind.

This was not the first time someone had broken in. At first she had thought it was just carelessness, things left where they shouldn't be by servants unfamiliar with her household. But this was clearly not the negligence of servants. Several crates had been knocked over, two of them opened and rifled, and a small stub of a candle in a tin holder had been found in the debris. Someone had been here again, in her house, looking for something in particular, and since he hadn't found it, Charlotte faced the frightening certainty he would be back.

"He is getting careless," said Lucia, breaking the silence. "Have you no idea what he searches for?"

Charlotte sighed. "None. These crates were only just delivered last week. Sometimes I wonder if *he* knows what he's looking for."

Lucia nudged a vase, lying spilled from its crate, with her toe. It rolled over to expose the lightning bolt of a crack that split the side. "Perhaps it is good. Perhaps he grows impatient, and will make a mistake."

"Perhaps he'll grow impatient with sneaking in, and just burst in during luncheon and hold us hostage until he finds whatever it is he wants." Charlotte picked up the vase, and paused, frowning at some dark spots on the carpet underneath. "Does this look like blood to you?"

Lucia leaned over with a rustle of silk. "Oh, do you think he hurt himself, and that is why he caused such a disturbance?"

Charlotte looked closer. It was possible. Out of hurt or frustration, the burglar might have gone a bit mad and started breaking things. But it had almost led to his capture; if the butler had been a quicker, younger man, she might be facing her tormentor right now. The thief had broken in several times, always very quietly, and left few traces of his presence. He could have been stealing her blind, for all the evidence he had left behind. These crates would most likely have sat untouched for weeks, just like all the others had, and he could have taken anything from them, leaving no one the wiser. Why would he endanger himself now?

She skirted the smashed crates, trying to view the scene dispassionately. She could tell which crates he had opened, since these were all newly delivered and no one else had disturbed them. Two had been opened and then closed, very carefully. One had been opened and partially closed, and another was left standing open. Why did he go on a rampage in the middle of his search?

Charlotte shook her head in despair. "Perhaps he thought his object would be in these last few crates. I'm not expecting any more, thank goodness; I haven't the space for these."

"Why do you not unpack them, then?" Lucia lifted

a small statue from the open crate. "The house is so dull."

"If I unpacked them, the house would look like a museum." *It would look like Italy,* Charlotte silently corrected, and she was trying to leave Italy behind. The truth was, she didn't want any of the things in those crates; she just hadn't figured out what to do with them. She hadn't expected Piero to leave them to her in the first place, but his will had contained a clause specifically directed at her, enjoining her to keep it all in remembrance of his affection for her. After that, she hadn't been able to say no when the solicitor offered to ship everything to England for her. If Lucia hadn't been with her, and the explanations difficult, Charlotte would have personally pushed every box overboard into the ocean on the voyage. Thieves were welcome to take any of it, but instead they simply broke in to make a mess, it appeared.

"Well, since there's nothing to be done, I'm going to bed," she said with a sigh. "I shall see you in the morning."

"How you shall sleep, I cannot guess." Lucia shuddered, hurrying out of the room behind her. Upstairs Charlotte stopped to check on Susan, who was sleeping soundly but all curled into a ball, just as she had done as a small child. Charlotte's heart felt heavy; she was trying so hard to be a proper guardian, and in less than a month she had allowed her niece to be taken in by a fortune hunter, and now to be terrorized by burglars in her own home. For the first time she considered braving London, for Susan's sake. So far she had put it off, telling herself they would wait until Susan was old enough for a season, but perhaps she was wrong. She gently tucked the blanket around the sleeping girl, and retreated to her own room.

The fire had gone out, because the maids were too frightened to go about the house. Charlotte sighed, stirring the ashes with the poker and coaxing just enough heat to light the candle. She put it on the dressing table, and began removing her jewelry, pressing her fingers to the back of her neck where it ached. Then her eyes fell on her bed, and she froze in place.

Someone had been in her *bed*. The bedclothes were rumpled, and a depression was clearly visible in the duvet. The maid would never have left it that way. Charlotte's skin crawled, and her breath came loud and harsh as she imagined a stranger in her bedroom, among her most personal possessions, in her bed. Shaking, she inched over to the bed and yanked back the covers by the corner, a scream poised in her throat. The duvet floated harmlessly to the carpet.

She jerked the pillows off, one by one. Nothing. She shook out the sheets and ran her hands under the mattress. Nothing.

Charlotte's knees gave out and she collapsed into the pile of bedding. Relief and fear twisted in her belly. So far she had never seen any sign of the burglar upstairs, and the violation of her private haven was unexpected. She realized she had grown lax in her handling of the burglaries; since no one had been hurt and often there was little evidence of intrusion, she had almost come to accept them as harmless annoyances.

She got to her feet and began a systematic search of her room for anything at all out of the ordinary. At the end, she was sure the thief had gone through her clothing, although she couldn't find anything missing. The maid hadn't cleared away the laundry and mending before the uproar, and all her unmentionables were spread out atop the pile. Charlotte resolved to throw them all out first thing in the morning and buy new ones. She couldn't bear to wear them after he had touched them.

The only thing missing, in fact, was the one thing that gave her hope. An emerald necklace was gone from her jewel case. Perhaps he was a petty thief after all, and had only gotten brave enough to come upstairs this time. Charlotte hoped this were the case, for she couldn't stand the thought of an intruder roaming her house at his ease. Jewels he could have, for all she cared; they could be replaced, and if he had satisfied whatever urge drove him, perhaps this would be his last break-in.

She put her bed to rights, giving everything a tremendous shake as if to rid it of the intruder's touch. It took her a long time to fall asleep, and when she did, it was to dream of the vengeance she would like to take on the man who had violated her privacy so vilely.

She hid her feelings from Susan the next morning. When her niece came down to breakfast, Charlotte smiled warmly, determined to go on as if there were no cause for concern. She would deal with the thief on her own. "Good morning, Susan."

"Good morning, Aunt Charlotte." Susan gave her an uncertain smile in reply. It was her first friendly greeting in days, and Charlotte felt a surge of delight. When she had gotten word of George's death, along with the news that he had named her guardian of his only child, Charlotte had nursed a secret hope that Susan might come to be a dear friend, a mixture of the younger sister she'd always wanted and the daughter she'd never have. Susan had been only a child when Charlotte left England, but Charlotte had remembered her niece fondly in the years since.

"Shall we go shopping today? I have need of a few things." Charlotte had ordered her maid to dispose of her undergarments that morning. She had only what she had worn the night before. "I've been thinking about the yellow muslin you liked," she added, trying to build on the good feelings. "Perhaps we should look at it again."

Susan looked up in surprise. "Really? You—you said it was too daring for a girl my age."

"Well, I'm reconsidering. Shall we?" Susan nodded, her face brightening. Charlotte turned her attention to her breakfast with a lighter heart. Perhaps she had been too strict with Susan; the yellow dress was a little provincial for her taste, but Susan was old enough to begin choosing her own clothes and developing her own sense of style. The dress, and of course new shoes to go with it, possibly a new bonnet and some gloves . . .

"Your pardon, madam." The butler had come into the room. "Tom found this in the garden." He held out a silver flask. Charlotte took it, her eyebrows rising in surprise. It was an expensive polished flask such as a gentleman would carry.

"Where, Dunstan?"

He cleared his throat softly. "In the honeysuckle, madam. Outside the music room." Charlotte stared at it. It wasn't hers, so it must belong to the burglar. The burglar, a gentleman?

There was a sharp clink of silver on china, and a gasp. Charlotte glanced up to see Susan, pale-faced and wide-eyed, staring at the flask in her hand. "Is that . . . Is that where the intruder was?" she asked faintly.

Charlotte tucked the flask into her lap. "Don't worry, dear. He shan't be able to come back." She nodded to the butler, and he bowed out of the room.

"Oh, no." Her niece wet her lips. "May I see it?" Charlotte hesitated. "Please?" Susan looked quite distraught. Reluctantly, Charlotte handed her the flask. Susan snatched it from her hand, turning it over and letting out another strangled gasp. Then she wrapped her napkin around it and sprang to her feet. "May I be excused?" She edged toward the door.

Charlotte frowned. "I need the flask, Susan. I shall send around to the magistrate at once. He'll want to see it and discover who owns it."

"Oh, no!" Susan shook her head frantically, clutching the napkin-wrapped flask to her chest. "I'm sure it has nothing to do with the intruder. It couldn't!"

"Susan," said Charlotte slowly. "Give it to me." She put out her hand.

Susan backed up, her breath rapid and loud. "No, no . . . I . . . I think it may be mine, Papa gave me one once, such as this."

"Then let me look at it." Charlotte rose from the table and took the flask from Susan's stiff but unresisting fingers. It still looked like an ordinary flask, Charlotte thought in puzzlement, turning it over. Why would Susan want to hide it from her?

She went still. An elegant script "D" was engraved on the side, along with a snarling dragon. The beast was almost worn away, but the plumes of fire spouting from his snout made it clear what he was. Charlotte raised her eyes to Susan's. "Whose flask is this, Susan?"

Her niece blinked rapidly. "I told you, Papa gave me one."

"Does this belong to Mr. Drake, by any chance?" Charlotte controlled her voice with great difficulty. Susan shook her head with a small whimper. "Then whose, Susan? It was not your father's."

Susan opened her mouth, then closed it, looking wretched. Charlotte was beyond caring. If that lowlife, that so-called gentleman had broken into her house and handled her most personal items, she would settle for nothing less than his head on a pike. How *dare* he molest her underwear?

"He wouldn't break into our house, Aunt Charlotte," pleaded Susan. "Mr. Drake is a gentleman!"

"After you went to bed, I discovered some of my jewels were missing. Mr. Drake is desperate for money."

"He wouldn't do this!" Susan cried.

"He would if he had given up on marrying you and your fortune." Susan sucked in a gasp, and Charlotte regretted saying it so bluntly. Before she could retract it and try again, Susan flung open the door and ran from the room.

Charlotte examined the flask again, her fury mounting. Susan couldn't believe her dear Mr. Drake was a thief, but of course that's what every fortune hunter was, deep down. The infuriating man couldn't even take a hint and leave town in disgrace like a proper coward. He had to stoop to petty thievery. Had he taken her necklace in retaliation?

She uncurled her fingers from the flask and set it on the table. She should go to the authorities with the flask and demand his arrest. She should march directly to his door and tell him what she thought of his craven sneaking around. She should invite him to return to the scene of his crime, and meet him with a pistol in her hand. She should *not* break into his rooms and vandalize *his* belongings while she retrieved her necklace.

But that's what she did.

Chapter Four

It shocked Charlotte how easy it was to get into his rooms. A quick scramble up the overgrown apple tree, and she was in through an unlocked window. For a housebreaker, he was very lax about his own residence, she thought, dusting off her trousers.

The room she found herself in was a modest sitting room, obviously furnished by the landlady. Charlotte smirked at the thought of tall, masculine Stuart Drake relaxing in the flowery chintz chair, tatted cushions all around. He must be truly desperate to take such a frilly room.

He was desperate enough to break into my house, she reminded herself, then set to work. She intended to find her jewels, leave a snide little note in their place, and then, time permitting, wreak some havoc, just as he had done to her. Charlotte hoped she would have plenty of time to cut his entire wardrobe to shreds.

She was about halfway through her search when the sound of a key in the lock made the blood freeze in her veins. Praying it would only be a servant coming to turn down the bed, she flattened herself against the wall where the shadows were deepest. She held her breath as a man came into the room, his head bent as he tugged off his gloves.

She closed her eyes. Just her luck, Stuart Drake himself.

He stepped inside and closed the door behind him. There were rustles of cloth as he discarded his overcoat, and a quiet curse as he fumbled with the flint. The spark caught, and the candle glowed briefly before he moved in front of it, blocking most of the light. He paused, head tilting to one side, then went and closed the window she had left open. He stood there for a moment, contemplating it, then gave a little shrug and went to the fireplace.

Charlotte knew a moment of hideous indecision. How was she going to escape without him noticing? There was no way she could open the window and climb back down the tree without making noise. If he would just go into the other room she could slip out the door. He seemed to be home for the evening; whatever had happened to gambling, drinking, and whoring all night like a normal rake?

He had stirred up the fire by now and added a log. With a weary sigh, he sat on the edge of a chair, almost directly across from her, and rubbed the back of his neck. For a moment he stared pensively into the flames, shoulders slumped. Motionless, hardly daring to breathe, Charlotte felt a strange tug of sympathy at his despairing pose. Even though she knew him to be the worst kind of scoundrel, he looked like a man worn down with care and worry, utterly at the end of his rope. And so damnably handsome, in the flickering firelight.

She closed her eyes to keep such thoughts at bay.

Handsome is as handsome does, she tried to tell herself. *Think of all the terrible things he's done.* But instead, her mind recalled the feel of his hands, sliding over her shoulders; the sound of his voice, low and seductive in her ear; the weight of his body, pressing into hers . . .

A loud snap broke her thoughts. Charlotte's eyes flew open. He was on his feet again, prodding the log farther into the flames. It was beginning to light, and the room was no longer dark. He lit a lamp, and a bit more of Charlotte's shadow cover fled. If he turned around, he would clearly see her.

He went into the other room, taking the lamp with him. She sagged against the wall, weak with relief, then quietly picked her way toward the door. Just as she reached for the knob, the room lit up again, and she glanced back without thinking.

"What the—?" She caught a glimpse of pure astonishment on his face before she lunged at the door in a panic. Charlotte seized the doorknob and even had it open a few inches before the door was slammed shut and she was thrown against it.

"What the devil are you after?" he snarled, pushing his face up beside hers. "Who are you?" Pure fear squeezed her heart for a second; he didn't sound or feel at all like a cowardly fop. Which of course he was. She made herself stay still, keeping her head down, biding her time. He grabbed her collar and one arm, pushing her across the room toward the fireplace. "Followed me home, did you?" he muttered. "I hope you're feeling more talkative tonight." He pushed her down into a chair, knocking off her hat.

Charlotte barely heard his swift breath of surprise as she shoved, setting him back on his heels before bolting for the door. He recovered from this surprise just as quickly, though, and caught her less than halfway across the room, tackling her to the rug, where her struggles were quickly proven useless.

"Well." He sat back on his haunches and looked down at her. Charlotte glared back venomously. "What an unexpected pleasure."

She tried to buck him off, without success. He was sitting on top of her, and had her wrists in an iron grip. "Let go of me!"

"I don't think I will," he said. "Not just yet, anyway. To what do I owe the honor of your visit? I would have let you in if you simply knocked on the door, you know; there was no need to sneak into my bedroom."

"I don't want to be in your bedroom," she hissed. "You know why I'm here—I want my necklace back! I know you stole it."

That wiped the smile off his face. "What makes you say that?"

She smirked, pleased to have rattled him. "You're not as clever a thief as you think." He seemed to consider this for a moment, his gaze narrow and calculating. "Let go of me, return my necklace, and perhaps, just perhaps, I shan't call the authorities," she added.

He focused on her again, and his grin returned, darker this time, wicked and sensual. "Oh, won't you?" he murmured. "And I thought you'd come to apologize for being a nasty little gossip."

Rage overpowered Charlotte. Writhing and snarling, she fought against his grip, his weight, his smile. She kicked and bucked and rolled, called him the foulest names she knew in every language she knew, and only ended up several minutes later spread flat on her back, arms above her head, beneath the considerable weight of one hateful, despicable, aroused man.

It was that last realization that finally ended her struggle. She could feel the hard length pressed against her belly, unprotected by layers of corset, petticoat, and gown. Thin drawers and breeches were all that separated them, and Charlotte was horrified by the tight knot of heat deep in her belly at that thought. She fell still, breathing hard.

Stuart knew better than to think she was surrendering. Good Lord, the woman was a hellcat, scratching and spitting at him until the only way he could protect himself was to hold her down with his own body. And now he was enjoying himself. Just the feel of her beneath him was almost worth what she had cost him. Almost, but not quite.

"I find myself in a bit of a quandary," he told her. Her eyes narrowed, but she didn't respond. "I ought to summon the authorities and let them haul you away for housebreaking. It's against the law, you see, and very dangerous."

"You would know, having done it yourself!"

"However," he continued, "I don't really want to let you go yet. Not until I've repaid all you've done for me."

"Get off me or I'll cut your throat," she said in a low voice. Her eyes glittered with fury, but she didn't move. Too bad, Stuart thought; he'd rather liked her squirming. "Let me go this instant and I won't call the authorities on *you* for breaking into *my* house."

"Ah, but you aren't quite in the position to be giving orders, are you?" he said sympathetically. "I seem to be on top, so to speak, and I rather like it that way." He shifted his hips against hers, half to prove his point and half to satisfy the clamoring of his body, and a tiny, inarticulate sound escaped her before she cursed him again, more volubly than before.

"No doubt," he said when she stopped. "But that doesn't answer the question: what am I going to do with you?" He shifted his grip on her wrists, holding them with one hand. She struggled briefly, until it became clear that he could hold her just as well with one hand as with two. Gently he stroked the loose dark curls away from her face, laughing softly as she looked away. His fingers lingered on the curve of her cheek and the line of her throat. She had impossibly soft skin, and he leaned closer to inhale her scent, fainter than usual.

"I know what I would like to do with you," he murmured in her ear. She said nothing, but her breathing accelerated. Stuart shifted, sliding one knee between hers. Instantly her legs clamped together, but too late, and she shook as he settled himself more comfortably atop her, his thigh between hers. "I like your trousers," he whispered. "Very much." He palmed the curve of her hip, and she jerked.

"I was wrong about you," Charlotte spat, still not looking at him. "I thought you were merely a common whore, trading on your looks and manner to gull women out of their money. I didn't expect you forced yourself on them as well."

"A common whore?" He frowned. "I doubt it. I admit to relying on my good looks and charming manners, but what of it? Women do as much when looking for a husband. And my intentions are always clear, about marriage or . . . other things." He paused, his fingers still playing idly up and down her side. Charlotte bit the inside of her lip—hard—to keep from betraying any reaction to that touch. Because she did not want to respond to it, or to him, and she especially did not want him to know that her body was responding in spite of her wishes.

"Still," he went on in the same thoughtful tone, "I can see how one might mistake my intentions in this instance. I believe what I would like is very clear." He slid his hips into the V of her thighs and grinned wickedly at her tremor of alarm. "But forcing myself on women? Oh no, never. Especially not on you. You, I think, will have to ask very nicely indeed."

"You're hurting me!" Charlotte burst out. How she hated this man cradled between her legs, using her body against her. She didn't know what to do, squeeze or relax, and tried to kick him instead. He reached back and caught her knee, pulling it up until it was hooked around his waist. "Ouch!" she protested, even though it didn't hurt at all, and even felt appallingly right.

His grip loosened, and his hand slid down the underside of her thigh toward her hip. "I don't think I'm hurting you any more than you're hurting me," he whispered, his breath hot on her cheek. "And I don't think you would be here at all if you were truly frightened of me."

"I am not afraid of you," she shot back. "I despise you, and all men like you. You're nothing but a bunch of cowardly swindlers, duping innocent, naïve girls out of their fortunes."

He raised his head and looked at her, his mouth tight. "You're not a very good negotiator." He rose up on his knees above her so quickly she didn't have time to resist, and hauled her to her feet. Charlotte struggled again, with a hard kick to his shin and a quick elbow to his stomach, but he simply bent her arm behind her back until she went up on her toes with a gasp.

"And that was not very nice, either," he said, breathing hard. "Come with me, little cat."

Whimpering, Charlotte obeyed, letting him propel her into the next room. His bedroom, she realized as he shoved her onto the wide bed, tugging his cravat loose. As it came free, he grabbed her wrists and looped the linen around them, then stretched her arms up above her head again, and began lashing the cravat to the bed.

Panic rolled through Charlotte in a nauseating wave. Tied to his bed, she would be helpless, humiliated, trapped. She yanked desperately, to no avail. Grim-faced, he tightened the knot with one last tug, and then unleashed a terrifying smile at her. Heart slamming, Charlotte tensed, watching him with an almost feral fear as he got off the bed.

Then he walked away. Striding to the windows, he began unknotting the cords that held back the draperies. One fell closed with a *shush* of velvet, deepening the shadows. "You have nothing to worry about," he said, going to the other window. "I won't hurt you. In fact, I won't even touch you. I'd rather wait until you ask me, perhaps even beg." *Shush*, the second drape closed. "Yes," he said more decisively, tugging the drapes all the way closed. "After all you've done, I should like to see you beg."

"Let me go," she said again. The room was totally dark now. She had no idea where he was or what he was doing. His hand closed around her ankle and she nearly jumped out of her skin.

"No," he said with a hint of laughter. "Not yet." He

pulled, and Charlotte swallowed her protest, letting him tie her legs. The drapery cords, no doubt. The dark must be just an added bonus to him. Trussed like a Christmas goose, unable to see or anticipate any of his actions, she was completely at his mercy.

"I promised I wouldn't touch you," came his voice, very near her ear. She jerked, turning toward it and pulling away from it at the same time.

"Tying me down doesn't count?" Ah good, some of the freezing scorn had come back to her voice, at least.

"No more, then. Let's just talk, shall we?"

"I won't pay you a pound." It popped out of her mouth before she could consider the wisdom of it. But money was what he wanted, and she absolutely refused to give him a single shilling.

He laughed, a low chuckle that was more threatening for sounding genuinely amused. "I don't want to talk about money."

She thought hard. "I can't retract what I said about you. Lady Kildair would never let go of gossip like that. But if you leave, I shan't try to follow or blacken your name elsewhere."

"Goodness, did you plan to?" Another quiet laugh. "How vindictive. I suppose then I'm doubly glad you decided to break into my rooms."

Disconcerted, Charlotte seized on the only other thing that came to mind. "If you think to tumble me, you'll sadly regret it."

"Tumbling you . . . Now there is something I could talk about. In fact, I could talk a great deal about it. Would you like to know all the things I want to do?" Charlotte turned her head away, uselessly. She couldn't cover both ears at once. "It's your own fault," he went on in the same relentless, velvet-soft voice. "You really made an impression that night in the library. You asked if I would have made love to you if you hadn't stopped me, and I think the answer is yes. God knows I want to now, even after you've ruined all my prospects and assaulted me in my own home."

"It is your own fault for preying on Susan!"

"That's a very harsh way to phrase it. I met her under the most proper circumstances and was a perfect gentleman at all times. But of course you don't really care about all that; the mere fact that she has money, and I have none, has aroused your wrath. Isn't that a bit hypocritical, wanting your niece to marry someone with money when you've gone to some lengths to prevent me from doing the same?"

"I don't care if she marries a wealthy man or a poor one," snapped Charlotte. "I want her to marry a man who loves her, and not just for her inheritance." She could hear him smile.

"Ah yes, love. I already admitted I did not love her. But I did mean to be a decent husband to her. She would have made me wealthy, and I would have been grateful to her for it."

"Gratitude is not the basis for a good marriage."

"It seems far more fair to me than many others," he replied, unmoved. "Good breeding, family alliances, lands and titles . . . Gratitude at least gives the husband a reason to please his wife past the wedding day. Whatever faults you lay at my door, never lay forgetfulness, or ingratitude. When someone does something to me, or for me, I never forget it."

Charlotte heard the implied menace in that statement, and felt a deeper kind of fear. That recklessness she had glimpsed in him earlier was shining through, and she knew with absolute certainty it was true: he never forgot his debts, for slights or for favors.

"But now, enough about that." His voice deepened, warming and chilling at once. "Let us discuss the matter between *us*, Madame Griffolino. I owe you, for your little performance the other night. It was very good, I must say. No one's ever tried to seduce me before the supper dance."

"Why did you break into my house?" she demanded, trying to turn his attention from seduction. Holy God, he wasn't going to try to do the same to her, was he? She was utterly confident of her ability to resist when she was in control of her own body, but now she was roped down flat on her back, and had no way to turn the tables. Charlotte was aware of her own sexual power over most men, and she had the advantage over this one in knowing already that he wanted her. But he had taken that power away by immobilizing her, removing the flirtatious little gestures, the coy looks, the half smile she knew how to use against a man.

He clicked his tongue in reproof. "No, no, you have asked enough questions. You, *signora*, are not leading me anymore." There was a faint sound, then a candle flared to life. Charlotte blinked, relieved for the light. He sat in a chair, pulled close to the bed. This room, she saw, was plainly furnished, almost spartan. Only the bed could be called luxurious.

As she watched, he unbuttoned the top of his shirt and loosened the collar. He had already removed his jacket, and now reclined in his chair in just his white shirt and trousers. He met her eyes, and another devastating, fiendish grin curled his mouth.

"Gads, I've never seen a woman look so vicious. One would think I planned to ravish you in fact."

"This," she announced in an ominous voice, "is kidnapping. On top of housebreaking, robbery, and conniving to carry off my niece. If you do not release me this instant, I shall swear to the magistrate that you abused me in the most cruel and vicious manner possible."

"Ah, yes, but how did you get into my rooms? I have two perfectly respectable acquaintances who will swear they accompanied me home from the tavern at half past ten. I would be very happy to fetch either of them so they might also swear that you are here, with no time for me to have gone all the way to your house, kidnapped you, and brought you back here. So either you came here willingly, or you came here for illegal purposes, neither of which will reflect well on you."

Charlotte cursed him again, pulling against the cravat binding her wrists until her arms ached. He watched with faint amusement. "I shall picture this every time I wear that cravat," he said when she lay still again, panting and furious.

Charlotte turned her eyes to the ceiling, swallowing her anger. He enjoyed it, she realized; he delighted in being able to make her so angry. She wanted to thwart him in that, but how? If she ignored him, who knew what he might do to provoke her. And it wasn't her nature to lie still and quiet.

"Yes, that's right," Stuart said, leaning forward to see her better. Her dark eyes flashed toward him. "The memory of you in my bed will forever be linked to that cravat."

She said nothing, but he could feel the violence of

her emotions. This woman was beautiful when she was
calm and in command of herself, but when she was
angry, oh Lord, she was a sight. Her color was high,
her breasts, unbound by any corset, quivered with
each indignant breath, and her dark eyes glittered.
His gaze traveled the length of her body, stretched out
on his bed. She was slimmer than he had thought, although no less rounded. With her arms over her
head, her jacket was bunched around her shoulders
and under her chin. Stuart reached out and began
unfastening the buttons.

"Take your hands off me!" she cried, trying to twist
away from him. Stuart frowned, concentrating on the
buttons until the last one was free. She wore just a thin
linen shirt underneath, and he deliberately let the
sides of the jacket fall open to the sides.

"I said I wouldn't touch you, and I won't." He
moved the candle closer. "Looking never hurt
anyone." She thrashed a bit, but only succeeded in
working the jacket farther open. Stuart smiled.

"But if I were to touch you . . . Oh, what would I
do then? You know I want you; would you like to
know how it would be? What I would do to please
you? I want to please you; I don't go to bed with
women just for my own satisfaction." Pure malice
sparkled in her glare. He propped his elbows on the
mattress. "And you would be a challenge, wouldn't
you? I expect you would deny yourself any sort of
pleasure just to spite me."

"I cannot imagine myself finding any pleasure at
your hands!" Charlotte hated his self-assured smile
almost as much as she hated the niggling feeling
that she lied. Piero had told her he could hardly

believe she was English, that her passions ran hotter and closer to the surface than any other English-woman he had met. He meant it as a compliment, that she was more continental, more Italian; Charlotte interpreted it as confirmation of her father's parting words to her. *An unnatural woman*, he had called her, without temperance or restraint in her words or her deeds. And he had been right.

Her feeling toward Stuart Drake ran so hot at this moment, she couldn't avoid the unsettling thought that if he could harness that feeling and use it for his own purpose, she would be in very deep trouble indeed. "I won't listen to another word," she vowed. "You're a cad, a no-account rake who—"

"Hush." He touched one finger to her lips, just firmly enough to silence her. "If you won't be quiet, I won't restrain myself to looking," he added with a pointed glance. "I shall interpret your next word as agreement." Charlotte clamped her lips shut and looked away.

"I know you dislike me," he went on softly. "I don't care much for your behavior, either. So ruthless, so unrelenting. But then, in bed, those qualities might be more promising. Such fire, and spirit! No fainting miss but a tigress, I'd wager, and I wouldn't mind if the kitten showed her claws a bit."

His finger left her lips and traveled over her chin, down her throat. At the collar of her shirt, it lifted, although Charlotte could swear she still felt the warmth of it on her skin.

"You have a lovely throat." His voice had become a quiet growl. "So smooth and soft. One would never know it hides a steel core. The curve where it meets your shoulder, there"—she shivered involuntarily at the faint stirring of air above her shoulder—"it cries out for a man's mouth. A man could feast on the slope of your shoulder." His finger tugged lightly at the collar of her jacket, and Charlotte opened dry lips to protest, but then it drifted away.

She flinched when it landed on her breastbone, just below her throat. "You're touching me," she said through clenched teeth. His finger rubbed back and forth slowly for a moment, then lifted.

"Ah, yes, so I was. My mistake." He was leaning over her, his face in shadow. All Charlotte could see was the gleam of his eyes. "Your pulse is so fast," he said softly. "Here." Again his finger dipped, almost but not quite touching the hollow at the base of her throat. "Does your heart beat faster, to imagine what would happen if I kissed you, here?" He bent lower, and Charlotte felt the hot rush of his breath across her skin. She struggled against the bonds that held her to conceal her body's visceral reaction.

"Stop," she gasped. "Please!"

"Your waist is so narrow," he went on relentlessly. "I could almost wrap my hands around it entirely." The worn linen of her shirt moved, sliding over her belly. He wasn't touching her, but he was touching her clothing, making it move over her skin in a caress worse than the touch of his hands. "I could lift you, over and over, and let you ride me," he whispered. "Do you like it on top, Charlotte? Do you like your lover spread beneath you, in your power? Do you hold him down while you take your pleasure, or do you show yourself off to him while he pleases you?" Charlotte made an inarticulate sound as his hands drifted, snagging on her shirt and pulling it over her breasts.

"I can see you rising above me, taking me inside

you. Would you move slowly, I wonder, or fast? I
couldn't lie down, of course; I can see your nipples,
Charlotte," he murmured, working the shirt from side
to side, letting it abrade her breasts. She had thrown
away all her undergarments, and there was nothing
underneath the shirt to protect her from its friction.
Charlotte closed her eyes, taking deep breaths in an
effort to calm her screaming senses. "Open your
eyes," he said. "See how perfectly you fit my hands."
She shook her head, squeezing her eyelids tighter.
"Just . . . like . . . this," he said softly, and she felt the
lightest touch along the lower curve of her breast as
he cupped it. She flinched, and his laugh was almost
a groan. "And when you mount me, I want to suckle
them. Gently at first . . ." His thumb moved, swirling
lightly over her rigid nipple. Charlotte bit her tongue
to keep from arching her back and pushing against
that thumb. "Then harder. The faster you ride me, the
harder I'll suckle."

Charlotte prayed for lightning to strike him. For
lightning to strike *her*. She prayed to go deaf, to faint,
or simply to fall asleep, anything at all to rescue her
from the havoc he was creating in her. He was the
lowest scoundrel, and yet her mind was betraying her,
weaving his words into vivid moving images that made
her body liquid with desire. She *could* see herself
mounting him, his large body resplendently nude in
her imagination. She *could* feel him driving deep into
her, and the hot, wet rasp of his tongue on her skin.

"But you need to be shown who's master." His voice
got even softer. "After you've had your turn on top,
I'll have mine. I want you against a wall, where you
have nothing to hold on to but me. Your arms around
my neck"—there was a zing of sensation along the

underside of her raised arms—"and your legs around my waist." His fingers feathered her knee, and Charlotte caught her breath. He was touching her again, but the word *stop* lodged in her throat. She couldn't bear his touch, but she might explode without it. "And I'll hold you here." His hand slid lightly over her thigh. "And here." His other hand stroked her hip. "You'll be at my mercy. I want you to touch yourself where I enter you. I want to feel your fingers holding me while I'm deep inside you." Charlotte gasped, picturing it in spite of herself and feeling herself growing slippery wet at the thought. "I want you to bring yourself to climax there, with your back against the wall, and your ankles locked behind my waist, and me inside you. And when you come, I want to hear you scream."

His fingers danced up her inner thigh, and Charlotte raised her hips in shameless invitation. Her hatred of him was all mixed up in the unnatural, blatantly sexual response she had had to him from the start, and her body was begging for release from the tension.

As if he knew, his fingertip slowly traced the crease between her legs, maddeningly light.

Stuart inhaled sharply as his fingers slid deeper between her legs, at her instigation. She was his, ready for the taking, although in his current state, it would be over in the blink of an eye. He didn't want her for a few seconds, he wanted to start at the beginning of what he had described to her and stretch each step out for hours. Knowing she wanted him drove him mad; the sparks that flew between them every time they met were a sure indicator—to him—of their inevitable collision in bed. And here she was, in his bed, aroused by the very same fantasies that made him burn.

But she was tied down. She didn't want to be aroused. She didn't want to want him. He only meant to teach her a lesson, not to rape her. Whatever his failings, Stuart did consider himself a gentleman, with some notion of honor. Never in his life had he had to take advantage of a woman to get her in bed, and he still meant what he said earlier: he wanted her to come to him. On her knees perhaps, but willing from the start.

She moved then, pushing against his hand again, and Stuart flinched at the dilemma before him. Seduce a woman who would surely hate him for it in the morning, or give up his one and only chance to have her willingly beneath him.

He withdrew his hand, slowly. She moaned, moving in a restless, seductive way that made his mouth go dry. Her eyes were still closed and her dark curls tumbled haphazardly over his pillows. Stuart hesitated again. Surely it was asking too much of any man to let her just walk away. He was sure he had only to kiss her to bridge the gap between arousal and desire.

All right, he told himself. *Untie her. Make it clear she can leave if she wants to.* If she were still there in five minutes, of her own free will, he would be perfectly within the bounds of honor to seduce her. Reaching for the cravat that bound her hands, Stuart lowered his mouth to hers.

Chapter Five

A loud knock sounded just as he took hold of the loose end of the cravat. Stuart paused. On the bed, Charlotte was breathing in shallow pants, her eyes closed, still lost in his words. As he preferred to be. Stuart decided to ignore it.

"Drake, damn you, open the door!" The voice, slurred by drink, changed his mind. Stuart sighed as Charlotte's eyes fluttered open and she blinked, coming to herself in a moment. Her chest rose as she drew breath to scream.

"Don't," he told her. "They are my friends, and they are also received. Keep quiet or everyone in town will know you were here tonight." Some of the familiar hostility returned to her expression, but he was already on his way out of the room. He pulled the bedroom door closed behind him, and went to let Jameson and Whitley in.

They almost fell over each other into his sitting room. "I say, Drake, gone to bed already?"

"I was tired, Whit." He extended a hand and

helped the very drunk Angus Whitley to his feet. "What brings you here?"

"A carriage," said Whitley with a stupid grin.

"You lost."

Jameson yawned. "All the women wanted to know where you'd gone. We couldn't even get a smile."

"Lost badly, then." Stuart glanced toward the bedroom. It was highly unlikely he'd be able to pick up where they left off, but he didn't like leaving her. She had been quiet so far, but the more time she had to think about it, the more likely she was to scream or cry out for help. Stuart really didn't want to have to explain to his friends why she was tied up in his bed. "I'm all done in for the night. Take yourselves home and sleep it off."

"Drake, this country life is killing you," announced Whitley, staggering to the mantel and foraging for a box of cigars. "Let's go to London. Tomorrow."

"I can't go to London," he said dryly.

"Rot," said Whitley, waving one hand. "That sorry tale's surely blown over by now." He picked up a cigar box. Stuart dragged one hand over his face. It was easy for Whitley to disdain the gossip; many of his friends had. But Stuart knew the rest of society would not. His own father had told him not to come back until he had made something of himself. So far, all Stuart had made of himself was an accidental thief.

"Sorry or not, I'd rather not stir up—" His explanation was cut short by Whitley's disbelieving exclamation.

"Drake, you devil! Empty pockets, indeed! No funds to play deep, with this in your hands?" He held up Charlotte's emerald necklace. Stuart clamped his mouth shut to keep from swearing; he had completely forgotten he had put it there while he tried to figure out how to return it.

"I say, Drake, I'll take my two hundred pounds back, then," drawled Jameson, sprawled on the sofa. "Whose neck did you buy this for?"

"You know how it is," he said vaguely, moving to take the jewels from Whitley. "A gentleman shouldn't say."

"How much is this worth?" Whitley tossed the necklace past him to Jameson. Now that there was something interesting afoot, both were more alert and less drunk than before. Stuart didn't want anyone knowing he had that necklace. Both Whitley and Jameson had met Charlotte in the last few days, and either might recognize the emeralds as hers. He took the box from Whitley with a scowl.

"All right, all right, just curious! You're at your last pence for weeks, and suddenly you've got a handful of gems. Surely not for the heiress. Wait until after the wedding for that."

"That's right, I should. The necklace, Jameson." He held out his hand. He should just hand it back to Charlotte, now that she had proven she was willing to break into his house. How she knew he had it, Stuart couldn't guess, but now that he was reasonably sure she wouldn't report him to the magistrate, he could return them without delay.

Jameson was frowning at the necklace, turning it back and forth. He leaned forward toward the fire, then scratched his fingernail over several stones. "Where'd you purchase this, Drake? A reputable place?"

"Not precisely," he hedged. "A friend of a friend." Still Jameson examined the necklace.

"I hope you got a good price, then." He looked up. "You know it's a fake."

Stuart stared. "No. Not at all."

Jameson met his eyes a moment longer. Then he dropped the necklace into Stuart's outstretched hand with a shrug. "Well, I could be wrong. Sometimes old stones look fake."

Stuart closed the box gently. It was dark in the room, and he hadn't a jeweler's glass, and he was drunk. But still . . . Jameson knew jewels, having bought a great many for his mistresses over the years. "How do you know?"

"They're scratched. Even good paste won't stand up to pressure. But I haven't a loupe, and the light is poor. It could be my imagination."

"What a tangle that is," said Stuart quietly.

"Let's find out, shall we?" proposed Whitley, puffing at a cigar he'd found. "There has to be a proper jeweler in this town."

Jameson shrugged. "Up to Drake, really. His blunt thrown away. His heiress who'll pout if she winds up with paste."

"Of course he wants to know!" Whitley declared as Stuart opened his mouth to demur. "How could he not? The man's been cheated." Jameson looked at him, and Stuart closed his mouth. If he showed no concern, his friends would remark it more than if he flew into a fury. As it was, he could only admit to a growing curiosity.

Did Charlotte know the emeralds were paste? If so, why had she come after them? Surely it was more trouble than the necklace was worth. And if she didn't know . . .

Stuart turned and went into the bedroom. Charlotte lifted her head at his entrance. "Who is here?" she whispered, her voice tight with anxiety.

"Some friends. We're going out for a bit." He picked up his jacket from beside the bed.

Her mouth opened in outrage. "And you're just going to leave me here, like this?" She started twisting against her bonds, and he held up one hand.

"Be patient. You can't leave while they're waiting in the other room." He pulled on his jacket and fiddled a moment with the cuff. "Perhaps you should wait until I return."

"No!"

Stuart winced at her loud whisper, and glanced at the door in apprehension. There was just the murmur of Whitley and Jameson talking, so he reached for the cravat around her wrists.

"Don't leave right at once," he said, working on the knot. "And stay to the main streets. It's not safe to walk alone at this time of night."

"Just untie me!" she hissed, wriggling again. "I know how to take care of myself!" Stuart paused to give her a wry look. She glared back. "Would you please hurry?" she bit out.

Stuart scowled at the knot. He had tied it securely, and her struggles had pulled the cloth tight. "I'm trying," he muttered. "Hold still—"

"Drake?" In one stride Stuart was across the room, narrowly blocking Whitley at the door. "Don't go back to bed," he joked.

Stuart grinned sheepishly. "I wasn't about to, Whit." He cast an apologetic glance back at Charlotte as he pulled the door closed behind him, just barely hearing her whispered "You'll regret this."

It took less than an hour to find a jeweler who could be roused from his bed. The fellow grumbled a bit, but examined the necklace and informed them that sadly, the stones were forgeries, good ones, but still worth very little. Stuart pocketed the necklace without a word, and refused his friends' offer of a ride. Jameson gave him a searching look as they parted, but said nothing, and Stuart walked home.

He wondered why Charlotte Griffolino wore paste jewels. The most likely reason, of course, was that she had sold the real ones. Women often did it, when they needed funds: have a copy made, then sell the original. Husbands or lovers were often none the wiser, and it provided a secret supply of money to women who otherwise had none. But why would she do something as dangerous as break into his rooms in search of jewels worth next to nothing? Surely her dislike of him didn't extend to risking her neck just to spite him.

The only explanation Stuart found reasonable was that she couldn't bear for anyone to know she wore paste, not even the fool who—mistakenly—stole them. But why? Stuart could understand wanting them back, and wanting to punish the person who took them, but why would she care what he thought of them?

If she didn't know they were fake, why not? She seemed like a worldly woman; how could she not have her jewels examined and insured? Had someone given her real ones as a gift, and then exchanged them for these? Perhaps there never had been real gems, and her wealth was all a front. Except for her undergarments; Stuart might be fooled by a false diamond, but he knew women's clothing, and her lingerie was real, and expensive. None of it made sense, or at least not in a flattering way, and he let himself in, still trying to puzzle it out.

She had fallen asleep. Stuart stood over her for a moment. She looked sweeter, calmer, in sleep, not at all like a hardhearted harpy. Her hands were still wrapped around his cravat, and even though he had tied her ankles with loose knots that would have eventually come undone, they were also still tied. She hadn't really tried to get free. He untied them gently, delaying just a moment longer until he woke her.

It was none of his business why the jewels were fake, or whether she knew it or not. Everyone had a right to their own secrets, even a woman who had done her best to expose his.

He sat on the bed beside her and reached for the cravat. Her eyes flew open and she gasped. Stuart smiled grimly, working at the knot. "Never fear, I am letting you go."

"How gentlemanly of you," she said bitterly. "Tying me down and then walking out and leaving me here for hours! I shall be quite amazed if my maid hasn't called the watch."

"If you didn't tell her you were going out tonight, dressed as a man, to sneak into my rooms, why would she even be looking for you? I've barely been gone an hour." The cravat came loose. Her eyes narrowed, catlike, as she hastily swung her legs over the side of the bed, rubbing her wrists. Stuart dug into his pocket and produced the necklace. It was a tacit admission of guilt, but he didn't have the heart to keep them from her, not after the look of breathless wonder on her face as he whispered his fantasies in her ear.

She snatched the jewels from his hand. He waited for her to complain about them being fake, to accuse him of switching the real emeralds. "Is this all?"

Stuart frowned. "That's all. I didn't take anything else."

"Then what were you doing in the music room?"

Ah yes, the music room. "Looking for a way out," he said. "But someone was in there and nearly slashed my throat."

"Who? Who was it?" she asked immediately.

"How the devil should I know?" Stuart raked his hair from his forehead. "He was opening crates. I didn't do anything to him, but he jumped on me with a knife. Gave me a lovely scar, no doubt." He opened his bandaged palm for her to see.

She glanced at it. "What did he look like?"

Stuart shrugged, suddenly tired. "I never saw his face. Small fellow, but strong."

"Did he speak? What did he wear?"

"I didn't take the time to converse, what with keeping his knife away from my neck." Stuart got to his feet and fetched a long cloak from the wardrobe. "Put that on. It's gotten cooler, and you shouldn't be recognized."

"I want to know who was in my house!" she exclaimed.

"And I've told you, I don't know." He tossed the cloak at her and went into the sitting room, slapping his hat low on his head. "Come along. I've had enough excitement for the evening."

"Not until you tell me everything." Charlotte was trying not to choke on a bilious fury that she had responded in a raw, sexual way to nothing more than the sound of his voice. That he could turn a woman— a mature, experienced woman, no less—into mush just by talking to her only confirmed her distrust of him. This man would have destroyed Susan, and Charlotte was not at all sorry for blackening his name.

But she did want to learn what he knew about the other burglar. For some reason, she believed his claim that he had only broken in the once, and taken only the necklace. It explained everything perfectly: why her bedroom had been disturbed for the first time, the wreckage in the music room, the obviously unfinished search of the newly arrived crates. Charlotte was almost relieved, in fact. If Stuart had been the one in her room, and had kept the other burglar from following his usual pattern, at least she wasn't dealing with a thief who was getting more dangerous. And if Stuart had seen the other man, there was a chance she could solve the whole mystery once and for all.

So she planted her feet in the doorway and waited. He heaved a sigh and faced her with his hands on his hips. "I've told you all I know. It was a small fellow." He indicated his own shoulder height. Still an inch taller than Charlotte, but perhaps small to him, she had to admit. "And slender, or wiry. Strong, and reckless as the devil, for he tacked right into me. He had a knife, probably a boot knife, maybe six inches, and used it without hesitation. He had a sort of lantern that gave only a little light, and he was searching inside a crate. I didn't see him remove anything, or even what was in the crate he had open, and when the servants came running, he ran over me and disappeared. Are you satisfied now?" He flung his hands wide.

"He didn't say anything?" Charlotte pressed.

"Not a word."

"Did he smell strange? Were his clothes unusual?"

He shook his head. "I couldn't tell you. What with his knife at my throat, I didn't take as much note as I might have otherwise."

"But you must have noticed something," she said

urgently. "You're the only person who's ever seen him, and if you can't—" She stopped as his head snapped up.

"He's broken in before?"

Charlotte tugged the cloak around her, regretting asking him anything. She should have known he would be too preoccupied with saving himself to notice anything helpful. "A few other times."

"Why?" Now he was staring at her.

Charlotte scowled. "I don't know. He searches, but never takes anything, as far as I can tell."

"What has the magistrate done?"

Her mouth tightened. "Nothing was ever taken. Many times there was no proof anyone had been in the house. My servants aren't attentive; they leave doors and windows open without a thought. What would a magistrate tell me?"

"Then why don't you have men guarding the house?"

Now it felt rather stupid to tell him she hadn't felt threatened, as he had firsthand knowledge of the fellow's knife. "I didn't think it would do any good."

"It could hardly do any harm. He had a knife. What if you or your niece should come upon him next time?"

Charlotte didn't need to hear any more condemnation of her fitness as Susan's guardian. She was perfectly aware of her deficiencies in that regard. "I'll consider it. Take care they don't catch *you* next time."

He gave a short, caustic laugh. "Don't worry, I won't be back. Shall we go, or are you staying the night?" He twirled her battered hat around his finger. Charlotte strode across the room and snatched it from him, jamming it on her head.

"Just a moment," he sighed, stopping her when she

would have opened the door. He lifted the hat from her head, and plunged his hands into her tangled curls. He combed his fingers quickly through her hair, and with a few quick twists, looped it up atop her head, and then pulled the hat firmly over the mass. "There," he said, opening the door and waving her through.

He walked her home quickly, just about as fast as she could walk without running. Trotting along beside him, Charlotte felt terribly awkward. She still despised him—she told herself so with every other step—but some odd sort of bond had been forged between them tonight. A bond of lust is not a good thing, she reminded herself, trying not to consider the way he had handed her necklace back without a word, or the way he had run his hands through her hair before hiding it under her hat.

Stuart Drake was a puzzle. On one hand, he was an admitted fortune hunter, after Susan only for her money. The rumors of his behavior in London were truly appalling, and he had broken into her house and stolen her necklace. Those facts alone should render him abhorrent to her. But on the other hand, he could have treated her so much worse tonight than he had. She had been completely at his mercy, and he could have had her arrested, or beaten her soundly, if not done something even worse. And though he had tied her down on the bed, he had kept his word and not touched her. Aside from chafed wrists and seriously wounded pride, she had ended up much as she had started off this evening.

Almost, anyway, Charlotte corrected with a frown. She didn't know how she could ever face him in the light of day now. It was almost as awkward as if she had actually gone to bed with him. Charlotte never knew what to say to her lovers in the morning, even though those relationships had all been well-defined at the beginning, unlike this one. It wasn't even a relationship, she thought in disgust. He had only forced her to admit she was attracted to him. Which might have been the basis for an affair at one point in her life, but no longer; Charlotte was determined to be a respectable woman now that she had Susan.

"Tell your servants they are to check every door and window before they go to bed," he said suddenly, interrupting her thoughts. "Threaten to sack them without a reference if you find any overlooked. Tell the butler it's his job to inspect the house at night, and make sure he does it. Tunbridge Wells isn't the fashionable place it used to be, and anyone who loses a position now will be hard pressed to find another soon."

"I've already told them that," she began, but he shook his head, still walking, eyes straight ahead.

"They've been lax. I got in through an unlocked window. It's possible one of them is in league with the thief, and is leaving him an entry. You said there's often no sign of intrusion?" Charlotte nodded uneasily; it had never occurred to her that one of her own servants might be allowing the thief into her house. "Then check the locks yourself every night until you're satisfied they're following your orders." Across the street from her house, he stopped and turned to face her. The streetlamps cast a dim light onto one side of his face, leaving the other in deep shadow. "And summon the magistrate," he said seriously. "The man had a knife, and he didn't take much time to discover upon whom he was turning it. Next time it could be one of your servants, or you yourself. If I hadn't been quite a bit larger than he, I'd have had my throat cut."

"All right," said Charlotte, subdued by his reasoning and by the intensity in his tone.

"Good," he said. "Wait here. I'll check the house from the outside, to see if anything seems amiss." Before she could say another word, he strode across the street, his cloak swirling out behind him. Charlotte clung to the shadows, suddenly thankful he had walked her home. What if the thief was in her house again, at this moment? She would have walked in without a thought, perhaps surprising him with a knife in his hand. She pulled the cloak up around her ears, finding herself in the odd position of being grateful for another person's interference in her life.

After what seemed like a very long time, Stuart's tall, loose-limbed figure reemerged from her garden. Charlotte breathed a sigh of relief as he crossed the street toward her, unharmed. "Everything seems fine," he said. "Perhaps the maids had some sense scared into them. You have a key?"

"I left it under the gatepost," said Charlotte. "Just tonight," she added as his expression darkened.

"I wouldn't make it a habit." He seemed on the verge of saying something else, but didn't. There was a moment of silence. "Good night, then."

"Good night." Charlotte stepped into the street, paused, and turned around. "Why *did* you steal my necklace?"

He sighed. "I didn't mean to. I apologize."

Charlotte's mouth dropped open. "You didn't *mean* to? You just happened to be in my room, looking in my jewel case, and it just *happened* to find its way into your pocket? Did you think I'd believe that? You went through my *clothing*." His mouth thinned, and he looked away. "Then why were you in my house in the first place?" Charlotte asked, reverting to a cold, mocking tone.

He remained silent for a moment. "I thought Miss Tratter had something of mine," he said at last. "I was wrong." He paused. "How did you know I had the necklace?"

Charlotte fumbled in her pocket for the flask. "You left this in my garden." She threw it at his feet. He looked down at it, and let out a weary sigh. "Good night, Mr. Drake," she said coolly.

"Good bye, Contessa," he replied, head still bowed.

Charlotte turned on her heel and left. She retrieved her key from its hiding place and let herself in without looking back. Only when she had bolted the door behind her and hurried up the stairs to her room did she realize she was still wearing his cloak. She debated tossing it out the window to him, then decided she would simply send it back tomorrow. It would be an invitation to disaster to seek him out again. Charlotte much preferred to keep things as they were, lodged in comfortable animosity, than risk discovering anything more that might challenge her view of him.

Out in the street, Stuart scooped up his flask and examined it ruefully. It was dented, just like his pride. Trust a woman to tie him in knots and then turn up her nose at him, just to make it really hurt. For a brief, few minutes this evening, he had felt like a man with a purpose. And while Charlotte had probably discarded most of his suggestions by now, at the time she had listened as if she respected his opinion. Even though there was no good reason whatsoever for it, Stuart thought he might miss the woman; for all her faults, she appealed to him, and not just physically. Although he certainly *would* regret for a very, very long time what might have happened had Whitley and Jameson not turned up.

That was no less than he deserved, though. Breaking into her house had to be one of his worst decisions. He had been stabbed, almost caught and arrested, and accidentally stolen an emerald necklace; all that, and he hadn't even gotten the ring he wanted. No piece of jewelry was worth any of those things, and Stuart decided he should leave well enough alone. Charlotte Griffolino had brought him nothing but trouble from the moment he laid eyes on her, and he didn't need to invite more by going after that ring again.

He shook his head and walked home through the silent streets. Time to forget what might have been and move on to the pressing question in his life, namely, what he was going to do now. The invitations that used to flood his breakfast table had dwindled to a trickle, then stopped altogether within days of Charlotte's visit to Lady Kildair. He had gone from an eligible, if poor, match to a pariah in a week. He had already accepted an invitation to a supper party at the Martins' the next evening, which a prouder man would now decline to keep, but Stuart had literally spent his last farthing. If he didn't attend the supper party, he couldn't be sure of dinner. Since it would have to be his last night in Kent, he would go, and take his leave in style.

He might even get lucky, and she would decide to stay home.

Chapter Six

"Did you get it?"

Charlotte groaned and pulled the covers over her head at Lucia's excited question. It was too early to be awake, let alone to recount her evening's adventure. Her friend ripped the blankets from her hands and Charlotte opened her eyes to see Lucia peering down at her from barely six inches away.

"I have been on tender hooks all morning. Did you get it?"

"Tenterhooks," corrected Charlotte.

Lucia waved her hand. "Tell me or I shall drink your *caffe*."

Charlotte immediately sat up, reaching for the steaming cup. As soon as they had taken up residence in England, Lucia had marched into the kitchen and taught the cook how to make proper Italian coffee. If Lucia did nothing else to earn her keep, Charlotte thought as she took a long greedy sip, she could still stay, just for the *caffe*.

Lucia sat back in her chair, pulled right to the side

of the bed, and waited until Charlotte lowered the cup. "Now, tell me. Was it a success?"

"I got the necklace back," she said. "It was so easy to get in, I'm surprised he isn't burgled nightly."

"Yes, yes." Lucia's eyes gleamed with mischief. "And did you take the scissors to his trousers?"

Charlotte took another restorative drink of coffee. She had told Lucia she intended to cut strategically revealing holes in Stuart Drake's trousers, but now she was unable to think of his trousers without remembering how he filled them out. "No."

"Oh, what a pity." Lucia pulled a face. "I was looking forward to the unveiling."

"Lucia."

"Do you know, I have been considering the matter. I do not think he is too old. You are not so very old, after all, and he seems to be a fit and virile man."

"He's a fortune hunter," Charlotte reminded her. "He wants a rich bride."

"But I am rich in experience."

"I suspect he prefers pounds sterling."

"Besides, I do not wish to marry him," Lucia went on. "Only to make merry with him." She laughed in delight at her wit.

Charlotte got out of bed, taking deep breaths as her body protested. Wrestling with Stuart had taken its toll, and she was stiff and sore. Her arms and her back ached. She thought fleetingly of the nights she had climbed out her window in her father's house and run across the meadow to be with the man she thought she loved. Then she had stayed with him all night, only sneaking back into the house just before dawn, and somehow she had still gone about the day as if she'd gotten a full night's rest. Now she could barely get out of bed, even though the clock indicated she'd slept several hours. She must be getting old. Either that, or the delusions of love had been stronger than any amount of *caffe*.

"With any luck, he'll be gone soon." Charlotte pulled on her dressing gown, her arms almost creaking out loud. She needed a hot bath, she decided, and rang for the maid.

Lucia sighed wistfully. "Ah, well. So. You were gone an eternity. I fell asleep waiting for you to return."

"Did Susan—?"

"No." Lucia waved her hand. "She never woke. Nor did she speak to me. I have done nothing to her, and still she turns her nose in the air to me. If she were my child, she would have a beating for her insolence."

"Please don't talk about beatings," said Charlotte, lowering herself gingerly onto her dressing table chair. Her hair was a wild mess, matted curls standing up in all directions. She picked up her brush and went to work, wincing as she raised her arms over her head. "Susan is still grieving for her father as well as becoming accustomed to life with me. It's been very hard for her."

Lucia sniffed, but let it drop. "So you got it back. He will leave town, so you are done with him, yes?"

"Yes." Charlotte gave up on her hair. The maid could do it.

"You are not telling me details," scolded Lucia. "Why did you tease me with such a tale, of him ravaging your lingerie? Where did you find it? Did you ravage his unmentionables?"

"He came home early," said Charlotte after a moment. "He caught me. We had an argument, but

then . . ." Heat unfurled low in her belly. "We talked."
Oh, how he had talked. "And he gave it back."

"No! You talked?" Lucia put down her cup with a
loud clink. "I almost forget you are English at times,
but there is no doubt of it, if you can break into a
handsome man's bedroom and simply talk to him."

"He didn't want to be arrested for stealing the
necklace." The maid tapped at the door, and peeked
inside at Charlotte's summons. "Draw a bath," Charlotte told her. "As hot as possible."

"Was he not angry to find you there?"

"He was." Charlotte crossed the room again and
got back into bed to wait for her bath. She didn't even
hope it came quickly.

"Did he hurt you? *Cara*, he is such a big man, with
such strong arms. And his hands! Do you know, his
hands remind me of a Russian count I once knew,
who could give a woman such pleasure . . . ! His fingers were so long—"

"He saw the other burglar," Charlotte interrupted,
not wanting to hear about Lucia's lovers or how much
Stuart Drake reminded her of them. Although he did
have very nice hands, now that she thought about it,
long-fingered and strong; surely they could be as sure
and demanding as they could be teasingly gentle . . .

"The other one?" said Lucia after a pause. "I
thought he was the one."

"There was another. Mr. Drake only broke in the
once, he claims, and I see no reason to doubt it. I suspect he wanted to punish me for denying him Susan
and her inheritance, but he would not admit it. He
ran across the other burglar in the music room, rifling
through the newest crates. They fought for a moment,
and then Dunstan came and both thieves fled."

"Did he see the other man clearly? Can he describe him?"

Charlotte shook her head. "No. He says not. All he could say was that it was a small fellow." She gave Lucia a sour look. "About my size. Am I small?"

Lucia shrugged. "For a man you would be. I prefer a man to be tall. There is nothing so delicious as the weight of a large man—"

"He noticed nothing else except the man's knife." Charlotte didn't know why she had grown so maidenly lately. For the three years she had known Lucia, they had always discussed men, often in ways that would have made the men blush if they had known. It had been one of the things Charlotte prized about her friend: her utter frankness and inability to be shocked. Married to Piero, Charlotte had lived surrounded by men, and Lucia was often the only female face she saw. When she had decided to return to England and Lucia had asked to visit, Charlotte had invited her immediately.

But perhaps the English side of her that had lain dormant for over a decade was reemerging now that she was in England again. Every time Lucia brought up Stuart Drake and began listing his appealing features, Charlotte tried to change the subject. She had been attracted to the wrong man before—she seemed to have a real talent for it, in fact—but he was the first one she shied away from dissecting with Lucia. And nothing on earth would make her tell Lucia what he had done last night. Hopefully Lady Kildair would accomplish her mission, and Stuart would be out of town in a matter of days. Once he was gone, she could concentrate on mending her fences with Susan and establishing her own life here in England.

"A knife?" Lucia bolted out of her chair, her voice squeaking with alarm. "A madman with a knife is loose in our house? What shall we do?"

"We shall make sure he cannot get in again," said Charlotte. "The servants seem to have been terrified the other night, for when I came home, St—" She stopped herself from telling Lucia he had walked her home. "The doors and windows were all locked," she finished. "And they will be, every night from now on, or I shall sack every servant until I find some who can remember to keep the house secure."

"Did he use the knife on Mr. Drake?"

Charlotte nodded. "He sliced his hand. If Mr. Drake hadn't been so much larger than he, the thief would have cut his throat."

There was a long silence. Lucia sat down, uncharacteristically somber. "He wants something important."

"But what the devil is it?" Charlotte exclaimed impatiently. "It would be so much easier if he left a note just asking for it."

Lucia was blinking rapidly. "Do you know what is in those crates?"

"More or less. Piero's valet packed everything. I haven't even opened most of them."

"Perhaps we should unpack them." Lucia's voice was deadly serious. "Spread everything out and see if there is something extraordinary, something a man would kill for."

"There are three rooms full of crates, barrels, and trunks," said Charlotte. "By all means, start unpacking. I can't face it."

"Why are you so reluctant? Our lives are in danger."

Charlotte knew Lucia was right, but she still couldn't

do it. "I don't want to see those things again," she said vaguely. "I've been thinking of giving them away."

"To a museum?"

Charlotte hesitated. "No."

"To whom, then? They are priceless objets d'art."

If only you knew, Charlotte thought. Thankfully, the servants arrived with the tub then, and began filling it with steaming water. Lucia went to have a calming cigarette in the garden, and Charlotte lowered herself into the scalding bath for a long soak. Perhaps she should hire some more men to guard the house; they might even catch the thief. She was sure there was nothing worth stealing in the crates, but the knife worried her. Once the thief had satisfied himself the crates held nothing, he might come upstairs and take out his frustration on her, or on Susan or Lucia. Charlotte had thought Kent would be a perfectly safe, dull place for three women to live alone, but it seemed she was wrong.

Well. She would give it another day's thought. If there were signs that the thief tried to get in while the house was locked tight, she would hire the guards. In the meantime, she had promised to take Susan shopping, and Charlotte intended to keep her promise. Although her niece had been somewhat sullen yesterday after breakfast, the trip to get the yellow dress had cheered her, and she had been almost cordial at dinner. Today Charlotte planned to take her to get shoes to match the dress. And if two women couldn't get along while shopping for shoes, when could they?

Stuart knew he was making his hostess uncomfortable. Cordelia Martin's eyes had almost popped from her head when he made his appearance, although she recovered in time to greet him. She had invited him, and he had accepted; it wasn't her fault he had fallen so low, but then again, it wasn't really his fault, either.

He found Jameson quickly. Although he didn't want anyone to think he was slinking away like a dog with its tail between its legs, he also didn't want to get thrown out. More than one back was turned in his direction as he made his way through the room. Jameson grinned when he saw him.

"Drake, old fellow! Simply capital to see you tonight."

"Snuff it," he advised his friend, taking a glass of wine from a passing footman. "This is my farewell to Kent. I'd rather not end it lying facedown in the street."

"Don't say you're abandoning the field!" Jameson shook his head with a soft tsk. "Thought you had more backbone than that."

"It's not backbone I lack right now."

"I'll spot you a hundred," said Jameson carelessly. "Kent would be as dull as a Lenten sermon without you."

Stuart forced a sour smile. "Many thanks, but I try to keep my debts under a thousand."

"Ah." Jameson became absorbed in his own glass of wine. "Back to London, then?"

"Regrettably," muttered Stuart, draining his glass. He lifted it significantly at a footman, and the servant hurried over to exchange his empty glass for a full one.

Jameson cleared his throat, looking around the room, anywhere but at him. "Well, best of luck."

Stuart knew it was sympathy that made Jameson

uneasy. Jameson couldn't believe a few paltry rumors had actually ruined him; stand firm, he had advised Stuart, and it will blow over. Stuart wasn't so sure—it didn't seem Charlotte did things by half measures—but it didn't really matter. The mortgage on Oakwood Park was due in a month, not nearly enough time for him to find another bride. He would have to admit defeat and return to London, and do his best to worm his way back into his father's good graces. If he began now, he might yet be able to keep his property.

"Ah," said his friend suddenly. "Your heiress has arrived. Give her one more go, why don't you? She looks dashed pretty tonight."

Stuart hesitated. Against his will he looked, from the corner of his eye. She was there, glorious in green with black lace. Miss Tratter was at her side, as was the tall, voluptuous Italian woman who lived with them. "I think I've burned my bridge with the aunt, so to speak," he said, watching the three women greet the Martins.

"Not quite the wizened shrew you were led to expect, is she?" Jameson was watching Charlotte with interest. Stuart was trying not to, both to avoid meeting her eyes and to keep from remembering how she looked in his bed.

"She's far from wizened," was all he said.

"I should say . . ." Jameson's voice tapered off, and Stuart tore his eyes off Charlotte. His friend's gaze had fixed on her, focused and intent, and Stuart was opening his mouth to ask, rather testily, what was so intriguing, when he saw what had caught Jameson's eye. Not Charlotte, even though she did shimmer like an exotic bird in her green silk, but the emerald and diamond necklace around her throat. "Not," finished

Jameson in a quiet, thoughtful tone. He shot a quick glance at Stuart, who was gulping down his wine and wishing he'd already left for London.

"Not many necklaces like that in Kent, I expect," said Jameson after a moment.

"No," agreed Stuart grimly.

"A woman like that is sure to have the stones appraised sooner or later."

"No doubt." Stuart seized another glass of wine, wishing it were whiskey. This, of all nights, was an excellent time to get foxed. "Pardon me."

He walked away before Jameson could ask outright if he had knowingly given a woman paste jewels, or why that woman was Charlotte Griffolino instead of Susan Tratter. Luckily Mrs. Martin had invited half the town to her supper party, and he could slip away without being noticed. Of course, half the town was already doing its best not to notice him even if they came face to face with him. Stuart stepped onto a balcony overlooking the garden and pulled the drape shut behind him. He must have offended the deity to have every little thing in his life go so spectacularly wrong.

"Drake!" Stuart closed his eyes wearily, then turned around. Susan stepped forward, her face shining. Stuart stopped her from throwing her arms around him by catching her hands and raising them to his lips instead. "Oh, you look terrible," she cried. "Has it been just dreadful for you? I've barely slept a wink, thinking about how Aunt Charlotte humiliated you! She's hardly left me alone for a moment since then, or I should have come to see you at once. I shall never forgive her, never!"

For a moment Stuart thought she meant Charlotte's

sabotage to his reputation, but then he remembered the dance at the Kildairs'. "It's been a difficult week," he said vaguely.

She nodded, her eyes glistening. "I've told her ever so many times you're not the scoundrel she thinks you are, but she refuses to listen. It's been so long since I've seen you anywhere, and people are saying the most dreadful things about you now—"

"Miss Tratter," he tried to interrupt.

"But of course I don't believe one of them," she rushed on. "I know you're not capable of ruining a young lady during her grandmother's garden party, let alone abducting some girl to Dover! I'm sure they were both plain, freckled girls anyway, but of course you would have married either if you had done anything to ruin them, unintentionally of course, because I know you are a man of honor."

"Garden party?" Stuart repeated incredulously. "Abduction?" Was that the story Charlotte had started? Anne Hale was a persistent flirt who was never content with just one man's attention. Even after she had contrived to walk with him in the park, she had been trying to catch the eye of another gentleman. When she lost her shoe, Stuart found it and slipped it back on her foot. True, she had lifted her skirt higher than necessary—the girl had no subtlety—but he hadn't touched her stockings, as the rumor had reported in London. Now he had ravished her in front of a party of elderly ladies?

And abducting Eliza Pennyworth! He hardly knew her, and never would have met her had she not been in love with an old schoolmate of his, Aiden Montgomery. Her family refused to allow them to marry, and arranged a match with a wealthy cousin for Miss

Pennyworth. In desperation, the lovers had decided to elope. Montgomery would have to desert the Royal Navy to do so, though, which shocked Stuart; Aiden had wanted a naval career his whole life, and had just risen to first lieutenant. Not wanting his friend to lose everything, Stuart had offered to drive Miss Pennyworth to Dover, where Montgomery's ship was docked. The couple could marry quickly and quietly, Montgomery could keep his rank, and Miss Pennyworth would be safe from her family's ambitions. Miss Pennyworth agreed eagerly, and Montgomery wrung his hand in fervent gratitude. But it all came to naught when her brother caught them a mere ten miles from Dover, dragging Miss Pennyworth back to London where she was unceremoniously married to her cousin. Montgomery's ship sailed two days later, and Stuart had borne the gossip in silence, knowing his had been the kindest fate of the three.

Susan shook her head and put her finger on his lips to silence him. "You don't have to deny it. I don't believe it, and it doesn't matter, anyway. I still love you."

Gently he removed her hands from his face and jacket. "Miss Tratter, I think it is time . . ."

"For us to run away together?" she asked, so bright with hope he couldn't bear to look at her. "Oh, I can pack my bag in an hour! That will teach Aunt Charlotte to treat me like a child. Where shall we go, to Scotland? Or to London? I just know I shall adore London, when we live there."

"For us to face the truth," he corrected quietly. "Your aunt will never give her consent to my suit."

"She can go hang," declared Susan.

"Nevertheless, I fear . . ." Stuart paused, thinking.

"I fear we are doomed to be apart, divided by fate and misfortune."

She contemplated that for a moment. "But if we elope . . ."

He shook his head. "It would be no use. We are a pair of star-crossed lovers."

"Oh," she breathed, understanding dawning. "Like Romeo and Juliet."

"Yes." Stuart heaved a tragic sigh.

"Pyramus and Thisbe," she said softly. "Heloise and Abelard!"

Stuart cleared his throat. "Yes, something like that. My only consolation is that you will bear it more nobly than I shall."

"I won't," she said, tears springing to her eyes again. "I shall die of a broken heart."

"No!" He brushed a light kiss on her hand before letting go of it. "That would make it worse for me. Say only that you will be happy. I could not bear it if I thought you miserable."

"Then I shall be," she promised in a wobbly voice. "But you! What shall you do?"

He looked away, over the dark garden. "I do not know. I cannot think beyond tonight." That was true, he thought wryly; none of his options at this point were pleasant to contemplate.

She reached out to him, then clasped her hands before her. "I shall miss you," she said in a small voice.

"And I you," he said with a sad smile. That wasn't strictly true, although if he ever did think of her, it would be kindly. She was a nice girl, but he couldn't see himself married to her now, not even for twenty thousand pounds. The thought of her fiery aunt would be enough to keep him from her bed forever, but he didn't have the heart to tell her that. He was just congratulating himself on his stroke of genius in casting her as the tragic heroine, and trying to think of a way to ask for his ring back, when the drape was abruptly torn back.

"How dare you?" said Charlotte with quiet malice.

Susan gave a guilty start, but put up her chin. "It was destiny," she said. Stuart could see she was warming to her role.

Charlotte didn't even glance at her. "Susan, you are excused."

The girl's expression turned mulish. Stuart gave her another sad, solemn look, and bowed slightly. "Good evening, Miss Tratter."

She dropped her pout and curtsied. "Good evening, Mr. Drake," she said in martyred tones. "Farewell!" She started to brush past her aunt, head held high.

"You may go to the carriage," said Charlotte in a frosty voice.

Susan turned, mouth opened in surprise. "Why? We've only just arrived."

"And you have disobeyed the only thing I asked of you." Charlotte had yet to take her eyes off him, so she didn't see the angry sparkle in her niece's eye.

"You don't understand anything!"

"I understand all too well."

"Oh!" Susan stomped her foot. "You think you know everything, but you don't!"

Finally Charlotte looked at her. "Go to the carriage," she said slowly, enunciating each word. The girl flushed, then headed for the door, casting one last look over her shoulder at Stuart.

Once she was gone, Charlotte stepped onto the

balcony and let the drape fall shut behind her. Stuart wondered what it would be like to see her without arguing with her, or perhaps only arguing when he stood a chance of winning.

"You needn't have done that," he told her, crossing his arms. "She was beginning to like the idea of being as tragic as Juliet."

Charlotte frowned. "She is not Juliet, she's a girl who is too trusting to see you as you are."

"Unlike you, who have seen me at my most elemental." She blinked, and then glared at him. Stuart grinned, feeling reckless again. Why not tangle with her one last time? He had absolutely nothing to lose now. "Or should I say, heard me, for I don't believe we *saw* quite enough of each other last night." He noticed she didn't quite meet his eyes. He found this rather pleasing. It meant their encounter last night had unsettled her. It had certainly seared itself into his memory.

Charlotte opened her mouth and then closed it, unable to say what she wanted to say to him. *Don't look at me,* she wanted to scream at him. *Don't make me think of all the things you said.* "Stay away from my niece."

He lifted one shoulder. "I was simply getting a breath of fresh air. She happened to want the same, it seems."

Susan had disappeared almost the moment they arrived. Charlotte had counted upon Mrs. Martin not inviting him, and hadn't worried about it for several minutes, until she saw Lord Jameson, one of Stuart's associates, alternating between watching her and staring at this balcony. "I did not expect to see you tonight," she said, raising her eyebrow contemptuously. "I thought Mrs. Martin was better informed."

He laughed. "She was, but too late. The fault is mine, for keeping an engagement agreed to in the calm before the storm." He leaned back, bracing his hands behind him on the railing. "So perhaps I should leave, you're about to suggest. Perhaps. I could consider it . . ."

"Pray, don't waste much time contemplating the question," she said coolly. "The answer is rather obvious."

His grin flashed white in the darkness. "Will you throw me out yourself?"

"I dream of it nightly," she replied with a superior smile.

"Then do it." Before she could react, he had taken her hand and raised it to the back of his neck. Charlotte pulled, shocked, and he massaged her hand until her fingers opened and lay flat against his skin, held in place by his. "Take me by the back of the neck and toss me out," he whispered, stepping even closer. He had to stoop slightly to keep her hand on his neck.

Charlotte tugged harder, appalled by the way her heart accelerated. "Let go of my hand."

"Ah, you're the ear-boxing type." He had her other hand, and flattened it across his cheek so that her fingers brushed the hair behind his ear. Charlotte gasped; her reflexes had abandoned her completely, for he'd gotten her hand against his face even before she thought to resist. And now she was stuck, cradling his head unwillingly in her hands.

"Let go, or I *shall* box your ears."

"A tempting offer," he said. "Although not as tempting as this." He slid her hand from his cheek to meet the hand behind his neck, and transferred his grip to hold both her wrists there with one hand.

Charlotte strained backward, then stumbled into him, pulled closer as he straightened. "That is much better," he said with another soft laugh.

Charlotte turned her face away. "Stay away from my niece," she said again, doing her best not to touch him while she tried to pull loose.

"I'm as far away as I can get," he murmured, his breath stirring her hair at her temple. "You should be pleased; I've given her up entirely."

"You were out here with her tonight," said Charlotte, staring fixedly at the ivy climbing the side of the house and trying to pretend she wasn't pressed up against him.

"If you're going to eavesdrop," he said, taking a step and backing her into the ivy, "you should do a thorough job of it."

"I heard enough." Now she was trapped, an ivy-covered brick wall behind her and Stuart before her, just as hard and unyielding. She considered screaming, and all the attendant furor over another public scene between the two of them, and had just decided in favor of it when he cupped her cheek in his free hand and turned her face up to his.

"You heard what you wanted to hear," he said, "because you won't admit the truth. You don't want me to marry your niece because you want me for yourself." She opened her mouth to scream, and he kissed her.

Charlotte jerked, bumping her head on the wall. He stepped forward again, his feet on either side of hers, fixing her in place. His fingers plowed into her hair, holding her steady as his mouth moved over hers. She clamped her lips together, but he had anticipated her, and his tongue came into her mouth so firmly and masterfully, she quaked. All her reactions were slow; it was almost as if her body and mind alike had paused to wonder at his truly marvelous kiss. She hadn't been kissed this well, and this thoroughly, in a long time. Perhaps never.

Charlotte felt herself drift. She did hate him, she really did, but he had left her quivering with desire last night, and maybe it would be fair to let him ease some of the need he had created in her. *It's just a kiss*, she told herself, letting go. *It means nothing.*

Stuart heard her sigh and wondered what it meant. She was soft and warm in his arms, perfectly female although as stiff as iron, and then she changed. The fists behind his neck unfolded to grip his shoulders, and she went up on her toes, pushing into him. The passive form in his arms came alive, clinging as if she would never let go. And her kiss . . .

Stuart had never been kissed like this by any woman. Even the most experienced courtesan seemed tame in comparison. She twined her tongue around his, sucking it deeper into her mouth in such blatant imitation of intercourse, he felt faint. And more alive than ever before in his life. He leaned into her, pinning her against the wall and leaving his hands free to explore at will.

He palmed the full curve of her breast, his thumb teasing her nipple through the silk. Her moan was acquiescence and delight and encouragement all rolled into one. Stuart stroked his other hand over the curve of her shoulder, around her waist and down to pull her hips against his. Her back arched a little, and he felt again her incomparable warmth pressed against his erection. He was a fool for it, but this woman affected him like no other.

"Come home with me," he whispered in between light kisses down the soft curve of her jaw. "Let me show you all I forgot to mention last night."

His voice shattered the spell. Charlotte froze, horrified to realize she was letting the man who had broken Susan's heart make love to her. It wasn't just a kiss, it was a betrayal, of her niece and of her vows to herself. "No." She uncurled her fingers from his shoulders and turned her head away when he would have kissed her again. "Stop. Please."

Slowly his embrace loosened. She stepped away, straightening her dress to avoid his eyes. "Someday," he said thickly, "you're going to have to finish what you start."

"No," she replied, reaching behind her for the drape, "you're wrong. I intend to finish what I started, protecting Susan from you and all fortune hunters."

"I don't mean your niece, and you know it," he said as she slipped back into the drawing room. "We're not done, you and I." The other guests had gone into the music room, and she walked rapidly out of the house. Lucia would fend for herself, and Charlotte wanted to be away as soon as possible. Stuart's last words taunted her, and worried her; what would it take to finish things between them? And why did he have to speak aloud her deepest, darkest fear: that she did want him for herself?

Chapter Seven

Susan didn't say a word on the way home, and ran up the stairs as soon as they got there. Charlotte delayed a few minutes, trying to quiet her guilt at kissing the same man she had commanded Susan not to speak to, and to calm her still-fluttering reaction to that kiss. Then she went upstairs and tapped on Susan's door. When there was no response, she opened it a crack.

"Susan? May I come in?"

"Why bother asking?" came Susan's bitter reply. "You'll only do what you want to do anyway."

Charlotte bit her lip and eased into the room. There were no candles burning, and the room was very dark. Silhouetted against the open window was Susan, her back to the door. She didn't turn around as Charlotte closed the door.

"I apologize," she began quietly. "I know you were looking forward to the Martins' party."

"No, you were. I thought it would be a dreadful bore, but no one asked if I wanted to go."

"But dearest, it's the best society in town." Charlotte

was surprised and a little hurt. She thought Susan wanted to go out at nights. She was trying her best to provide appropriate entertainments.

Susan sniffed. "Dull old Tunbridge Wells. What I wouldn't give to leave it at once."

Charlotte had no reply to that. She knew her niece longed to see London, and by next spring, when Susan was eighteen, Charlotte told herself she would be ready to go. She changed the subject. "I am sorry if I embarrassed you in front of Mr. Drake."

Susan said nothing for a long moment. "Why do you hate him so much? You hardly know him." Her tone was flat, almost devoid of emotion. Charlotte hesitated; she had expected another blazing row, not this quiet resentment.

"Because he reminds me of someone I once knew," she said slowly. "Someone who made me believe he loved me, when I was young. Just about your age, in fact. And when I had fallen completely in love with him, I discovered he was after nothing more than my inheritance."

"Who told you? Some interfering relation?"

Charlotte sighed at Susan's scornful question. "My father, who did me a great favor by exposing the man."

"And then you ran away to Paris to nurse your broken heart," said Susan. "How terribly you suffered."

No, Charlotte wanted to tell her, *my father sent me away because he couldn't stand to have such an immoral child in his house. He foisted me and my humiliation off on a distant cousin and refused to acknowledge me for the rest of his life. It wasn't my idea at all.*

Susan suddenly whirled around, fists at her sides. "How do you know he's only after my fortune?"

"He is destitute," Charlotte began to explain, but Susan snorted impatiently.

"So I may only marry someone with more money than I've got. How am I supposed to meet such a man, here in bloody boring Kent?"

"You're only seventeen."

"And how old were you, traveling across Europe by yourself? Papa used to tell me about you when I was a child: 'Aunt Charlotte, who lives in Paris,' then Nice, then Spain and Italy."

"It wasn't as romantic as you think," Charlotte warned.

"And I have never even been so far away as London," Susan went on savagely. "How I long to be out of here! I am always too young, or too rich, or too—too . . . Oh!" She dashed one hand across her eyes. "Just go! You don't know anything about me or what I want, and you can't make me live my life to atone for all the mistakes you made in yours!" Charlotte felt as if Susan had struck her; was that how it appeared to her niece? "I wish my father had never made you my guardian!" With a flounce of her skirt, Susan turned her back again.

"I am trying my best," said Charlotte softly after a moment. "I'm sorry if you don't agree but your father did appoint me your guardian, and I shall continue to do what I think best. I hope you will understand one day." Susan huffed loudly, but said nothing.

Reluctantly Charlotte turned and left. She went down the hall to her own room and sank onto her dressing table chair. For the first time, she was intensely glad she didn't have children of her own. She would have been a wretched mother, to judge from the way she got along with Susan. Perhaps she had been foolish to expect to become friends immediately, but she simply didn't understand why Susan viewed her with such animosity. It couldn't be just Stuart Drake, although he was a major obstacle; Susan argued with her over everything. Charlotte's suggestions about everything from the height of her slipper heels to the best time to walk in the park displeased Susan, and Charlotte simply didn't know what to do. She couldn't just allow Susan to do anything she liked, but it was breaking her heart to argue with the girl constantly.

Charlotte sighed, catching sight of herself in the mirror. She didn't even look like a maternal woman. Her skin was still golden from the Italian sun, and her face was artfully painted with cosmetics. Her hair was arranged in the contrived disarray Piero had favored, claiming it made her look more alluring, and not in the neat, proper curls English ladies wore. And her dress . . . She had always loved colors, and wore them with abandon. She looked, Charlotte realized numbly, like an expensive courtesan. What had been stylish and bold in Milan appeared brash and vulgar in England. No wonder she was failing so miserably. Charlotte dropped her head into her hands and said a silent plea for George's forgiveness, for failing in her every effort to raise his daughter the way he would have wanted.

She could do better. She *would* do better. George had trusted her with his beloved daughter, and she couldn't let him down. George was the only person who hadn't condemned her all those years ago, when her youthful indiscretion had exploded in scandal.

When her father banished her to the Continent for her behavior, George had made sure she was safely on a decent ship, and told her he would miss her. Charlotte hadn't expected him to save her—he had had a wife and baby to take care of—but he was the only person who sympathized with her, a scared seventeen-year-old girl thrust into the world alone. And all her years abroad, George had written to her, somehow finding her once or twice a year no matter where she roamed.

Charlotte pulled the combs from her hair. She removed her jewelry and slipped out of her brilliant gown. It was time to start looking her age, or at least dressing it. She was used to being the focus of attention, particularly male attention, but it was time for her to assume her proper place with the matrons.

The next morning, she scrubbed her face but left it bare, pinned her hair into a simple twist, and wore her plainest gown. It was a deep bronze—hardly ordinary, but it was the simplest one she owned. Charlotte brushed one hand wistfully over the bright silks and muslins, then closed the wardrobe door and went down to breakfast.

Lucia stared at her. "What happened? Has someone died?"

"No. Why?"

"You look dreadful. Have you run out of rouge?"

Charlotte reached for her coffee. "English ladies don't wear so many cosmetics, so I decided not to, as well."

"Then you did not see Mrs. Fitzhugh last night,"

said Lucia. "She must have used a butter knife to apply it. English ladies wear cosmetics, just not well."

"Nevertheless, I am giving it up for a more dignified style. I am not a young woman anymore."

"All the more reason to wear it," said Lucia *sotto voce.* "Without it, you look so . . ." She put her head to one side, grimacing. "Bucolic."

Charlotte shot her a dark look. "Susan hasn't come down yet?"

Lucia shook her head. "I would not know if she did. She does not speak to me."

Charlotte sighed. Naturally, Susan would resent Lucia, who behaved with every bit as much license as Susan envied. When she had invited Lucia to visit, she had never thought of the bad influence her friend might be on her niece. "Perhaps she's sleeping late. We had another argument last night."

"It is hard not to argue with her. The child is spoiled."

"She is at a difficult age, in difficult circumstances."

"Her papa would have taken a strap to her, and you know it. You are afraid she will never like you if you are harsh with her."

"I've ordered her to stay away from Mr. Drake, haven't I?" exclaimed Charlotte.

"For all the good it has done, no one would know." Lucia rose. "I go to the lending library this morning. What book would you like?"

"The library?"

"*Si.*" Lucia smiled coyly. "A young man I met last night has offered to read me poetry there. Such adventures I have when you abandon me with the English."

"Enjoy it. I'll wait for Susan." Lucia left and Charlotte finished her breakfast in silence. Of course she wanted

Susan to like her, and of course she didn't want to be too harsh with her. She didn't want to be as strict as her own father had been with her, because she truly believed she would have behaved properly if he had trusted her more. But neither could she allow Susan to run wild and ruin her reputation while she was still too young to know better. Perhaps if she simply explained that to Susan, her niece would understand better.

She waited all morning, but Susan never came down. When luncheon came and went and still Susan hadn't appeared, Charlotte braced herself and knocked on Susan's bedroom door. There was no reply. An hour later there was no reply, and finally Charlotte knocked one more time. "Susan, please come out." Still silence. "Then I am coming in," Charlotte warned, putting the key in the lock.

She needn't have bothered, for the room was empty. Charlotte's stunned gaze veered from the open window to the undisturbed bed, and then she rang furiously for Susan's maid. The girl came running, wide-eyed.

"Where is Miss Tratter?" Charlotte yanked open the curtains. A sturdy trellis climbed the wall nearby, not a difficult distance to reach for an agile young person.

The maid wrung her apron. "I dunno, ma'am. She never rang for me this morning, and since you told us not to enter until rung for . . ."

"Why did you not tell me she never rang?"

The girl shrank from Charlotte's wrath. "Well, I didn't . . . That is, I didn't know it was important. Miss Tratter often sleeps late, and I didn't think . . ." Her voice died as Charlotte flung open the wardrobe doors.

"Check for anything missing. Don't forget the new

things we just bought this week." The maid ran forward to do as told. Charlotte sat down at the writing desk and went through it swiftly. There was nothing out of the ordinary, and she moved to the bureau, which also yielded no information.

"A few dresses are gone, ma'am," said the maid hesitantly. "They could be in the laundry, though; shall I check?" Charlotte nodded, and she scurried out the door.

The butler appeared as Charlotte pressed her hands to her forehead in growing panic. Where could Susan be? Where would she go? "Madame?" Dunstan inquired. "Is aught amiss?"

"Yes, Dunstan, Miss Tratter seems to have gone missing." Charlotte's voice trembled on the last word. God in heaven, what would she do if something happened to her niece? "Have you any idea, any sign of a break-in?"

He shook his head. "No, ma'am. I shall check again at once."

Charlotte paced the room, struggling to keep calm. First she must make certain no one had taken Susan; she cursed her laziness in not hiring guards the morning after Stuart had advised her to do it. She didn't want to believe Susan had run away, but abduction wasn't preferable.

A bit of white caught her eye then, a triangle of paper sticking out from under the bed. She snatched it up, and read her own name in Susan's writing across the front of the letter as she tore it open.

Aunt Charlotte,
    I cannot bear it any longer. Can I stay here, when my heart goes hence? I must follow my love, no less

than Juliet did. I know you can't understand—I'm
sorry you won't be at my wedding—but if this is the
way it must be, so it must be. Good-bye,

Susan

She was still standing motionless with shock when
the maid hurried back in. "The dresses aren't in the
laundry, ma'am. Shall I—?"

"I'll kill him," said Charlotte softly. Slowly her fingers
closed, crumpling the note. "I shall kill him with my
bare hands."

"Madame?" squeaked the maid in alarm.

"You are dismissed," said Charlotte as she brushed
past the girl. She went straight to her room and took
a mahogany box from under her bed. With fury burning in her heart, she took out a pistol and loaded it,
praying she wasn't already too late.

Stuart's last day in Kent was turning out much
better than expected. He had just enough money left
to pay the rent due, which meant he could leave
without sneaking away in the dead of night. His valet,
whom he had sent on forced furlough a fortnight
earlier for lack of funds to pay his salary, returned
unexpectedly, and Stuart gratefully set Benton to
packing the linens and other furnishings. He continued
packing his clothing, only pausing when he folded his
old cloak.

He lifted it and took a deep breath. Yes, it still
carried just a trace of her perfume, and the warm,
rich scent made his blood heat in memory. It had
been lying in a heap on his doorstep the previous

morning, but at least she had returned it. *What a missed opportunity*, he thought, wishing he had known things would go this way. If he had anticipated anything like the kiss they shared the night before, he would have made a greater effort to seduce Charlotte the night she broke in. Heiresses could be found the width and breadth of England, but a woman like that came along once in a lifetime, if a fellow was lucky.

A loud pounding interrupted his thoughts. Benton had gone to take the trunks already packed to be shipped back to London. Stuart put the cloak in his trunk and went to open the door.

"Where is she?" Stuart paused at the sight of the pistol in Charlotte's hand, pointed straight at his heart. Good Lord, this woman had nerve, but he couldn't deny the sudden jump in his pulse at the sight of her.

"I've no idea what you're talking about." He turned his back on her and strolled toward his room.

"Do not walk away from me." Charlotte's voice shook with fury. "I *will* fire!"

He glanced over his shoulder. "And I could not stop you since I am, as you see, unarmed." He went into the bedroom, and she followed with a rustle of skirts, slamming the door behind her. Her chest rose rapidly, her eyes glittered, and her face was flushed. She was magnificent.

"Tell me where Susan is, or forfeit your life."

Stuart burst out laughing. "Did you rehearse that line? It's very good, but a little melodramatic. Next time, try it with less emotion; when holding a gun, it's more frightening to your victim to be calm."

She snorted. "You're hardly anyone's victim. Where is my niece?"

Stuart shrugged, only mildly curious. "I've no idea. I haven't seen her since last night. Why? Have you lost your charge, Aunt Charlotte?"

"You think you can swindle me as well, don't you?" She shook her head with a caustic laugh. "I'm not fooled, not a whit. I should shoot you now, as a kindness to all women, but will give you one more chance: tell me where she is, and I'll let you live."

He sighed, tossing more shirts into the trunk. "As magnanimous as your offer is, I can't accept it. I have no idea where your niece is."

"Then where are you going?" She raised her chin. "You're packing. Do you deny you're leaving town?"

"The sooner the better."

"Where are you going?"

He hesitated. "To London. Alone," he added as triumph flared in her eyes. "Feel free to follow and see for yourself. But I'm leaving on the afternoon mail, and really must finish packing, so if you don't plan to leave, would you hand me those boots?"

She hurled the boots at his head. Stuart caught one and ducked the other, then tucked both into his trunk. Charlotte said nothing for a minute, pacing restlessly about and peering around all the furniture. Stuart continued his packing even though awareness of her sizzled along his every nerve. He had never wanted a woman who held a gun on him before; it was rather perverse, but undeniably exciting. Under her watchful gaze he folded his trousers and shirts, whistling a tune under his breath just to annoy her. This woman, he decided, had gotten her way for too long. She needed someone to put her in her place.

"Very well, you may go to London," she announced suddenly. "I shall go with you. In fact, I shall take you.

And when we find Susan, you'll tell her everything about your cruel plan to marry her for her fortune. You'll tell her about your attempts to ruin other heiresses, and how you were banished from London by your own father for your wild ways. And you'll beg her pardon for deceiving her into trusting you."

Stuart leaned against the bedpost and studied her. She looked quite disheveled, her dark curls falling out of a loose knot and her cloak askew. "That's the real matter, isn't it? You're upset she trusted me."

"Don't be ridiculous. She was tricked by your lies."

"You told her to avoid me like the plague, and still she sought me out as soon as your back was turned," he said as she aimed the pistol again. "This, my dear, smacks of wounded pride."

"It's not your pride I'll wound." Charlotte wanted to shoot him just to take the smile off his face. How dare he mock her?

"All right. I'll go to London with you, since you're holding a pistol on me, and you can satisfy your suspicions that your niece eloped with me— that is what I'm accused of, is it not? And if I've lied to you"—he opened his arms in a deceptive gesture of defenselessness—"you may take your revenge in any way you choose."

"I shall," vowed Charlotte.

"But if you're wrong . . ." He shook his head, a wicked smile on his lips. "Then I shall get what I want. You. For one night."

Her heart stuttered for a second. What unbelievable gall. She would never agree to such a thing. Give herself to him for a night! She would sooner give herself to a hungry bear. She swiftly considered the chance that he was telling the truth. But no, it couldn't be. He had already proven himself a liar and a manipulator, a master of getting his way with women. He had been on the balcony last night with Susan, and Charlotte hadn't heard a whisper of another man from anyone, not from Susan, not from the servants, not even from the gossips. It had to be Stuart Drake who was responsible for Susan's disappearance, Stuart Drake who knew where she was or where she was going, and Stuart Drake who had just made a breathtakingly outré suggestion to call her bluff. If he thought she would be intimidated or deterred by such a thing, he was sadly mistaken.

"Fine," she said coolly. "Let's be off."

He was motionless for a moment, staring at her. Then he turned back to the trunk and began throwing things into it left and right. "Give me twenty minutes."

Charlotte hired a private carriage while Stuart stood chatting with the innkeeper as if he hadn't a care in the world. She glared at him as she finished counting out the coins. The breeze ruffled his dark hair across his forehead, and a grin curved his sensual mouth; fine lines crinkled around his eyes when he smiled like that, taking the edge off an otherwise wolfish expression. *A friendly wolf,* she thought suddenly, *that's what he looks like, with his long thin nose and wide mouth. Except such a thing didn't exist, and she would do well to remember it.*

She watched as the luggage was loaded into the carriage: Stuart's enormous trunk and her small valise. She had hired a boy to take a note to her house, and Lucia had sent three gowns, all her new lingerie, and a fortune in jewels. What Lucia thought she would do with evening gowns and diamonds, Charlotte couldn't guess, but she couldn't leave and go pack for herself. If she relaxed her guard for a moment, he would be able to send word ahead to Susan, and Charlotte wasn't taking a chance of that. He made a show of offering to help her into the carriage, but she kept a firm grip on the pistol and waved him in ahead of her.

She sat across from Stuart, where she could keep her eyes on him, and he infuriated her by dropping his hat over his eyes and going to sleep. She almost fired the gun out the window, just to restore a little healthy respect to his demeanor, but since she didn't have a second loaded pistol, she decided against disarming herself just for the satisfaction of scaring him.

They lurched and bumped toward London as the daylight waned. Charlotte allowed them to stop for only the quickest of meals, and Stuart woke up to accuse her of starving him. "This is a very poor kidnapping, if you ask me," he said, contemplating the apple and hunk of bread she handed him. "You might have at least brought along a hamper."

"This is not a picnic." Charlotte ate her own apple with one hand. Her wrist ached, but she wouldn't put down the pistol. For all his appearance of casual indolence, he might just be biding his time. And if he disarmed her, God only knew what he would do to retaliate.

Not that he seemed to care about it, one way or the other. He just lounged on his seat, watching her. As the light faded, the shadows slanted through the carriage and made him appear more feral and dangerous, with only his eyes, and occasionally his teeth, gleaming in the dark.

"Go back to sleep," she snapped at last. He chuckled.

"You don't like to be watched, do you?" She glared at him. He nodded thoughtfully. "I thought not. Odd, really, since you aren't exactly the quiet, inconspicuous type. Not in that dress, at any rate."

Charlotte clenched her fist to keep from twitching her cloak over her bronze gown. She would not let him rattle her that easily. "My attire is purely my own concern."

He grinned. "Oh, I wasn't complaining. I rather like it. Particularly the gown you wore to the Kildairs' party. Lovely."

Charlotte, who knew full well that dress displayed her figure to its best advantage, sniffed. "I thought you found it rather drab, if your sudden interest in removing it was any indication."

"You don't know much about men if you think I wasn't interested," countered Stuart with deliberate innuendo. "I've dreamed of seeing you in that dress again."

"Every man may have his dreams, I suppose."

"Oh, yes I do." His teeth gleamed in his wicked smile. "Most of them don't involve you *in* a dress, though. Shall I tell you about those?"

Charlotte laughed in disbelief. "You have no shame."

He lifted one shoulder. "Not much, anyway. It gets in one's way. I thought you would have figured that out by now. Besides, you were the one who decreed an end to the lies between us. I'm merely following your wishes."

"My wishes?" she exclaimed. "I think it was your wishes—your wildly impossible wishes—you were discussing."

"I find them highly possible, since when you lose our wager . . ." His eyes drifted down, and Charlotte realized her body had responded again to his voice, soft and growling. A memory of all the things he said he'd like to do to her came vividly to mind, and gave her an inner tremor. She was suddenly acutely aware of the rocking of the carriage, and the way his body was sprawled across the opposite seat, one foot propped beside her. He reclined with his hands folded over his stomach, totally at his ease as he watched her watching him.

"It's a long ride to London," he said in that low, gravelly voice that acted on her like a physical caress. "Shall we surrender to the inevitable?"

"It's not inevitable," she retorted, disgusted to hear how husky her own voice had become. Why was she always attracted to the worst possible men?

One corner of his mouth quirked up. "You know it is. Have you ever made love in a carriage?"

Charlotte tried to quell the heat rising in her body. "Yes, I have," she said as carelessly as possible. She was an experienced woman, after all, not some naïve girl who would fall for his seduction. "I didn't much care for it."

White-hot desire flared in his gaze. "Come here, then, and allow me to persuade you otherwise." He extended one hand toward her. Charlotte turned away, refusing to look at him. "It's a long ride," he coaxed. Unfortunately her gaze landed on his lap, where his arousal was clear beneath his tailored trousers. Her mouth went dry and she squirmed a little in her seat, horrified that she was aroused, too. Was he saying it was a long trip to London to sit in discomfort, or offering her another sort of long ride?

"If you say another insulting word, I'll shoot you after all."

He laughed. "Admit it, Charlotte, you want me. You want me as much as I want you."

"I most certainly do not," she snapped. "You conceited, amoral, lying, thieving—"

"I didn't say you *wanted* to want me, only that you do." He sounded too damn amused.

"I want you to tell me where Susan is. After that, I shall be very happy never to set eyes on you again."

"That's not very good motivation for me to tell you, is it?"

Charlotte lifted the pistol, shaking with fury. "You bastard!"

"Hey!" Alarm suddenly colored his voice, and he ducked as she pointed the weapon directly between his eyes. "Be careful!"

"Where is she?" she shouted.

"Damned if I know!" he yelled back, arms still thrown up defensively around his head. "Put the pistol down!"

For a mad moment Charlotte held the gun in place. Then she realized what she was doing and lowered it abruptly, unable to believe she had fallen so far. It was one thing to wave the pistol around and threaten to shoot him, and another to put the barrel to his head. She huddled in her cloak, trying to hide her trembling. She had endangered someone's life. She wanted to fling the pistol out the window, but then she would be left defenseless, and might never find Susan. That, above all, must guide her actions: finding Susan.

"I just want my niece back," she said unevenly. "I

don't want to shoot you, but you have to tell me where she is. Once I have her back, I don't care about anything else. Tell me now, I beg you."

"I've told you I don't know." His voice rang with frustration.

Charlotte closed her eyes. "I don't believe you."

"Why do you dislike me so much?" he asked after a moment's silence.

"You know why," she said before he had even completed the question.

He snorted. "Yes, you hate any man who considers a woman's prospects before offering her marriage. Because of course women never marry men for their money, or for their titles."

"I cannot admire that, either," she said softly.

"But I, for some reason, have been singled out in your dislike. You have publicly insulted me, got me hounded out of Kent—out of *Kent*, for God's sake—broken into my lodgings, pulled a pistol on me, and now kidnapped me. What, may I ask, makes me so much worse than the typical man who needs money so badly he'll marry it?"

Charlotte struggled with the question. What did make him different? "I suppose . . . I suppose it's because you made Susan fall in love with you."

"How could I make a girl fall in love with me, if she didn't want to?" There was a note of exasperation in his tone.

"You did," Charlotte insisted. "You courted her and made her think you loved her in return."

"I never said one word to her of love," he said. "And of course I courted her. That's what a man does before he makes an offer of marriage."

"Yes. But women are courted all the time without thinking they're in love." Charlotte spoke quietly, almost to herself. "Susan's too young to suspect it's all lies, and too romantic to guard her heart. She's innocent and naïve, and thus loves blindly and absolutely, overlooking not only small flaws that don't signify but also large flaws, like the fact that her love was unreturned. Her affections have disarmed her, and she could be so easily destroyed by the discovery that she's been a fool."

For a moment the only sound was the rattle of harness and the creak of the carriage straps. "Who broke your heart, I wonder?" Stuart murmured speculatively.

Charlotte froze. "If you won't tell me where she is, you may as well remain silent." That seemed to quell his curiosity, and the carriage was quiet for the rest of the trip.

Chapter Eight

When the rumbling of the wheels changed to rattling over city streets, Stuart sat up. "We've arrived. Where now, captor mine?"

"Clapham Close, number ten." Charlotte had recovered from her momentary madness by now. Everything would be fine; she had done the right thing. He hadn't been out of her sight once, and she intended to keep him there until Susan appeared. Charlotte didn't expect it would take long, but she had to find her niece first, before he had a chance to tell her more lies.

He went still. "Oh?"

She jerked the pistol. "Your valet sent your things there. You were going there. Therefore, that's where we will go."

He sat back and stared out the window the rest of the way.

A short while later, they came to a stop, and the driver opened the door. Stuart climbed out first, then turned to offer her his hand. Holding her skirts in one hand and her pistol in the other, Charlotte ignored it. With a shrug, Stuart started up the steps of the large townhouse. She tucked her weapon under her cloak as he rang the bell.

"I've still got my pistol. Don't think you're safe."

The smirk he gave her was more strained than insolent. "I've never felt less safe in my life."

The door opened to reveal a footman in starched livery. He blinked, then opened the door wider. "Good evening, sir."

"Good evening, Frakes," said Stuart, strolling through the door. Charlotte followed, her skin prickling with unease as she took in the state of the house: elegant, handsomely furnished, fully staffed by servants. Was this truly the home of a fortune hunter? It was possible, she tried to reassure herself. No doubt the whole house was mortgaged to the hilt and the servants paid on borrowed money. The butler appeared, looking rather flustered.

"Good evening, Mr. Drake. We did not expect you."

"No, I'm sure you didn't." Stuart was shedding his coat, and he turned to Charlotte, raising one brow in question. She gripped the front edge of her cloak tighter and glared back. Stuart handed his coat to the footman, and turned back to the butler. "Is anyone at home tonight?"

"Ah, well, sir, I'm not sure," said the butler almost apologetically. Charlotte sent another surreptitious glance around the hall. Something was wrong. This was not the right house. It couldn't be.

"Ah well. Don't let it worry you, Brumble," said Stuart.

"Where is Susan?" hissed Charlotte, more and more ill at ease. Yes, it could be a façade, but she just wanted her niece.

Stuart turned. "I told you before, I've no idea. You wanted to come to my home, and here we are. I trust you are satisfied?"

"I shall be satisfied when I see my niece safely returned!"

He sighed. "God save me from unreasonable women . . ."

Charlotte was infuriated, and worried, and prodded him with the pistol. "This cannot be your home."

"I promise you, it's the closest thing to it. I've nowhere else to go, and you know I sent all my baggage here." He spread his hands wide. "This was my destination all along, sad to say."

"Back again?" rumbled a cold voice. They turned in unison to see a tall, gray-haired man with a sour expression. His eyes were fixed on Stuart, who winced almost imperceptibly before assuming a cocky smile.

"Surely you didn't think I would last the whole Season in Kent, Terrance. You know how dull those country assemblies are."

The man limped forward, leaning on an ebony cane. He looked highly displeased to see Stuart. "You could use a little dulling."

"Oh dear, I always thought a sharp wit my best asset."

The man snorted. His eyes landed on Charlotte, and she was thrown even further off balance by the malice in his expression. "How dare you bring your bit of skirt into this house?"

Stuart shifted his weight toward her at the same moment Charlotte took an unconscious step in his direction. Their elbows bumped, and Stuart steadied her with one hand without looking at her. Charlotte didn't pull back; her intuition was telling her she had just made a very serious mistake, and she had the terrible feeling that she would need more than forced cooperation from Stuart. "Not a bit of skirt at all," Stuart replied, curling his fingers more securely around her arm.

"Stuart!" Another voice, female this time, echoed in the hall. A short, plump woman hurried forward, her arms outstretched in greeting. Stuart finally looked away from the gentleman. "Oh, how delightful," cried the woman, embracing him. "I had no idea you were coming back to town. Why, if you'd sent word, I would have held dinner for you!"

He kissed her cheek. "Hello, Mother. I had other concerns and must confess complete disregard for dining."

"Ah well, I shall always hope." The woman's smile dimmed just a bit. She glanced at Charlotte, who was feeling rather faint. *Mother?* Stuart's mother? This was his *parents'* home? "Who is your guest, darling?"

"Allow me to present a friend of mine, the Contessa Griffolino. Charlotte, my mother, Mrs. Drake."

"It is a pleasure to meet you, Contessa," said Stuart's mother politely. Her expression had grown even more acutely intrigued at Stuart's use of her Christian name, but Charlotte barely noticed.

"Mrs. Drake," she said, faintly.

"And my father, Mr. Terrance Drake," added Stuart, in the same half-mocking tone he had used when he spoke directly to his father. Mr. Drake glowered at them both, but his wife glanced at him, and he jerked his chin down in unwilling imitation of a bow. "We've come on urgent business," Stuart went on. His grip was tight on her elbow. "Madame Griffolino's niece has disappeared, and we fear she's run off to London.

I offered my assistance in tracking her, and we left Kent in a hurry hoping to overtake her."

"How dreadful," said Mrs. Drake at once. "You must be so worried."

Charlotte barely nodded. She had made a terrible error—Susan wasn't here, and might be halfway to Scotland by now, or France or anywhere, with some unknown person. She had let her prejudices against Stuart affect her judgment, and now she had lost Susan.

Stuart slipped one arm around her waist as he felt her sway. Her face was blank with shock, and he could only guess at what was in her mind. Whatever her failings, the woman cared for her niece, and Stuart suddenly felt a bit ashamed of himself for teasing her and trying to seduce her when she must have been worried out of her mind about the girl.

"We both are, Mother," he said, to fill the silence. "Terribly. There aren't many clues to her disappearance, and we left Tunbridge Wells in such a rush, we haven't anywhere to stay." He was supporting more and more of Charlotte's weight. In a minute he would be the only thing holding her up. Discreetly, under cover of her cloak, Stuart extracted the pistol from her fingers. She didn't make even a whimper of protest.

"Why, Stuart, if you think it would—" Stuart didn't hear the rest of his mother's words as Charlotte finally collapsed. With a quick motion, he caught her under the knees and lifted her. She hadn't fainted, but was simply stunned, her eyes wide and unfocused, her body limp.

"She's overcome," he said quickly to his mother. "Might we have a moment alone?"

"See here," began Terrance warningly, but his wife interrupted.

"Of course! The poor woman! Bring her into the library, Stuart." Stuart followed his mother down the hall, ignoring his father's glowering. In the library, he set Charlotte down on the chaise, and accepted the small glass of brandy his mother handed him. She hovered behind him until he sent her a speaking look. When she had closed the door, Stuart drew out the pistol he had hidden under Charlotte's cloak and set it safely to one side.

"Charlotte." He gripped her shoulders, but she looked right through him. "Are you going to be ill?"

"She's gone." Her lips barely moved. "But where? She said . . . following her heart . . . I was sure . . ." She fumbled in the pocket of her cloak, and withdrew a crumpled note. Stuart smoothed it flat.

What a mess. It appeared the girl really had eloped, although obviously not with him. Clearly Susan hadn't been as in love with *him* as she had professed. It had been the life she thought he was offering her, much the same way he had wanted the financial independence and security she offered him. That was no more than he deserved, Stuart conceded. But faced with the fact, he suddenly felt quite terrible that he hadn't made a greater effort to convince Charlotte he had nothing to do with it. When she told him Susan was gone, Stuart had assumed the girl had simply run off and would likely turn up at a friend's home, if she didn't return on her own. He had let his uncontrollable interest in Charlotte quiet his better judgment, and given in to her demands because it suited his desires.

He cleared his throat. "Have you any idea whom she might mean?"

Her eyes focused on him. "Romeo. And you told her she was Juliet." Stuart felt worse and worse.

"Have you no other information?" he asked gently. "When did she disappear? Did she take anything? Have you questioned her maid, or the rest of your household?"

She shook her head, wilting again. "The maid knows nothing. Some of Susan's dresses are missing, but not many. I spoke to her last night, when we returned home; she never came down to breakfast or luncheon, and I assumed . . . and I did not go to her. But she ran away—and I've no idea with whom, if not with you . . ."

"Were there no other suitors she might have favored?"

"You were the only one she ever mentioned," she whispered.

"Are you sure she would have come to London?" he asked quickly, trying to turn the subject from him.

She closed her eyes. "Susan talks of nothing but going there. It's her fondest dream." Now that he thought about it, Stuart realized, he knew that. All Susan's conversation had revolved around their future life in London, with its shopping and society and entertainments. Perhaps there wasn't a man at all, and she had simply set out on the adventure she dreamed of.

If that were the case, though, she shouldn't be hard to find. Since she hadn't been kidnapped, she would likely go out and see the sights; haunting the theaters and shops would turn her up in a matter of days. She probably had little money, and might be found simply by waiting at her family solicitor's office. They could hire an investigator as well—Stuart stopped himself, realizing he was planning a search when Charlotte would hardly welcome his participation.

"I'm sure she'll turn up soon," he tried to console her. "A few days away, and she'll see the error of her ways."

"A few days?" Sudden fury banished the emptiness in her eyes. "A few days! What sort of person do you think I am, to sit and wait a few days? My niece is *lost*, gone, spirited away by some lying, conniving villain! How like a man, to suggest sitting and doing nothing." She shot to her feet, setting Stuart off balance. "I shall not wait. I have to find her!"

A vision of Charlotte charging alone into every nook and cranny in London filled Stuart's head. He stood and caught her arm when she would have brushed past him. "Where do you plan to look?"

She tried to shake him off. "Everywhere!"

"You're mad," he said in disbelief. "What will you do, break into every house you suspect? Most people aren't as kindly disposed towards housebreakers as I was, you know."

"I did not ask your advice."

Stuart grabbed her other arm and forced her to look at him. "I will not let you charge off on your own."

"You have no right to stop me." Charlotte struggled in his grip. "She's my niece, and my responsibility. You have no right—" A sob of terror caught in her throat, terror that almost overwhelmed the humiliation of being so grossly wrong. Dear God, what if she had *shot* him? They would have hanged her. Well, they would have hanged her anyway if she had killed him, but it would be a thousand times worse if she had actually shot an innocent man. She would have been thrown into prison and then hanged, and there would be no one in the world to search for Susan. Her poor niece would simply vanish, and no one would care.

She pounded against his chest, and he caught her hands. Another sob welled up, and another, and then Stuart closed his arms around her, pressing her face into his shoulder. "There," he murmured. "Don't despair. It's not hopeless."

"I've got to find her—I can't just wait around—she may be in danger. . . ." Trapped in the circle of his arms, she clutched at him convulsively.

"I know." He held her even tighter, forcing her to be still. "But you must stay calm and rational, to find her as soon as possible." Charlotte dimly acknowledged the sense of his words through her haze of panic, and sucked in deep breaths, trying to compose herself. "We'll find her," Stuart added softly. "I swear."

She lifted her head in pure astonishment. "We?"

He rested his forehead against hers. "She can't have gone far. A thorough search, begun immediately, should have a very high chance of success."

Charlotte could only stare. He was offering to help? Stuart Drake was offering to help her? What would make him do that, after the way she had treated him? She searched his face, but there was nothing but kind concern there. Her chin wobbled a bit; it would be easier to say no, to leave and never see him again, but she couldn't. She would be a fool to refuse any help, no matter what it meant to her pride. Not when it was Susan's safety at stake.

"Thank you," she said quietly. Her throat was raw from unshed tears and she blinked back a few more as he urged her into her seat and pressed a tumbler into her hand.

"Things will look better in the morning, and there's nothing you can do tonight at any rate. Now drink." Like a doll, she nodded, suddenly too drained to move. She sipped the drink—an excellent brandy— and barely noticed when he left.

Stuart let himself out of the library, still not sure what had possessed him to do that. He must be a glutton for punishment, not only putting aside his own problems but in such a way that would throw him together with Charlotte even more. Not that he dreaded it; on the contrary, he looked forward to it far too much. He needed to keep a clear, steady head if he wanted any chance of restoring his fortunes in time to keep Oakwood Park, and she had the very opposite effect on him.

But as usual, he hadn't been able to hold his tongue. Charlotte's distress had pricked his conscience, and he felt truly awful at his own role, however peripheral. And once he had her in his arms, he really wasn't able to control himself anyway.

His mother was pacing in the hall outside, and pounced on him as soon as he closed the door. "Stuart, whatever is going on? You never answered my letters. I was so worried, after the way you left, and now you appear with an Italian woman, out of the blue—"

"She's English," he said. "Her husband was Italian. She's devastated by her niece's disappearance."

"Why, of course, the poor woman, but—" She stopped as Terrance stomped toward them, dragging his foot more than usual. Stuart never learned what had left his father with a limp, but when Terrance was angry or upset, it grew more pronounced. At the moment he was practically lame.

"See here," rumbled Terrance. "You know what I have to say. Take your woman and go, before I have you thrown out."

"She's not my woman." Stuart wished he hadn't allowed Charlotte to lead them here. At the time it had seemed fitting that she get such a royal comeuppance, but now he was sorry. "We had nowhere else to go."

"Of course you were right to come here," said Amelia Drake firmly, giving Terrance a reproachful look. "And you must stay. Was it an adventurer, Stuart dear?"

"I think it must be. The young lady has a large inheritance."

"You're not staying here," Terrance announced.

"Good heavens, has hell frozen over? No? Then of course I'm not staying here," said Stuart with affected surprise before his mother could speak. There had been a tremendous argument the night Terrance had banished him, one that left his mother weeping. The least he could do was cause as little trouble as possible now.

Terrance glared at him, then limped off. Amelia followed Stuart to the door. Her hands kept fluttering out to touch him, smoothing his sleeve and then his shoulder. He stopped to give her one last kiss. "Take care of her, Mother. I'll call tomorrow."

Amelia clutched his hand. "She's important to you, isn't she? Of course I would help her anyway, but you've never . . . Well, of course it's none of my concern, but is she . . . ?" Her face was at once worried and hopeful as she gazed up at him.

Stuart didn't know what Charlotte was to him. He couldn't very well tell his mother he thought about bedding her every time he saw her, but they didn't really have any other relationship. "I've promised to help her. That's all."

"Of course you did." Amelia sighed. "Stuart—your father—he's been worried about you, too, these last few weeks, and I just wanted you to know . . ."

"Don't worry, I know." He winked, taking his hat and coat from the butler. "I've missed you, Mother."

Her expression cleared, and she beamed up at him. "Dear boy. I'm so glad you're home."

"Good night, Mother." He left her there by the door and walked down the steps. At the bottom he paused to think. Charlotte would be fine—his mother would see to that—but where was he to go? He had no money, and no chance of getting any from his father tonight. His plan to humble himself and beg for another chance had been pretty well scotched, thanks to Charlotte and her pistol. His trunk, as well as Charlotte's valise, had been taken into the house, and the coach was gone. Turning up his collar against the fog, Stuart turned and started walking.

Twenty minutes later, he climbed the steps of an imposing mansion in Mayfair. He rang the bell and waited until the footman opened the door.

"Good evening. Is Ware in?" The footman bowed, taking his card. Stuart waited in the cavernous hall, amusing himself by counting the suits of armor. How Ware managed to live in this tomb was beyond him.

"Drake." Stuart looked up. The Duke of Ware himself was coming down the stairs. "What the devil brings you to town?"

He grinned. "The usual. A woman."

The duke's eyebrow arched. "Really? I thought that was the reason you left."

Stuart shrugged. "A different woman."

"Ah. Well, come in. I've just got rid of Percy for the night. Fancy a hand of cards?"

"No, thank you," said Stuart. "I can't afford even penny stakes." He followed his friend up the stairs to the luxurious study. A fire crackled merrily in the grate, and the remains of a dinner tray sat on the desk atop a perilous mountain of papers; his secretary might have just left, but it seemed Ware wasn't finished working. The duke went to the cabinet and poured two drinks while Stuart edged toward the fire, warming his hands.

"What sort of woman is it this time?" Ware handed him a glass and waved him toward the chairs in front of the fire.

Stuart took a long sip, closing his eyes in contentment. He hadn't had whiskey this good in a long time. "Not the usual sort. It's too long a tale for tonight, I assure you."

"I see."

"I doubt it. I'm both the villain and the knight errant."

"Indeed," was all Ware said, sipping his whiskey. Stuart wondered when the man had become so bloody controlled. Jack Lindeville had once been the biggest hellraiser in London, leaving even Stuart behind. Sometime in the last few years, though, he had become a cipher, and Stuart wondered if he'd made a mistake coming here.

"I came to ask whether Philip is still in Vienna," he said. "He promised me the use of his rooms, should I need it, and it seems I need it."

"Philip," said the duke, "is no longer in Vienna; if I recall correctly, he is in Florence, or perhaps Rome.

I am not kept closely apprised of his plans. And of course you may use his rooms, or stay here, if need be."

That offer, though well-meant, was impossible to accept. Ware ignored the gossips, but the duchess did not. Stuart knew he would not be welcome in her home. "I don't want to intrude. Philip's still got the house in Cherry Lane?"

"Yes. There are no servants. It's been shuttered since he left four months ago. Are you sure you wouldn't rather wait until tomorrow, after it's been aired?"

"No, tonight will be fine. I don't mind the dust." Ware simply met his eyes for a moment, then got up and went behind his desk to get the key. Stuart wondered fleetingly if Ware ever got lonely in this mausoleum of a house with only his mother for company and a desk that was never cleared of work. Once he would have asked, but not now. "Many thanks, Ware."

"Have you resolved your financial straits, then?" The duke's question came just as he reached the door.

Stuart's fingers closed painfully around the key. "I'm afraid not. Not yet."

"Ah." Ware hesitated. "Barclay called on me the other day."

Stuart's heart plummeted. Barclay was Ware's banker, as well as Stuart's own. He must have finally heard of Terrance's actions. Stuart waited with dread.

"He had been unable to reach you," the duke said when Stuart made no reply. "He has heard of your difficulties." Stuart closed his eyes in resignation. If Barclay knew he had no chance of paying back the loan or the mortgage on Oakwood Park, Stuart had already lost it. "I told him I would guarantee the loans," said Ware then.

Stuart's eyes popped open in astonishment.

Ware's steady gaze met his. "You need only time. I have never known you to break your word."

Stuart swallowed, but nodded. "And I will not this time. Thank you."

A trace of his old grin crossed Ware's face, and he inclined his head. Stuart left and walked the few streets to Cherry Lane, where Lord Philip Lindeville lived. Philip called it his "rooms," but to Stuart it was a house, only slightly smaller than his parents'. He let himself in, not surprised to find it spotlessly clean; even an empty house was cleaned by the Ware servants. The wealthy really were different.

He peeled off his clothes in the spacious master bedroom and fell into bed. He ought to be hungry, but had no appetite. He had hoped Barclay wouldn't hear of his troubles; his next payment wasn't due for a few weeks yet, and Stuart was holding tightly to his belief that somehow, something would work out that would enable him to pay it. Nothing had so far, of course, nor even the promise of something, but thanks to Ware he wouldn't be called to account immediately. As grateful as he was to his friend, Stuart wished he had been able to get himself out of this spot all by himself.

And Charlotte. Stuart sighed, staring at the ceiling. What was he to do about Charlotte? Helping her hunt for her missing niece would only complicate his circumstances, but he could still feel the limp weight of her in his arms, still see the look on her face. He had never guessed she could look so defenseless. Stuart tried to recall what Susan had told him about her aunt, but all he had paid attention to were the things that turned out to be wrong: Charlotte was neither old, nor wizened, nor stone-hearted. She was as fierce as a mother cat when it came to Susan, silly spoiled chit that she was. He ought to thank Charlotte for keeping him from marrying her, he thought as he drifted off to sleep. It was the one indisputably good turn she had done him. And leaving her to search alone was out of the question.

Charlotte woke the next morning feeling at once much better and much worse. The previous evening had blurred in her mind until she wasn't quite sure what had happened after they had reached London. The only fact she remembered with painful clarity was the magnitude of her mistake; by assuming Stuart was responsible for Susan's disappearance, she had lost valuable time investigating other possibilities, and now it could be too late. It had just been so easy to believe Susan would run away with Stuart Drake.

But here she was, in his parents' home, of all places, and hadn't the slightest idea where to start looking for Susan. Her valise stood at the foot of the bed, and Charlotte opened it, her heart sinking as she surveyed the gaudy clothing Lucia had packed. It didn't seem right to go downstairs to breakfast wearing red silk and diamonds. With a sigh she turned to her bronze gown from yesterday, lying neatly across a chair. It would have to do until she could send for more.

She dressed and brushed her hair, wishing Lucia had sent her cosmetics. She could certainly use them today, to cover the dark circles under her eyes and the paleness of her cheeks. She opened her door and went in search of her host.

The house was elegantly decorated, a home of comfortable wealth. It reminded her a great deal of her father's house, all those years ago, and she wasn't sure if this was good or bad. The more evidence she saw of wealth, the more she wondered why Stuart had none. Charlotte had believed the gossip, that he had tried his father's patience until the poor man had no choice but to cut off his wastrel son. There was something uglier than that in the way they had spoken last night, though, just as there had been something finer in Stuart's offer to help her. Was he an immoral rake who seduced young women until his own father turned him out, or was he a gentleman who could offer to help her even after she had almost shot him? Charlotte didn't know anymore.

A maid directed her to the breakfast room. It was at the back of the hall, tucked behind the main dining room. Just about to enter, Charlotte heard raised voices and paused. She didn't want to walk in on a private argument.

"Not in my house, I say," raged a harsh man's voice. Charlotte pictured Terrance Drake's stern face, dark with anger, and almost turned to go back to her room.

"Now, Terrance, you're being unreasonable," said a female voice; Stuart's mother, Charlotte guessed. Unlike her husband, she sounded quite calm, even pleased.

"He's not bringing strange women into this house! She could be anything, his mistress, his whore, or some gullible chit who's fallen for his lies. I will not allow it."

She was not going into that room. She would pack her few things and leave; the butler would be able to direct her to a hotel. Charlotte's face burned with humiliation that they were discussing her. What had Stuart told them, to make his father so furious? She took two steps back down the hall, resolved to leave all the Drakes behind, when another voice stopped her.

"She's not my whore," said Stuart. "She's a widow responsible for her willful niece who's up and run off with a scoundrel, and I am gallantly offering her my aid. I assure you, she is as disgusted as you are by my failings and would be quite appalled to hear you accuse her of consorting with me."

"Anyone with you must be suspect," growled his father. Charlotte realized her mouth was hanging open. Did Stuart's father *hate* him? She turned around and walked into the room, unwilling to leave him to face such animosity while he was defending her.

"Good morning," she said clearly. Mr. Drake glared at her before turning back to his breakfast. Mrs. Drake beamed at her. Stuart was already on his feet, coming toward her.

"Good morning," he said, sketching a brief bow. Between them, where his parents could not see, he pressed her hand quickly and lightly. "Did you sleep well?"

"Yes, thank you." She smiled, determined not to display their differences. He seemed taken by surprise; he blinked, then escorted her to the table and seated her. Charlotte turned to her hostess, whose eyes were flitting curiously from her to Stuart and back. "Thank you, Mrs. Drake, for your kind hospitality. I was not at all myself yesterday."

"Naturally!" Amelia waved one hand. "How terrible for you. You are welcome to remain with us for as long as it takes to find your poor niece."

"Thank you, but I don't wish to intrude. Perhaps you could direct me to a hotel—"

"Of course not!" Amelia declared. "You must remain here. I insist. Stuart, help me to persuade her."

"Madame Griffolino is quite capable of making her own decisions." Stuart set a plate in front of her and gave his mother a warning glance. Flustered at being served by him, Charlotte looked up, straight into his midnight-blue gaze. "Have you any more ideas where Susan might have gone?"

"No, I—"

"But Madame Griffolino," said Amelia with too much enthusiasm, "you simply must stay! A hotel is so impersonal. You shall be like one of the family here."

Charlotte glanced up, aware that Mr. Drake was glaring at her as if she were Jezebel incarnate. It didn't seem to her that family was very well received here. Beside her, Stuart sat down and continued eating, apparently unruffled by the hostility. If it didn't bother him, why did it bother her? "It's really not necessary to invite me into your home," she murmured to him.

"He's not staying here," snapped Terrance.

A muscle twitched in Stuart's jaw. His mother spoke in a high, rushed voice. "Stuart never stays here, if he can help it. Why, we haven't seen him for breakfast in years! Such a pleasure it will be, to have two young people about the house."

Stuart shoved back his chair. "We should call on your solicitors directly," he told Charlotte. "Susan may approach them for funds." Even though she had yet to eat a bite, Charlotte nodded, and he all but yanked her chair from the table. He hurried her out the door, pausing only to toss her cloak around her shoulders and hand her her bonnet.

On the street, he seemed to relax, and slowed his pace to hers. He folded her hand securely around his elbow. Charlotte realized he intended to walk. "We can stop for a bite if you're hungry. I didn't intend to take you from your breakfast."

"Please stop." Charlotte tugged, and he stopped, but didn't release her hand. "It's quite kind and generous of you to offer as you did last night, but I would understand . . . that is, I cannot hold you to it. I was . . . unfair, and did not intend to coerce your help—"

"You coerced nothing. I offered sincerely." He reached out and tucked a loose curl back into the confines of her bonnet. "I've already inquired about an investigator; I can give you his direction, if you wish, but I would like to help you."

She stared in amazement. "But . . . why?"

A slight smile curved his mouth as he studied her. "Let us say, I'm trying to redeem myself. You've still got your pistol if I fail. Truce?"

She thought of searching for Susan alone, in a strange city. She thought of having no one to talk to, for the search must be conducted discreetly to preserve as much of Susan's reputation as possible. Stuart's hand was so firm and steady on hers, so comforting. Her resolve to release him from his offer wavered, and crumbled.

"Truce," she agreed.

His hand tightened for a second. "Good." He gave a short laugh, almost awkwardly. "Thank you. I want to help." He cleared his throat. "Shall we, then?"

Charlotte nodded, taking his arm again. She felt

awkward herself, accepting thanks from the man she had held at gunpoint yesterday. He ought to have been angry, or vengeful, or even smug, as she would have been in his place. Instead he offered to help. Insisted on helping. It poked yet another hole in her image of him, and made her wonder again just how wrong she had been.

Chapter Nine

For a week, there was no news. The investigator, Mr. Pitney, was unable to turn up the slightest clue to Susan's whereabouts. Stuart sent his valet, Benton, back to Kent, and he was also unable to discover anything. Lucia wrote in nearly illegible Italian with no news of anything except the young Englishman, who had progressed from reading her poetry in the lending library to taking her to the tea room.

He moves with the pace of a snail, her letters complained.

> *Already an Italian would have seduced me. But I cannot complain too much. He is a sweet boy, and when he finally acts, I will be ready—more than ready! Of Susan, I hear nothing, but, oh! The town is alive with talk of you. Are you truly Mr. Drake's mistress now? What a game you play, letting me think you hated him, when you wanted him yourself! I do not condemn your taste, naturally, and if you ever find he is too old—*she had underlined *old* twice—*I will be pleased to divert him. The English,*

*they need longer to learn the art of love; my young poet
requires a manual . . .*

"Any news?" Charlotte jumped at Stuart's question
as he entered the drawing room. She folded Lucia's
letter quickly, trying not to think about what she had
just been reading.

"Lucia has begun unpacking all the crates," she
said. "The house looks like an Italian villa."

He dropped onto the chair opposite her sofa. "Did
you ever catch your thief?"

Charlotte shook her head. "Lucia hopes to catch
him by displaying everything and waiting up at night
with a pistol, but he hasn't returned."

"No?" Stuart looked thoughtful, then smiled
slightly. "Thank God I'm in London. Whitley has his
hands full, I see."

"Whitley?"

Stuart's grin turned wicked. "Angus Whitley is
courting your friend; didn't you know?"

Charlotte looked down at her letter, surprised. "I
didn't realize you knew him."

Stuart nodded. "He went into Kent to keep me
company, but I didn't expect him to last a month."

"Neither did Lucia," murmured Charlotte. "How
old is Mr. Whitley?"

Stuart's eyebrows shot up. "Nine-and-twenty, I believe. Why?"

She smirked. "Lucia thinks a man is at his best
before thirty."

He closed his eyes, a long-suffering expression on
his face. "I've come to propose a new course," he said,
changing the subject. "Pitney hasn't uncovered a
breath of information, and it's been six days. If you're

still certain she came to London, I think we should try something else."

"What?" Charlotte put aside her letter. "I still believe London is the most likely place she would be, the place she would most likely agree to go with someone."

"It makes the most sense," Stuart agreed. "If we still have no leads in a few days, we should consider other places, but for now London is our best hope." She nodded, watching him expectantly. Stuart gripped his hands together and drew a deep breath. "I think you should go out in society."

"You can't be serious," she said in disbelief. "I am not in town to see the sights and dance until dawn. I could never enjoy it, as long as Susan is missing—"

"Not for your own enjoyment," he interrupted, having expected this. "Although it wouldn't do you any harm. Fretting and worrying all day isn't healthy. But there are two strong reasons that it may aid our search. First, there may be helpful gossip floating about. One hears everything about everyone in London, sooner or later, and you are the one best able to discern what might be useful, since you know Susan best."

"I don't really know Susan so well," she confessed, lowering her eyes. "If I did, this mightn't have happened."

"Nonsense. Charlotte, it is not your fault." She nodded, but didn't look up. "My other reason is more complicated," Stuart went on, choosing his words with care. "I've been thinking a great deal about the way she disappeared. What sort of man could persuade a girl to run off with him? To persuade her to elope with him, he must be a charming fellow; young girls might not consider a man's prospects, but they do pay attention to his face and manner."

Charlotte gave him such a dour look, Stuart belatedly realized he had just described his own relationship with Susan. He hurried on.

"But we have no idea who he might be. You're certain there were no suitors from her home." He paused, and Charlotte shook her head. "Then she met him in Tunbridge Wells," he went on. "My intuition says she would be flattered by a man who appeared to know a great deal about her, and who approached her romantically. A mysterious stranger, charming and handsome, who appears and sweeps her off her feet with words of love."

"Or adventure," added Charlotte. "Susan craved adventure. Her father was a scholarly man, and raised her very quietly. I suspect she hoped I would be more fun."

Stuart nodded. "Right. He woos her dramatically, whether she knows him or not, and she's upset at you, so she's easily persuaded. If he offers her romance and adventure, she might accept on impulse."

"Yes," said Charlotte after a pause. "On impulse. Susan would do that."

"How long had you lived in Tunbridge Wells?"

"A month. I returned from Italy in late spring, and collected her from Honeyfield, George's property. I wanted her to wait a year before she had a Season in London, and so we went into Kent."

"I knew her a fortnight while you were away, and then a week after," Stuart said. "That leaves only a week. Since she was still . . . er . . . attached to me the night before she disappeared, it doesn't seem likely he was someone she had considered previously."

"But who?" Charlotte jumped to her feet and began pacing. "The servants never saw her pay any mind to anyone but you."

"Why did you have the servants spy on her?" he asked, diverted.

Her mouth thinned, and a slight frown touched her brow. "To protect her. I still had matters to attend to in London, both my own affairs and Lucia's as well as George's estate, and I worried I would miss something significant. So the servants were supposed to report to me about her health and so on, and if she was an object of interest to fortune hunters."

"Ah. I see," he murmured.

Her frown deepened. "They told me about you, yes. As did Susan, in her own way."

"And you rushed back to put an end to my suit?" This was rather interesting, Stuart thought, sitting forward.

"I didn't hear much good of you in town," she retorted. "Seducing women, carriage racing, gambling and drinking—"

"I am a blot on humanity," he agreed. "But no worse than most men. And you repeated all this to Lady Kildair, I presume?"

"I simply wanted you to leave town," she said, dodging the question. "I was sure it would show Susan the error she had made."

"Am I really that bad?"

"You were wrong for Susan," she said stiffly, her back to him. "But . . . perhaps . . . I overreacted somewhat."

"Well." He sat back, seeing he wouldn't get much more. She hadn't wanted to admit even that. "Such praise will go to my head. Shall we return to the question of recovering your niece?"

"A charming, brash fellow," she said at once. "Unknown or slightly known to Susan? Couldn't it be someone she knew and trusted?"

"Was there any such person in town?"

"No." Her shoulders slumped. "Not anyone who's since disappeared."

"What was his motive in making off with her, then?"

"Her fortune, undoubtedly."

"But she's not of age, and you control her funds for several more years." Stuart moved to the edge of the sofa. "So either he has funds of his own to last until then, or he thinks to convince you, perhaps by presenting Susan as his wife, possibly with child." Charlotte shuddered. "Or, there could be some other reason entirely," he continued, watching her closely. "A thief wanted something from your house."

All the color left her face. "Surely you don't think he wanted Susan."

Stuart shook his head. "No. He was searching the crates. If he had wanted only her, why bother? He wanted something specific, and he wanted it badly." He closed his scarred hand in reflex. It was still painful.

"But the crates are filled with Piero's collection of art. That can't be what the thief was seeking."

"Why not?" he asked in surprise.

Charlotte turned away. "Why, he looked in every crate and took nothing. If he had wanted something from Italy, he would have taken it."

"Perhaps he thinks you've hidden it," he said slowly. "Perhaps he thinks Susan may be able to help him get it."

"Why Susan instead of me? Why not send a ransom note if so? Why run away with her? Why not court her in Kent, near the object of his desire, until he gets what he wants?" Charlotte began pacing again, her nerves taut. "I can't believe that happened—surely she wouldn't trust a stranger—surely she wouldn't have been so foolish—"

"Stop." He had come up behind her, and now took hold of her arms with a gentle shake. "We don't know, we are only guessing. Until we find her, no possibility can be discarded, no matter how unflattering or unlikely."

Charlotte gulped. "Of course not. I just . . ." She shook her head. "I feel I shall go mad from not knowing!"

"I know."

For a moment she thought he would draw her into his arms, let her rest her head against his shoulder. Charlotte was shocked to realize she wanted him to. How had she come to rely on him so much in only a matter of days? When the task of finding one girl in the teeming city had seemed overwhelming and impossible to Charlotte, Stuart had stepped into the breach, finding an investigator, setting his valet to searching, asking questions and posing possibilities Charlotte would never have considered herself. And while he had presented her with these choices, along with his own thoughts and advice, he had let her make all the decisions. Really she couldn't have asked for a better person at her side.

But then he released her, and she stepped away to cover her absurd disappointment. "If the thief kidnapped Susan, he did so to make you suffer. If you don't appear to be suffering, he may give himself away out of pique."

Charlotte hesitated. What he said made sense, if the thief and the kidnapper were one, but she couldn't believe that. The thief had wanted something from Italy; Susan had no knowledge of or connection to Italy at all. The fact that the burglaries had stopped at the same time Susan disappeared was coincidental. It was more likely his encounter with Stuart had scared the thief away. As if sensing her thoughts, Stuart added, "And if Susan simply eloped or ran off, she may hear of your doings and come to you."

Charlotte's mouth twisted in a heartsick smile. Yes, jealousy would bring Susan out of hiding. Jealousy had sent her into hiding, after all. Charlotte had told Stuart she would do anything to get her niece back, and he had taken her at her word. Even the thought of going into London society, which made her stomach knot, was worth it. Charlotte had lived a scandalous life and she knew it; proper ladies did not jaunt about Europe by themselves, or with their lovers. Her husband had been an old man, and no one would doubt she had married him for money. If people connected her to her past, it would ruin her, no matter how modestly she was living now. But what did that matter next to Susan's safety? "What do you suggest?" she murmured.

She heard Stuart let out his breath. He turned her to face him, his hands lingering on her shoulders. "The most visible place possible," he said gently. "The opera, or the theater."

Charlotte held herself perfectly still. If she had to do this, let it be in true Italian fashion. "The opera."

* * *

Stuart arrived early that night. He firmly believed everything he had said to Charlotte that afternoon, and would have wagered heavily that this would yield results, if he had had anything to wager. Pitney's men had scoured the seedy side of London, been to Dover and a number of other ports, and even gone to Gretna Green, destination of more than one eloping couple. But all had turned up nothing so far. Either Susan had been swept away by a genuine suitor who had secreted both of them away in some lover's hideaway, or the mysterious thief had something to do with her disappearance. It was too strong a coincidence that the burglaries had stopped at the same time something infinitely dear to Charlotte had vanished.

Still, he barely managed not to pace as he waited. His other reason for wanting to escort Charlotte was more selfish, and he was loath to admit it even to himself. He disliked seeing her tense and worried, wracked with guilt over something he privately considered outside her control. He wanted her to laugh and smile again, to be the woman who had so fascinated him. As he had watched her quiet suffering this past week, he had come to feel a great deal more than lust for her. She was brutally honest and forthright, and when it wasn't directed at him, he liked her dry wit. Even when it was, he had to confess, he still appreciated it. The woman gave no quarter, but she asked none, either, and Stuart respected that.

Naturally, he had repressed his baser urges. She was in a terrible spot, after all, and he had promised to help her. She was vulnerable now, and he couldn't take advantage of that. He wasn't a thorough-going cad, after all. Stuart told himself again he simply wanted to make her smile, for her own sake, and that this evening was about finding Susan above all else. He had no plan, intention, idea, or even desire to seduce her. None.

"Will I do?" He spun around to see her coming down the stairs. "You said to dress conspicuously."

Stuart stared. She wore red silk that clung to her curves yet swayed with every step. Ropes of pearls hung around her neck, dipping into the generous cleavage revealed by the gown's low neckline. Her dark curls were pinned in a loose tumble atop her head, more pearls twined through them. She stopped in front of him, adjusting her long white gloves.

"Mr. Drake," she admonished, a wry smile pulling at her mouth. "You're staring."

Stuart blinked. "Am I? How terribly rude."

"I suppose I must forgive you, since that was the desired effect. We want everyone to notice us, correct?"

"They'll notice you, at any rate." This was a call to arms, to Stuart's way of thinking. He wasn't a cad, but he also wasn't a monk, and she knew it. All right, so it had been his idea to go out tonight, and he had encouraged her to dress elegantly, but surely any other woman would have managed it without being this . . . entrancing. Or maybe not; Stuart was beginning to acknowledge his peculiar weakness for this particular woman. He draped her velvet cloak around her shoulders with great care, and she gave him a sleepy-eyed smile that seemed to confirm his instincts. Whether he imagined things or not, this looked to be a very promising evening.

* * *

Stuart had secured an invitation to join the Duke of Ware in his box, one of the most prominent in the Royal Opera. He told her he had already spoken to the duke about their hopes for the evening, and when they arrived at the opera, he led her up to the box directly.

When they reached it, Charlotte took the foremost seat without hesitation. She even tugged it closer to the railing, in the process leaning over and giving anyone watching a spectacular view of her bosom. By the time Stuart took the seat beside her, she had taken up a pair of opera glasses and was scanning the crowd. "Have you any idea where he might be?"

Stuart leaned forward and took the glasses from her. "He needn't be here himself, although that would of course be very convenient. We need the gossips to see us, and that they will."

Charlotte snatched the glasses back. "Then you don't think he'll be here?"

"He may. All I want to do is establish your presence in town." She still frowned at him, annoyed. "Suppose he does attend the opera," he said in exasperation. "Suppose he is here tonight in this very building. How the devil would we know?"

Charlotte turned her back to him, raising the glasses again. Perhaps she had made a mistake choosing the opera. It had been her choice, but she ought to have tried to think what a kidnapper might prefer. Still, people *were* noticing them. She saw a pair of women, heads together and fans shielding their mouths, their eyes fixed on her. In another box sat a man and woman, the man reclining in his seat and watching her with heavy-lidded eyes as the woman spoke directly into his ear, her eyes also on Charlotte. Other people in other boxes were aware of her, some with avid curiosity, some with contempt. Charlotte knew exactly how she looked, and she reminded herself she wanted to inspire their interest, whether good or ill.

She put down the glasses. "What do we do now?"

"Enjoy the opera, I hope." He was sitting very close to her.

"Do you enjoy opera?"

"I might. This is my first."

Charlotte almost fell off her chair. "Your first?"

He looked out over the crowd in the pit. "Yes, as a matter of fact. Not all of us have your cultural experiences, m'dear."

"There is an opera house in the heart of London," said Charlotte dryly. "I believe it has stood here for many years."

He affected surprise. "Has it? How extraordinary."

Charlotte shook her head in disbelief. "What entertainments do you prefer then?" He gave her a smile so beatific it was obscene, and she threw up one hand. "I do not wish to know after all. Please do not tell me."

"As you wish. I have always preferred to be a man of actions, not merely words." His voice dropped into a soft rumble, and his blue eyes gleamed.

Charlotte stiffened. His words alone had left her twisted almost double with desire; heaven preserve her from any actions. She started talking just to prevent him from doing so. "The first time I heard opera was in Venice. Everyone went; the opera house was filled with people of all stations. I was assured no one paid much mind to the production onstage until someone began to sing, and in the main this was true. But when the prima donna came onstage, the entire hall grew quiet. I had never heard anyone sing so beautifully, like the angels in heaven must sing. She made the audience weep with her, laugh with her, and care for her with their whole hearts. My only thought from that night on was to see and hear more, and I never missed a performance by that soprano." She stopped, remembering again how mesmerized she had been that night, how completely swept away by the passion in the music.

She looked over the growing crowd toward the stage, where the heavy curtains still hung closed. Lucia had said it was like waiting for a new lover, those minutes backstage before the curtain opened: a mixture of nervous apprehension and sheer elation. Charlotte was acutely conscious of Stuart beside her, dangerously attractive in his eveningwear. She felt that apprehension very strongly, but also some of the elation; she should not be so intrigued by him. Lucia, no doubt, would say it was an omen that she was with him for his first opera. Charlotte wondered if Stuart would be as moved by the music as she had been.

"Your friend," said Stuart quietly. "Madame da Ponte?"

Charlotte started, jerking her thoughts away from new lovers and omens. "Yes. I have still never heard anyone sing as beautifully as she did."

"Does she no longer sing?"

"No." He said nothing, and for some reason Charlotte told him why. "That is my fault. I introduced one of my husband's companions to her, and he was instantly besotted. In trying to win her favor, he gave her some Turkish tobacco, and then she was instantly besotted—with the tobacco. She began smoking it several times a day, and her voice was never the same. Other singers, younger and more grasping, contrived to take her roles. I invited her to come to England when I got word of my brother's death, and she accepted, I believe, to salvage her fame before it was entirely gone." He said nothing, but she felt his eyes on her, and abruptly changed the subject. "This box is ideally situated for our purposes," she observed, leaning forward again for a view.

Stuart let his gaze rove over her back. Her gown was even lower in back than in front, and his eyes traced the line of her spine up to the heavy knot of dark curls. Her shoulders were entirely bare, and he wondered what she would do if he leaned forward and kissed the back of her neck, right at the necklace clasp as he undid it and let the pearls slide down . . .

She sat back, squaring her shoulders. The pearls settled in a wide arc that caught just on the edge of the red silk. "You are not to blame for the tobacco," said Stuart, willing them to slip into her cleavage, not that he needed any other excuse to look there. He could hardly look away from her at all. "It was her choice to smoke it."

She flicked open her fan, no longer looking at him. "I do not suffer from terrible guilt, Mr. Drake. I merely think it a great pity. Have you never regretted the unforeseen consequences of your actions?"

He was spared a reply by the arrival of their host. The orchestra was beginning, and Charlotte had turned her attention toward the stage and her back toward him. Stuart gave one last lingering glance at the necklace clasp, acknowledging that this was not the place. But what would Charlotte do, if he acted on his impulse? He suspected part of her would welcome it. The other part of her would undoubtedly pull a pistol on him, though, and Stuart had had enough of that. His entire acquaintance with Charlotte had been one of unintended consequences, but Stuart couldn't say he regretted it.

The opera was not the best production Charlotte had ever heard. Between acts Stuart brought wine, but they remained in the box, highly visible. A few men stopped by, but only those who knew Stuart or the duke. Charlotte was relieved when the opera began again, and Stuart resumed his seat beside her.

The prima donna was an Italian woman with strong, heavy features. Charlotte thought she might have heard the woman sing in Italy once, a minor role in Rome. Her inflection was florid and her tone slightly nasal, nothing like the clean pure beauty of Lucia's voice before the cigarettes had stolen it. Letting her mind drift from the overwrought arias, Charlotte wondered what Lucia was doing, and if Mr. Whitley had made enough progress to persuade her to begin singing again. If Lucia came to London with even a shadow of her voice restored, she would be a sensation.

Since she wasn't paying attention to the opera, her ears gradually became attuned to the low voices behind her. Stuart, who had sat in perfect silence through the first acts, had begun a quiet conversation with the duke, who sat behind him. Without meaning to, she began listening.

"I received a notice from Barclay yesterday," murmured Ware.

A long pause. "Ah," said Stuart simply, but Charlotte sensed a great deal of dismay in that small word. Who was Barclay? And why would Stuart be upset by mention of him?

"I expect he simply didn't know where to reach you," added the duke. "He had already sent to Oakwood Park."

A longer pause. "I cannot afford to pay him yet," said Stuart, his voice somewhat strained.

"I understand." A very long pause. "I do not mind," said the duke so softly Charlotte could barely make out the words.

"No," said Stuart more harshly. "*I* mind. I'll find a way."

The opera ended, and everyone applauded. Charlotte turned her head just enough to see him from the corner of her eye; his face was set, his eyes melancholy. He didn't notice her watching for a moment, and when he did the sadness disappeared at once.

"Simply brilliant," he said, leaning forward to rest his arm along the back of her chair. "What was the story? Ware and I have a wager: is it secret lovers?"

"All Italian opera revolves around secret lovers," said the duke with a faint smile.

"In this instance, you are wrong." The Duke of Ware was the most beautiful man Charlotte had ever seen. Tall and golden-haired, his face appeared sculpted by Michelangelo himself. Charlotte had to remind herself not to stare every time he spoke to her. His eyes were a mesmerizing mixture of blue and gray, but his smile barely touched them. He had been formal and polite to her, and although he and Stuart were clearly old friends, there was a reserve about him that made Charlotte wonder how the two of them had ever gotten along. "The lovers are not secret," she said. "They are to be married. The other characters try to cause trouble between them."

Stuart turned to the duke. "I was counting upon an evening of lovers' laments. How disappointing."

"As you do not speak a word of Italian," teased Charlotte, "you may persuade yourself you have had one. Perhaps I did not tell you the truth."

He shifted, nearer. His arm rested lightly against the back of her shoulders. "But I know you did."

"Absolute trust?" The duke's eyebrow went up as he turned to Charlotte. "That is a rare thing indeed to give another person." Disconcerted, she looked away, right into Stuart's eyes. For a moment, neither moved, and she knew in that moment the duke had put his finger on it. She did trust Stuart. It left her delighted, and uneasy, and more than a little surprised. Was it natural to trust him now, when she had so recently distrusted him completely? Was it wise, to depend so much upon him after she had done so much to make him dislike her? Or was she fooling herself, persuading herself he was a better man than she'd thought simply because it would allow her to justify other feelings?

"Yes," she said, tearing her eyes from his. "Exceedingly rare." There was a moment of silence. "I am sorry there were no lover's laments, for the sake of your wager," she said to fill it. "I enjoyed it all the same."

"As did I," murmured the duke. Charlotte looked up to see he was regarding her with a strangely intense expression. For a moment those magnetic blue gray eyes searched her face, almost hungrily, as if looking for some particular resemblance or feature. She wanted to look away but somehow couldn't.

"Well, splendid! Perhaps Ware will abandon his long-favored theater haunts for the opera."

Charlotte started at Stuart's lighthearted remark. The duke's expression closed immediately, becoming distant and cool.

"Perhaps." He stood. "Pray, excuse me, Madame Griffolino, Drake." He bowed and moved away, leaving Stuart furious at himself and yet unable to forget how Ware had been looking at Charlotte. Ware hadn't looked at a woman that way in years. What the devil would he do, if the reclusive duke finally came out of his shell to pursue her? How could he compete with a man like Ware? And should he even try to, when he had so little to offer Charlotte himself?

"He's very lonely, isn't he?" said Charlotte softly, watching the duke.

"I suppose." Stuart's frown turned to a scowl. It rubbed him the wrong way to hear her pity poor Ware, who lived in the finest house in London with his every need and wish satisfied at once. Ware, who could have any woman in England for a snap of his fingers. Ware, who had the influence and wealth to take London apart brick by brick until Susan was found.

Stuart sprang to his feet, hating himself for thinking such a thing. Ware was his friend, a gentleman who would never . . . He looked at Charlotte, lush and sensual in her crimson gown, her ropes of pearls sliding tantalizingly into her cleavage. Friend and gentleman or not, a man would have to be blind not to be attracted to her. "Shall we go?"

She looked up in astonishment. "But we haven't

spoken to anyone! I thought you hoped to hear gossip that might help us find Susan."

Stuart shifted his weight. "People come to the opera to talk about each other. It should be easier to let the kidnapper hear of you than for you to hear of him. I doubt we'll hear anything of Susan here."

"Oh." She wilted a bit, and Stuart felt like a cad all over again. He knew the chance of hearing something among the ton was very small, but he'd hoped going out would be good for Charlotte . . . just not so good she ended up a duchess. It was jealousy, pure and simple, and he hated himself for it, but he couldn't deny it. Not even the reminder of how acute his own troubles were becoming could distract him. And Stuart didn't quite know what to make of that.

Chapter Ten

Charlotte was early to breakfast the next morning, not surprised to find Stuart there ahead of her. He had taken breakfast at his parents' house every day, although thankfully Mr. Drake had been absent since that first morning. And because she knew he would be there, Charlotte came down as well; it would be rude to avoid him, after all his help. So she told herself, even as her heart lifted a little at the sight of his welcoming smile.

"No word from Pitney," he said, seating her. "I expect to see him later today, though."

Charlotte sighed, her moment of happiness fading. "He's had no news at all."

"Don't be discouraged. He's good at finding people; it was the one skill I particularly required. Pitney may seem slow, but he's following his method, and has all but guaranteed results." He took his own seat. "Have you any news from your friend?"

Charlotte poured a cup of tea. "No. All her letters are filled with gossip and—and other news." She avoided his gaze, not wanting to share all the details of Lucia's fascination with his friend Mr. Whitley, or her lurid questions about Stuart. "But nothing of Susan."

"Well, we didn't expect much. Don't take it too much to heart. The center of our effort is still in London." He looked up with a slight toss of his head to clear the hair from his eyes, giving her a quick smile. Charlotte stared, arrested by that careless motion. There was something so familiar, so *intimate* about noticing he needed to have his hair cut. No man had ever been so informal around her; they had always been turned out in their best, to impress and seduce and awe. Even Piero had refused to see her each day until his valet groomed him. But Stuart had sent away his valet to look for her niece. His hair was too long because he was neglecting himself to help her.

Even though she knew very well that Stuart had sent his valet back to Kent, it had never fully sunk in how much that signified. Not only was Stuart helping her, he was doing it at great inconvenience and cost to himself. He had sent away his only servant, imposed on his friends, and subjected himself to the hostility of his father's house, all to help her find Susan.

No one had ever put themselves out for her. For the most part Charlotte simply accepted this fact; it relieved her of any obligation to put herself out for someone else, after all. But here sat Stuart, helping her almost as if he did it just for the sake of helping her. As if her happiness were all that mattered to him. As if he cared about her.

"Did you enjoy the opera?" she said, flustered by her thoughts.

"Very much," he said. "I never would have thought

to spend an evening listening to singing, but it was splendid."

"I'm so glad. I have always found the opera enthralling." Something in her tone must have betrayed her less musical thoughts, for Stuart looked up.

"I, too, found it most stimulating," he said, his eyes darkening as he leaned toward her. "I'm so glad you suggested it; I couldn't have enjoyed it half as much with anyone else. I should be very happy to escort you, any time you wish to go."

"I can never hear enough opera," she warned, allowing the ambiguity to continue. He leaned closer still, his gaze never leaving hers.

"I cannot tell you how delighted I am to know that, and how much I would like to satisfy your . . . desire for more."

The butler interrupted. "A message for you, madam."

Charlotte dragged her gaze from Stuart's and took the note. "It's from Susan!" she cried, recognizing the handwriting.

Stuart bolted from his chair. "Brumble, who delivered it?"

"A very grimy lad, sir," called the butler as Stuart ran from the room. The front door slammed as Charlotte tore open the letter. A smaller note fell out, but she ignored it, her eyes racing across Susan's uneven writing.

Dear Aunt Charlotte,

I am writing to assure you I am well and happy. I am to be married soon! I expect you're still unhappy about the way I left, and I apologize for that, but you must see I had to do it. Soon I shall send for my clothing and other belongings, but for now we have

not taken a house, and have no room. London is
everything I dreamed and more! I shall write again,

Susan

She ran into the hall in pursuit of Stuart just as he
came back into the house, breathing heavily. "I
couldn't catch him," he said, his voice sharp with frustration. "Brumble!"

The butler appeared at once. "Yes, sir?"

"If any other lads deliver messages for Madame
Griffolino or me, take hold of him and don't let go
until I speak to him." The butler bowed, and Stuart
turned to Charlotte. "What does the note say?"

Charlotte handed it to him. A deep frown creased
his brow as he read, and he waved her back into the
breakfast room. When they were alone, she put her
hands on her hips. "Well?"

Stuart began pacing, tapping the letter against his
chin. "He's told her he wants to marry her; we were
right about the romance and adventure. But who is
he? We still have no idea who could have lured her
away so secretly and suddenly."

"I realize that," she snapped, snatching back the
note—her only contact with Susan in a week—and
holding it reverently close to her chest. This message
proved her niece was alive and well, and in London.
"She's indisputably in London. How do we find her?"

"Send for Pitney," he said at once. "Frakes can describe the messenger. If we can locate the boy who
brought it, we're one step closer to the person who
sent it."

"That could take days! There must be hundreds of
grimy lads in London!"

"Thousands," said Stuart. "Patience, Charlotte. Pitney knows the city, and the lowest citizens in it."

"But what shall *we* do? Summon a carriage. Surely if we drive quickly, we might come across the boy . . ."

Stuart was shaking his head. "He's gone. We could drive every inch of London and not see him."

"But I have to do something or I shall scream!" Charlotte gripped the letter like a lifeline, hysteria bubbling up in her throat. She had thought not knowing anything was the worst thing, but that was wrong; knowing a little, but not enough to act, was far more agonizing.

He sighed and ruffled one hand through his hair. "Besides telling Pitney . . ." He shook his head. Charlotte abruptly remembered the other scrap of paper that had fallen out of Susan's letter. She went down on her knees and crawled under the table to retrieve it. "What are you doing?" Stuart lifted the tablecloth to peer at her as she unfolded the coarse paper and gasped out loud.

"What?" Stuart all but dragged her from under the table and pried the paper from her fingers. "What the devil is this?"

Charlotte smoothed the page and translated from the Italian.

> *Scarlet whore, you have taken my treasure and I have taken yours. While you display yourself to the English gentlemen, your Susan sits by my side, weak and willing. When you return the Italian treasure, I will give her back to you.*
>
> *Someone who watches.*

"Bloody hell." He snatched the paper back and scowled at the crimped writing. "What's the Italian treasure?"

"I have no idea." Charlotte was shaking, with elation and fear. "But he was watching us last night." She seized the note and pointed, even though he couldn't read it. "Scarlet! My red gown! He's nearby! And Susan is with him!"

He looked up then, his eyes gleaming. "He is. You've provoked him into showing his hand. Well, well. He's an Italian. He must have followed you from Italy. And he's most likely the thief who broke into your house."

"But what does he want?" She clasped her hands to stop their trembling. "I haven't any treasure."

"He obviously thinks you do." Stuart frowned at the note again. "He stole Susan away when he couldn't find it himself."

"Oh, my poor girl!" Charlotte all but sobbed. "What can we do now? To know she is in London, so near, and I have no idea where!"

"Patience," he said with fearful calm. "We know what to look for. I shall set Pitney and Benton on this at once. Now that they have some firm leads, I expect at least one of them to make great progress. Your friend is still in your house in Kent, is she not?" Charlotte nodded. "Write to her immediately. Tell her to pack up everything you brought from Italy and send it here as soon as she possibly can. I'll send a note to Benton; he can help. He's a master of packing quickly."

"Why? Oh—of course!" she said with growing enthusiasm. "Whatever he wants must be in the things from Italy. Shall we do what Lucia did, set it all out and wait for him to break in and steal it?"

"No, we are going to discover what the bloody hell he's after," said Stuart grimly. "And then we'll be able to deal with him on an equal footing. He knows he doesn't stand a chance of getting it from you if he injures Susan, so she's safe as long as he thinks we have it. Are you certain there's nothing else from Italy besides the things in Kent, perhaps at a solicitor's office or sent to a friend?"

"No, everything was shipped to Kent. If his object is in my possession at all, it's in Tunbridge Wells."

"Then we'll find it and somehow let him know we're ready to negotiate. I'll also have Benton ask after any foreigners in Kent; you might ask the same of Lucia, particularly Italians. If he is your thief, he must have stayed close by, in order to watch your house and know when you left."

"I'll write to her immediately," Charlotte promised, desperate for anything to occupy her mind. "But what else—?" Stuart silenced her with one finger over her lips.

"I'll go to Pitney at once. Write to your friend." He removed his hand and surprised her by pressing a quick kiss in its place. "The more we find out about the kidnapper, the better Pitney's chances of finding him." He kissed her again, longer and harder this time. Without a moment's hesitation, she surged against him. Fear, she was finding, could be a powerful aphrodisiac, leaving her body tense and taut in anticipation of *something*. Desire came to life in an instant, supplanting her worries and concerns and focusing her entire being on Stuart, and the way he always affected her.

He caught her tightly around the waist when she opened her mouth, and Charlotte felt her knees give out as his other hand slid up to cover her breast. She had never wanted a man this way, never craved his presence and his touch so desperately. She clutched at him, straining to get even closer. He cupped the curve of her bottom, pulling her against him, and she moaned, her leg twining around his of its own volition. She wanted this, she wanted him, and she wanted him now.

As she pulled on his neck, completely willing to make love there on the carpet, he fell forward with her still clinging to him, catching a nearby chair to keep them upright. The table's edge pressed her hips into his, and Charlotte rubbed against him shamelessly. Stuart ended the kiss with a gasp.

"I can't make love to you here." His shoulders shuddered. "God knows I want to, but I can't."

Charlotte released him like a hot coal. "Stuart—"

"Someday," he said, low and fierce, "we have to finish this. You're driving me mad."

Before she could recover, the door opened. "Good morning," trilled Amelia. Stuart turned, hiding Charlotte from view for a moment as she yanked her dress back into place. Good Lord, they had been on the brink of making love on the breakfast table, on his *parents'* breakfast table, where anyone might walk in on them. She was behaving worse than the most promiscuous courtesan, and being an abominably rude guest as well.

"We've received a note from Susan," Stuart was

telling his mother, as calm as if nothing had been happening. "She's well, and in London. The fellow persuaded her to run off with him by promising to marry her; she wrote to Charlotte of her impending wedding."

"What a cruel trick!" Amelia's eyes flashed. "The poor girl! Why, she's been practically kidnapped!"

"And held for ransom," Stuart agreed. "It seems she doesn't even know it yet."

"Good heavens! What will you do to stop him?" Amelia cried, appalled.

"We received a message from him as well," Charlotte said. "He wants an Italian treasure he thinks I have. In exchange for the treasure, he'll release Susan." She glanced at Stuart. "I shudder to think what will happen if I don't have it."

"You do," he said firmly. "Somewhere. He must have been certain of it, or he wouldn't have risked searching your house repeatedly, not to mention taking Susan. It mightn't even be valuable, but it's important to him."

"I hope you're right."

He flashed his usual cocky grin. "I'm always right, m'dear; haven't you noticed by now?" He headed for the door. "I'm off to find Pitney. Write Lucia at once."

"I will," she promised. He smiled briefly, and was gone.

Alone with his mother, Charlotte slipped into her chair to finish her breakfast, still on her plate. The memory of what had distracted her from it made her feel terribly awkward, and she sipped her cold tea in feigned nonchalance. What would Mrs. Drake say about discovering them locked in an embrace? Good

Lord, she had almost ravished the woman's son! In broad daylight!

"You've grown quite fond of Stuart, haven't you?" asked Amelia. Charlotte glanced up guiltily, not surprised to find herself the subject of keen scrutiny. "He's a handsome boy," continued Amelia. "I don't blame you. All the Drake men are handsome devils."

Charlotte cleared her throat, not quite meeting her hostess's gaze. "We have become friends."

"Now, now. We are both grown women. You are not, I think, naïve or inexperienced. I give you leave to admit you are attracted to my son."

Charlotte opened her mouth, then closed it. She had no idea what to say.

Amelia reached for the teapot and filled her cup, the steam curling around her wrist. "But I must warn you," she added with a sympathetic glance, "he will never marry you."

Charlotte's eyes almost popped from her head. "I assure you, I—I had no idea of any such thing," she stammered. Marriage? To Stuart? He wanted a wealthy young bride; she enjoyed her freedom and independence. Marriage between them was ludicrous, even in theory.

But then, Mrs. Drake likely meant it as a warning to Charlotte not to harbor hopes of tricking Stuart into marriage. With her past, no mother would want her for a daughter-in-law, Charlotte realized. She was tarnished, soiled. Stuart might find her appealing enough to take to bed, but his mother was right: he would never marry her, because she wasn't the sort of woman a respectable man married.

It was a lowering thought. Despite all her efforts to become more respectable, she was still beyond the pale. No matter how she changed her hair or her dress, she would always be the one who had run wild in her youth. She was caught, stuck between her earnest wish to reform and the past she couldn't escape.

"I say that not out of my own wishes." Amelia sipped her tea, still watching her. "Some men are simply not capable of responsibilities like a wife and family, and Stuart is one."

Charlotte wasn't sure she believed the first part, but she was quite sure Stuart would have married Susan in an instant if she had consented. While the thought of them as man and wife made her ill, it ran counter to what his mother claimed. He had told her he would have been grateful to Susan, and Charlotte knew he wouldn't have abused her niece; he would have seen to it that his wife was comfortable, at least. "I cannot agree," she said slowly. "I think he craves responsibility."

Amelia shook her head. "Stuart has never craved responsibility. He wouldn't mind the appearance of it—a country estate, perhaps, or a stud farm—but he hasn't the slightest idea how to manage it. It's all he can do to take care of himself, and not well at that."

"But he has never had anything to manage." Charlotte didn't even know why she was defending him in this. Her opinion had been exactly the same, only a few days previously. "Do you not believe he would rise to the challenge, should the need be there?"

Amelia laughed, sadly. "No. I have known Stuart all his life, and although it pains me to say it, he will always rely on his charm and handsome face to make his way."

"He's been invaluable to me," protested Charlotte,

forgetting that she had once described him in those exact terms. "He's quite clever, and very determined."

Amelia sighed. "When a man is intent on seducing a woman, he can assume an infinite variety of guises. Gentle suitor, mysterious adventurer, knight in shining armor . . . They're all acted with one goal in mind, and that goal is not marriage. And the moment they achieve that goal, they're off to the next woman."

"That is true of some," Charlotte allowed after a moment. "But not all. Surely you, as his mother, must see the better parts of his character. I think you underestimate your son."

Something raw and desolate flashed across Amelia's features. She gave a short, sad laugh. "You don't know what you speak of. Stuart is just like his father."

Charlotte didn't find that too flattering; Mr. Drake seemed about the coldest, bitterest man she'd ever met. Was Amelia warning her Stuart would be the same in time? That would be the direst warning imaginable. "And do not be fooled into thinking the love of the right woman will make a man better than he is," continued Amelia. "Love is a fiction, for a man. He can never love a woman as much as she can love him. Above all, don't marry for love, my dear; it will break your heart. There is nothing so terrible as being married to someone who doesn't return your love."

"I don't love Stuart," she whispered. "And he doesn't love me." Although she was suddenly a little less sure of the former, the latter was undeniable.

"Good." Amelia lifted her teacup again, her polite smile restored. "It will save you a world of heartache. Other ladies have not been so fortunate."

"Other ladies?" Charlotte echoed in confusion.

Again she thanked her lucky stars she wasn't a mother; she wouldn't be able to survive her daughter falling for adventurers and fortune hunters, and she could never warn other women away from her son. Her maternal fancies had only covered children to a certain age, never into the years when they would be adults. When did a mother's responsibility end?

"Other ladies who have fallen for Stuart," clarified Amelia gently. "It ended badly for all of them. One was sent into the country in disgrace, and the other was quickly married to a cousin who was willing to overlook her dishonor."

"Anne Hale," said Charlotte, staring at her. "Eliza Pennyworth."

Amelia looked away. "Two young ladies in the course of a month. Terrance was justified."

Suddenly Charlotte didn't know. She had repeated the rumors to Louise Kildair, but by the time the gossip had circulated back to her, it reported Stuart all but seducing one girl in front of her horrified grandmother. The supposed elopement with Eliza Pennyworth had become an abduction. If her little bit of tattle could grow so monstrous in a week, how much might it have grown before she heard it the first time?

"Mrs. Drake," she began, "you have been very direct with me. May I ask a similarly direct question of you?"

"Of course."

"Why does Mr. Drake dislike his son so?"

Amelia's expression closed. "Terrance has been so disappointed in Stuart; he hoped to raise him to be a better man than—than he has become." Charlotte wondered at that stumble, but Amelia went on. "But

Stuart turned out wild—impossibly so. Everything Terrance wished him to do, Stuart refused, and everything Terrance warned him against, Stuart pursued."

"But he is a man now. Surely Mr. Drake will not hold the recklessness of youth against him his whole life."

"You are assuming he has reformed."

Her tone ended the discussion; clearly Mrs. Drake, for all that she loved her son, still believed the worst of him. Charlotte was amazed in spite of herself. Her father, at least, had needed the terrible truth proven beyond all doubt before he turned her out. Perhaps he had done her a favor, for Charlotte truly didn't know which was worse: being cast out never to return, or always subject to suspicions and judgment from the very family one was dependent upon. "I have found him quite honorable," she said slowly. "And I know rumors can exaggerate."

"My dear Madame Griffolino." Amelia took her hand. "Stuart is my only child. I adore him, and I confess, I invited you to stay here so that I might see him more. But I am not blind to his faults, and don't wish you to be. It is easy for us women to be swept away by feelings and emotions, and I would be very sad to see you betrayed. The terrible lesson of your own niece has persuaded me to speak."

Charlotte didn't know what to think. She did know, from cruel experience, how easily a charming man could steal a woman's heart. Most of what Mrs. Drake said was gospel truth, as far as Charlotte was concerned. But it was Stuart Mrs. Drake spoke of, not the heartless cad who had ruined her all those years ago or the nameless villain who had abducted Susan. Despite plentiful opportunities, and motive provided by Charlotte herself, Stuart had taken pains not to hurt Susan; he had convinced her she was *Juliet*, of all people, to avoid breaking her heart.

But he was a fortune hunter, by his own admission. There was nothing respectable about that. How could she see him as honorable, after the way he had coldly set his sights on Susan and her inheritance? How could she like him, when he was partly responsible for Susan running away?

Susan ran away because of you, whispered her guilty conscience, *not because of him. If not for him, you would be lost, with no idea whom to turn to for help.*

But that didn't mean she was falling in love with him. Even if he could arouse her like no one else could, he also aggravated her like no one else could. He wasn't put off by anything she said to him. He laughed when she threatened him with a pistol, and managed to turn a conversation on the opera into a sensual promise. Charlotte had flirted with too many men to have missed what he was saying: he still wanted her. But none of that was love.

She worried about it all day. For a time she considered going to bed with Stuart just to break the tension between them; why shouldn't two adults enjoy a discreet, mutually agreeable affair? Then she thought about Susan, and how utterly devoid of decency she was to think about her own pleasures while Susan was at the mercy of some Italian madman. But if she waited until she had her niece back, how could she have an affair with Stuart then, knowing how hurt and betrayed Susan would be? Charlotte confronted the possibility that there would never be a good time, and it made her want to weep. He was the only man she had ever wept over in regret.

Could that mean there was more to her feelings than desire? Ever since the one disastrous time she had given her heart, Charlotte had refused to let herself feel anything beyond desire for a man. She didn't want Stuart to be any different. She couldn't afford to let him be different.

What if he was, in spite of all her wishes to the contrary?

A brief affair, she decided, was the answer. She couldn't be in love with Stuart. She didn't want to marry him. She wanted him, true, but it was a purely physical need. Once they made love, the attraction would burn itself out . . . unless it were something more. If making love to him failed to move her heart, she would know it was simply lust. And if it did move her heart . . .

She would deal with that problem when it arose.

Stuart spent an exhausting day canvassing taverns and pubs. Charlotte had given him money for rewards, and despite distributing it liberally, he was unable to find the boy who brought the message. By evening, he was hot, tired, and frustrated. They had been so close to someone who could lead them to Susan's kidnapper, but had nothing to show for it.

After meeting with Pitney to confirm that neither had found the messenger, Stuart headed toward Mayfair. He was so tired, he wanted nothing more than to go home and fall into bed, but he had to tell Charlotte about the day. He also wanted to see her again, enough to brave the house when Terrance was likely to be there, a fact which made him somewhat uncomfortable. He probably wouldn't even be alone with her, but he was still walking half a mile out of his way, hungry and covered in dirt, just to see her.

She was waiting for him in the hall, a sight which made his mood considerably brighter. She took one look at his face, and her hopeful expression faded. "You didn't find him."

Stuart took her hand. "We put the word out over all London. The lad is sure to turn up soon. You mustn't lose hope."

"No." She nodded, looking distracted. "I've been thinking—"

"What are you doing?" Stuart winced at his father's growl. Beside him, Charlotte shrank a little. He turned around, keeping their clasped hands behind him. "Good evening, Terrance."

"If you're going to come here, behave with some civility," snapped Terrance. "We receive guests in the drawing room." He stood back in the drawing room doors, and Stuart led Charlotte in, trying not to drag his feet. He seated her on a chair, then took the other one for himself. Terrance sat in the middle of the sofa, his stiff leg stretched in front of him, and regarded Stuart with a cold stare.

"So. What mischief have you been causing today?"

Stuart shrugged. "Less than usual. You should be proud."

Terrance grunted. "Why were you standing in the hall?"

"I wanted to speak to Madame Griffolino privately."

"How many ladies have you disgraced with your private conversations?" Terrance glared at Charlotte for a moment. "Where have you been?"

Stuart sat back and draped his arms over the back of the chair, knowing it would infuriate his formal father. "Dens of iniquity and havens of vice."

"Do not mock me!"

"I wasn't mocking you," said Stuart. "I was telling you what you expected to hear. I do try not to disappoint, Terrance."

Terrance's frigid stare switched to Charlotte. "I trust you can see, madam, that your trust in this scoundrel is highly misplaced."

Charlotte blinked, then her eyes narrowed. "I have not been disappointed thus far."

"You will be." He turned to Stuart. "Was it the tables? You're due for a loss."

Stuart, who hadn't wagered a pound in months, shook his head with a soft tsk. "Terrance, please. There is a lady present."

Terrance's suspicious eyes swung to Charlotte and back, as if questioning her gentility. Stuart sensed an insult brewing, and moved to forestall it. "I came to inquire if I might take Madame Griffolino driving on the morrow," he said, crossing one ankle over his knee.

Terrance looked as though he were contemplating kicking Stuart's foot back to the floor. "How dare you sit in my drawing room like a common laborer? Show some respect."

Stuart dropped his foot. Charlotte, her face unreadable, got to her feet, forcing the gentlemen to theirs. Stuart turned to her as Terrance struggled out of his chair. "I should be delighted," she said.

Stuart bowed. "Excellent. I shall call for you after luncheon." If he couldn't see her tonight, he damn

well would see her tomorrow, where Terrance couldn't
follow. She met his eyes for a moment, then took a
deep breath and smiled, as if she had decided something. He raised one brow slightly in question, but she
gave a tiny shake of her head, and Stuart took his
leave, too tired to worry about it then. Ware had already offered him the use of a rig, and the Ware
horses were excellent. Tomorrow, he would take her
for a long, long drive, perhaps out of London, to a
quiet secluded place where he could finally have her
to himself, and then . . . Then he could try to discover
her real feelings.

Charlotte watched him go, her blood already
singing with excitement. Tomorrow, if all went well,
she would conquer this stubborn, persistent attraction
that threatened her sanity. Lucia had always advised
her that the best way to eliminate temptation was to
give in to it, and in this case, Charlotte was more
than willing to try it. It was the only way to save herself
from worse.

Chapter Eleven

"I thought you might like to escape London for a bit," he said the next afternoon after helping her into the carriage.

"Oh, no, I wouldn't want to go so far." Charlotte didn't have the patience to wait for him to seduce her. She intended to seduce him, as soon as possible, and didn't relish doing it alongside the road. "Shall we see the park?"

Stuart started to speak, but said nothing, clearly disappointed. "Of course." He drove in silence for a while, guiding the restive horses through the heavy traffic.

"It's a lovely day for a drive." Charlotte watched the other carriages and riders. Several gentlemen raised their hats to her, and she nodded in response, but no one stopped them.

"Yes. All London comes out in fine weather." Stuart sent the team around a stopped carriage filled with elderly ladies.

"I cannot blame them. Who would not want a long ride today?"

"Ah," he said with interest. "Do you ride? I shall have to see about a mount for you."

Charlotte smiled secretively. "I wish you would. It is one of my favorite things. There is nothing like a pounding gallop to refresh one's senses, or a brisk canter to set one's heart racing. Even a trot can be quite stimulating."

"I am delighted to hear that," said Stuart, still concentrating on driving. The park was crowded, and he had to rein in the spirited horses every few minutes. "Many ladies prefer a walk, so as not to disturb their bonnets."

"I rarely wear a bonnet," replied Charlotte. "I prefer my hair loose and free." Stuart said nothing, but his hands twitched on the reins. "And I've never found a sidesaddle pleasing. There is something exhilarating about clinging to my mount with my knees."

He cleared his throat and sent her a sideways glance. "You ride astride, then?"

She leaned into him as they went around a bend. "I always ride astride," she whispered. "I imagine the horse prefers it as well."

Stuart looked at her from the corner of his eye so long he almost drove into another carriage. The other driver shouted, Stuart jerked his attention back to the horses, and the oncoming carriage passed them with inches to spare.

"Oh, my!" Charlotte laughed, leaning into his arm as she clutched at her parasol. "You know how to make it exciting."

"I try." His eyes flickered from the road to her to the road. "I may have a suitable mount in mind for you," he said, turning out of the park.

"How delightful. Where is it stabled?"

"At Philip's house. Where I am staying."

"Lovely." She smiled. "Would it be a terrible imposition to take a ride now?"

"Not at all." He flicked the whip, and the horses surged forward. In minutes Stuart turned them into a mews and then into a small stable yard. He jumped down, reaching up to help her. She waited while he saw to the horses, then calmly, sedately, he escorted her into the house, where he took her pelisse in the most ordinary manner and hung it up. Charlotte looked around with interest as he shrugged out of his own coat, not surprised to see an elegant townhouse.

"Wait," he said then, taking her face in his hands. His burning gaze roved over her features. "This was your meaning, was it not?"

"Well." She gave him a coy, sideways look. "We did have a wager. Which you won."

Stuart's grip tightened. "Is that the only reason?"

Charlotte's smile faded. Slowly, her gaze locked with his, she shook her head.

"Saints be praised," he muttered, tossing his key and hat onto a nearby table. He grabbed her hand and led her toward the stairs. Charlotte picked up her skirt and ran after him, flushed and giddy. She felt young and reckless, having a clandestine rendezvous in the middle of the afternoon.

At the top of the stairs he stopped suddenly, catching her shoulders and pushing her back against the wall. His mouth came down on hers, hot and demanding, and Charlotte melted.

"I have wanted you for so long," he whispered, his breath flowing over her skin. "Tell me you want me. I have to hear it."

"I want you," she gasped as his fingers flew down the buttons at her back, then gathered the edge of her bodice and pulled it down, exposing her breasts. At Stuart's hiss of breath she pried open her eyes.

Slowly he sank to one knee, reaching out to cup her breasts reverently. Charlotte, who thought she had wanted him to take her fast and hard, changed her mind. This was better, much better; *let it last an hour*, she thought, as he bent his head and circled her nipple with his tongue. Her knees buckled, and she started to slide down the wall as he suckled.

"Stand up," he ordered, spreading one hand over her belly to anchor her to the wall. She nodded, slumping back into the wall and arching her back to give him full access. "Just like that," he breathed, replacing his mouth. Then his hand closed around her ankle and began sliding upward.

"Oh dear Lord," she gasped on a bubble of hysterical laughter. "I forgot—against the wall—"

Stuart looked up. "Is that what I said?"

"Don't you remember?" It was difficult to talk, with his hands moving over her.

He grinned. "There were so many to choose from, I couldn't remember which fantasy I told you about."

"So many?" His fingers reached the top of her stocking.

"Hundreds." His voice dropped. "Thousands." He reached higher, his eyes burning like blue flames as his fingers slid through wet curls. "My God," he said in a rough voice. "You're already—"

"Yes!" She pushed her hips forward, begging shamelessly. "Aren't you?"

"More than ready," he said, stripping off her dress with urgent efficiency. "But not here." He led her three more steps, jerking at his cravat, then seized her for another frantic kiss. In fits and starts they stumbled down the hall, shedding clothing as they went until finally Stuart flung open a door.

All restraint fled then. Stuart ripped off the last of his clothing and grabbed her around the waist to carry her, still in her stockings and shoes, to the bed. They fell in a tangle of limbs, all but devouring each other until Stuart broke away with a gasp.

"What?" Charlotte tightened her arms around his neck.

He gave a short, strangled laugh. "Give me a moment, or I'll end before we begin."

"We've already begun." Charlotte wriggled closer until he grabbed her hips and stilled them, and then she kissed his neck, taking little nibbling bites. Stuart quivered in her arms before turning onto his back, his lips moving as if in prayer.

Charlotte sat up, piqued. "What are you doing?"

"Kings of England," he said without opening his eyes. "After Edward I came Edward II, disemboweled with a hot poker on the orders of his queen. Then Edward III, founder of the Order of the Garter. Next Richard II, deposed by his cousin Bolingbroke."

"But Stuart," she said, drawing her fingertip over his chest and down his belly, "we have all day."

"Henry IV," he said stubbornly, seizing her hand to keep it from going lower. "Welsh rebellion led by Owain Glyndwr."

Charlotte sighed and rolled on top of him. His erection surged against her belly, but he kept murmuring kings. Slowly, more and more pleased with herself, Charlotte slid down, pausing when he was cradled intimately between her breasts. She did love this: the anticipation, the play at seduction and delay before the first time, the inevitable cataclysmic consummation that followed. She levered herself up onto her elbows and lifted her head. Stuart was motionless; even his lips had stopped moving. His face was almost fierce with restrained desire, the tendons of his neck taut. His body was magnificent, hard and lean and completely bare. Charlotte smiled slowly, rocking back and forth, sliding him between her bare breasts. He was hot, so hot, and smooth as satin against her.

"What are you doing?" he growled through his teeth. His hands were in fists at his sides, his knuckles bone white.

"Watch," she said softly.

His eyes flew open and he lifted his head. "You can't mean . . ." His question faded into a moan as she took him into her mouth, closing her lips tightly and stroking with her tongue. She kept her eyes on his face, feeling a rush of desire at his thunderstruck expression as he watched her make love to him with her mouth. She had never asked a lover to watch before, but then, she had never felt so at ease with a lover. There was something about Stuart that invited confidence, something that made her feel secure.

Abruptly he shuddered, and gasped aloud. "Charlotte," he croaked, "you can't . . . Christ in heaven . . . don't . . . stop . . ." She stopped long enough to smile, then lick him slowly, and he lunged forward, bowling her over onto her back. One of his arms tangled with one of her legs, and he forced her knee up high, spreading her wide open. With one harsh breath, he drove into her, sleek and hard and slick from her tongue. Charlotte gasped, surprised in spite of herself at how exquisite he felt inside her. He shuddered in her arms, then held still for a moment. "Thank God we have all day," he muttered, pulling back for another hard thrust, and another. Charlotte strained against him, meeting him with the same frenzy and desperation. Soon, too soon, he convulsed in her arms, throwing back his head and going still.

He rolled onto his back, taking her with him. Charlotte cuddled against him for a moment before sitting up and easing free. He might be limp with satisfaction, but she was still as tense as a coiled spring.

"God Almighty," he groaned. "I was told you were a wizened old woman."

She smiled, settling her knees farther apart. "I'm not as old as you."

He watched her fingers in fascination. "Is that a challenge?"

"If you like." She raised one hand to caress her breast and half-closed her eyes. "Let that teach you to recite kings to me."

"Never again," he said. She shook her head, past speech, rushing toward climax, feeling him growing hard beneath her. After a moment, his hands grasped her waist. "Let me." He lifted, then lowered her, thrusting up into her. Charlotte fell forward, catching herself on his chest as his thumbs slid around hers and toppled her world off its axis. He wasn't even moving, but her whole being was centered on where their bodies joined.

"Uhhn . . . oh Gahhh . . . aaaaah . . . there . . ." She wasn't making any sense, and Stuart loved it. Her long dark curls spilled over her shoulders, bouncing and swaying as she rode him. She was lush and tight and every bit as hot as he had expected; even more so, he corrected himself as she jerked upright, frozen in ecstasy as her body closed around his with a molten rush. When she began to collapse, he turned over again, folding her knees back to her chest and settling himself firmly atop her.

She opened her eyes a little. "Again?"

He nodded, beginning a slow but steady rhythm. "Finish what you start. Only this time, we'll do it together."

She wiggled, but his weight held her in place. "I can't do anything like this."

Stuart grinned. "I rather like you this way. I can go so deep . . ." He thrust in illustration, and her neck arched.

"Oh . . . I . . . see . . ." Her hands closed on the sheets. Stuart had never felt so far inside a woman, or so connected to one. Already he could feel her beginning to tighten around him again, and he moved faster, waiting until he felt himself on the brink before sliding his hand between them, and this time, when he fell into oblivion, he knew she came with him.

"Piero was an old man," she told him later when they were lying on their sides, face to face. "He called himself a count, but I doubt he really was. He had buried two wives already, and didn't want to die alone. He asked me to marry him after Carlos abandoned me in Milan with nothing more than my luggage."

"Who was Carlos?" Stuart asked, winding one of her curls around his fingers. He couldn't stop touching her, her face, her hands, her hair. She was so stunning, one arm folded under her head as she lay naked but for the sheet. One night would never be enough; all he could think of was how to keep her.

"He was a Spaniard I met in Nice. I thought he was wonderful, and when he asked me to go to Italy, I went without a thought. It seemed very romantic and impulsive, and he was such a good—" She stopped abruptly, and Stuart mentally filled in *lover*. Perhaps this wasn't really a conversation he wanted to have right now, as it seemed certain to leave him knotted with jealousy. "I only found out later the French were after him for smuggling munitions to Spanish guerrillas," she went on with a wry smile. "I have the worst taste in men."

Had, he wanted to say. "And he left you?"

She nodded, the smile fading. "Without a farthing. One night he was there, and in the morning he was gone, along with most of my jewels. I carried on as if nothing was wrong, but I was terrified. I had no money and was alone in Italy. Piero saved me."

"At least he was not a fool, like Carlos." He said it lightly, and she gave him an almost shy smile, as if she didn't get many compliments.

"He was generous and kind, and I was beyond grateful. It was the best three years of my life in many ways."

Stuart wasn't sure he could take it if Piero the elderly count also turned out to be a magnificent lover. "A love match?"

She laughed. "Oh, no. A mercy match. And, I suppose, a gratifying one. He was a collector of beautiful things, and I was simply one of them. Lucia says I was his doll, his excuse for buying fine silks and jewels and feminine things a man wouldn't need. He had exquisite taste."

Again he wondered about the paste jewels, but said nothing. "So he was a good husband."

"I suppose. He was . . . incapable. The doctor said it was his heart, but I thought it was his lungs. He had a cough that never completely went away, and his skin would turn blue at times. It was clear he was dying."

"What a horrible way to die," Stuart said.

She nodded, her eyes growing sad. "He wasn't in much pain, he said, but when he was confined to a chair it was difficult for him."

"I meant being married to you and yet incapable," Stuart said, leaning forward to kiss her lightly. "I would cut my own throat within a month."

She blushed, pleased. She blushed beautifully, and Stuart realized he had never seen it before. "But he . . . Well, perhaps I shouldn't say, as he's gone to his final rest, but he did feel that loss keenly. He didn't require me to be faithful. In fact, he preferred otherwise. He . . . He liked to watch."

"And he wasn't carried away by an apoplexy immediately?" Stuart couldn't stomach the thought of Charlotte making love to another man, let alone contemplate watching it. Even thinking about it made him want to spit on the old lecher's grave. "Did the others know he watched?"

Her face was scarlet now. "Some. Some liked it. Some did it to flaunt their abilities in front of him."

"Charlotte." He hesitated. "Did you like it?"

The sadness returned. "Not especially. Because I knew he watched, it became a performance, a duty I owed him. He would point men out and ask if I wanted to seduce them, and after a time I felt obliged to say yes. It became his only joy in life, the last few weeks. No one ever seduced me."

"The Italians are mad," he declared, deciding he'd had enough. Her past was her past, and no one could change it now; there was little point in worrying about it, and even less reason to hear the details. "I've thought of absolutely nothing but seducing you since the moment I saw you, and if anyone else wanted to watch, I would gouge out his eyes."

"It's quite different," she agreed shyly, winding her arms around his neck. "Knowing it's only between us."

It always will be, he promised her silently. She lifted her face and he kissed her, then gathered her close. It felt so right, simply lying here with her, and Stuart admitted to himself he wanted that almost as much as he wanted to make love to her. Which was highly unusual for him, especially in light of their wager for one night only and the fact that his fantasies about her now numbered in the thousands. *No one ever seduced me,* she had said; perhaps, if someone did, she would stay with him. And of all Stuart's problems, keeping Charlotte was becoming the most pressing.

She awoke to fingers moving over her back. For a moment, Charlotte lay perfectly still, relaxed and half-asleep, feeling his fingers drifting over her spine. It was a gentle touch, but not a caress, as if he were touching her just for the joy of it. She opened her eyes the tiniest bit; her hair had fallen in a tangle over her face and shoulder, and with her head pillowed on her arms, she could see him without his knowledge. Stuart's expression was open and almost wondering as he smoothed one palm over her bare shoulder. It wasn't the smug expression of a man who had triumphed in his desires; it was the expression of a man amazed at his good fortune.

She closed her eyes. One night, he had said of their

wager. What if he asked for more? What if he didn't? Was it better to end it now, before she fell any harder, or should she stake everything and continue with him? It was a terrible choice; every fiber of her being yearned to see where this curious friendship and powerful attraction might lead. But all reason and propriety dictated that she put an end to it as soon as possible, before Susan could know of or be tainted by her actions.

Of course, Susan hasn't been found yet, and no one need know about this, her heart whispered. *Why deny yourself for no reason? Especially since you've already come this far . . .*

She gave a soft moan, stretching a little. His fingers paused, then resumed, this time with bolder purpose. "It isn't evening yet, is it?" she mumbled.

"No, it's not," he said at once, easing closer to her. His erection slid over her hip, and Charlotte stretched again, arching her back. He felt so good against her.

"Are you sure?" She pushed hair away from her face. "It's dark out."

"It's cloudy." He traced the furrow of her spine, all the way down and under. She caught her breath as his fingers became gently but surely more intimate.

Charlotte lifted her head, tossing her hair over her shoulder. He was leaning on one elbow, a smile on his lips and raw desire in his eyes. She cocked her head toward the window. The drapes had never been drawn, and she could see the pale moon, hanging low in the sky. "You lit the lamps."

"I wanted to see you," he said, a note of laughter in his voice. "Since it's grown so cloudy." He moved on top of her, sweeping aside her hair to press a kiss on the back of her neck as his knee pushed her thighs apart. "I swear it's still day."

"Stuart, it's evening," she said, trying and failing to keep the regret from her voice. "We can't pretend . . ."

"Yes, we can," he said with authority, pushing her face back into the pillows. "Keep your eyes closed, and you'll never know the difference." His weight lifted off her, and then he grasped her hips and pulled her onto her knees, her head still on the pillows. With one hard thrust, he entered her, and Charlotte moaned, fisting her hands on pillows.

His fingers ran over her back as he controlled the pace. When she tried to speed up, he slowed her with a firm hand at the small of her back, and when she resisted, he pinned her shoulders down, holding her still beneath him. As his thrusts grew harder and deeper, and Charlotte began to feel herself quake inside, he leaned over, sliding one hand down to where they became one.

Charlotte gasped, jolting up onto her hands and trying to move with him. He forced her gently but relentlessly back onto her elbows.

"Just feel it," he muttered, his breath short and harsh. "You don't need to do anything this time but feel."

Charlotte felt. She couldn't escape feeling. Her nerves were raw, stripped bare and screaming for release. She closed her eyes and forgot about everything but the feel of his hands and the demands of his body. She rested her forehead on the mattress and rocked back, flexing her spine to take him even deeper, and climax burst over her. Dimly, she felt his hand tighten on her hip, and then he shuddered with his own release.

He fell to the side, holding her against him. Charlotte lay there, cocooned in his arms, happy and replete.

She could stay with him; she had nearly convinced herself. There was no reason why two unmarried people couldn't enjoy a discreet affair. Although . . . where? She couldn't very well invite him into her own bed when Susan would be sleeping next door. And Stuart had no permanent lodging of his own. Something niggled at the back of her mind, and she asked before she thought it through.

"What is Oakwood Park?"

He rested his cheek against the back of her shoulder. "Hmm? Where did you hear about that?"

"The night we went to the opera. Is it yours?"

He was silent for a minute. "No."

"Why did Barclay think you would be there?"

Stuart flinched, then rolled away from her and got out of bed. "Leave it, Charlotte. I don't want to discuss it." He pulled on his dressing robe, never meeting her eyes. Charlotte sat up, holding the sheet to herself. "Who is Barclay? Why must you pay him? Are you in danger?"

He gave a mirthless laugh. "Not mortal." He caught sight of her face and sighed. "Oakwood Park is a small estate I wanted to own, but cannot afford. Barclay is my banker." He shook out her petticoat and laid it on the bed. "Are you hungry?"

Charlotte continued to stare at him in confusion. "But the Duke of Ware said Barclay had sent to Oakwood Park, looking for you. Why would he do that? Why must you pay your banker?" Comprehension hit her then, as Stuart continued sorting out clothing and saying nothing. "You own it, don't you?" she said numbly. "You have to pay the banker because you already have a mortgage."

"This conversation is over." His tone was final. He knelt down and fished his boots from under the bed.

"If I had consented to your request for Susan's hand, you would be able to afford it," she said, unable to stop thinking out loud. No wonder he had been so furious with her. "Instead you might lose it, all because of me."

"Charlotte." He scrubbed his hands over his face. "Stop."

"You would have been a good husband to her, wouldn't you?" Her throat was tight. "And if she had married you, she wouldn't have run away . . ."

He jerked his head up, appalled. She turned away and started to scramble off the far side of the bed, but he grabbed her before she got there, flipping her onto her back and holding her down. "You did nothing wrong," he said fiercely, his face mere inches from hers. "You were right about me—I wanted to marry her for her money, not for her charm or for her beauty or for love. You were right to mistrust me, to protect her. She ran away because she's a girl, too young and impatient to see the sense behind your decisions. She would have been miserable with me, and I with her." His voice fell. "Not the least because I couldn't have looked at her without thinking of you."

Charlotte scrunched up her face and clenched her jaw. She would *not* cry.

Stuart sighed, his shoulders sagging. "Yes, I bought it. I'll be an old man before I inherit Belmaine, and I can't face the rest of my life waiting upon Terrance's pleasure for my every farthing. If the farms could be made productive, I would have an independent income, not to mention a home of my own." He paused. "But it needs a great deal of work—the whole property's been neglected for years—so I had to borrow from Barclay. And without my income from Terrance, I can't afford to pay it back."

"Oh, Stuart, I am so sorry," she whispered. And she was, desperately. Not for refusing him Susan, although her reasons were more complicated now, but for spreading such tales about him to ruin his chance of marrying well. If only she hadn't jumped to such terrible conclusions about him.

One corner of his mouth lifted. "It wasn't your fault. I just . . ." He sighed. "I misjudged Terrance. I didn't expect he would react so strongly to the chattering of gossips, particularly since he always disdained them as idle tattlers who spun tales out of thin air."

"But then he may reconsider," she began, but Stuart was already shaking his head.

"I don't think I can count upon Terrance to come to my aid."

Something about his tone warned her not to pursue it. She wet her lips. "What will you do, then?"

Stuart didn't say anything. He just looked at her, his eyes dark. With regret? Then he shrugged, his somber expression falling away. "I'll manage somehow. Bad pennies stay in circulation forever, you know."

Charlotte wanted to ask again, to press for a better answer, but didn't. If he had wanted to tell her, he would have when she asked the first time. It really wasn't any of her concern, she told herself. She was only his lover, after all, a temporary relationship—as she very well knew it had to be. Stuart had every right to solve his troubles in his own way . . . including marrying an heiress.

When she tried to get out of bed this time, he didn't stop her. When she slipped on her dress, he moved behind her to button it. She bit her lip at the feel of his hands on her back, fastening the buttons he had all but torn open a few hours earlier. Suddenly she was glad he hadn't told her. She didn't want to know. A heavily mortgaged estate, in need of extensive repairs, meant he needed a great deal of money, and she didn't want to think of how a gentleman of no profession and no income might raise such a sum.

"It's late," she said to end the deafening silence. "I think I should go to a hotel."

He sighed, his fingers pausing at the back of her neck. "Charlotte, that will make it look even worse. Why don't you just announce to the world you spent the day in my bed?" She flinched. "Go back to my parents' home. They want to think you came back as chaste as you left. Going to a hotel will only throw it in their faces that you didn't. Everyone in town will know what it means."

Her shoulders slumped. "Truly?"

"Truly." He took her hand, and she met his eyes for the first time in several minutes. "My parents are sure to be out anyway, and shan't notice your return."

Charlotte let out her breath. "All right. But if your father says one word . . ."

Stuart waved it off. "You handled him beautifully the other day. Terrance needs someone to cut him down to size now and then."

She hesitated some more, then nodded. Stuart pressed her hand, then released her to keep from taking her back to bed and banishing the closed, tense look from her face. The short drive to his parents' house was quiet, and true to his prediction, both his mother and father were out. Charlotte bade him good night in a subdued voice and hurried up the steps without glancing back.

Stuart watched her go, wishing Charlotte hadn't asked him what he would do next. He had been trying to avoid that question for over a week now, diverting himself with the search for Susan and his growing feeling for Charlotte herself—and what a diversion this afternoon had been. But he would have to face reality sooner or later, and he feared the answers wouldn't be any more to his liking than they had been when he left for Kent.

Terrance was not about to reconsider. Stuart had probed, very delicately, and discovered that not only had his father not softened, his mother had come to agree with him. That put to rest Stuart's hope that living an austere, penitent life and enlisting his mother's aid could persuade Terrance to relent in time. It was quite ironic, Stuart thought glumly, that she had loyally championed him through all the disreputable things he *had* done, and now abandoned him when he was essentially innocent. He had helped Eliza Pennyworth run away, but that was it. Was there something about him that made people want to believe the worst?

But that was neither here nor there. Stuart had known he faced long odds winning back Terrance's good graces; arriving unannounced with Charlotte hadn't improved them. But the next logical course of action, marrying an heiress, had never seemed less palatable. And that, too, was due to Charlotte.

He drove to Ware House. The carriage, like everything else in his life now, was borrowed; he handed the reins over to a groom and left, even though he properly should have called to thank Ware again.

Stuart knew he was extremely fortunate to have such a friend—Ware had guaranteed his loans, opened his brother's house, and lent him an elegant carriage harnessed to some of the finest horseflesh in London—but it was getting to be too much. Stuart was tired of being a perpetual borrower, always asking favors of his better situated friends. He was determined to stand on his own feet this time, or fall trying.

He reached Philip's house and let himself in. The house was as quiet and still as always, but now it seemed lonely as well, empty. He climbed the stairs, recalling vividly where he had stopped to kiss Charlotte, where he had removed her gown, where she had said she wanted him. In the bedroom he smelled her perfume and the lingering scent of their lovemaking, and wished he had wagered for a year instead of a night.

Stuart sat on the edge of the bed, unconsciously touching the pillow she had used. She would never stay with him for a year. As soon as they found Susan, Charlotte would take her niece and leave, returning to Kent or some other place where any scandal couldn't follow. As much as Stuart dreaded that moment, he couldn't bring himself to wish the search would fail. That would destroy a part of Charlotte, and Stuart didn't want that, no matter what it cost him. But when she left . . .

Almost unwillingly, Stuart began to examine his motives for helping Charlotte look for her niece, why he had spent the last week combing London for Susan while his financial situation grew more dire by the day. It was the gentlemanly, honorable thing to do, of course, and that was part of the reason; he also felt some responsibility, even guilt, for the girl's disappearance, since it was his courtship of Susan that had caused the rift between aunt and niece. But the remaining part—the greater part—had nothing to do with honor. He had offered to help Charlotte because he wanted to be near her. He wanted to help her, and make her happy again. He wanted to see her smile at him, feel her fingers on his skin, breathe the soft warm scent of her perfume, and he wanted to hold her in his arms every night for the foreseeable future.

That was what was upending all his plans. Before Charlotte, marrying a wealthy young girl had seemed perfectly reasonable—not ideal, but certainly prudent. Now he couldn't imagine a girl who could hold a candle to Charlotte, and he wasn't sure he could bear it, knowing what he would be missing. He could still marry an heiress—already the stain of the scandal was wearing off—and then he could keep Oakwood Park, restore it the way he dreamed of, and have the independence he craved. But he wouldn't have Charlotte.

Stuart thought again of Oakwood Park. It had been his dream for years, since he had been a young man recently out of university and had finally realized that his life would be one of waiting; his grandfather was still hale and hearty at eighty, and Terrance no less so in his fifties. While some of his friends, notably Ware, had professed they could wait decades before inheriting their responsibilities, Stuart had always wished he wouldn't have to wait quite *so* long. One of his secret habits had been getting orders to view properties for sale and assessing them as if he were buying them, imagining how he would improve them and run them. Oakwood Park had stolen his heart, and he had taken the leap, on faith and credit and cold determination to make a success of it.

But this time the vision of his own hearth and home seemed as cold and lonely as Philip's house. Would it be worth it, riding across his own fields back to his own manor, when the woman waiting for him wouldn't be the woman he wanted? For some time the answer to that question had been yes; the woman he had wanted, after all, had been anyone who was wealthy enough to make the fields and manor his. At this moment, though, he rather thought it would be an unbearable existence, because . . . because . . .

Gingerly, Stuart let himself think the dangerous thought. He was falling in love with Charlotte. It was more than a little frightening. He didn't know anyone for whom love had worked out well. Ware had been in love, years ago, and had gone through hell when the girl broke his heart. Was still in hell, to all appearances. Aiden Montgomery had been so madly in love he had been ready to desert the Royal Navy, and had also ended up with his heart broken. Stuart wanted no part of that pain.

He feared it might be too late already, though. Even as he stood on the brink of ruin, about to lose the estate he had poured all his energy and money into for the last year and be left homeless and penniless, all he could think of was Charlotte with someone else, someone like Carlos or Piero or another faceless man Stuart hated already. He wanted her, very selfishly, for himself, even as he admitted he had nothing to offer her *but* himself.

He smiled humorlessly. What did it even matter what he felt for her? He didn't have the slightest idea if she returned his feelings, or ever could, after the way they had met. He had no doubt her loyalty and affections lay with her niece. He could hardly fault her for that; he loved her for it, in fact. Stuart knew how rare that sort of devotion was, even among family, and had nothing but admiration for Charlotte's steadfastness even in the face of Susan's rebellion.

Stuart fell back on the only choice open to him. First, he would worry about finding Susan; until that happened, Charlotte would never be truly happy, and it would keep his promise to her. Then, when her niece was safely returned and things had settled down, he would determine whether she cared for him, and what, if anything, he could do about his feelings for her.

Chapter Twelve

Charlotte delayed going downstairs as long as possible. The maid, out of habit, did not bring her breakfast. Charlotte almost sent for her trunk and started packing, but Stuart was right—she couldn't simply leave—and so she went down to eat as she had every morning.

It was late morning, and the breakfast room was empty. The sideboard had been cleared, but a servant brought her toast and tea. There were two letters lying at her place, and Charlotte read them while she ate.

The first was from Lucia, in reply to Charlotte's letter.

Italians, oh! How I long for Italians in Kent! Sadly, there are none but myself, to my knowledge, although this has made me something of a curiosity. Or perhaps I mean celebrity? Whichever, I dine out on my accent many nights, which is lovely although the English have the blandest diet in all the world. Even the Russians eat better.

Charlotte skimmed the rest of the page until she reached Lucia's answer to her other question:

> *There have been no more housebreakers since you left. The house is secured like a royal treasury, and alas, no men have come to ravage my lingerie, not even Mr. Whitley. I have unpacked all the crates and boxes, which has improved the house greatly; you should not have left such beautiful things in straw. But though I waited up four nights with a pistol ready, no thieves came. Only for you would I pack it all away again, but I shall do my best. I also had the pianoforte tuned, for all that it is a poor instrument, but before you ask, no, I have not found my muse. Mr. Whitley, I fear, may prove to be Cherubino, better at proclaiming his affections than demonstrating them . . .*

Charlotte put the letter aside for closer reading later, somewhat diverted by the thought of Lucia resuming her singing. The other letter was addressed in a vaguely familiar hand, but she didn't place it until she opened it. Her heart flipped as she realized it was from Stuart. He had heard from Benton, in Kent; a slender, dark-skinned man, thought to be a Spaniard, had stayed just outside of town in a tavern room. He had left abruptly at the same time Susan ran away, but as he had paid his rent a month in advance, the landlord hadn't paid much mind. Armed with this information, Stuart wrote, he intended to find Pitney at once and help him continue the search. He promised to send word as soon as he could, and signed it simply "S."

Charlotte was rereading it, tracing each sharp spiky

letter, thinking of the hand that had made them, when her hostess entered the room.

"Good morning, Madame Griffolino," chirped Amelia, beaming.

Charlotte folded the letter. "Good morning."

"It's a lovely day. Would you care to visit Bond Street with me?"

"Oh, no, thank you." She shuffled her letters in agitation. This was too much to bear. She was breakfasting with her lover's mother. "Mrs. Drake, I greatly appreciate your hospitality, but perhaps it would be best if I removed to a hotel. I cannot impose on you forever—"

"Nonsense!" Amelia cried. "You must stay here! A lady, alone, at a hotel? It simply isn't done."

"I could summon my friend from Kent," Charlotte tried to say, but Amelia raised one hand.

"But you are already settled here! Please do stay; I am so pleased we can help you in any way during this trying time."

"That is very kind of you, but you have already been kinder to a stranger than anyone could require—"

"Madame Griffolino." Amelia grew suddenly absorbed in her cup of tea. "Please stay. I beseech you."

"I wouldn't . . ."

"I have seen my son more in the fortnight you have been here than I saw him in the previous year," said Amelia into her tea. "I'm not such a fool to think he'll take breakfast with me once you leave."

The Drakes, Charlotte thought, were the strangest family she had ever encountered. Mr. Drake threatened to throw her into the street almost within her hearing, and his wife begged her to stay. What went on between them, when they discussed their differing positions? Charlotte would have wagered heavily in Mr. Drake's favor, and yet he had done nothing but glare at her on occasion. She gave in as gracefully as she could. "Then I shall stay, so long as my presence is not a burden."

"Not at all!" Amelia's smile was wide with relief and, Charlotte realized with even more discomfort, suppressed tears. "You are welcome to stay as long as necessary to find your niece."

Charlotte indicated the letters beside her plate. "Stuart sent word this morning that his valet has heard of a foreigner living near Tunbridge Wells this past month, who may be Italian. He and Mr. Pitney are setting to finding him at once. I hope Susan is found very soon."

"Of course. I pray she is found soon, and is unharmed."

Charlotte didn't even want to think about what she would do if Susan returned injured in some way, or even, heaven forbid, with child. If she had been persuaded she was to marry soon, Susan might have been persuaded to allow him unspeakable liberties. Charlotte grimaced at the irony of that; she was a fine one to wring her hands over Susan giving herself to a man who had no intention of marrying her.

The difference, of course, was that Susan still had a chance to make a respectable marriage. Charlotte intended to do everything in her power to keep this horror from coming to light. That was why she had allowed Stuart to persuade her to go out in society. If anyone's reputation had to suffer, let it be hers; Charlotte fervently hoped that if any scandal came to be attached to them, her own more notorious past would distract people from Susan's disappearance.

She excused herself and returned to her room. She re-read her letters, smiling at Lucia's laments on Mr. Whitley's continued hesitation. But the tuned pianoforte was encouraging. Charlotte wrote a reply, thanking Lucia for her news and dropping strong hints about the fevered reception even mediocre opera singers enjoyed in London. One thing Lucia couldn't stand was praise unfairly given.

The letter from Stuart was less satisfying, because it was shorter and she could send no reply. She wanted to demand to know what he had learned, and this time she wanted to accompany him on his search. Sitting in this house day after day was a nightmare, and while Charlotte could admit she had been too hysterical to be of much help in the first days of Susan's disappearance, now her emotions had boiled down to cold, hard determination. For all that Stuart had come to her aid almost nobly, Charlotte wanted to feel as though she were doing something herself. Writing to Lucia and waiting for word from Susan didn't suit her. Even if she gained no ground in the search, she would feel better about it. Right now she had nothing to do but think about all her troubles, which was not the most comforting thing at the moment.

By luncheon, Charlotte was a wreck. Her stomach was so knotted with anxiety, she couldn't eat. Stuart had sent no word, and although it was unreasonable to expect him to do so every hour, the waiting shredded her patience as well as her nerves. She lay on her bed and tried to rest, but her eyes refused to close. She stared at the ceiling, her mind inevitably turning to thoughts of last night.

She was in deeper trouble than she'd feared. Making

love to Stuart hadn't satisfied her lust, as hoped. Just thinking about his hands moving over her skin was enough to make her hot and restless. Charlotte could accept that; it was often that way at the beginning of an affair. What bothered her more was the memory of Stuart's expression when he thought she was asleep. No man had ever looked at her that way, as if she were precious and amazing and completely beyond his expectations. As if he couldn't believe he'd been lucky enough to find her. As if he might be different than every other man in her life.

She hid her face in the pillow. It was happening again. She was falling in love with a man who wouldn't marry her. At least this time she was thirty and not seventeen, with no illusions about the future. For Susan's sake, she had to remain decent and respectable, and for his own sake, Stuart had to marry a wealthy bride. Whatever passed between them would have to be brief and clandestine, stolen hours or minutes that wouldn't satisfy her. For a desperate moment she wished Susan wouldn't be found for weeks, giving her a chance to savor her time with Stuart.

Slowly the tears pooled in her eyes. She was irredeemably wicked now, wanting to sacrifice her poor, innocent niece in favor of her sinful desires. She wiped the tears away in disgust. Crying about it would do no good. She had learned that lesson years ago. When her father sent her away, she had cried and cried, begging him to change his mind and let her stay, but he had walked away from her without a word, and her whole world had vanished in the blink of an eye.

She lurched off the bed. There must be something she could do to distract herself from the misery of her private life. She had promised to attend a ball tonight with Stuart, but that was hours away. With any luck, he would have good news of Susan, which would put an end to things regardless of her feelings. She must make herself hope for that.

In desperation she went to the library. Charlotte had never been much of a reader, preferring to do things rather than read about them. She had barely slept last night, she must be tired, and if she found a dull enough book, she would fall asleep and not have to think.

The Drake library was quiet and dim, appropriately dreary, to her mind. She wandered the shelves, squinting at titles. The room was shaped like a horseshoe, situated next to a glassed-in rotunda garden, and the light diminished almost to the point of darkness as she went around the curve. To her surprise, there was a window at the far end, shrouded in draperies. She pulled them aside a little, still hoping for a book on agricultural methods or political history. The light streamed in and Charlotte turned to the shelves, then gasped.

Stuart stared back at her. She blinked, and leaned closer in disbelief. It was an exceptionally good painting, catching almost exactly the line of his nose and the arch of his brows. There was a hint of deviltry in his expression, although he was very staidly dressed. Charlotte frowned; the clothing was old fashioned, not staid, decades out of date. Not Stuart, then; a relative, though, for certain. She wondered who it was, and why his portrait was consigned to the darkest corner of the house.

"Curious wench, aren't you?" She whirled around with a strangled chirp, the sound of a scream uttered with her heart in her throat. Terrance Drake stood behind her, leaning on his cane and glaring at her with angry eyes. "Taken to exploring, have you?" he said, jerking his head at the portrait. "Not enough of your own to worry about?"

Charlotte folded her hands and raised her chin. "Not at all. I was looking for a book, and cannot see in the dark." She glanced pointedly at the drape.

"Hmmph." He stomped closer. "Go on. Ask. I can see you want to know." He nodded again at the portrait.

Charlotte didn't look at it. "It is none of my concern, of course. I was merely startled by the resemblance."

He turned to the painting, his expression even more bitter and venomous. "It's uncanny. In every way. As alike as twins, they are. Both rotten to the core."

"Now really," said Charlotte before she could stop herself. "He's your own son."

He snorted. "Blood cannot be deceived; I know him for what he is."

"Blood cannot be deceived, but it can be betrayed? I find it hard to agree with you, sir," she said coldly.

Mr. Drake continued to stare at the portrait as if he would like to tear it down and destroy it. "Your blood betrayed you, didn't it? Ran off with a scoundrel, didn't she? Turned her back on her duty to her family and did as she pleased. Bonds of blood meant nothing to her when her fancy called."

"She's just a girl," protested Charlotte in outrage. "I am her only family, and it is I who owe a duty to her, not the other way round."

"Seducers, liars, gamesters," rumbled Mr. Drake.

"Not an ounce of responsibility between them." He turned on Charlotte, pointing at the portrait. "My own brother! It was a blessing he died young. My son," he said with contempt, "is just like him. My father tolerated them both, and they both did nothing for him! If you are wise, madam, remain childless. Your niece has proven the weakness in your own blood; rest assured it will come out, if given the opportunity." His hand fell, and he faced the painting, radiating hatred. "Good day to you."

Charlotte fled, shocked to her core by such virulence and rudeness. Poor Stuart, her heart wept, to have such a father. What must it have been like, living in this house for years with all that dislike focused on him? His mother loved him, but even her affection was tainted. What would make a father hate his own son so badly, even wish him dead? And how had the son turned out as well as he had?

More and more she wished she had never said a word to Lady Kildair; it had been unfair to spread gossip of which she had no firsthand knowledge, and now she was soaked in shame at the discovery that it was likely all a lie. Stuart angered his father simply by being, and whatever else he might have done to provoke the man seemed beside the point, in Charlotte's mind. She certainly wouldn't go out of her way to please a man who hated her, father or not.

It was none of her concern, she tried to tell herself. There was nothing she could do but cause more trouble, prying into family secrets Stuart didn't want revealed. She would just have to control her curiosity.

* * *

The ball that evening proved to be a marvelous distraction. She never knew how she came to be invited to the Throckmortons' affair; the invitation had simply arrived. Of course it was Stuart's doing, and Charlotte reflected that he was fortunate in his friends if not in his family. The Duke and Duchess of Ware had invited her to accompany them, so she was well received, but she began to worry as they made their way through the crowded ballroom. She felt out of place again, and was more than a little apprehensive about being in society in the first place. Anyone who had known her family might recognize her. She stood stiffly beside the duchess, all her senses on alert for any ruinous whispers around her.

Fortunately, there seemed to be a competing, more scandalous, sensation. The Duke of Exeter had acquired a wife without so much as a hint of being ready to marry. Notice of the wedding had simply appeared in the *Times*, catching even the duke's lover off guard. Charlotte watched with private relief as Exeter and his new bride took several prominent turns about the room, attracting many eyes and more comments.

"Quite a to-do with Exeter," remarked the Duchess of Ware, flicking her fan. "Any number of people are saying a prayer of thanks to him. Murder and mayhem could happen tonight in this very ballroom, and no one would notice."

Charlotte allowed herself a small, guilty smile. "Indeed, Your Grace." A gentleman was approaching, and the duchess smiled at him.

"Here is Lord Robert Fairfield," she said, looking quite pleased. "Have you come to dance with my friend, young man?"

He bowed, eyes twinkling. "If she will honor me,

madam." He turned to Charlotte. "Might I have this quadrille?"

Charlotte hesitated, and the duchess waved her fan. "You may dance with Lord Robert, my dear. He is quite respectable." Charlotte didn't feel she could refuse then, so she nodded and gave Lord Robert her hand.

"Never fear," he whispered to her as they took their places. "Drake warned me about the duchess."

"What do you mean?" She glanced back. The duchess wore a smile of smug satisfaction.

"Why, she's guarding her son, of course. Thinks every woman in England is out to entrap Ware. Drake knew she'd have you dancing all night."

"Ah." Charlotte had wondered. "So Stuart arranged this dance as well?"

He grinned. "Drake offered me the opportunity to ask you, since he expected to arrive late. Once he's arrived, I shan't dare ask again."

Charlotte laughed before the dance turned her away from him. When the quadrille ended, the duchess introduced her to another gentleman who also turned out to be a friend of Stuart's, and she danced with him. Before she knew it, in fact, her dance card was full, and she was almost enjoying herself, touched at the lengths Stuart had gone to for her.

Stuart arrived at the Throckmorton ball very late. Grimy and tired from a day spent walking the docks and crowded alleys of London looking for Italians, he got home to find he had forgotten to bank the fire, and it had gone out. It took a long time to heat water even to lukewarm to wash and shave, and then he had to walk to the ball because he had spent all the money he had gotten from Charlotte in search of information. His stomach rumbled as he climbed the steps of the Throckmorton home, and he said a prayer of thanks that the gossips had found something else to talk about, and he was nominally respectable again.

The ballroom was crowded, and he didn't see Charlotte or Ware. He wound through the guests, checking the terrace as well as the card room, but with no success. He had recruited all his friends—the respectable ones, anyway—to make sure Charlotte was well attended and protected from gossip. Stuart was aware her association with him would earn her little favor, but Ware had an entirely different consequence.

Finally he saw her, splendid in sapphire silk that molded to her body. She was fondling her fan and smiling up at someone in that coy, close-lipped way that made her seem mysterious and enticing, and so seductive. It almost brought Stuart to his knees, how beautiful she was.

"Stuart Drake, by all the stars, back in London at last!" A female hand curled around his arm as Stuart bit back a curse. Emily, Lady Burton, pressed closer as if to allow someone to pass behind her, but then she remained tight against him. Stuart sighed, and peeled her fingers off his sleeve, raising them for a brief kiss.

"Good evening, Em."

His former lover smiled. "Quite an evening it is, with all the scandals. First Exeter—Susannah Willoughby is fit to be tied, after telling everyone she would be the next Duchess of Exeter."

"Perhaps she should have waited for Exeter to make that announcement," Stuart murmured, still watching Charlotte. The way she was playing with her fan was nothing short of wicked. The woman ought not to be allowed to hold anything that way.

"Exeter would no more have offered her marriage than he would have offered to adopt her. I thought he would be the last bachelor in London." Her fingers crept back up his sleeve. "Except perhaps for you."

"As always, you are a font of information, Emily." Again he removed her hand. At one time he had found her forwardness exciting. How stupid had he been?

"Ah, but you've not heard the more interesting news," she purred. Too late, he identified the gleam in her eyes. Triumph. And desire. Good Lord. He had no desire to resume his affair with her. In fact, he couldn't wait to get away from her.

"Some other time, perhaps. I'm late meeting someone."

"But really, let me tell you," Emily insisted, dragging on his arm as he tried to leave. "You'll be very interested, I vow. The Italian countess you've been squiring about is really Miss Charlotte Tratter, daughter of Sir Henry Tratter. Don't you recall, the stuffy old man who used to be such a companion of your father's? Well, perhaps not; it was several years ago, when you had other interests." She sent him a smoldering glance, which Stuart ignored. Now she had his complete attention, although for the wrong reason. "Anyway, his daughter ran terribly wild, so wild they say her father sent her away to avoid being humiliated."

"How do you know that?" Charlotte had been sent away in disgrace? Stuart had assumed her free-spirited nature had led her to leave of her own choice. Of course, doing the simple math, he abruptly realized she must have been very young indeed when she embarked for Europe. Had she been sent away, or run away?

"Why, Mr. Hyde-Jones recognized her. Where is he? Oh, there." She raised her hand and an elegantly dressed gentleman crossed to them. He had the air of a fading angel about him, a once-beautiful man now losing his looks, and his hair. He kissed Emily's hand with a sanctimonious smile. "Jeremy, do you know Mr. Drake? Stuart darling, Mr. Hyde-Jones knew your countess when she was plain Miss Tratter. Isn't it a small world?"

"Yes." Stuart already knew Jeremy Hyde-Jones by sight, although he was surprised to see him here; the man was barely received. A gentleman by birth, Hyde-Jones had married not one but two heiresses, neither of whom had survived more than a few years. Stuart searched his memory and dredged up tidbits of gossip about the two Mrs. Hyde-Joneses. One had died in a suspicious fall down the stairs while heavy with child, and her husband had remarried with disrespectful haste. That wife had broken her neck in a carriage accident just last year. Her husband had been driving, but escaped without serious harm. Ever since, Hyde-Jones had been accepted, but only just; it was a great irony, in Stuart's mind, that it was due to the enormous fortune inherited from his wives.

But the man had known Charlotte when she was young. Curiosity won over distaste, and he bowed. "Mr. Hyde-Jones."

"Good evening, Mr. Drake." The older man's smile turned down in condescension. "I trust you aren't surprised to find your Italian is an Englishwoman after all."

"No," said Stuart. "I knew it at once. You knew her

as a girl?" Perhaps Hyde-Jones had been a friend of her father, or brother. He seemed too old to know Charlotte herself.

He seemed amused. "Yes," he replied with a glance at Emily, who still clung to Stuart's arm. "I knew her."

Emily laughed. "Jeremy, what a cipher you are! What would a man like you want with a girl like that? She must have been a child then!"

"I assure you," he said with the same curious smile, "she was not a child. Certainly not at the time our acquaintance ended."

An image of Charlotte at seventeen or eighteen flashed through Stuart's mind. He looked at Hyde-Jones with suspicion. The man was forty if he were a day. There were few things a man could want from a girl a decade younger than himself. Stuart could only think of two, in fact, and both made his hands curl into fists.

"I am sure you would find her greatly changed," he said. "It's been a dozen years since she was in England."

"Stuart, darling, you mustn't divulge a lady's age!" Emily poked him in the arm. "Certainly not ladies of a certain age."

"Oh, but some ladies improve with age, like fine brandy," he said automatically, not paying her much attention. Hyde-Jones was watching Charlotte with far too much interest. At Stuart's comment, he turned back.

"I certainly concur. She's grown into quite a beauty. I never would have expected it."

"Ah, yes," said Stuart carefully. "So often it is the plain, awkward ones who grow into the true beauties." He didn't like this man, and he didn't like the way

Hyde-Jones was staring at Charlotte. "Perhaps you did not see her often enough to judge her potential."

The man laughed silently. "I saw her often enough. I almost married her."

"Almost?" Stuart barely heard Emily's increasingly annoyed laugh. She tugged at his arm and he all but shoved her away. "Rotten luck she got away, eh?" Alarms were sounding in his head about this man, who stared at Charlotte like a hungry fox at a hen.

"Well, it wasn't quite bad luck," said Hyde-Jones with another sly glance. "Has Count Griffolino come to London as well?"

"He's dead," said Stuart through his teeth, wanting to add that a similar fate awaited Hyde-Jones himself if he tried to hurt Charlotte again. In the carriage ride to London, Stuart had asked who broke her heart; Charlotte hadn't said another word. He had asked to discompose her, and assumed she reacted out of pique, but what if he had hit a nerve? What if Jeremy Hyde-Jones had jilted her, and she had fled to the Continent in despair?

"Ah." Hyde-Jones's face lit with satisfaction. "How tragic."

"Yes, losing a spouse must be. My condolences on your wife's passing, by the way." Stuart stripped Emily's hand from his arm and shouldered past Hyde-Jones, ignoring the latter's lifted eyebrow. He made straight for Charlotte, who was currently dancing with Lord Robert Fairfield, one of his oldest friends. He stared at them until he caught Fairfield's eye, and gave him a curt nod. Fairfield returned it, sweeping Charlotte across the floor.

Stuart folded his arms and waited, impatiently. The

waltz had just begun, and it would be several minutes before Robert returned her. If not for the execrable Hyde-Jones, Stuart would be holding her in his arms right now; it was another black mark against the man. Whatever he had done to Charlotte, Stuart wanted to be sure she was forewarned of his presence, and of his renewed interest in her. And the next time he crossed paths with the scoundrel, Stuart could simply break his nose.

"Your pardon, Mr. Drake." A Throckmorton servant bowed, a silver tray extended. "This was just delivered, urgently."

Stuart muttered his thanks as he ripped open the note, elated at what it contained. Pitney had found the messenger boy, and the kidnapper's trail. A foreigner, Spanish or Italian, was traveling with a young woman, allegedly his widowed sister, who wore a heavy veil at all times. She was an English girl, though, and they had been sharing a small set of rooms on the fringe of Clerkenwell for the last several days. What next, Pitney wanted to know.

Stuart glanced toward the dance floor. Robert and Charlotte were still dancing. Charlotte would be wild to know this. She would also demand he reply as soon as possible. Stuart hesitated, then strode out of the ballroom. It would only take a moment to send a message, and he could collect Charlotte with the good news that they were closing in on Susan.

After the second waltz, Charlotte was ready for a rest. Her partner, Lord Robert again, led her from the floor and she flipped open her fan to cool her face. "Thank you, Lord Robert," she said with a smile.

"The pleasure was mine." He looked around, brow furrowed. "Drake was here just a moment ago. Looked as though he had hot coals in his shoes. I half expected him to steal you away in the middle of the waltz."

Charlotte laughed, but part of her warmed with delight at the image of Stuart sweeping her away into his arms. Finally, he was here! She couldn't wait to tell him—and show him—how grateful she was for all he had done this evening to ensure she enjoyed herself. It might seem like a small thing, but Stuart had thought of how she might feel in a ballroom of strangers. Lord Robert turned to her with an apologetic grin.

"He can't fault me for taking advantage of his absence. Will you honor me with a turn about the room?"

"Thank you, no," she said with a wry laugh. "I should like to stand here and fan myself for a while, if I may."

"Of course. Would you like some wine?"

"That would be very kind." He bowed and left, returning a minute later with a glass. Charlotte took a long sip as the music for the next set began, and Lord Robert regretfully excused himself to attend his next partner. Charlotte bade him farewell with a smile, certain Stuart would return soon. She stepped back from the dancers, wishing she had pinned her hair higher on her head. The heavy curls were like a wool blanket across the back of her neck. When Stuart returned, she would insist he take her for a walk on the terrace.

The thought brought a secretive smile to her face: alone with Stuart, in the dark garden . . .

"Good evening, Contessa. Or should I say, my dear Charlotte?"

All the heat fled from Charlotte's body at the cynical, idly amused voice at her shoulder. Slowly, gingerly, as if to keep from breaking, she turned.

And beheld the man who had ruined her life.

Chapter Thirteen

"Surely you remember me," Jeremy Hyde-Jones said with a knowing smile. "I remember you, although not quite this way."

"It has been my creed in life to learn from my mistakes and then forget them," she said coolly. "Good evening, sir." She turned back to face the dancers, although she didn't see a one. Why in the name of God hadn't she considered the possibility of meeting him again? She should never have gone out into society. It would have been better to hire a hundred investigators. Just seeing him again made her feel stupid and ashamed.

"Come, Charlotte," he said, moving closer. "After all we meant to each other?"

"I believe I meant little more than five thousand pounds to you," she said, staring straight ahead. Where was Stuart?

"You always were a passionate little thing." He said it with undisguised interest, staring at her bosom. "Although now there is a bit more of you to hold a man's attention. Your charms have only increased."

She looked up to where his guinea-gold hair was markedly receding from his forehead. When she knew him, he had been a vain man, with a fine head of hair. "And yours have only diminished."

His mouth thinned. "Still spirited, I see. I do admire a woman with an agile tongue. Have you learned anything useful, I wonder, since your youth? You had such promise."

"I have learned to kill the snake instead of playing with it," she replied. "Once bitten, twice shy."

"I remember the taste of your skin," he whispered. "Let me bite you again."

Charlotte recoiled, incredulous. "How dare you—"

"Ah, now, Charlotte, what did you expect me to do? Your father pointed a gun at me."

"Would that he had fired."

He chuckled. "But now there is nothing and no one to come between us." He smirked. "Drake is panting at your skirts, I know. Surely you have more discernment. He's completely under the hatches. His own family threw him out."

She opened her eyes wide. "How odd. Was that not your tale of woe, when you misled me into thinking you were a gentleman?"

"Now, now," he said, folding his arms. "There's no need to act the outraged offended spinster. I've heard of you through the years. You haven't scrupled about lovers before. Rumor even holds you enjoyed two men at once. Or did they enjoy you? You're fortunate I'm making a decent offer; a woman with your reputation won't last long in society, no matter who introduces her. And that reputation could grow so much blacker, if certain stories were to get out . . ." He reached out and flicked one of her curls. "I'm even willing to support you this time. Shall we negotiate an hourly wage, or a lump sum? I can afford it now."

Charlotte stood motionless and silent even as something inside her wailed in agony. How could she counter lies like the ones he promised to spread? She foresaw a host of debauchery he would ascribe to her, orgies and worse. Even if no one actually believed it, they would still delight in the gossip. It was bad enough to be condemned for what she had done, but to suffer for sins she hadn't committed . . .

And Stuart. Her knees almost buckled as she imagined what Stuart would think when he heard. His father would be enraged that Stuart had brought such a woman into his house, and Stuart would be cut off . . . disowned . . . run out of town with yet another scandal at his heels. He could never dare associate with her again, if he wanted any chance of respectability. Most likely he would quickly marry someone irreproachable, a sweet proper girl who would redeem him with her goodness, the wife he needed to give him the life he deserved.

If she had been alone, Charlotte would have collapsed. Even though she had told herself she would lose Stuart eventually, she had never imagined it would be so abrupt or so soon or . . . or ever. She couldn't imagine watching him walk out of her life forever. She needed him in a way she had never thought possible. He had given her so much of what she had long since told herself she would never have.

Charlotte felt hollowed out by hatred. The man smirking at her had ruined her life once, and now he would do it again. He would cost her Stuart, her chance of a decent life in England, and even Susan.

More pain lanced through her at that thought; she would lose Susan, even when the girl was found. Charlotte could never allow her own blackened name to sully Susan's. She would have to leave her niece with a hired companion, and return to the Continent in exile, remembered as wicked Aunt Charlotte. After a decade of flitting about, she had hoped to be home at last, and now she would be forced back to her nomadic life in even worse disgrace than before.

"Tell me," she said slowly, to keep her voice steady, "did you think I would take you back, after the way you lied to me? Did you think the foolish child you seduced wouldn't grow wiser in all these thirteen years? What makes you think a woman of my experience would want a man like you?" Charlotte laughed in scorn. "It was a lark to you. A country escapade to pass the time, or a quick path to riches, whichever way it turned out."

"Don't blame me," he retorted. "You wanted me as much as I wanted you. Your fortune was attractive, I grant, but you were a beautiful young woman, and not a child."

"I was barely seventeen."

His jaw tensed, then relaxed. "That was, as you say, thirteen years ago. You have, as you say, grown up. I have a fortune of my own now. We could explore the possibility that things might have ended differently, if your father hadn't—"

"Hadn't saved me," she cut him off. "The next time I see you I will have my own pistol ready, and I haven't my father's restraint." She dashed the contents of her glass into his face, too enraged to savor the incredulous fury that contorted his expression. "May you burn in hell." She dropped the glass at his feet with a splintering crash, turned on her heel, and walked away.

She did not see Stuart on her way from the ballroom. She did not see Lord Robert, or the Duke of Ware, or anyone she recognized. She barely saw where she was going. Somehow she walked out of the Throckmorton home and down the steps, and when she found herself at the Drake house, she hardly knew how she had gotten there.

The footman opened the door at her knock, and seemed surprised to see her again so soon. Or maybe not; Charlotte didn't pay him much mind as she brushed past him, ignoring his confused look when he realized she hadn't come in a carriage or worn her wrap home. The numbing shock that had sustained her so far was wearing off, and her only wish was to reach the privacy of her room before she broke down.

Charlotte stumbled up the stairs, her breath coming in painful gasps. Her throat felt closed, as if she were choking, and she yanked at her necklace until it came off. She was ruined—unquestionably, irredeemably ruined. Her foot caught on a stair tread, and she fell onto her knee, slumping against the wall. Everything she held dear, gone. Every hope and dream, dashed. Every repentance and regret, wasted. When she had left England the first time, she had been too young and stupid to consider such far-reaching consequences of her actions. When the shock of being sent away had worn off, Charlotte had vowed to live her life day to day, enjoying whatever came her way. She hadn't intended to become wild and immoral; it had somehow happened a little bit at a time without her noticing how far from her upbringing she had strayed. And once there, it was too hard to go back.

The news of George's death, and her consequential guardianship of Susan, had sobered her. It had come close on the heels of Piero's death, when she was at loose ends already, and Charlotte had seen it as her chance to start again. Her home and family, through her brother's trust, had been restored to her, along with a great responsibility. But though she had tried and tried, her every action since had been wrong.

She leaned her forehead against the baluster, engulfed in despair. She had meant to be a kind and loving guardian to Susan, and the girl had despised her and run away. She had meant to be chaste and respectable, and had fallen into an affair with Stuart, who had made no secret of his plan to marry someone else. She had meant to live quietly, above reproach, and now Jeremy Hyde-Jones would drag her name back down into the mud.

Two maids descended on her then, exclaiming in concern. Charlotte paid them little heed; what did it matter if her gown was crumpled, when her life was coming apart at the seams? She let them help her up to her room, too shattered to protest. Then she sent them away, refusing tea, brandy, and a hot bath.

When the maids had gone and the room was quiet, she sat and considered what she should do now. She couldn't leave without finding Susan and ensuring her safety, but neither could she allow Stuart to continue helping her. The sooner she parted from him, the better; with luck, he could claim to have been mistaken in her, mislead and deceived. People would believe it, once Jeremy spread tales of her supposed depravity. She knew Stuart was unlikely to accept the necessity of that pretense, though, so she would have to persuade him. And it would take all her strength to do it.

Stuart jostled his way through the crowd to where he had last seen Charlotte and Fairfield. Neither was there. He looked around, and caught sight of Fairfield among the dancers. Charlotte must be with the duchess, he thought, but no: Her Grace was still holding court across the room, alone. Where the devil had she gone? Stuart saw the terrace doors, a mere twenty feet away, and took a step in that direction, his pulse quickening at the thought of intercepting Charlotte in the garden, and with such news from Pitney. Before he could take another step, however, something else caught his eye.

Two servants were falling over themselves helping a man wipe wine from his clothes and face. Jeremy Hyde-Jones, livid with fury. Another servant crouched nearby, sweeping something into a dustpan. Stuart's blood chilled. It didn't have to involve Charlotte. The man could have offended anybody in the room. But Charlotte was nowhere to be seen. And she had almost married him years ago.

"Drake, there you are." Fairfield came up beside him, pausing when he saw what Stuart saw. "Is something wrong? Where is Madame Griffolino?"

"I was pondering that very question." Stuart watched, stone-faced, as Lord Throckmorton himself strode over, his face creased with polite concern. Hyde-Jones spoke to him with an angry gesture, then calmed down, speaking for another minute. Throckmorton listened and frowned, then nodded and went back the way he had come.

"I left her here, Drake," said Fairfield in an undertone. "I expected you would return at any moment, and she urged me to go."

"Never mind," murmured Stuart. "See if you can find her, and stay with her until I find you." Fairfield nodded and disappeared into the crowd. Stuart took a deep breath, rolling his shoulders back until the tension eased slightly. He forced a careless smile to his lips and sauntered over to Hyde-Jones, who still bore a dark red stain down the front of his waistcoat. "I say, terrible waste of good burgundy, Hyde-Jones."

The man looked up, his scowl fading when he recognized Stuart. He smiled. In fact, he positively gloated. Stuart's hand fisted in spite of himself, and he shoved it into his pocket. "Ah, Drake. How fitting. Your countess has shown her true color: scarlet." He indicated his waistcoat as he dabbed one more time at his face before tossing the towel at one of the servants. "But then, perhaps you don't know her sordid history."

Stuart's eyebrows shot up. "Sordid? You must be joking."

Hyde-Jones laughed softly. "Thought you'd found a wealthy widow, did you? She may be, but mark my words, that widow is black through and through."

"See here," protested Stuart. "You ought not to say such things about a lady." Hyde-Jones sent him a sharp glance. "She has a past, I admit," he added, "but sordid? Black through and through? Surely that's overstating the matter."

Hyde-Jones tilted back his head to look down at him. "Ah, yes, your father is another martinet," he murmured. "He wouldn't look fondly on a whore in the family, would he?"

Stuart didn't have to feign his astonishment. "I beg your pardon."

"A whore," repeated Hyde-Jones with relish. "Whatever she's told you, I assure you the truth is ten times worse."

"Good Lord. I'd no idea." Stuart gestured toward the terrace doors. "Shall we . . . ?"

Hyde-Jones smirked. "Of course." He strolled out, and Stuart followed, meeting the Duke of Ware's eyes across the room for a second. Robert Fairfield was at his side. Stuart pushed the terrace door gently closed behind him.

"I pity you, really," went on Hyde-Jones in the same patronizing voice. "How disappointing it must be, to discover she's beyond the pale."

Stuart counted to five. "But she has other charms, of course." He lifted his gaze to the sky, nodding as if in fond remembrance. "Other delightful charms. A man in my position can't be too particular. Surely you understand."

"The charms are real enough." Hyde-Jones chuckled. "And more bountiful than I remember. I enjoyed them myself once." He raised one hand, palm up. "But if you dislike sharing them . . ."

He couldn't stop the fury that must have darkened his face. Stuart was a very good liar if he did say so himself, but he couldn't quite control himself in this. Hyde-Jones, though, seemed amused.

"No more, no more," he said, smiling broadly. "Although she did seem amenable to the possibility, if you take my meaning. Perhaps if she reverts to form, we both might." Stuart's jaw had gone numb from being clenched so hard. Hyde-Jones stepped closer, his eyes gleaming with malice in the moonlight. "She whored for her living, all those years abroad," he said softly. "How else does a disgraced woman support herself in such luxury?"

"How, exactly, was she disgraced?" asked Stuart through his teeth. Out of the corner of his eye, he saw Ware step onto the terrace and close the door behind him.

The man's eyes shifted to the duke, then back. "She was wild and immoral even then. Her father disapproved and banished her."

"And you, no doubt, were devastated to lose your bride." Stuart flexed his fingers. "What very bad luck you've had, losing brides."

The other man's expression hardened. "I resent your implication. I spoke only as one gentleman to another, intending to spare you the shame of making a fool of yourself over her." He turned on his heel, back toward the ballroom, and came face to face with Robert Fairfield, who was standing in front of the door, arms folded across his chest. Hyde-Jones hesitated, darting a quick glance back at the duke, then started walking toward the steps down into the garden.

"How did you discover her true nature?" Stuart followed him. Hyde-Jones frowned over his shoulder. "Did her father tell you when he banished her? Surely a man wouldn't spread tales of his daughter's misbehavior."

Hyde-Jones stopped at the bottom of the steps. "It was clear what had happened when she vanished and never came back."

Stuart arched one brow. "Indeed. And you didn't

wish to hear your intended bride defend herself? Perhaps it was all a misunderstanding."

Anger flashed in the man's eyes. "There was no misunderstanding," he snapped. "She seduced me. I knew what sort of woman she was."

"Seduced you? A girl of seventeen seducing a man of thirty or more?" Stuart moved closer. "What kind of fool do you take me for? I suppose your first wife simply tripped on a bit of loose carpet, and your second wife jumped out of a speeding carriage of her own volition."

"How dare you?" said Hyde-Jones through clenched teeth. He was shaking, with fury or fear, Stuart didn't know. Or care. The sick feeling he had had from the moment he realized Charlotte had disappeared had blossomed into rage, and he didn't need to hear any more. He could kill the man for nothing more than the fact that he had ruined Charlotte when she must have been a young and trusting girl, just as romantically foolish as Susan.

His first punch carried them both to the ground, rolling into a nearby hedge. Hyde-Jones was a well-built man, but in the style of a poet: tall and lean. Stuart, who had never pretended to such elegance, was built broader and heavier, as well as ten years younger. He barely even felt the blows Hyde-Jones managed to land. When Ware pulled Stuart back, Jeremy Hyde-Jones lay on the ground, bleeding from the nose and mouth and holding his stomach.

"Enough," murmured Ware, hauling him to his feet. Stuart shook him off, but didn't make another move. He yanked at his jacket, setting it right.

"I suggest you enjoy the Continent," he said to the man on the ground. "If we meet again, I might be

inspired to see if I, too, can get away with murder."
Hyde-Jones made a muffled growling sound, but
wisely stayed on the ground. Stuart glanced at
Robert, who shook his head, and turned to Ware.
"Would you . . . ?"

The duke nodded, watching Hyde-Jones grimly.
Ware would make sure the man either left town or got
what he deserved. Stuart would have no qualms
telling people Hyde-Jones had confessed to murder-
ing his wives; spreading gossip was not illegal. It
was almost certainly true, anyway, and Hyde-Jones
couldn't refute it without reigniting curiosity and renewed interest in events he surely wanted to languish
in obscurity. The man was hoisted by his own petard,
threatening to spread tales of Charlotte's past. Stuart
muttered an excuse to Ware and headed back into the
house.

He hammered on the door of his parents' house
twenty minutes later. "Has Madam Griffolino returned?" he demanded, pushing past Frakes. One of
the Throckmorton footmen had seen Charlotte leave
without her cloak and on foot. Stuart was at the end
of his rope; if she wasn't here, he didn't know where
else to look.

"Yes, sir. She has retired for the evening. Sir!
Mr. Drake!" The butler sounded scandalized as Stuart
took the stairs two at a time. He tapped at her door,
then pushed it open.

She was standing at the window, her back to the
door. She was still gowned in her blue silk, but Stuart
could see the tension in the set of her shoulders and
in the hand that gripped the drapes.

"Charlotte?"

With a small start, she glanced over her shoulder. "Mr. Drake. What will people think?" The muted mockery in her tone made him pause. "I have retired for the evening," she said, turning back to the window. "Good night."

"I had to see you," he said, closing the door and removing his hat. "Are you all right?"

"You *had* to?" She gave a short laugh. "Come back when you can afford me, Mr. Drake. I paid my wager in full."

Stuart stared. This was not his Charlotte. This was the woman with the heart of stone who had gossiped him out of Kent, who had accused him of getting ahead on his looks and charm. This was the woman who had infuriated him, and inflamed him, with her scorn. "I am not here because of that. I want to talk—"

"I know what men want," she said coldly. "Don't pretend you don't want the same."

"Stop it," he said in a low voice. "I care about more than getting you in bed."

Her eyebrow went up, and her lip all but curled in disdain. "More? How demanding. Take care to marry a very wealthy woman, who will be able to support your care for 'more.'"

Hyde-Jones must have hurt her terribly to make her act like this. She was baiting him, trying to lull him into revealing something. She had done it to him before, in the Kildair library. But what was she after now? Surely by now she had come to see him as more than just a man who wanted under her skirts. "Why? How much would it take?" he asked, watching her closely. Not a quiver or a flinch disturbed her stillness.

Except for the rise and fall of her bosom, she didn't move at all.

"More than Susan has," she said. "I meant everything I said before: I'll put a pistol ball in you before I let you marry her."

He told himself she was angry. He told himself it was because of Jeremy Hyde-Jones. He told himself it was the strain of Susan's disappearance. It didn't matter; her words still stung. He stripped off his gloves and shrugged out of his coat, buying time to restrain his temper and keep himself from lashing out in retaliation. "The thing is," he explained slowly, "I don't want her. Not now."

"Your good sense is commendable, if long overdue." She turned back to the window. From the neck down she was perfectly reflected in the glass; only her face was hidden, shadowed by the draperies. He couldn't tell what she was thinking or feeling, nothing at all of the woman she was inside. All he saw was a woman's lushly curved body, elegantly gowned. How many men had seen her only this way, he wondered suddenly, how many men had never cared to discover the real Charlotte inside the siren's façade?

Slowly he crossed the room to stand behind her, the way he would approach a spooked horse. She didn't move. Lightly, he laid his hand on her shoulder. Although she appeared calm, her muscles were taut, her body rigidly held. He eased closer, letting more of his hand rest on her. Still she didn't move. *Don't be angry at me*, he wanted to say. *Tell me what's upset you, so I can slay your dragons and comfort you.* But who would believe that of Stuart Drake, reckless ne'er-do-well who lived on the edge of trouble and scandal? Even he couldn't believe it.

"Better overdue than never," he said instead, lamely trying to lighten the mood. At his words, she jerked away from his hand.

"Do not patronize me," she sneered. "I am not a child to be jollied into acquiescence. How dare you laugh at me for showing some sense of honor and keeping Susan from the likes of you!"

"Charlotte," he said evenly, his patience running very low in spite of his best efforts, "calm yourself. I'm not making sport of you."

Her eyes narrowed, glittering, but not with tears. "Go home, Stuart. I don't want you here."

"I know you saw Hyde-Jones tonight," he said, making one last attempt at reason. "I know you knew him years ago."

"I have *nothing* to say about that."

Stuart swore. "What am I supposed to do? Leave you here to lick your wounds in misery while I go home and wonder what he did to you, to make you turn against me like this? Do you think I could, after what's happened between us?"

"Nothing has happened between us," she snapped. "Nothing!"

Stuart stopped, poleaxed. It wasn't nothing to him; it was the very opposite of nothing. It had come to be everything to him: seeing Charlotte, making her smile, appreciating her sly wit and dry humor. He would rather be here, quarreling with Charlotte, than in bed with any other woman. And it couldn't mean nothing to her. He knew there was more between them than that. "Don't say what you don't mean, Charlotte."

"How dare you think I didn't mean it? I'm not a

romantic sort of person, Stuart. I have desires like any other woman, but I'm not the faithful sort. Last night it was you, tomorrow it will be someone else; men are all the same to me," Charlotte taunted. Why wouldn't he *go*? The longer he stood there looking so honorable and patient, so *decent*, the harder it was to hold herself together. The sooner he realized he deserved better than she could offer him and left, the easier it would be for both of them.

At her words, his face darkened, and he took a step toward her. Charlotte jumped back, keeping the distance between them. "Don't tell me it didn't mean anything to you," he said. "Don't tell me I don't mean anything."

"It was nothing but an evening's entertainment," she fired back, taking another step backward. Stuart followed, his anger obviously mounting. She scurried around a chair, putting it between them.

"Liar!" He shoved the chair away. "Men are all the same to you, are they? So I could be any man, any of the dozens you've taken to bed to fulfill your *desires*."

Charlotte gasped at the savagery in his question. She flung the first thing her fingers touched, a china figurine on the dressing table. Stuart ducked, and it crashed against the wall behind him. "Hypocrite! How many women have you taken to bed for the same reason?"

"Do you want me to say it meant nothing to me? Is that it? If I confess you're just the woman I want now, just the woman who happens to have taken my fancy this week, will it make it easier for you to turn your back on me?" He advanced on her, dark and terrifying. She had never really seen Stuart angry, not smirking, teasing, flirting Stuart, but he was furious now. Beyond furious. Charlotte retreated again, hovering on the verge of hysteria, and found herself in the corner. "I won't, Charlotte. If you're going to toss me out, you'll have to prove to me that I don't mean anything to you."

Chapter Fourteen

Charlotte tried to push past him. Stuart caught her around the waist. "Let me go!" she cried, struggling.

"Not without a fight." He deposited her with a thump on the dressing table. He wasn't gentle at all, and Charlotte sucked in her breath at the impact. Grim-faced, Stuart took advantage of her distraction to press her arms behind her back and hold them there. He took hold of her chin with his free hand and forced her defiant gaze up to his.

"I admit," he said in a low, harsh voice, "I wanted you that way once. You hurt my pride and publicly humiliated me, and I wanted revenge. I am not a saint. But neither am I an immoral cad with no sense of honor. I have never taken advantage of you, I have never demanded more than you were willing to give, and I have done my damnedest to help you find your niece." She turned her face away, trying to remain cold with indifference, or at least the illusion of it, but he jerked her back. "Tell me how that makes me as black as the other men in your life. Carlos, who used you to escape the French and left you penniless in Italy? Piero, who used you to fulfill his twisted desires?"

"I'm surprised such an honorable man would want such a woman," she lashed out. It only made things worse that it was all true; Stuart was one of the few decent men she had known in her life, and she did find it hard to believe he would want her for more than a few nights. No one else ever had. Jeremy Hyde-Jones had wanted her money, and the others had wanted her body. "I have no shame, and no discernment! My base nature overrules whatever sense a woman has, and leads me down the path of sin. You should be grateful I'm tossing you over now, instead of later, when you'll be accustomed to having me. Normally I like to torment my victim before I cast him aside, but since you're so admirable, I'll let you walk away now."

"Right," he said to the air above her head. "The hard way, then." He lifted her chin again, and Charlotte clamped her lips together, anticipating a brutal kiss, but he didn't. His lips brushed her temple, lingering there for a moment. His breath stirred her hair, lightly, and she bit the inside of her cheek to keep from giving in. She was prepared to fight him, but how, when he was being so gentle?

He kissed the corner of her eyebrow, the bridge of her nose, and the curve of her cheek. She tried to turn away, but he held her chin firmly. "Let me go," she said one more time, pleading in spite of herself. "Make it easier for both of us . . ."

One corner of his mouth quirked. "Easier for you, perhaps. It would not be easier for me." He continued pressing light, gentle kisses over her face, moving slowly downward. Charlotte shivered as he found the sensitive spot below her ear.

"Stuart . . . admitting we're attracted to each other doesn't mean . . ." He kissed the hollow at the base of her throat, his tongue swirling over her fluttering pulse. "It doesn't mean anything else," she finished in a gasp. "Stop!"

"If I stop," he murmured between kisses along the exposed slant of her shoulder, "you'll have the footmen drag me out the door. And then, I'll wager, you'll never see me again."

"I shouldn't." It was hard to think, now that he had released her chin and his free hand was exploring. He traced her shoulder blades through the silk of her gown with the same careful touch as last night. Had it only been yesterday that she lay in bed with him, feeling treasured? "I won't!"

"You would if you could," he corrected, lifting his head to look her in the eye. "But I won't let you."

"I'll scream," she threatened, not certain she could do it. Her throat was so scratchy she could hardly speak above a whisper. If she screamed and the servants came, and found them like this, Stuart would be disowned for good. His father, she suspected, was simply waiting for an excuse, and ravishing a guest would probably be enough of one. And she didn't want Stuart to be hurt any more; that was the whole reason she was trying to end things.

A faint smile lit his face. "You'll scream, all right," he agreed. "But only when I let you. Only when I make you." His nimble fingers slipped the gown off her shoulder. He had undone the back of her dress without her noticing it at all. "And I won't do that until you admit there's more than desire between us."

"I consider you a friend," she said wildly as he placed his lips against the suddenly unprotected skin.

"Good," he said, tugging the sleeve down with one finger. Charlotte pulled at her hands again, but his grip hadn't relented. The unbuttoned silk slid slowly down, finally catching on the trim of her chemise. He brushed it aside, then pulled on the other sleeve. In a moment the bodice of her gown slid into her lap. Charlotte made a faint noise of alarm.

"And—and a confidant," she blurted. He was leaning into her, urging her back. Charlotte resisted until she lost her balance, and fell back against the mirror, his arm still around her, holding her hands at the back of her waist. She had to stop this, stop him, before things went too far. Already her body was responding to his touch, like a flower to the sun. Charlotte fought to keep her wits about her. *You have no future with him*, she reminded herself. *This was doomed from the start*. It was a mistake to have an affair at all.

"Very good," he said, with a tinge of amusement. "I like that role, confidant. An excellent beginning."

"And . . . and . . . and a steadfast, loyal, friend," she babbled, trying to squirm away from the increasingly intimate kisses. His hair fell over his forehead, brushing maddeningly over her bosom as his mouth found its way toward the swells of her breasts. "You've been so kind and helpful and really quite heroic in helping me search for Susan, even though I treated you so abominably at the beginning, and therefore you're also quite forgiving and kind . . ."

"Charlotte." He raised his head. At some point he had knelt on the chair, and they were almost eye to eye. "Stop babbling."

"But I can't tell you what you want to hear!"

He shook his head. "Can't, or won't? Convince me, then; persuade me you don't care. I won't make love to you again just for the sake of satisfying your *desires.* I'm not a plaything, Charlotte, I'm a man." He cupped her cheek to focus her distraught eyes on him. "And you are not a whore. You're a woman who has the same needs and desires as other women, including the desire to be loved. That's what it's always been with you. You want to love, and to be loved. You let Susan behave like a spoiled brat because you wanted her to love you as much as you love her." Charlotte's mouth fell open in shock. Stuart went on relentlessly, his blue eyes earnest. "That's what drove you to take all those other men to bed, wasn't it? Did you ever make love to someone you didn't at least hope to fall in love with? Carlos, the romantic who swept you off your feet? All the men who might have brought you happiness in your sterile marriage?" His voice dropped. "Jeremy, the dashing gentleman who dazzled a young girl longing for adventure?"

Charlotte bucked and twisted. "Let me go! You don't know anything! How dare you recount my life as a series of pathetic, lovelorn mishaps? My dealings with other people are my concern, and none of yours. You're a fine one to talk, in fact! Your own father hates the sight of you, and your mother thinks the worst of you even as she adores you. I'll not take advice from someone who lives on borrowed money in borrowed houses—"

He cut her off with a kiss, the hard, demanding kiss she had feared earlier. Now she welcomed it, and the sanctuary it provided from Stuart's too-perceptive words and her own cruel response. Even as he kissed her, the tears seeped from her eyes. What had she done, flinging his father's dislike in his face? What sort of person was she now, defending her own wounded heart by shredding his? How was this supposed to make things better, pushing away the one person she desperately wanted close?

Abruptly Stuart broke away. He grasped her face, his thumbs under her cheekbones, his fingers curling under her jaw, forcing her to look up at him. "I am not like those other men," he said in a voice taut with emotion. "I am not trying to seduce you for an evening's entertainment. I am not using you. I want you to be happy, damn it, even if not with me. I'll leave if you want, but don't tell me you, even *you*, think so little of me. I love you, for God's sake."

Charlotte could only stare up at him, her breath coming in short, stunned pants. He loved her? Stuart *loved* her?

Stuart suddenly blinked, his grip loosening, as if just realizing what he'd said. He snatched his hands from her face and took a step backward. "Ah, Lord," he muttered, turning away. "I'm sorry. I didn't mean . . ." His shoulders slumped, and he didn't look back as he collected his coat and shrugged into it. He stooped to pick up his hat and gloves, and Charlotte realized he was going to leave. She hovered on the brink of wrenching indecision; if she admitted she loved him, to him and to herself, she risked a broken heart. For thirteen years she had refused to let herself be that vulnerable. But if she said nothing, he would leave, and she would suffer a life of wondering what might have been. Which was worse, the never-ending ache or the felling blow?

"Stuart?" He didn't pause. She teetered, and fell. "Stuart, wait! Don't go!" Charlotte jumped off the dressing table and ran after him. "I love you, I do! Don't leave me now!" She was sobbing by the time she reached him, almost blinded by tears as he caught her in his arms.

"Don't say what you don't mean," he whispered. "I didn't want to pressure you."

She shook her head, her face hidden against the side of his neck. "It frightens me how much I mean it."

He gave a short, unsteady laugh. "Then we're even. I've never felt this way about anyone."

"I'm sorry," she said, lifting her head. "For what I said earlier. I don't think so little of you, and it was cruel of me to say—"

"It was," he agreed. "But I understand. You wouldn't be yourself if you didn't fight with every weapon at your disposal." He brushed away her tears with his thumb, then kissed them away. For a moment they just held each other until Charlotte, feeling his body stirring, looked up.

"Do you—?"

"Yes," he said, kissing her lightly on the mouth. "I do." And her gown slipped, sliding to the floor as Stuart's hands brushed her hips. "Do you?"

"Yes." She spread her hands across his chest, running them up to his shoulders to push his coat off. Stuart pulled one arm, then the other free, managing to work her petticoat loose at the same time he loosened the laces of her corset. Both joined the dress on the floor.

"Let me please you," he whispered, running his fingers over her bare back.

Charlotte shivered. "You do."

At her words, he smiled tenderly, then lifted her and carried her to the bed. He took her face in his hands and kissed her, softly and sweetly. Then he gave her a wicked grin.

"I love you," he said, unknotting his cravat and jerking it off. "But I owe you." He slipped her chemise over her head and caressed her shoulders, his gaze growing dark and intense. "Watch. See how beautiful you are." He ducked his head and Charlotte caught sight of herself in the full length mirror, directly opposite them. She watched, transfixed, as Stuart's dark head lowered to her breast, and she saw the desire that flushed her own face as he began to tease her nipple with his tongue. And when he began to suckle, she watched his hands move to her knees and slide back and forth along her thighs, easing them apart.

She gasped for breath, watching as his hands touched her, intensifying the physical sensation. She had watched other people make love, but never herself. Unsteadily, eyes still glued to the mirror, she began to fumble with Stuart's clothing, wanting to see more of him as well. With a soft chuckle, he helped her until he was as exposed as she was. This time she watched Stuart's face, her chest tight at the fiercely tender light in his eyes.

With his fingers spread wide across her belly, he eased her down onto her elbows. He moved, his shoulders sliding between her knees, and Charlotte took a long shuddering breath of anticipation. His hands slid under her hips, holding and lifting, his breath warmed her intimately, and still the first stroke of his tongue made her cry out.

"Shh," he whispered. "I shan't go on if you can't be quiet."

Charlotte pressed one fist to her mouth, her body jerking helplessly as he lowered his head again.

"Stop," she wheezed in a strangled voice. "I can't be quiet! Stop!"

"You can," he said. "You will." And this time, when he applied himself, he didn't stop. Charlotte nearly choked on her cries of pleasure, her heart full to overflowing and her body singing. This was what it was like to be with a man who loved her, a man who wouldn't leave her in the middle of the night or treat her as a mindless ornament. A man who wanted only to please her.

Stuart sat back on his heels, his hands smoothing over her. He slipped one finger inside her, rubbing slowly, and Charlotte twisted her hips, desperate for more. He laughed softly, then removed his hand. She lifted her hips, beseeching, but he continued playing with her. He pressed into her, just a little bit, then withdrew to slide up and down, tantalizing. Aching for completion, Charlotte leaned up on her elbows to protest.

He had taken himself in hand and was watching as he retraced the paths his fingers had taken, a look of absorbed concentration on his face. As she moved, he looked up. "Watch," he muttered, his voice so guttural it was almost incoherent. He placed himself against her and thrust home. Charlotte almost lost her balance at the feel of him inside her at last. He pulled out, so far she could see the distance between them, and then slid back in.

Her arms gave out, and she collapsed. Stuart loomed over her, covering her with his body. He caught her hands and stretched them to the sides, pinning her in place as he moved, riding her with long, sure thrusts. Charlotte could hardly breathe as he plunged into her, his weight pushing her into the mattress. There was nothing but Stuart in her world, and she wrapped her legs around his hips, holding nothing back.

"Charlotte," he gasped. His eyes were so dilated they were nearly black, and a fine sheen of sweat dampened his brow. "My God, I never knew . . . never dreamed . . ."

"I love you," she said, dropping her hips to heighten the friction between them. "Only you." It was all she needed; her body contracted, and she threw back her head with a mute shriek. Stuart's hand slipped beneath her arched back and he, too, froze, caught in the same ecstasy. A moment later he lowered himself, still holding her close.

Stuart lifted the long tangled curls gently from her neck, and pressed his lips in their place. "Is that what he said about you?" he whispered. "Those terrible things about having no heart and no shame?"

She lay under him, utterly spent. "Everyone did. I was afraid it was true."

"It's not."

After a moment she turned her head. "But everything you said was true. I did fall in love too easily, at least once. I never wanted to feel that way again."

Stuart went still. Her eyes were shadowed and disillusioned. Even though she faced him, she seemed to be seeing something else. "He was a gentleman from town, visiting friends in the country. We met at a picnic, and a fortnight later he said he loved me. He said he wanted to marry me. When my father forbade him to visit, I climbed out my bedroom window at nights to see him. I was so naïve. My father never told me anything; he simply told me what to do, and I never wanted to listen. And when that man told me he was leaving, and asked me to come with him, I said yes."

Her voice dropped. "We made it as far as an inn some ten miles away. I don't know if my father tracked us, or if that man told him, hoping to force his consent, but Papa discovered us there, posing as man and wife."

Stuart groaned inwardly. "He took your virginity."

Charlotte didn't flinch. "My father offered him five thousand pounds to leave. We were still in bed; I couldn't get out to get dressed, not while my own father was standing there. When Papa offered him money, that man simply asked for more. Not for a farthing less than ten thousand, he said. Papa had a pistol, and he brought it out. You'll go for five, or you'll never go anywhere at all, he said. So he got out of bed and put on his clothes, took the bank draft my father handed him, and left. He never looked at me again."

And Stuart understood then just why she had hated him so fiercely at the beginning. She had been acting on knowledge gained the hard way, and now that he knew the whole truth, Stuart couldn't fault her for anything. What must have gone through her mind, when she saw history repeating itself with her niece?

"My father dragged me home in utter silence. I was devastated, both at the realization I had been completely wrong and because Papa refused to look at me. When we got home, he sent me up to my room, and told me to pack my things. I was very scared, but did it—I was too frightened not to. He sent for me an hour later, and . . ." She closed her eyes. "He told me I was unnatural," she continued in the same flat voice. "Ungrateful, ungovernable, and immoral. I was ruined—he had seen the evidence with his own eyes—and he couldn't bear the sight of me. I was to go to Paris, to a distant cousin of my mother, and stay there until I was summoned home."

"He never sent for you?" His heart ached for her.

"He died four years ago. I never received a word from him. My brother George wrote to me, and he always gave me news of Papa, but never a message from him. Besides, by then I was everything he had named me: intemperate, unrestrained, and wild. Whatever the gossips say about me is probably true."

"No," he said softly. "It isn't."

"I had hoped, coming back to England with a new name, I would be able to put it behind me. If I lived an upright, blameless life, I thought, people will forget, or not connect me with the scandal. I never told anyone, not even Lucia. My father almost surely told no one, and George would never have breathed a word. The only person who would be able to tell—"

"Hyde-Jones," Stuart finished when she stopped. "Damn."

She sighed. "I didn't let myself consider that I might meet him again—how could I let my fears stand in the way of finding Susan? And it had been so long, I thought he could hardly care or even recognize me now. But now, even if I find her, she'll be ruined, too, by association." She covered her face with her hands. "Oh, what have I done? Why must everything go wrong?"

"It isn't your fault." He pulled her close again, into the curve of his arm where she fit just perfectly. "Everyone has something in their past to hide." He kissed her temple, feeling that protective urge again. What a life she must have led, thinking herself irredeemably wicked and unloved. He thought of all the men who had used her and cast her aside, and then he imagined them all drawn and quartered, their heads impaled on pikes along London Bridge.

And he was the first person she had told. After thirteen years, she had trusted him, of all people.

"You must have noticed Terrance hates me," he said before he could think better of it. She didn't move, but her breathing changed. "You must wonder why."

"You don't have to tell me," she murmured. He waited, gathering his thoughts. "But I do wonder," she admitted.

"I don't know for certain," he began slowly, "but I have an idea. When I was a child, we lived at Barrowfield, my grandfather's estate. My mother still lives there ten months of the year. She only comes to London for the Season. Grandfather dotes on her; always has, as far as I can recall.

"I lived there, too, until I was old enough for school. That summer, Terrance came to Barrowfield, which was highly unusual for him. I barely knew him as my father, for my grandfather filled that role most of the time. But Terrance came, and he took me for a ride. I had just gotten a gelding from Grandfather, and was quite proud of my riding abilities. I must have been eager to show Terrance. I remember he didn't say much until we reached a narrow pass that wound around a ravine. There was a steep drop, and he made me dismount and walk to the edge.

"I had been there many times, of course, being as daring and reckless as most boys. But Terrance made me stand there, and he told me he thought I should call him Terrance now, instead of Father. I didn't want to—it seemed unnatural, after all—and asked why. He looked me up and down, for I had grown quite a bit since his last visit, and said he couldn't have a son so tall. I thought it must be a lark, but from that day on, whenever I called him Father, he corrected me."

Charlotte had listened in unmoving silence, but now she raised her head. "Did you never discover why? What did your mother and grandfather say?"

He shrugged. "I never knew. My mother put me off every time I asked her, until I realized she didn't want to answer. Grandfather simply threw up his hands and mumbled something about 'unyielding Terrance,' but that was all. It was quite accepted by everyone else that I call him Terrance, and so I became accustomed to it.

"Then one day, just before I left for school, I overheard the maids talking. They were giggling over something Grandfather had done for Mother—he had fresh flowers cut for her room every day, and he would often give her gifts, sometimes quite extravagant ones. One maid declared that Belmaine—my grandfather—must love her more than Terrance did, and the rest all laughed. Another suggested he always had, and that was why Terrance resented me so."

She frowned. "Surely they didn't mean . . ."

"I suspect they did. What would make a man dislike his own son so much he wouldn't even let the boy call him Father? What if it weren't his son at all, but his father's?"

Charlotte sucked in her breath. "Then . . . you're his brother?"

He shrugged again, not quite meeting her eyes. "I've no proof. But it explains why Mother only lives with Terrance during the Season, for appearances' sake, and why Grandfather adores her so. Whether he seduced her after she married Terrance or before, I cannot say; my birth was barely nine months after they married. For the life of me I cannot decide which Terrance would regard as the bigger sin, but my own belief is after, when she was already married and Belmaine couldn't have her himself."

So many things whirled around in her brain; it was a plausible, if terrible, explanation. "Oh, Stuart . . ."

Stuart pulled her back down into his arms, still stroking her shoulder. "Don't pity me, Charlotte. In all likelihood I was raised by parents who loved me."

"But to wonder . . . to know everyone suspected you were a—"

He put his finger on her lips even as Charlotte stopped short. "Either way, I'm Belmaine's heir, and he would never let Terrance interfere with that." His hand fell away and he gave her a gentle kiss. "The past doesn't change who you are. It might shape your character, but it doesn't dictate your future, unless you let it."

He pulled the covers over them, keeping her nestled against him. For a moment both were silent, quietly savoring the nearness of the other, the complete confidence they had shared. The old wounds didn't hurt as much, as if the raw edges of her pain had joined the raw edges of his pain, and each had soothed the other.

"Stuart?" said Charlotte hesitantly. "Tell me about Oakwood Park." His hand paused at her shoulder for a long minute.

"It's in Somerset." His fingers glided down her arm again. "A quiet little farm, really, barely a hundred and twenty acres. I purchased it from a Scot who'd never even taken the time to visit; he wanted rid of it, since it was several hundred miles from the rest of his properties. It came into his family as part of a marriage settlement, but no one had lived there in decades."

He told her about the land, acre after acre of rich soil that had been allowed to go wild but should be arable by next spring, ready for the fields of wheat and barley he hoped to plant. He told her about the house, which needed renovations but was still sound, all except the east wing, whose roof had collapsed some time ago. "We've already taken most of it down," he added. His voice stayed quiet and even, but Charlotte could hear the pride and enthusiasm in it. "When it's all gone, there should be a fine site for an orangery. My mother has one at Barrowfield. And I did want to plant an orchard; aside from the namesake oaks, it's virtually all farmland." He fell silent, and she knew he was thinking of all the work, all the time he had put into Oakwood Park. He loved it. And at that moment Charlotte said a small prayer that he would be able to keep it, somehow, even if she didn't like what it might take. He deserved no less. How could she deny him a second chance, a fresh start, when she was trying to make one herself?

He gathered her closer, his breath warm against her neck in a soundless sigh. "You have to leave, don't you?" she whispered.

He smoothed her curls beneath his cheek. "Not yet."

"Thank you," she said after a moment. "For telling me."

Stuart's smile was bittersweet. "It was my pleasure." Strangely enough, it had been, even though it had only convinced him to sell Oakwood Park. Telling her about the time and effort he'd put into the estate, about the plans and hopes he'd had for it, had only underscored the difference between a parcel of land and the woman in his arms. He loved both, but couldn't have both, and so Stuart chose the one that loved him back: Charlotte.

He didn't feel any sense of loss, although he expected that would come when he signed away the deed. Telling Charlotte had been like a last tour of the property, a farewell visit. He couldn't bring himself to do what it would take to keep it. Tomorrow he would begin making discreet inquiries, and hopefully he could get a price that would enable him to pay off Barclay in full. Then . . . perhaps Ware needed another steward, or a caretaker for one of his properties. He had been raised to oversee Barrowfield one day, after all, and his experiences at Oakwood Park had only helped. He could manage an estate, and it would provide a home and an income—enough to support a wife.

He remembered something then. "Charlotte," he said softly. "I received word from Pitney tonight." She started, then flipped over, her face pale and anxious in the candlelight. "It is good news," he rushed to assure her, then told her what the investigator had learned. "Susan will be home soon," he finished.

Silently, she kissed him, gently and sweetly. He thought to tell her then about his decision on Oakwood Park. But the words were too hard to form, and he decided to wait until he had spoken to Ware and made arrangements to sell the property. For something this important to him, he needed more than a feeling, more than blind confidence that things would work out in the end. He needed a plan, something definite he could promise her.

He held her until her breathing was soft and even and he was sure she slept. Even then he didn't want to leave, but there would be no end of trouble if Terrance found him here. When Charlotte rolled onto her stomach and off his arm, Stuart reluctantly slid out of bed.

He sorted through the discarded clothes, dressing himself and laying Charlotte's things across the chaise. He looked around again, and scooped the broken china figure into his pocket; he would try to replace it before his mother noticed. Then he tucked the blankets securely around Charlotte, brushing one last kiss on her temple. The faint tracks of tears down her cheeks made his heart ache. He doubted she cried often. Then Stuart carefully slipped out the door and left.

Chapter Fifteen

"What the devil are you doing in my bed, Drake?"

Stuart rolled over and blinked awake. Lord Philip Lindeville stood over him, arms folded over his chest and looking a great deal like his ducal brother, only darker. "Pip," he said groggily. "Welcome home."

"And to you! I heard you'd been run out of London by a mob of angry papas."

"Not quite." Stuart sat up, scrubbing the sleep from his face. "Ware gave me the key."

Philip waved one hand. "No matter, you're welcome to stay. Just not in my bed." He dropped into a chair and leaned back. "So, who is she?"

"She?" Stuart reached for his robe. The sound of servants bustling about the house filtered in through the open door. Within an hour they would have one of the other bedrooms cleaned and aired for him. Stuart had gotten used to the quiet and privacy, but of course Philip was accustomed to servants.

"The woman who brought you back to town." Philip smirked. "An heiress? Or a temptress?" He twirled a silk parasol over his head, fluttering his eyelashes. Stuart scowled.

"Where did you get that?"

Philip closed the parasol and held it to his nose. "It was in the hall, under the hat rack. I wonder how a lady could have dropped her parasol there and not missed it. She smells divine, though."

Stuart grabbed the parasol, resisting the urge to smell it himself. Charlotte hadn't mentioned missing it, but she must have had one the day they went driving. He tucked the delicate bit of silk and wire under his arm protectively. "Never mind that."

Philip stood. "By the by, I invite you to stay, but not to move in. Benton is downstairs with four wagons of crates, and I doubt they'll fit. I brought back a few things myself, and—"

"Benton's here?" Stuart retrieved clean clothing from the wardrobe.

Philip helpfully kicked a stray boot in his direction. "I sent him to the kitchen. So sorry I can't be more accommodating, but once my own luggage arrives—"

"You've been more than accommodating, Pip." Stuart ran one hand through his hair in distraction. Four wagons! What in the name of God had Charlotte brought with her from Italy? He remembered the tiger skin, and shuddered. "I'll send Benton on to Clapham Close with the wagons. We have to unpack everything as soon as possible."

"At your father's house? Have you gone mad?" Philip exclaimed. "Are you even allowed to enter?"

"My mother always receives me." Stuart shrugged. "Many thanks, Philip."

Philip still stared at him in amazement. "What's this about?"

Stuart opened his mouth to explain, at least in part, but ended up shaking his head. "Someday I'll tell you. It's much too long a tale."

"Filled with exotic beauties, I trust." Philip leveled a stern look at him.

Stuart winked. "I wouldn't have it any other way."

"Lucia!"

Her friend swept into the drawing room with a smile. "*Cara*, how good it is to see you again. But you look so tired and pale!"

Charlotte smiled self-consciously, aware of Mrs. Drake hovering anxiously in the background. "It's early by town standards." Lucia gave her a doubtful glance, and Charlotte hurried to present her friend to her hostess. Mrs. Drake welcomed Lucia politely, if nervously, then excused herself.

Lucia watched her leave. "She is not pleased to see me." She seated herself with a swirl of skirts. "So. What has happened?"

"A great deal since I wrote you last. The investigator has found where Susan's been staying, although not where she is now."

"Then you do not need Piero's collection?" Lucia rolled her eyes. "I knew it would happen this way. I spend three entire days packing what I have just unpacked, ordered about by your Mr. Drake's man, then fly to London in a very shabby coach, only to find you have no need of my help."

"No, we still need the crates," Charlotte assured

her. "Stuart is persuaded the kidnapper is watching this house. If he sees the wagons arrive with Piero's things, he'll know what he wants is here. Hopefully he will show himself again, in his desperation to get it."

"Oh?" Lucia smiled slyly. "Stuart?"

Charlotte flushed. "He's been a great help to me."

Lucia nodded. "*Buono*. That one knows what a woman needs." Charlotte glared at her. Lucia shrugged, looking pleased.

"I did not expect you to come yourself." Charlotte changed the subject. "I thought you were enjoying your stature in Kent."

Lucia clucked, reaching for her cigarette case. Charlotte couldn't keep back a sigh at the sight of it. "I have come to help you, of course. Kent had become quite dull. Mr. Whitley decided to return to London, and I saw no other attraction. Not that he retains much attraction; such a mistake I made, allowing you to persuade me not to pursue your Mr. Drake. I knew at once he would be a man of action, not just words."

"You came with Mr. Whitley, then?"

Lucia nodded, no longer looking pleased. "I have sent him off to make arrangements at a suitable hotel. He is quite good at talking, that one. With luck he will arrange all day until he has no voice left."

"Oh dear." Charlotte bit her lip to keep from laughing. Lucia gave a disgusted snort. There was a commotion in the hall before Charlotte could think of anything else to say, and Stuart threw open the door, grinning widely.

"Good morning. I trust you're ready to unpack."

Charlotte found herself smiling. It was so hard not to smile back at Stuart. "Good morning. Have you met my friend, Lucia da Ponte? Lucia, Mr. Stuart Drake."

Lucia got to her feet as Stuart bowed. "Signora."

"A pleasure," purred Lucia. "I have not heard enough about you."

Stuart hesitated, glancing at Charlotte. "I trust we shall remedy that soon enough." He gestured at the door. "Forgive my ill manners, but I'm certain everyone understands the need for haste. If we unload the crates into the hall, we can bring the things in here. Have you a complete inventory?" Charlotte shook her head. "Then someone should create one, as the things are unpacked."

"I shall do it," said Lucia, settling back into her seat. "I don't wish to touch straw ever again."

Charlotte followed Stuart into the hall, where two footmen were dragging in the first crate. "Good heavens," she said, peering out the door and trying to count the crates in the wagon outside. "I'd forgotten how many there were."

Stuart took her hand, lifting it to his lips for a moment. "Did you sleep well?"

She blushed at his quiet question. "Yes."

"Any regrets?"

Her blush deepened, but she didn't look away. "No."

He smiled. Relieved, she realized; he hadn't been sure of her reply. He brushed his lips once more over her knuckles before releasing her. "Change your gown; I'm quite fond of this one, and would rather it didn't get ruined."

When Charlotte came back downstairs, Stuart was talking with his mother. Amelia was wringing her hands and watching the slow but steady accumulation of wooden crates and trunks in the hall. Charlotte paused. The enormity of what was at stake hit her then. There was nothing else they could do, and yet the fear returned that the thief sought something she didn't have. All Stuart's arguments made sense; an Italian who had been searching those crates almost surely wanted something from Italy. But what could it possibly be? The thief had opened every box and not found what he wanted. Was there some small valuable secreted somewhere? How could they hope to find it when he hadn't been able to?

Then Stuart saw her. For a moment he just stared at her with an almost besotted expression, then blinked and finished whatever he was saying to his mother before hurrying up the stairs to her. That look, though, steadied her in a way no words could. She didn't have to face this alone. Someone was with her, and would be until they found Susan.

"I should apologize to your parents," she whispered to him. "It's a terrible inconvenience."

Stuart was already shaking his head. "The kidnapper has been watching this house; we want him to see the wagons arrive, so he knows his prize is at hand. There's plenty of room here, and Mother understands the important thing is to find your niece."

Charlotte bit her lip. "I fear we won't find it."

He squeezed her hand. "We will."

"But how? He hasn't given us a clue, and I can't think of what he might want. What will we do if we find nothing valuable? Something in one of those crates cost me my niece, and I have no idea what it was." She closed her eyes, and felt his lips at her temple.

"Something in these crates will return your niece to you," he corrected gently. "You must think of that."

Charlotte heaved a sigh and opened her eyes. "Then let's begin."

For hours they worked. Vases, statues, sculptures, and paintings emerged from the straw, all recorded by Lucia before Benton placed them in the drawing room. Charlotte examined each piece carefully, looking for anything out of the ordinary, but it all looked the same as it had in Italy. She wished again with all her heart she had left everything behind. Piero's bequest had been so oddly phrased, entreating her to keep every piece; had he known there was something in it that would cause her such trouble?

By luncheon one wagon was empty and another half empty, and the drawing room was growing crowded. By midafternoon, when the third wagon was emptied and they began unloading the fourth, the drawing room was filled, Lucia was complaining of sore fingers, Charlotte was ready to pitch the lot into the street, and even Stuart's good humor had faded.

"I heard Marcella Rescati sing," she told Lucia to break the monotony as she pulled out a heavy urn. Straw showered the floor, which was filthy despite the best efforts of the maids who swept it constantly.

Lucia's eyebrows flew up as she noted the urn. "Marcella Rescati? *La porcellina?*"

"*La porcellina?*" Amelia asked innocently. She had begun helping, Charlotte suspected, to hasten the process and to protect her drawing room carpet. But then she had begun admiring the pieces, more and more effusively, and was now as engaged as everyone else, even to the straw in her hair.

"The piglet," Lucia told her. "Because she has the nose of one, and her highest register is a squeal. What did she sing?"

"Susanna, in *Figaro*."

"Susanna." Lucia flicked one hand. "I trust she was laughed off the stage."

"No, she was very well received." Charlotte handed her urn to Benton and glanced at Stuart. "How did you find the opera the other night?"

He shrugged, prying the lid off another crate with an iron bar. "She sounded perfectly fine to my ears."

"Pah." Lucia snorted. "Your English ears."

"Charlotte's ears are as English as mine," he pointed out.

"She has been to Milan and Venice, and heard opera the way it is meant to be sung."

"The English must take what they can get," said Charlotte. "There aren't many true opera singers about."

"There are not many in the world. It is a gift, to sing opera, and no ordinary piglet can open her mouth and squeal it." Lucia frowned at the small statue Amelia held up, scribbling a line in her inventory.

"Of course not. But if the closest one can get is a piglet . . ." Charlotte shrugged as she wrestled with a statue. It was heavy, and she dragged it forward, kicking the straw away as she did. It caught on the edge of the crate and pitched forward; Charlotte barely caught it before it hit the floor. An edge cut into her scraped, sore hands, and she pushed it back upright with a thump, where it rocked back and forth for a moment.

"*Attento!*" snapped Lucia. "What good is all this work if you break things? That might be the treasure."

Hot and dusty, her arms and back aching, Charlotte looked at the statue. It was one she particularly disliked, a smirking Mercury whose expression had

always made Charlotte's skin prickle, as if the thing
were really watching her. Piero had kept it in his bedchamber, and had actually spoken to it at times. Even
now it seemed to be grinning at her, mocking her, and
she just couldn't take it anymore. "This is no treasure,
Lucia. It's a forgery. Just like all these other things."

"What?" said three voices at once. Even Benton,
Stuart's sphinx-like valet, stopped and stared at her.
Charlotte dropped onto the bottom stair, too tired to
stand any longer.

"Piero was a forger," she said wearily. She flung out
one arm, encompassing the clutter of statuary and
other art crowding the hall. "These are fakes."

"Are you certain?" demanded Stuart. "How do you
know?"

"He told me." Charlotte leaned against the newel
post. It felt terribly good to sit down without holding
something. She had had enough of handling Piero's
creations as if they were priceless masterpieces. She
had never wanted them in the first place, and each
one that appeared only reminded her of those years
and months of her life when she had been so lonely.
Stuart had named the essence of the matter last night:
Piero had used her to fulfill his fantasies. He had
supported her lavishly in return, but she had lived a
life designed to please him, not herself. Only now,
after Stuart had shown her what it was like to be
loved just as she was, did she realize how alone she
had been in Italy.

And she wouldn't protect his name any longer.
Piero had sworn her to secrecy, arrogantly proud even
as he let people believe his art collection was real. He
had probably left it to her because anyone else would
have found him out and denounced him as a fraud.

And because of all he had done for her, when she was in desperate need of help, she had kept his secret. But that was before. Charlotte was afraid her respect for a dead man's request had fooled too many people, and cost her too dearly.

"What the devil!" Stuart dropped his bar with a clunk. "All of it?"

She nodded. "All of it."

"Surely not, Madame Griffolino," protested Amelia, holding a small marble bust close to her chest as if to protect it. "They're so beautiful!"

Charlotte gave her a sour smile. "He had talent, but no imagination. Apprentices learn the craft by making copies, and Piero simply never stopped. All the beautiful things he wanted to possess, but couldn't—either because they were too expensive, or too fragile, or too well known—he replicated for his own enjoyment." She waved at the statue she had almost dropped. "Piero's favorite piece. It stood in his bedchamber."

Stuart frowned, stepping over packing debris to take a closer look at the statue. It portrayed a young man half seated, half standing, cradling a harp in one arm while he plucked it with his other hand. His laurel-crowned head was tilted down toward the instrument, but his eyes looked up, as if catching someone watching him, and the faint suggestion of a sly smile curved his sensual mouth. "I would have never suspected. Why would he create forgeries? This looks quite good."

Charlotte pointed at the god's arm. "Except his left

arm is longer than his right. His leg is scarred, where the polishing wasn't good, and the lyre is too small."

Lucia threw down her pen. "*Dio!* The old cheat. And he gave me many things as gifts!"

Charlotte shrugged half-heartedly. "At least he did not sell you any."

"Then you knew all along the thief would never find anything valuable," Stuart said slowly, his expression darkening. "And he broke in repeatedly, yet you never did anything. What were you thinking, Charlotte? What did you think the thief sought?"

"I didn't know! I suspected he wanted something smaller, easily carried away, gold plate or a jewel-encrusted reliquary. Most of these are large items, framed paintings and statues. It would be difficult to carry Mercury through the streets unremarked, genuine or not."

Stuart continued to frown in disapproval. "You took a terrible risk."

"Until you crossed him, he did nothing threatening," she said sharply, pricked again by the guilt that she had ignored the thief until it was too late. He hadn't been fooled by Piero's counterfeits, but had stolen the one treasure Charlotte had, her niece. And unless she could produce something of genuine worth from these crates, she might never get Susan back.

"Well, what are we to do with this, then?" Stuart threw up his hands. "If you say it's all worthless, how shall we bargain with the kidnapper?"

"Why, have it appraised, Stuart dear," piped up Amelia. She looked around sadly, still cradling her bust of Cupid. "Hopefully some of it will turn out to be authentic."

"It won't," said Charlotte in disgust. She got up and stretched, bumping into the statue whose flaws she had exposed. In frustration and anger, she pushed it over, venting her feelings on the carved marble. It wobbled, then tipped, and fell to the floor with a tremendous crash. The god's head broke off and split in two, one half sliding across the floor into a pile of straw, the other half coming to rest at the bottom of the stairs.

Stuart drew breath as if to scold her, then sighed. "One less for the inventory," he said, leaning down to lift the headless Mercury. He grasped it by the neck and heaved it to its feet again. "This chap's hollow," he said with some surprise.

"The pinchpurse," said Lucia with disdain. "A real sculptor would never use less than a perfect stone."

"Rather fitting, though," Stuart said, trying to move the ruined statue against the wall out of the way. "A hollow god for a fraudulent artist." He gave it one last shove, and more marble crumbled from the neck. Stuart brushed the rubble away as a maid hurried up with a broom, but he stood, transfixed. "Charlotte."

"What is it?" She took one look at his expression and hurried over to peer into Mercury's chest. Just as Stuart had said, the statue was hollow, but deliberately so. The edges of the cavity were smooth and straight; someone had bored a hole down through the middle. She leaned closer. "It . . . It's not empty!"

Cries of interest echoed in the hall, and everyone crowded around to see. Carefully, Stuart extracted a tightly rolled sheaf of paper from the hollow. It was old and yellowed, torn around the edges and well creased. He glanced at Charlotte. "Have you any idea?"

She shook her head. "None."

"What is it, Stuart?" Amelia asked. Her face was flushed with excitement, and Charlotte realized she must have been quite pretty when young.

"I'm not sure, Mother." Stuart carried the roll of paper into the dining room and gingerly unrolled it on the table. The paper was thin, but held together except at the edges, where small sections simply crumbled into dust.

"They're studies," said Charlotte, holding the edge as Stuart continued unrolling. Smaller sheets of the paper sprang loose and curled back upon themselves, and she had to keep catching the edges. They were the sort of drawings a painter would make before setting his brush to canvas, for practice or for planning. The images, though, fairly leaped off the paper, all the more so when they were life sized. Wild-eyed horses plunged over each other, their riders locked in mortal combat. Men in battle dress impaled each other on javelins, and cowered beneath shields under the hooves of rampaging horses. There were pages of arms upraised with spears, hands clasped about sword handles, headless figures contorted in death throes.

"Very brutal studies," observed Stuart, paging through the sketches of severed limbs. "But why were they hidden? Did Piero make them?"

Charlotte shook her head helplessly. "He was a better sculptor, but he did paint. These would be made before an original painting, though, and he didn't have the patience for that."

Stuart cocked his head, studying the profile of a man clearly exhorting his troops to charge. "Perhaps this was to be his masterpiece? His one burst of creative genius?"

Charlotte snorted. "Who would consider that a treasure, besides Piero himself?"

Then Lucia reached between them, and put her finger on the crest of a heraldic standard. "Anghiari."

"What is Anghiari?"

"Anghiari," explained Lucia, giving Charlotte a meaningful glance, "as any Florentine would know, was a famous battle long ago in which the Republic defeated the Milanese army." Charlotte waited expectantly; Piero, like Lucia, had been Florentine, and very proudly so. "The magistrati commissioned two murals to commemorate their victory: the Battle of Anghiari and the Battle of Cascina. Michelangelo would paint Cascina, although he never did. Leonardo—a Florentine himself—would paint Anghiari, but his technique was flawed, and his work was lost."

"What do you mean, lost?"

Lucia flicked her fingers. "Lost. The paint dripped from the wall."

As one, all four turned to the drawing again. The detail, down to the bulging veins in the horses' nostrils, was astounding. "Do you think these are his? Leonardo's?" asked Charlotte in a hushed voice.

Lucia lifted one shoulder. "I do not know. His cartoon was copied by many others; even then Leonardo was recognized as a great artist."

"So this is the treasure?" Amelia clutched at Stuart's

arm, still gazing reverently at the drawings. "Goodness, how much is it worth?"

"If it is Leonardo, it is priceless," said Lucia, seating herself.

Stuart turned to Charlotte. "Is it possible?"

Charlotte hesitated. Could Piero have come across a priceless set of drawings and hidden them to avoid sharing them? He was capable of the last part, she thought, and Mercury was an ideal hiding place. But how on earth could he have gotten the drawings in the first place? One didn't simply walk into a gallery and purchase them. "I don't know," she said at last. "But I find it hard to believe. He didn't have a single authentic piece when I knew him. Everything was a fraud."

"Well, that explains the jewels," Stuart muttered, letting the drawings roll back into themselves in resignation.

"What do you mean?" asked Charlotte, surprised.

He shifted uncomfortably. He hadn't quite meant to blurt that out. "You didn't know some of your jewels might be, ah, paste?"

Her hand flew to her throat, even though she wore no necklace. "No!"

"Er, yes. The, ah, diamond and emerald necklace . . ." She continued to gape at him. Stuart cleared his throat and busied himself with rolling the papers.

"How did you know, Stuart?" asked his mother.

"When he stole it, no doubt," said Lucia from her chair. Stuart glared at her in annoyance; he was not in the mood for her teasing at the moment.

Amelia gasped. "You stole it?"

"Not precisely," mumbled Stuart. "I gave it back." He spread the drawings open again. "I for one think these may be authentic. They fit the description of a treasure, and they were hidden securely in a place no one would expect, since, as Madame da Ponte said, most sculptors use solid blocks of marble. No one would suspect anything might be hidden inside."

"Then you have found the treasure," said Lucia. "Of course you cannot give it to this madman."

Amelia twisted her hands. "To whom do they belong, then?"

"To the people of Florence," said Lucia. "It is their battle. Also, they paid for them three centuries ago."

"I doubt they're authentic," said Charlotte. "I simply can't believe it. They must be drawings from the original, and Piero may have hidden them because he planned to copy them and sell them. I always suspected he dealt in false antiquities and art, although he never admitted it." She turned to Stuart. "And if even my jewels are fake, then I am doubly sure. He was a fraud, through and through."

Stuart began rolling up the drawings again. "We have to be certain. Continue unpacking, and see if anything else interesting turns up."

"What will you do?" Charlotte asked, helping him.

"I'll see if I can authenticate these, or prove them false." He gathered up the sheaf of papers and went into the front hall. Charlotte followed him.

"That may be impossible," she warned him. "A good forgery—"

He stopped, and put up one hand. "It may be," he agreed. "But we should try. Even if they're false, we may be able to pass them off on the kidnapper as authentic; he doesn't seem to know just what the treasure is, after all. He's already seen most of the rest of the things, when he searched your house—and I have more to say on the subject of ignoring inherently dangerous people like burglars, by the by—and he didn't seem fooled by it. But this he can't have seen."

"Then why can't we use it to draw him out now?" cried Charlotte impatiently. "If it doesn't matter . . ."

"It matters," he corrected her as he took his hat from the butler. "If these are authentic, they *are* an Italian treasure, and no one man, especially a thief, should own them. And we should know what we're dealing with before we risk them."

"Of course, but . . ." Charlotte gripped her hands together, looking at the drawings longingly. "Couldn't we let him know now, just in case? How long will it take to authenticate them?"

"There is someone who may know," he said. "I studied under him at Cambridge."

"I'm coming with you," she said at once.

He grinned. "I knew you would."

Charlotte turned to Lucia and Amelia, who had followed them into the hall by now. "We're going to see someone who may be able to tell us if they're genuine," she told them.

Lucia waved her hand. "Go, then. Shall we continue here?"

"Yes, yes." Charlotte nodded as the footman hurried forward with her bonnet and gloves. "We'll be back soon." The footman opened the door, and as they left, Charlotte heard Lucia ask, "Shall we continue smashing more things?" and Amelia's horrified gasp.

Stuart hailed a cab, and helped her into it. "Oh, Stuart, do you really think this is what he wanted?" she asked as they bowled along.

"Hopefully we can persuade him it is. If he was watching the house just now, he's seen us leave in a hurry after unloading all those wagons. With any luck, he'll come to us now." They looked at each other, brimming with barely concealed excitement.

"We may have Susan back soon," said Charlotte softly. "Oh, how I hope your friend is at home!"

Chapter Sixteen

As it turned out, he was not. Almost ill with disappointment, Charlotte allowed Stuart to hand her into the carriage. About to climb in himself, he suddenly stepped back out. "One moment," he said, then hurried back up the steps to ring the bell again. Charlotte watched as he exchanged a word with the butler who had just crushed her hopes, and then Stuart loped back down the steps, a wide smile spreading across his face.

"Old Sherry's gone to his club," he said, swinging up to sit beside her. He leaned forward and gave the driver his parents' address. "I'll try him there."

"I want to come, too."

He shook his head. "You won't be allowed entrance. I'll take you home and go myself."

"But—"

He kissed her. "No," he said softly but firmly. "I will not allow you to sit in a cab by yourself for an hour. Sherry's a good fellow, but a bit of a rambler. It may take a while to work a definitive answer out of him."

Charlotte uttered a particularly vile curse in Italian,

but made no other protest. At the Drake house, Stuart helped her out and held her hand a moment longer than necessary. "I believe we've found what he wants," he said. "Whether or not the drawings are authentic. We're close to finding Susan, but must be patient to the end. A move too sudden may send him off in a panic. Promise me you'll wait for me to return."

"Promise me you'll be back within an hour," she retorted.

"Charlotte," he warned, although his eyes crinkled as he spoke.

"All right. But you must hurry!"

"For you, I will hurry." He turned her hand over and kissed her palm, the heat of his mouth seeping through her glove.

"For you, I will wait," she said, a trifle breathless. With one look he managed to remind her of last night, all that he had said and done. As if he knew, he leaned forward, his blue eyes alight with laughter.

"I love you," he whispered.

It still seemed incredible to Charlotte. She smiled, swaying toward him, momentarily forgetting the mysterious drawings, the tension of the last week and the next hour, all the guilt and regret and doubt that had frayed the edges of her conscience. His lips brushed hers, too lightly, and then he jumped back into the carriage.

She watched the cab leave, a vaguely silly smile still on her face. At the corner Stuart leaned out and waved. Charlotte raised her hand in reply, and he was gone. She turned and climbed the steps, where the footman already stood beside the open door.

In the hall, it was quiet. The straw had been cleared away, and the false treasures still sat undisturbed, even the decapitated Mercury. For a moment Charlotte contemplated it; it was a fitting end to the miserable little sneak, she decided.

Amelia came into the hall, stopping short when she saw Charlotte. "Well? What did you discover?"

"Nothing. The gentleman wasn't at home." Charlotte took off her bonnet and gloves. "Stuart's gone to try Mr. Sheridan's club."

"Oh, dear." Her face fell. "He's sure to be at the club. Gentlemen are always at their clubs."

"Let us hope," said Charlotte. "Has Lucia gone?"

Amelia nodded. "She returned to her hotel to rest once it seemed pointless to unpack the rest of the things."

Charlotte turned and walked into the drawing room, where Benton was packing some of Piero's collection, with less care and more speed than before. "You may go," she told him. "This can wait. You deserve a rest, after bringing it all to London so quickly."

He bowed. "Yes, madam. I was pleased to be of service. How unfortunate it was not more useful."

Charlotte considered that as he left. If it led to Susan's return, it would be useful, or at least no longer a liability. She wondered what Piero had intended her to do with it; had he thought she would eventually find the treasure? He hadn't left her anything else of value. Even though she hadn't counted on much from Piero, she had always kept the jewels in the back of her mind as a comfortable reserve, one she had been considering using. Her mother had left her an inheritance which provided a modest income, but Charlotte had spent a great deal of money looking for Susan. In fact, unless she planned to begin spending her capital, she would soon be as penniless as Stuart.

A sad smile twisted her lips. What a pair they were, their fortunes worsening by the day. Since the moment he told her he loved her, Charlotte had been hoping—dreaming—things would work out well for them. Unfortunately, she just didn't see how that was possible. At this rate they wouldn't have two shillings between them by the end of the week.

Whatever else she might be, Charlotte was a realist. Regardless of what she might be willing to give up for love, she could hardly expect Stuart to give up not only Oakwood Park but any chance of prosperity. He had said he didn't want to be a dependent his whole life, but he hadn't meant to be poor instead. No matter how much they loved each other, she feared what genteel poverty might do to them. Would he come to wish he had married better? Even if he didn't blame her, could she bear to see him so disappointed?

She didn't think so.

But he had never offered her anything, anyway. He had told her he loved her, but that didn't mean he wanted to marry her. She ought to know by now that passion didn't necessarily translate into marriage. She should treasure this rare connection between them for what it was, and not pin her hopes on anything more. Losing Stuart wouldn't be the end of her life; she would have Susan back—hopefully soon—and that responsibility would occupy her time and thoughts. And if there was always a small place in her heart that never got over him, well, she would accept that. Unlike the other broken hearts she had suffered, this one would have been worth it.

Amelia bustled in then with a maid and tea in tow,

and Charlotte thankfully turned her attention to her hostess. Unfortunately, Amelia mostly wanted to talk about the terrible trick Piero had played on her by leaving her a collection of forgeries. Charlotte had many things to say about Piero and his frauds, but none she felt comfortable expressing in front of Mrs. Drake. If just a few of the paintings or sculpture had been real, she would have money, enough to support herself, enough to live without regard for fortune. Enough even to marry the man she loved.

"A message, madam." The butler had come in to hand her a note. Charlotte seized it with relief.

"Why, it's from Stuart," she said, reading. She glanced up at Amelia. "He asks me to join him, but says nothing of what he's learned."

"Not at all?" Amelia asked in astonishment. "How could he?"

Charlotte frowned as she studied the note. "This is not the house we called at earlier." Stuart had said he was going to the man's club, where she would not be admitted. If it wasn't Mr. Sheridan's home or his club, what was it? "I wonder where he's gone."

Amelia sat on the sofa with a little sigh. "Are these really all forgeries?" she asked yet again, wistfully. The bust of Cupid she had held earlier sat on the mantel, smiling beatifically as if enjoying the joke he had played on them.

Charlotte continued to frown at the note. There was something about it that struck her as odd, but she couldn't put her finger on what. Perhaps she was just piqued because he hadn't told her anything. There was nothing suspicious about the message, it was just brief. Frustratingly brief. *Come to me at once*, it said, and included a direction. Like the other message he had sent, it was only signed with a sharp, slanted "S."

"Mrs. Drake," said Charlotte slowly, "does this note seem odd to you?" She held it out.

Amelia leaned forward to see it. "What do you mean, odd? It really doesn't say much, does it . . ." Her voice trailed off as she read the message again.

"What?" asked Charlotte, sensing a change in her hostess's demeanor.

"It's only . . . Well, this does not look like Stuart's hand." Charlotte's head snapped up. "But of course I do not see his handwriting often." Amelia retreated immediately at her expression. "It may have changed; he does not write me often. Perhaps he wrote this more quickly than usual, or . . . Oh dear."

"I have the note he sent the other day," said Charlotte. "Let's compare." Amelia agreed, looking relieved, and Charlotte hurried up the stairs to her room, but couldn't find the message. Where could it have gone? She was quite sure she had placed it in the drawer beside the bed, right under the window.

Charlotte stared with narrowed eyes at the window, which overlooked a stretch of garden. Slowly, gently, she drew back the drape. The window was unlatched, and opened soundlessly at her touch. A wall-scaling thief would have no trouble getting into her room. Just as he had had no trouble climbing into Susan's room.

She spread out the note again. This, then, was not from Stuart. It was from the kidnapper. She rifled through the drawer looking for the note from him, but it, too, was gone. Only Susan's cheerful message was in the drawer where all three had once been.

Charlotte was so still the beat of her heart felt jarring. The thief had been in her room, searching her belongings again. Not only did he come and go as he pleased in her Kent house, steal her niece away, and follow her about London, but he broke into her host's home. Would she never be free of him?

With jerky movements she opened the wardrobe door and retrieved her pistol. She loaded it with practiced efficiency, and stalked back down the stairs.

"Have you found . . . Oh!" Amelia's eyes flew wide open at the sight of the pistol. "What are you doing?"

"This note"—Charlotte waved it—"is from the kidnapper. The last message from Stuart as well as the message from the kidnapper are missing from my room. He broke into your home and stole them, and now has sent me a forged message to lure me to him."

"Oh, but my dear!" Amelia's face was white. "You must wait for Stuart! He would never forgive me if you were injured!"

"You must tell him where I have gone." Stuart had been gone barely half an hour; she couldn't possibly wait. She couldn't let Stuart go in her place in any event. If she didn't respond at once, the kidnapper would know she hadn't been fooled, and might take it out on Susan. Charlotte read the note one more time, memorizing the direction before handing it to Amelia. "I cannot wait. The man who has my niece has proven himself capable of anything, and I will not send Stuart in my place on an errand which would surely endanger him."

"But it is equally dangerous for you!"

"Not half as dangerous as it is for the kidnapper," vowed Charlotte. "And if I do not go, he may harm Susan." She strode into the hall, and almost collided with Mr. Drake, who was just coming in.

"Your pardon, sir." Charlotte brushed past him and handed her pistol to the dismayed butler as she put on her cloak.

"Impertinent chit," grumbled Mr. Drake. He caught sight of the pistol and scowled. "What the devil are you doing with that?"

Charlotte lifted her chin. "It was my father's," she said calmly, deliberately misinterpreting his question. "I inherited it from my brother. I am taking it to shoot the villain who has abducted my niece." She tucked the pistol into the folds of her cloak. "Good day, Mr. Drake." She turned and marched out of the house, hearing Mr. Drake bellow for his wife. The footman scrambled to hail a hackney, and she climbed in, a cold, deadly calm creeping over her. No more waiting and worrying; one way or another, things were coming to a head.

Stuart stepped out of the carriage in front of the Cantabrigian Society for Antiquarians, a club composed of former Cambridge fellows who had a passion for history and the arts, the older the better. The man Stuart was looking for had been a founding member, and had zealously recruited his former students to join him. Stuart, naturally, had preferred other activities, but he did still have a passing interest in the subject.

He walked through a number of bright, sparsely furnished rooms. In the dining hall, he came upon an argument between two society members. One was standing, an upraised fork in his fist as if to stab his companion, who was arranging the other silver into military formation, shaking his head vigorously. As

Stuart approached, the argument grew more heated. The man with the fork began stabbing at the silver on the table, and the man who had arranged it leaped to his feet and began shoving it around the dishes.

"Mind you don't let him take your wineglass, Sherry," said Stuart with a chuckle. "He's massing for a flanking maneuver around the salt cellar."

"Ah, young Drake!" Jasper Sheridan's eyes lit up. "Have you come to join our society?"

Stuart smiled. Sherry was a stout little figure resembling nothing so much as a hedgehog, which had been his nickname among the students at Cambridge. His hair, considerably grayer now, stuck up in a ruff about his round, apple-cheeked face. Stuart recalled him charging around on the balls of his feet, leaning slightly forward as if against a strong wind. He was a curious character, Sherry was, but he was also a leading scholar of Roman history, and had a special interest in art. "Unfortunately not. I haven't the mind for it."

"Nonsense! We require only enthusiasm." Sherry chuckled, putting down the fork. He excused himself to his companion and motioned Stuart over to a vacant pair of chairs. "And we never hold examinations, although you made a fair showing. Most of the time, that is."

Stuart remembered that. He had just missed taking a first in history because he'd gone out drinking with several friends and shown up the next morning for his last examination with Sherry sporting a blackened eye and a splitting headache. At the time it hadn't bothered him much, for he hadn't expected to depend on his studies, but privately, Stuart had long since admitted he would take back that night of revelry if he could. "I hadn't the mind for it then, either, I fear."

"Fustian. You had the mind, just not the discipline." Sherry pulled out his pipe and began filling it. "I don't hold it against you, mind. So few of your mates did have the discipline necessary to become a scholar. Young Fielding, I recall, and that Cateborough chap was quite studious. Too bad he was only as bright as figgy pudding. Well! Enough of that, what brings you to the Society?" He lit his pipe, settling back into his chair.

"I've brought something that might be of interest to you," said Stuart. "A friend of mine recently discovered some drawings of a most unusual nature, and was curious about their origins."

"Ah, well! Drawings, you may recall from my lectures, are sometimes difficult to judge, since they are rarely finished works."

Stuart grinned. "I haven't forgotten everything, Sherry. But these drawings are . . . unusual."

"You said that." Sherry pulled on his pipe. "Well, well, let's see, then." He fished his spectacles from his pocket, and fitted them on his ears. He waited as Stuart gently unrolled the sketches on the low table before them. For a moment Sherry just frowned at them, turning his head from side to side.

"Do you know, you may have something here," he murmured. He reached out one hand to trace some lines in the air above the paper. "This musculature . . . the perspective . . . the detail in the hair . . ." He shifted the rolls of paper, examining a number of pages. "Where did you get these?" he demanded, suddenly focused and intent.

"They were hidden inside a statue of Mercury."

Sherry's eyebrows shot up. Stuart nodded. "Yes, I know, the god of thieves. The previous owner of the statue was a known forger; the Mercury itself is almost surely his work. When the statue tipped over, the head broke off because the neck was almost entirely hollowed out, and these were inside."

"Indeed," said Sherry, turning back to study one drawing Stuart hadn't noticed before. Sherry stood up and patted his pockets, frowning. "Hang on, where's a mirror?"

"A mirror?"

Sherry pulled the bell. "A mirror. There's some writing here, very faint, but I believe it's written in a mirror image of proper writing." A servant came over to them. "Bring a small hand mirror and a magnifying lens," Sherry told him. "And ask Bingley to join us."

"Sherry," said Stuart quickly, "this is a very private matter. I'd rather know your thoughts before consulting others."

Sherry waved him off with a sharp glance. "Nonsense. If these drawings are what I suspect—and, I wager, what you suspect; you always were a bit sharper than you let on, young man—Bingley's opinion is the one you want. Devoted his life to Italian art, Bingley has."

"Well, all right then," said Stuart lamely, put in his place as effectively as if he were still Sherry's pupil. Sherry continued to study the drawings until the servant appeared with a small mirror and magnifying lens, Bingley on his heels.

"What is it, what is it?" Bingley's head swiveled back and forth on his scrawny neck. "Something new?"

Sherry indicated the drawings. "Odd bit of work here, Bingley. What do you make of it?"

Bingley almost toppled over, so quickly did he lean over the table. Stuart almost reached out to catch the man, thinking he would fall face-first onto the drawings. "I say, old chap, I say," he murmured reverently. "Quite good this is, quite good. Is it a mirror?"

"I believe so." Sherry crowded over the table with Bingley, and Stuart watched as they tilted the mirror and magnifying lens over various sections of the topmost drawing, speaking to each other and to themselves in phrases and words that meant little to him.

"Why, this is simply extraordinary," declared Bingley after a long while, looking up at Stuart. "Where on earth did you find these?"

Stuart related the story of the hollow statue again. Bingley's head bobbed the whole time. If Sherry was a hedgehog, Bingley was a grasshopper: long-limbed and skinny and ready to leap at any moment. "Mercury, how droll," Bingley murmured at the end. "Fascinating, fascinating. And whose are they?"

"The Mercury belongs to a friend of mine." Stuart hesitated, then moved to the edge of his seat and lowered his voice. "She is being blackmailed for an unknown Italian treasure. She knew the Mercury was worthless, and believes these drawings most likely are as well. But the penalty the blackmailer is threatening is very high. I need to know if these drawings are authentic, or could be construed as a treasure in any way. What say you, Sherry? Bingley?"

Sherry puffed on his pipe. "I say they are. I'm not a scholar of painting, but I've seen a bit in my day, and these are uncanny in their resemblance to other drawings known to be Leonardo's."

Bingley was holding his chin. "Oh dear, oh dear," he muttered. "Well, I think they quite likely are

Leonardo's, but I am not certain. If we take them around to some other experts, we would have a better idea."

"I haven't the time," said Stuart. "I need to know immediately. Someone's life hangs in the balance."

"What have you got yourself into, young man?" asked Sherry with a keen glance. "A woman, blackmailers, mysterious drawings, someone's life in danger?"

Stuart waved it aside. "Then the drawings are good enough to make even an expert suspect they're genuine. I suppose that will have to do. Thank you, Sherry. Mr. Bingley." He reached for the drawings.

"Well, see here, we should discover the truth!" Bingley exclaimed.

Stuart paused, then extracted one of the drawings and handed it to him. "Take this, then. I cannot let them all go—if that proves authentic, I shall bring the others to be examined as well." He rolled them up again, very carefully.

"Those are quite probably priceless," warned Sherry. "You'd best be careful, Mr. Drake."

Stuart flashed him a cocky smile that completely hid his own misgivings. He was going to risk these drawings, but it seemed unavoidable. Unless the other forged artwork also turned out to be filled with lost masterpieces, this was their only hope. He meant to do his utmost to protect the drawings, but if Susan's safety came into question, Stuart knew which way he would go. What were some sketches, lost to the world for centuries anyway, against a girl's life? "I'll do my best, Sherry."

"I was hoping for something stronger," said Sherry dryly.

Stuart nodded. "It's the best I can offer. I'll call on you in a few days to see if you've learned anything."

Stuart left the unreassured Bingley and Sherry and returned to his parents' home, thinking furiously. Somehow they had to get word to the kidnapper that they had found something; Stuart preferred to leave it unclear exactly what. Let the man wonder. Then they would have to lure him out of hiding, some place where he could be ambushed. But he would be on guard against that, and even if they caught him, they would need to find Susan. Catching the man meant little without recovering Susan.

Stuart had only bits and pieces of a plan worked out when he got home. He swung down from the carriage, holding the rolled drawings carefully. They would need an unquestionably secure storage place; perhaps Ware would be able to guard them.

He jogged up the steps, startled to find his mother waiting in the doorway. "Oh, Stuart, darling," she cried, her face pale and worried. "Thank goodness you've come. I knew you would return soon; I begged Madame Griffolino to wait, but she wouldn't, not once the note came. She left it for you, so you could follow."

Stuart thrust the drawings at the footman. "What are you saying, Mother?" He grabbed her shoulders. "What did Charlotte do?"

"She left," said his mother with a hiccup. "She received a note, supposedly from you, but we realized it wasn't because the handwriting wasn't right. Then she went and got her pistol and left." She began fumbling to unfold a piece of paper. Stuart snatched it from her and read it quickly.

"Damn." He crumpled the note. "Damn it! She promised me."

"Oh, but I tried to persuade her!" His mother clasped her hands. "You must go at once—she may be in danger—Stuart!" But Stuart was already gone.

Chapter Seventeen

The house was ordinary, a respectable looking townhouse in a quiet part of town. Charlotte marveled at the cunning of the kidnapper; she would have walked right up to the door and rung the bell without suspicion. Certain she was being watched, she pretended to do just that, although instead of ringing the bell, she tried the door. It opened at once, and she slipped inside, her pistol at the ready beneath her cloak.

The house appeared empty. The walls were bare, the floors were uncovered, and there was a thin film of dust on the newel post; Charlotte stepped out of her slippers to prevent her steps from echoing. Cautiously, peering around corners for ambushes, always listening intently, she searched the ground floor. The whole house had an eerie, deserted air, as if it had been empty a long time. Every now and then the trace of a footprint would show up in the dust on the floor, but it was difficult to follow them since all the drapes were closed.

There was nothing and no one on this floor. Taking

a deep breath, Charlotte picked up her skirt and hurried up the stairs, flattening herself against the wall at the top as she waited for her breath to slow. She surveyed her surroundings with a great deal more trepidation. The hall turned back toward the street, lined with closed doors. Anything could be hiding behind any of them, and she did not look forward to opening them.

Then she heard a faint noise, like footsteps. She inched forward, always keeping an eye on the stairs. As she rounded the corner, she saw light spilling from an open door almost at the end. Expecting a trap, she moved even slower, raising her pistol.

Slowly the room came into sight. It was a large, bright room, painted a cheerful yellow. Someone was in there, walking about. Step, step, step, pause; step, step, step, step, pause. Pacing, perhaps . . . lying in wait. Hardly daring to breathe, Charlotte eased forward and peered into the room.

It was Susan. Charlotte couldn't restrain a gasp, and her niece turned, an expectant smile on her face. At the sight of Charlotte, or perhaps at the sight of her pistol, her eyes rounded, and she clapped her hands to her mouth.

Charlotte pressed a finger to her lips, and after a quick glance inside, ducked into the room, her heart pounding. Here the danger was greatest, she sensed. But Susan was alone in the room; like the rest of the house, it was unfurnished except for a low table, where, incongruously, tea for two was spread. Charlotte moved behind the door and lowered her finger.

"Aunt Charlotte!" burst out Susan, amazed. "Whatever are you doing here?"

"Susan, we have to leave," she said firmly and quietly. "Come now. We can talk later."

"No!" her niece protested. To Charlotte's anxious eyes, she looked perfectly well and unharmed. Her clothing was somewhat bedraggled, but if the only thing the villain had done was deny Susan a lady's maid, Charlotte would fall on her knees in thankful prayer. "I won't! Daniel will wonder where I've gone. I didn't expect to see you so soon, but now you're here, you must stay and meet him. He's wonderful, truly, Aunt Charlotte. We're to marry soon, and might take this house. What do you think? It isn't quite—".

"Tell me about it later," Charlotte interrupted. "I've been so worried about you. How could you simply leave? He's not the man you think he is."

Susan's chin jutted mutinously. "But he is! Oh, you can't think that! Wait and meet him. He's only gone to fetch some biscuits so we can have tea, to see what it would be like to take breakfast in here." Her cheeks turned pink. "This would be my room. Isn't that romantic of him?"

Charlotte had heard enough. The man was out of the house. "We'll come back soon," she said, resorting to outright lies to get Susan safely away. "I do long to meet him, but first I must tell everyone I've found you! Goodness, you gave me such a fright, leaving with only a mysterious note. And you're to be married? How terribly exciting!"

"You—you're not angry?" asked Susan, mouth hanging open in surprise.

Charlotte widened her eyes innocently. "Why, no! You taught me such a lesson; who am I to stand in the way of young love? I've been so lonely and unhappy since you left, please do come with me, for a little while. From now on I shall do my best to be more understanding. Will you forgive me?"

"Oh." Susan frowned, nonplussed. "I suppose."

"I'm so happy to see you again," Charlotte gushed on. "You'll need a wedding dress, in fact a trousseau. These things take time, we must order at once or you'll never have it before the end of the Season."

"Well . . ." Susan hesitated. "Perhaps if I leave a note for Daniel?"

"I'll send one back directly," promised Charlotte, desperate to be out of the house. The moment she had Susan safe, she could let Stuart and Mr. Pitney track down this Daniel. "I've found the best modiste, but she's very exclusive and only considers new customers in the early evening. If we don't hurry, she'll be closed for the day."

"All right, I'll come. But I think there was a scrap of paper here . . ." Susan turned in a circle, looking about the empty room. "I do feel badly about leaving Kent as I did, but I knew you wouldn't approve, and I just felt I had to do something to direct my own life. Don't you agree, like when you left Nice for Italy? Sometimes a dramatic change is vital, and—"

"Susan, please," begged Charlotte, taking Susan's arm and literally pulling her to the door. "I've not seen you in weeks, and you'll be back soon. This dress simply must go. Your maid should be sacked at once." She was babbling, trying to get her reluctant niece moving. Still chewing her lip in indecision, Susan took a few steps toward the door, then stopped abruptly, a wide smile blooming on her face.

"Why, Daniel!" she cried. "Aunt Charlotte has caught up with us at last. But you'll be glad to know she isn't being unreasonable at all."

"I doubt she will be." A slender man with curling dark hair lounged in the doorway, a pistol in his hand. He had dark eyes and olive skin, a prominent nose and regal bearing; a lean and handsome young man with an arrogant air. He was, in fact, exactly as Charlotte would have imagined her late husband forty years ago. She sucked in her breath at the sight of him, the frustrating mystery cleared in an instant. The man stepped into the room, pushing the door closed. "Put the pistol down, Contessa."

Slowly, never taking her unblinking gaze from him, Charlotte laid her pistol on the small tea table. "Good heavens, Daniel," said Susan playfully. "You don't need your pistol now! Aunt Charlotte will give us her consent. Isn't that lovely? We can be married soon."

He glanced at Susan, then at the tea tray. "You did not drink your tea."

"I was waiting for you," she said, beginning to pout. "Daniel—"

"Where is it?" he said, looking straight at Charlotte.

"I've no idea . . . Dante." He jerked a little at the name, but otherwise made no protest.

"His name is Daniel Albright, Aunt Charlotte," said Susan, a considerable amount of her cheer fading. "Have you met before?"

"No," said Charlotte, her gaze still locked with his. "But I have seen him. He is not Daniel Albright, or at least he was not born Daniel Albright. He is Piero de Griffolino's great nephew, Dante d'Alabrini. He came to the villa once, a year ago or more."

"English whore," said Dante calmly, switching to Italian. "He gave it to you and left me nothing. Where is my treasure?"

"I haven't got your treasure," Charlottte answered

in English. "All Piero left me was his collection; worthless, every bit of it, as you no doubt know, since you broke into my house several times to search it."

"I want it back," he said, his jaw tight. "It is mine, and I won't let her leave until you tell me where it is."

Charlotte took a step to the side, toward Susan. "I won't tell you anything until she's safely away. How dare you kidnap my niece to make me give you a treasure I don't even have? How dare you tell her you loved her and wanted to marry her?"

Susan gasped. "What do you mean, Aunt Charlotte?" Without waiting for a reply, she turned on Dante. "Daniel, what treasure?"

He looked at her without emotion. "You should have drunk your tea," he said in English. He spoke it very cleanly, but with an unmistakably foreign lilt.

"It's most likely drugged," said Charlotte.

"Oh, no!" protested Susan. "Daniel wouldn't!"

"Oh?" said Charlotte evenly. "Then where are the biscuits he was supposed to be fetching?" Dante held only the pistol, still aimed at Charlotte.

"Please put the gun down, Daniel," said Susan slowly, her eyes fastened on the pistol even as her hand crept into Charlotte's. Dante looked at her, a flicker of contempt in his eyes.

"Your aunt is going to fetch my treasure at once. You are going to stay here, and drink your tea like a good child." He smiled chillingly, and Susan flinched. "You," said Dante, glaring at Charlotte again, "are to bring the treasure to this house by nightfall. We will not be here. When I see it is delivered, I will let her go to you. You are to tell your lover and his hired dog to stay at home tonight; it was clever of you to stay in and let them scour London for you. I spent many days waiting to see if I could simply snatch you off the street. But then, you've always been able to bend men to your will, haven't you?"

"I am not leaving without Susan," said Charlotte. She spoke as loudly as she dared, both in the hope that Stuart might arrive and hear her. "And if you shoot me, you'll never learn where the treasure is. If there *is* a treasure. Everything he left me was worthless, even the jewels. We've both been fooled. Piero was a forger and a liar; what would stop him from taunting you about some mythical treasure when he gave his own wife paste jewels?"

"Liar," he snapped, taking a step toward her. Hatred burned in his eyes. "You have it—he told me he would give it to you, to spite me! I don't care if he left you a thousand glass diamonds. The treasure was supposed to be mine! I know you have it. I saw the wagons arriving from Kent."

"I don't even know what you're talking about," said Charlotte, although she was beginning to wonder if perhaps the drawings could be authentic. "When did he tell you of this treasure? How do you know it exists?"

"He stole it from a collector in Salzburg. The man wanted it repaired, and Piero restored it, copied it, then left the copy in its place." Dante laughed in contempt. "A forger and a thief! May the old fraud roast with Master Adam." He grew deadly serious again. "Bring it tonight. If it is not here by midnight, she goes with me."

"You won't take her anywhere," declared Charlotte again. Susan clutched at her arm, trembling. "We are leaving this instant. And if you shoot me, you should know my entire inheritance from Piero will be hacked to pieces and burned. I couldn't bear to let anyone else be fooled by his fraud."

"I won't shoot you. I'll shoot her," he said, wagging his pistol from side to side as if to shoot either one of them. Susan whimpered, clinging to Charlotte's shoulder.

Charlotte folded one arm around her niece's shoulder and replied in Italian. "If you hurt her, I'll feed you your testicles. The world could use another castrato."

His eyes narrowed. Then he laughed viciously. "How protective you are of your little cub! If only you were a better mother. She ran off with me after two or three lines of poetry. Such weak, insipid creatures English girls are. The mere hint of romance, and they are easily plucked."

Charlotte said nothing. Susan peered at Dante over her shoulder, her eyes bewildered and afraid. Dante cocked his head, studying them with a lingering, cruel, smile. "Oh, she hated you. So unfair you were, so hypocritical. My thanks, Contessa; her eagerness to escape your tyranny made things much easier. I did not expect she would pack her own things to come with me. Do all English women give themselves so easily? Is that what my uncle liked about you?"

Charlotte held herself immobile, even though his words flooded her with guilt and rage. It was all true, she had failed Susan by being unfair and hypocritical. Susan didn't even know how hypocritical she had been regarding Stuart. Charlotte knew better than to argue the point with him, though, and expose any weakness. She needed to be calm and clear in mind.

Dante pivoted on his heel suddenly. He waved the pistol, forcing them away from the door and behind the tea table. "I will have my treasure, Contessa," he said. "Let us see what it takes to convince you."

Stuart fairly flew through the streets. He tried without success at various intervals to hail a hackney. It seemed an eternity before he reached the quiet, respectable street where his mother said Charlotte had gone. *Damn that woman*, he thought furiously; she couldn't wait an hour, but must charge off by herself to confront a madman. When he got his hands on her, he would shake her, and then hold her close, then shake her again, then hold her some more . . .

He stopped to get his breath when he reached the house. The door was ajar, and he slipped inside, all his nerves tingling. For a moment he listened; a faint murmur of voices, from upstairs. He ran lightly up the stairs, moving as quietly as he could under the circumstances. The upper hall turned away from the stairs, lined with doors. Cautiously, ready to duck at any moment, Stuart inched forward, and almost gave himself away as he rounded the corner and saw a figure hovering outside a slightly open door. *"Terrance?"*

His father turned, one finger to his lips. Obediently silent, Stuart came up beside him, and listened for a moment. Charlotte's voice, in clear, ringing English, and a man's voice, soft and foreign. *The Italian*, he thought in a mixture of elation and alarm. They had found the kidnapper! And Charlotte was in that room with him. Terrance waved one hand, and Stuart leaned forward.

"There are two ladies," whispered Terrance, his lips barely moving next to Stuart's ear. "He is threatening them, I think. Your friend is speaking clearly, but I cannot make out what the man is saying."

"He's Italian," Stuart breathed in reply. "How long have you been here?"

"I followed your friend from the house."

Stuart made a note to wonder about that later. "Have you any idea how he's armed?"

"I saw him arrive. A pistol."

Stuart nodded. "We have to get him out of there. Once he's away from the ladies—"

"Did you bring a pistol?" interrupted Terrance.

Stuart grimaced and shook his head. Terrance frowned, but not in irritation. "What will we do when he comes out?"

Stuart glanced down. Terrance carried his ebony cane, as usual, his long bony fingers wrapped around the lion's head knob. "Does it have a sword tip?"

Terrance followed his gaze. "Yes."

"I'll make a disturbance. There's a tall clock at the top of the stairs, I can shove it over the railing. Conceal yourself behind the door; when he comes into the hall and starts toward me, take him from behind with the sword. Mother said Charlotte brought a pistol as well. If she's able, she'll no doubt come out with it drawn."

"He has a pistol!" Terrance whispered harshly. "What if he simply shoots you?"

"Take him from behind with the sword," repeated Stuart grimly. "Do it. I'll take care of myself. Just make sure he doesn't get back into that room."

Terrance stared at him for a moment, almost incredulously. Stuart realized he had just had a serious conversation with his father for the first time in years, and he jerked his head toward the door, unsettled.

Think about that later, too, he told himself, moving quietly back down the hall to the carved clock. It had stopped, its weights hanging motionless, its warped back sloping against the wall. He managed to squeeze his hands behind it, and braced himself to pull it over. With any luck, it would crash over the railing and fall to the ground floor of the hall; in the worst case it would tip over and still make a tremendous noise. He tensed to pull, and looked up to give Terrance the signal . . .

Only to watch in horror as Terrance pushed open the door of the room and stepped inside, his cane outstretched.

"Stop, you!" To Charlotte's shock, Terrance Drake charged into the room, his gray hair standing up, his eyes wild. He brandished his cane at Dante, and a sword tip flashed in the sunlight. "How dare you assault these women?"

Dante stared in amazement for half a second, then raised his pistol and fired. The gunshot almost drowned out Susan's scream, and she collapsed, dragging Charlotte down with her. Terrance cried out. His cane clattered to the floor as he pivoted on his good leg and crumpled into a heap. Down on one knee, tangled with a weeping Susan, Charlotte couldn't see where he had been hit. Dante lowered his pistol and smirked at her. "Old fool," he said.

"What the—?" Stuart appeared in the doorway, taking in the scene in a second. With a curse, he charged Dante even as Dante lifted the pistol to smash Stuart's face. Charlotte surged forward, seizing the tea pot from the table and flinging it straight at the Italian.

It hit him in the back of the shoulder, jarring the pistol from his hand, and fell to the floor with a burst of shattered porcelain just as Stuart clipped Dante in the waist, taking them both to the floor.

Susan screamed again, and Charlotte shoved her down behind the tea table, diving for her own pistol. The two men rolled over, and Charlotte saw the glitter of polished metal as Dante raised a knife above Stuart's back. With one fluid motion, Charlotte cocked her pistol, sighted down the barrel, and fired.

The blast almost broke her wrist. Faintly, her ears ringing, she heard a man screaming. She dropped her pistol and turned to Susan, who was sprawled in the broken crockery, her hands over her ears. "Are you hurt?" Charlotte cried. Wide-eyed, Susan gave a tiny shake of her head. Charlotte was already scrambling over the remains of the tea dishes and the table toward Stuart and Dante, choking on the lingering smell of gunpowder.

Dante was lying in a fetal ball, sobbing. Blood dribbled from between his fingers where he clutched his lower arm. Excellent: she had hit him. A small, lethal dagger glinted on the other side of the room, several feet away. She ignored him and kept going.

Stuart was lying flat on his back, arms thrown wide and eyes closed. Charlotte stopped cold. "Stuart," she gasped. "Stuart, no!" She hauled his head into her lap, leaning close to see if he still breathed, pulling frantically at his jacket and waistcoat to see if his heart still beat. Her hands were shaking too badly to tell. "No!" she wailed.

His eyes fluttered opened. "Jesus, Mary, and Joseph, you have nerves of iron," he said in a raspy voice.

"Oh!" Her voice caught on a sob, and she kissed

him, hard. Although he still lay motionless across her lap, he returned her kiss, until Charlotte had to stop for another sob. "I thought I'd killed you!"

"No," he said, pushing himself into a sitting position and rubbing the back of his head. "Although you may have deafened me. I've never had a pistol fired within a foot of my head before."

"Don't tease me now," she cried, clinging to him. "I can't bear it . . ."

His face changed. "Shh." He pulled her into his arms, holding her tightly against him. "I'm fine," he whispered. "You saved the day."

"I didn't," she wept into his shoulder. "If I hadn't been so harsh to Susan, she wouldn't have been so susceptible to him. If I had listened to you, there would have been guards around the house and he never could have broken in and carried her away. If I hadn't been so suspicious of you—"

"Then you never would have kidnapped me at gunpoint and brought me back to London, and we never would have found her," he finished for her. "Remind me to thank you later for not shooting me on the way to town. I didn't think you had the nerve, but I admit my mistake here and now."

"Oh!" She slumped against him, then almost immediately sat up. "Susan? Susan! Where—?"

"I'm here," said Susan from her other side. She was still pale, and avoided looking to where Dante lay in a sobbing heap. Charlotte folded her niece in her arms as Stuart pushed himself off the floor. She heard the murmur of his voice as he talked to his father, and the deeper rumble of Mr. Drake's reply.

"Aunt Charlotte? I'm sorry." Susan's voice was

muffled. "I can't believe I was so stupid and believed him. I'm sorry I thought so ill of you."

"Hush, it doesn't matter." Charlotte cradled her close, shaking with delayed terror. She was dimly aware of Stuart turning Dante over, and strapping up his arm with something. Footsteps sounded on the stairs, and loud voices. People filled the room slowly, the neighbors who had heard the shot, the watchman they had summoned, a bunch of curious passersby, and a surgeon who happened to live nearby. Somehow Stuart sorted it all out, got rid of the curious and the neighbors, sent the watchman for help to take Dante away, and set the surgeon to tending both gunshot wounds. Through it all Charlotte held her niece, who didn't seem inclined to let go, either.

When the furor died down, Stuart came back to them, his boots crunching on the broken tea service. "Are you all right?" he asked, kneeling down beside them.

Charlotte nodded, smoothing Susan's hair with one hand. "Now I am." She looked up at him, alive and well and unhurt, his face taut with concern. Susan's limp figure was draped over her lap and shoulder, making her back ache. Her ears still hurt, and her wrist throbbed. She couldn't recall being so happy in all her life, and tears stung her eyes. "Now I am perfectly fine."

Chapter Eighteen

Stuart bundled Charlotte and Susan into one cab, and his father into another with the surgeon, staying behind himself to see to Dante. Charlotte could only give him a grateful look; there were too many people around to say anything. "I'll see you shortly," he said, rapping on the roof of the carriage. Charlotte smiled in reply as the driver snapped the whip. Stuart would take care of this as well as he had managed everything else, and she hoped Mr. Drake had gotten a good view of his son handling everything so competently.

By the time they arrived, Mr. Drake had already been taken upstairs to his rooms, and the house echoed with Mrs. Drake's cries of alarm and the running footsteps of servants. The hall was deserted, and Charlotte simply led Susan up the stairs to her own room. For now, all she wanted was peace and quiet.

Susan let go of her long enough to look around when the household uproar was muffled behind the closed door. "Aunt Charlotte? Is this . . . is this Mr. Drake's house?"

Charlotte nodded. "His parents'. We came to

London as soon as I realized you were gone, and his mother invited me to stay."

"Oh." Susan looked at her sideways, as if uncertain how to take that. "I thought you did not like him."

Charlotte flushed. "I accused him of running away with you. I thought, after the way you went to him at the Martins' . . ." She paused to steady her voice. "I blamed him for your disappearance, and when I realized my mistake, he proved himself a greater gentleman than I ever expected." *And a better man than I deserved,* she added to herself.

"Well." Susan cleared her throat. She sat on the chaise beside Charlotte, but an arm's length away. "It is terrible to be so wrong about someone, isn't it?"

"Yes." They sat in silence for a moment. Charlotte was resolved not to press Susan for an explanation yet. She hadn't gone through weeks of hell just to make the girl hate her again. "Are you truly unhurt?" she asked hesitantly at last. "He didn't . . . harm you in any way, did he?"

Susan fiddled with a fold of her skirt. "No. We told people I was his sister whose husband had died." She stopped with a shuddering breath. "But he didn't do anything to me. Nothing."

Charlotte closed her eyes. "Thank God."

"Aunt Charlotte?" Susan's fingers shook as they pleated and creased her skirt. "Are you terribly angry at me?" She sounded like a small girl, lonely and unsure, and peeked up uncertainly.

Charlotte shook her head. "No. Your actions I ascribe to youth and inexperience. I know, all too well, how it is to be young and feel as though no one understands you or respects you. I know how easy it is to fall under the spell of someone who offers to take you away from your quiet, circumscribed life and show you a world of excitement and wonder." She paused. "I blame myself more than I blame you. I never suspected the thief would use you to get what he wanted. I had warning after warning that he wanted something of mine, yet I ignored them all because I couldn't face opening those crates and dragging out the ghosts of a life I wanted to forget. I never . . ." Her voice faltered. "I never dreamed he would touch you."

"He said you would send me away to school," said Susan, beginning to sniffle. "That night, when we argued, he heard us. He climbed up the trellis after you left, and told me he had traveled in Italy and had heard stories of you, that you were a cold-hearted woman who never tolerated anyone who opposed you. I began to be frightened, for I had said very unkind things to you, and you had been so angry with me at the Martins'! He seemed so kind and sympathetic, and when I said I did not want to go away to school but had nowhere else to go, he said he could help me. He told me . . ." Her voice began to waver. "He told me I was the loveliest girl he had seen in England, and he felt so terrible that I would be shut away in some terrible school where the girls were all required to do embroidery and make soap all day. He made it sound as if I would be in prison, and I—I had been so cruel to you . . ." She scrubbed her eyes. "I didn't know how I could face you again, after the things I had said, and I was sure I would be punished for being so rude. He was very handsome, and he knew all Romeo's lines, and somehow, before I knew it, I was climbing down the trellis with him."

"Oh, Susan," whispered Charlotte, putting out a tentative hand. "I could never send you away! It's more awful than you can know, to be alone in the world at your age. I would never do that to you . . . as my father did to me."

"What?" Susan looked up, her eyes red-rimmed.

Charlotte bit her lip. "When I was your age, much the same thing happened to me," she confessed. "A handsome man, very elegant and charming, proposed to me. He said he would take me away from my strict father and we would live in grand style in London. But when my father offered him money, he left me without a backward glance. And my father was so furious that I had run away, he sent me to Paris with instructions that I was not to come back until sent for."

"But Papa said . . ." Susan's voice trailed off, bewildered. "He said you liked traveling."

Charlotte hesitated. "I suppose I became used to it. And I did enjoy some of it immensely. But it was not the life I would have chosen. I never saw my brother or my father again."

"Oh." Susan's eyes were round. "Never?" Charlotte shook her head. Tears streaked down Susan's cheeks. "You're really not going to send me away? Even after I was so spiteful and ran away and caused you so much trouble? You don't want to go back to Italy or France and not be bothered with me?"

"Oh, Susan, never," declared Charlotte passionately. "I left all that for you, the moment I got word of your father's death. All I wanted to do was be a good aunt to you, and hopefully, your friend."

"I'm sorry," whispered Susan. "I'm very sorry. I never thought you would stay. When he said you would send me away to school, I believed him because I had thought all along that you would get tired of me and want to go back to Paris or Rome or some other exciting place and I would be left with a governess or sent to some dreadful finishing school."

"I'm staying," vowed Charlotte, hugging her again. "Even if we don't always get on very well."

Susan sniffled some more, wiping her eyes with the back of her hand. "Did you really kidnap Mr. Drake at gunpoint when you thought he'd run off with me?"

Charlotte smiled a little. "Oh, yes. He was very difficult to frighten, though."

Susan gave a watery, uncertain smile in reply. "I imagine so. Was he very angry with you?"

Charlotte cleared her throat. How on earth was she ever to tell Susan about Stuart? And what *should* she tell her? Perhaps that was better left until another time. "I expect he's got over it by now."

"You did shoot Daniel, when he would have stabbed Mr. Drake." Susan grew quiet again, her face very pale. "Thank you, Aunt Charlotte. For looking for me."

Charlotte folded her into a fierce hug. "You don't need to thank me."

It took some time to get everything sorted out. Dante was finally taken away; he had shot a gentleman, if nothing else. Stuart didn't know how far Charlotte would want to pursue kidnapping charges, now that she had Susan back safe and sound. Perhaps it would be best to keep it quiet for the sake of the girl's reputation. Dante, who still didn't even know just what he had been seeking, raved to the authorities about his stolen treasure, but Stuart had dismissed it all as the ramblings of a madman. Once the constable hauled Dante away at last, Stuart walked back across town, back to Charlotte.

When he finally reached his parents' home, no one opened the door. Stuart rang twice, then knocked, and finally a maid threw it open, looking flustered. "Oh, Mr. Drake, sir," she said, bobbing a curtsey. "Mr. Brumble told me not to admit anyone but you."

"I think the danger has passed." Stuart closed the door behind him. "How is my father?"

"La, sir, he's fine. Mrs. Drake's already quizzed the surgeon, who said it wasn't fatal—" A sharp voice echoed down the hall, and the maid flushed. "Your pardon, sir, but I'm to fetch a poultice." She curtseyed once more and scurried toward the kitchen. Stuart climbed the stairs, hesitating at the top. His father had been shot; he should inquire after his health. A door opened, and he heard his mother's voice, firm and brisk, directing servants. Stuart deliberated, then turned toward Charlotte's room. Terrance was in good hands, and there was nothing Stuart could do for him anyway.

"Come in." Charlotte and her niece were sitting side by side on the chaise when he opened the door.

"I came to see you were both well," he said, then stopped. Charlotte had her arm around Susan, who looked tired and subdued but happy to be back with her aunt. It gave him a strange feeling in the pit of his stomach; Charlotte didn't need him anymore. What if her joy at Susan's return eclipsed her feelings for him? What if Susan's presence made their whole relationship awkward and uncomfortable for her? If she had to choose between him and Susan . . .

"We are," Charlotte answered his question, turning a brilliant smile on him. "All thanks to you." Every trace of anxiety had been wiped from her face; she was radiantly happy, fairly beaming. And Stuart knew then that whatever it took to win her, he would do, because he wanted her looking at him that way for the rest of his life.

He cleared his throat. "Not all, I assure you."

"Aunt Charlotte," said Susan, lifting her head from Charlotte's shoulder. "May I have a word with Mr. Drake?"

"Oh . . . of course," murmured Charlotte, surprised. Stuart braced himself, wondering what the girl wanted to say. She crossed the room, motioning him aside.

"Mr. Drake," Susan began, then paused, blushing.

"Yes?"

"I've been thinking," she said in a rush. "I owe you a great thanks for all your help—I was really so stupid—and I can never repay you." Stuart tensed as she glanced at him under her eyelashes, then back at Charlotte, who watched them with ill-concealed curiosity. Susan lowered her voice even more. "But I think I owe you another apology for the way I acted in Tunbridge Wells. My behavior was . . . well, childish. And it was partly because I was jealous of my aunt." Stuart started in surprise. Susan flushed. "I could tell you thought she was very beautiful the first night you met her, and it just didn't seem fair. So I threw myself at you, at the Martins' party, and I realize how foolish that must have seemed to you."

"Impulsive," said Stuart gently.

Susan grimaced. "I shall have to overcome that tendency, I suppose. But thank you for helping Aunt Charlotte."

"It was my honor," he said. "I owed it to you, for

making an offer of marriage when my heart was not fully engaged. You deserve more."

"I didn't want to believe she was right about that, too," whispered Susan.

"Miss Tratter . . . it is worth waiting for," Stuart murmured. She glanced up uncertainly. "Someone who loves you. That's what your aunt wanted for you all along."

She turned bright pink. "I realize that now. Thank you, Mr. Drake." She tugged a thin chain from under the high neckline of her dress. His mother's ring dangled from it. Susan unclasped the necklace and handed the ring to him, blushing even harder. "I meant to give this back to you."

Stuart took the ring with a rueful sigh as Charlotte came to them. Susan turned to her aunt. "May I go sit in the garden, Aunt Charlotte? I would like to—to be alone for a while."

"Of course," said Charlotte at once. "I'll be here." Susan nodded and slipped out the door, head down, leaving them alone.

"I think we shall get on better now," said Charlotte, watching her go. "I shall try to remember more what it is like to be young and full of dreams, and she might appreciate some of my caution, having experienced rashness."

Stuart nodded, suddenly at a loss. "I am sure she will."

Charlotte bit her lip, seemingly as uncertain as he was. "She ran off because she thought I would never stay in England. She was afraid I would send her to school, or leave her with a governess and go back to Italy."

"Ah." Stuart cursed his tongue, whose glibness had

gotten him in and out of trouble his entire life, for falling mute now. Now that he finally knew what he wanted, he couldn't find the words to express it. "It must be an enormous relief to you," he said. "Having her back, that is."

She smiled again, that beaming smile of pure joy. "And it is all thanks to you. I could never have found her without your help, Stuart, and I could—" She stopped, uncertainty flickering in her face. "I could never thank you enough," she finished quietly.

He forced a quick grin. "Your happiness is all the thanks I need." His grin faded, and they stood there staring at each other for a moment. Then Stuart took a deep breath, and plunged ahead. He had meant to wait, but suddenly found he couldn't. "Charlotte." He took her hand and studied it. "I've been thinking of us, and how we shall go on."

Her smile faded. "I see."

"It would be wrong for us to continue as lovers," he said. "With Susan in your house, it wouldn't be proper. I commend you for stepping in to raise her, and fully understand that you must adhere to respectability for her sake, as well as for your own."

"Yes," she said, her voice soft—with regret? "I must."

"But neither can I give you up." He looked up, meeting her wary gaze. "I cannot promise you much, but in every way I can, I swear to make you happy." He drew a deep breath, and gripped her hand even though she was gripping his even harder. "You took my heart some time ago, and I would like you to take my name, as well as myself, if you will have me."

"You—you want to marry me?" Charlotte stammered.

Stuart grinned a bit hesitantly. "I realize my past

isn't very respectable, but I shall take your example to heart, and reform—" He stopped at her stricken expression.

"But Stuart, you don't know. Last night, that horrible man, he threatened to say things about me. I fear my own reputation . . ."

"Your reputation is safe from him." Stuart clasped both her hands between his. "The last I saw Mr. Hyde-Jones, he was contemplating an extended tour of the Continent."

"What did you do?" she demanded, searching his face.

"Not half as much as I wanted to do. Suffice it to say, he shan't trouble you again." She was stiff a moment longer, then relaxed with a sigh of relief. "Have you any other objections?" he prodded with a smile, trying to hide how anxious he was about her reply.

"What about Oakwood Park?" Charlotte asked, her voice wobbling. "Oh, Stuart, I don't want you to lose it, not after all the work you've put into it—I know how much it means to you."

"Charlotte." He touched her lips. "I have to sell it; I can't afford it. I wanted it because I had nothing of my own, nothing to be proud of, anyway. And I do—did—love having my own property, and I did have such high hopes for it. But I won't lie awake at night regretting losing it as long as you are lying beside me."

"But Stuart—I have only a modest income. We could live at Honeyfield until Susan marries, but what then? Where would we go? What—?"

"Charlotte!" He smiled ruefully. "I intend to see if Ware might have a position I could take, perhaps managing one of his smaller estates. And if you prefer to live at Honeyfield, we'll do that. I'm not afraid of economy; Lord knows I'm used to it by now." He pulled her closer, resting his chin on top of her head. "And if all else fails . . ." He lifted one shoulder, his eyes falling on the paintings and statues stacked on the far side of the room. Someone had brought them up from the hall. "We could always open an antiques shop."

"What? They're all forgeries!" Charlotte protested.

"An antiques shop for those who can't afford authentic pieces, then. 'Tasteful Frauds for the Customer of Limited Means,'" he suggested with a crooked grin. Charlotte laughed, wiping her eyes as she cast aside her doubts and fears. Somehow, together, they would think of something. They had both survived too long alone not to be able to make their way together now.

A knock at the door interrupted a few minutes later. Stuart growled in frustration, but Charlotte giggled. "Yes?"

A maid appeared. "Your pardon, ma'am, but Madame da Ponte has come to call. And your father is asking to see you, Mr. Drake, sir."

"Show Madame da Ponte into the drawing room. I'll come down at once." The maid nodded and left, and Charlotte looked up at Stuart. "How is your father?"

He shrugged. "Fine, I'm sure. Mother's taking care of him."

"You didn't see him yet?" she gasped.

Stuart looked down at her. "I had to see you first," he said simply. Another luminous smile lit her face. Of all the times he had seen her, in all her various moods, she had never been more beautiful than now, even though her dress was dirty and disheveled and tiny bits of straw still clung to her hair. She was happy, he realized, completely happy for the first time in their acquaintance.

"Give him my thanks," she said. "I was never so astonished to see him charge into that room."

"As was I." Stuart frowned. "We had agreed he would wait in the hall while I lured Dante out of the room, then disarm him with his sword."

"Lure him out? How?"

"By knocking down the old clock. Dante would never have seen Terrance standing behind the door, and it would have been quite simple for Terrance to put the sword to his back."

"But Dante would have seen you," said Charlotte slowly. "And he would have shot you."

Stuart shrugged. "Likely he would have missed. I didn't plan to stand still and invite him to take aim."

Charlotte looked up at him. "He might not have missed. Your father didn't want to see you die, Stuart."

Stuart thought about that. Could Terrance have gone into that room to keep Stuart from risking his life? Stuart hadn't considered it possible at the time; still didn't, to be honest. Stuart would have endangered himself without hesitation to save Charlotte and Susan, but could Terrance have endangered himself to save Stuart? It defied twenty years of experience.

"Well, either way, it's a good thing the bloody blighter's in Newgate." He squeezed her hand. "You'd best see to Lucia before she begins breaking all the other statues looking for more hidden treasure." He paused. "Those drawings are most likely authentic, Charlotte; a real Italian treasure."

Her eyes widened. "Goodness."

"What shall we do with them?"

Charlotte lifted her hands helplessly. "I don't know. Lucia is probably right, they should be returned to Italy in some way."

"I agree." He released her hand. "We can decide that later. A few more days won't hurt, after all these years."

Charlotte shook her head and smiled, turning to leave. At the door she looked back. "What did Susan give you, just now?"

Stuart dug the ring out of his pocket and handed it to her. "It was my mother's. She gave it to me to give to my bride when I left London."

Charlotte's smile faded. Stuart took her hand, folding her fingers around the ring and holding them closed. "I gave it to Susan because my nerve was about to break," he said quietly. "Even before I met you, I knew it was a mistake to marry a girl I didn't love. But I thought that if I just got it over and done with, everything would be fine." He kissed her. "If not for this ring, though, we never would have ended up here." Her brow wrinkled in confusion. Stuart began chuckling as he thought it through. "Because this is what I broke into your house to retrieve, which brought you to my lodging, where we realized how perfect we are for each other—"

"Oh, really?" Now her eyebrows shot up in amusement. Grinning widely, Stuart went on.

"And then you assumed I was to blame for Susan's disappearance because you couldn't see how *anyone* could resist me—"

"Stop!" she protested, laughing.

"And then I helped you look for her because *I* cannot resist *you*," he finished. "And here we are, just as we were meant to be."

Her face softened, and he just had to kiss her again.

Smiling once more, she left, and Stuart went down the hall to his father's suite and tapped on the door, girding himself for anything but too happy to worry about it much. Quite likely he was about to be disowned once and for all, after having gotten Terrance shot. His father's valet opened the door. "How is my father?" he asked.

"Resting. You may come in."

Stuart hesitated. "If it won't tire him overmuch."

The valet shook his head, and Stuart stepped into the room. Terrance was reclining in a chair near the fireplace, his leg propped on another chair. It was draped with a quilt, hiding the bandages. He was staring out the window, his eyes half closed, his complexion pasty gray.

"I came to see how you are," Stuart began. The moment of cooperation at the vacant house seemed long ago. There was too much between them, after all, to expect one instance of accord to sweep it all away. "And to express my thanks for your help. Madame Griffolino and Miss Tratter send their profound thanks as well."

"She is Henry Tratter's daughter," said Terrance. "Is she not?"

"Yes," said Stuart, surprised. "And Susan is her brother's daughter."

Terrance nodded, his brow still lowered moodily. "I recognized her pistol; I gave that set to her father myself. Tratter and I were best mates at one time. A good man, Tratter was, uncompromising in his beliefs and proudly so. But he died with one regret. He sent his daughter away in a moment of anger, and repented of it the rest of his life."

Stuart shifted his weight. This was not what he had expected. "He never wrote to her. She believes he never forgave her."

"He was too proud to admit he was wrong. For years he hoped she would write to him, asking to return, but she never did. Then, when it was too late, he did try to find her, but she had vanished. The relations he sent her to had no idea where she had gone, and by then he was too ill to search."

"Her brother knew," said Stuart sharply. "If he had once humbled his pride and asked his son—"

"Yes, yes." Terrance sliced one hand in dismissal. "He did not. It was her place to come to him, to beg his forgiveness."

"Unfortunately she had as much pride and will as he did."

Terrance sighed. "It would seem so." He glanced down at his leg. "She shot that villain."

"Ah yes. Right in the hand, as he was raising his knife to my throat."

"Hmmph," Terrance grunted. "Good eye."

"Steady hand," added Stuart.

Terrance snorted—laughter?—and finally glanced at Stuart. "You're in love with her, aren't you?" Caught completely off guard, Stuart nodded. What did it matter to Terrance whom Stuart loved, or if he even fell in love at all? "Does she love you?" Again, Stuart nodded, slowly, warily. "Then you had better marry her, before someone else does," said Terrance. "She's got a spine, that one does."

"Yes. She does." Stuart cleared his throat. "I have already asked her to marry me, and happily she has agreed."

"Good." Terrance pursed his lips. "You may have

your income back. A good wife will keep a man out of trouble. Tell her she has my gratitude. She saved both of us, most likely, not to mention the girl." Terrance turned back to the window, and Stuart, thinking the interview at an end—and a better end than he had ever expected—made to leave. "And she has also reminded me that anger can be misplaced," Terrance went on. "Tratter sent her away, punishing her in place of the man who deserved it. He knew that, you know; tell her he knew. When his temper had cooled, he knew she had been taken advantage of, and that he had failed to protect her. By then it was too late; he had committed himself . . . but he knew the fault was not hers alone." His fingers twitched restlessly, then he waved at a chair. "Sit down."

Slowly Stuart sank onto it. He had a great apprehension about what Terrance would say next, and wasn't at all sure he wanted to hear it, not now.

"You are not my son." Stuart tried to keep his face impassive; he already knew it, after all. "You are not," added Terrance with a sharp look, "my father's son, either. I know you have held this belief for some time, and that many other people do as well."

Stuart sat, tense with surprise and dread. What, then, would the truth be?

"You," said Terrance, "are my brother's son."

Stuart blinked, searching his memory. "Your brother? He died before I was born."

Terrance nodded, leaning into the pillows behind him. "Eight months, to be precise. He seduced your mother, who was a young, trusting girl. She had always been in awe of him, and he used her for his own pleasure. No doubt she wasn't the first he had so used, but she was the first with a doting father.

"When she found herself with child, her father went to our father and demanded that Nigel marry her. Belmaine, to everyone's surprise, agreed, and ordered Nigel to make amends. But Nigel was proud, and he laughed at the suggestion. She was a farmer's daughter; he was the heir to Belmaine. Our father was angry, and gave him a day to come to his senses or be cut off.

"Nigel, you may think, was despicable. But our father had raised him that way, to think he was above the governance of others. Belmaine thought he could still control his son, but Nigel was a man in his own image, who would not listen to anyone. When Nigel heard he must marry the girl or lose his allowance, he stormed from the house. He declared he would go to London and find himself a wealthy bride, and as Belmaine couldn't completely disinherit him, Nigel would simply wait it out. He rode off, Belmaine thundering at his back about duty and honor."

Terrance paused. "The next morning, Nigel was found at the bottom of the ravine. His horse must have taken fright, for they had both gone over and broken their necks. Belmaine was devastated; his heir was dead. The farmer, seeing his chance of saving his daughter's honor fading, came to Belmaine again. He would accept two thousand pounds for his daughter to start a new life somewhere else with her child. Now, though, my father wanted that child. It was Nigel's child, the next true viscount. If the girl left, the child would vanish with her."

"So you married her," said Stuart almost inaudibly. Terrance smiled, one of the first real smiles Stuart could recall seeing on his face.

"I had loved her since she was fifteen," he said

softly. "She was a beautiful girl, so gentle and so merry. She never looked at me again, when Nigel began to pay her notice. I think she did love him, for she was never the same after he died. But I loved her, and I married her."

Stuart frowned at his feet. Under those circumstances, might he not hate the child, too? The proof of his wife's love for another man. If it were Charlotte . . . He ground one palm against his burning eyes. Would he be able to stop loving Charlotte, even if she carried another lover's child? Stuart didn't know, but he suspected, deep down, that he would never be able to look at the child with affection.

And his mother! His poor mother, left brokenhearted and married to another man for the sake of her child. She had never loved Terrance or Belmaine; all her sacrifice had been for him.

"We might have muddled through, she and I," continued Terrance in the same faraway tone. Long-lost happiness lent his features warmth, and made him appear younger, almost handsome. "She wanted you, desperately, and I wanted her to be happy. Once she bore the child, I told myself, we would begin again. We would have our own children, and she would forget my brother. I waited; I said nothing, did nothing, waiting for you to be born, for her to turn to me at last. But she never did. She died in childbed, leaving me to raise my brother's bastard as my own."

The bottom dropped out of Stuart's world. *"What?"*

Terrance looked away. "You were an infant and needed a mother. Amelia was a poor relation of your mother's. Belmaine approved, and the marriage was hushed up to allow us to pass the child off as hers." Stuart sat like stone. Terrance plucked at the quilt over his knees. "You are the image of Nigel. All my hatred of him was diverted onto you. He stole the girl I loved, seduced her and ruined her, and then his child killed her. When you were young, I tried not to see him in you, and to raise you not to be like him. But every time I looked at you, it was Nigel I saw instead, and when Belmaine suggested you and Amelia live at Barrowfield, I agreed. It was kinder to all of us."

"Why did no one tell me?" Stuart demanded without heat.

Terrance closed his eyes. "Amelia could not have children, we learned. If she had borne a child, my child, we might have told you the truth. But then, perhaps not; it was too cruel to shame them, the mother who conceived you in sin and the woman who raised you when she knew she would never have a son of her own body."

Stuart tried to absorb it. It made sense, in a way. The affection his grandfather had always had for his mother—Amelia, he corrected. The distance between his parents, and the bonds between them. Why Terrance had taken him to the ravine where his natural father must have died, and asked not to be called "Father." And most of all, why Terrance had turned him out; the rumors of Eliza Pennyworth's disgrace must have seemed like the ultimate insult to Terrance, who had already borne indignity upon indignity for Stuart's sake.

A soft noise behind him disrupted his thoughts. Stuart turned to see his mother, standing in the shadows. She held a tray in her hands, and her face was pale. "That's almost true," she said quietly. Terrance started at her voice, then put up one hand as if to hold her back.

"Amelia—please—"

"Terrance, did you really think it was because I couldn't have children?" She came forward. "I would have told Stuart years ago. It is his history, and his right to know. But you wouldn't allow it, because you still loved her, and I didn't have the courage to face that." She turned to Stuart, and her chin wobbled once.

"I do love you as my own child, and did so before I knew there would be no others. You were an innocent child, and bore no shame or guilt for what Nigel or Aimee did." Stuart said nothing, turning over his real parents' names in his mind: *Nigel and Aimee.*

"I did not still love Aimee," said Terrance.

Amelia turned to him. "You did," she corrected softly. "You always did. You never noticed me, even after we married, because you had no room in your heart for anyone but her. I married you because I loved you, but you never would have looked at me if not . . . if not for Stuart."

Stuart got to his feet. This was outside his story, and he didn't need to hear it now. "Excuse me," he murmured, heading to the door. He paused at his mother's side, and kissed her lightly on the cheek. "Thank you," he said.

"I am so sorry, Stuart. For so many things. I tried to be a good mother to you." Her smile was weak and full of sadness, and Stuart understood. She had been torn, forced to choose between the husband she loved, but who did not love her back, and the only child she would ever have, who wasn't even hers. Stuart glanced back at Terrance, who was still staring at Amelia with a stunned expression. What must the man be feeling, he wondered, having learned he had spent his whole life throwing away happiness and hanging on to bitterness.

"Amelia, I never knew . . ." he heard Terrance say as he closed the door. His mind awhirl with what he had just learned, Stuart went in search of Charlotte.

He found her in the drawing room, far from alone. Angus Whitley was fidgeting at Lucia's side. As Stuart paused in the doorway, the bell rang, announcing yet another guest. Whitley glanced up, and leaped out of his seat when he saw Stuart, practically sprinting across the room.

"Drake, thank God," he said fervently. "All's well, I trust? Come in, come in, take my seat. I've got to take my leave, an appointment, you know, haven't seen my parents in weeks."

"What's the matter?" Stuart glanced at Lucia. "I thought you were engaged here."

"Yes, well . . . The thing is, you see, Drake, she's quite overbearing," explained Whitley in a whispered rush. "Never lets a fellow take the lead, if you take my meaning. Exhausting work, keeping up with her."

"Well, I shouldn't let it worry you," said Stuart, trying not to laugh. "How old are you now, Whit?"

His friend's eyebrows shot up. "Thirty next month. Why?"

Stuart shook his head, grinning. "Nothing of import. I'll make your good-byes, if you wish."

"There's a mate, Drake." Whitley clapped him on the shoulder and slipped out the door, casting one more furtive glance at Lucia, who was deep in conversation with Charlotte and didn't seem to care if Whitley left. Stuart started across the room toward the two women, only to be stopped by a familiar voice.

"Good God, Drake, tell me that's not the woman

who's been sleeping in my bed," said Philip, staring. Frowning, Stuart twisted to follow his gaze.

"It was my bed at the . . ." But Philip was looking past Charlotte to Lucia, who sat in voluptuous profile. "Ah, no, not Lucia da Ponte. The woman with her, the shorter beauty."

Philip didn't take his eyes from Lucia. "Excellent. Well done. Introduce me." He started toward the two women, and Stuart followed obediently, thinking that Lord Philip had returned in Pip's place. The young man about town had grown into a young nobleman.

Charlotte sensed him approaching and turned with a smile. With something resembling a naughty smirk, Stuart bowed briefly. "Lucia, Charlotte, may I present to you Lord Philip Lindeville, an old friend of mine? Philip, the Contessa de Griffolino and Signora da Ponte, lately of Milan."

"Milan," said Lord Philip, bowing. "A marvelous city."

"Indeed," said Lucia, eyeing him with interest. They were of a height, and shared similar coloring. Lord Philip had dark hair, slightly long and wavy, dark eyes, and a lean build that spoke of youth and vigor; he was a darker version of his older brother, the Duke of Ware. He looked exceptionally well next to Lucia, Charlotte noticed. "Were you recently there, my lord?" Her accent seemed thicker than usual.

"Scarcely a month ago." Lord Philip had ceased to regard Charlotte at all by now. His voice dropped a register. "I have missed it immensely since I left, its culture and its people."

Lucia nodded languidly, displaying the arch of her neck. "As have I. It was my home for almost twenty years, but you see I have ventured forth in pursuit of English adventure."

"Excellent notion," said Philip. "I trust you have found one?"

Lucia sighed. "Alas, no. I believed so, but found I was mistaken. If not for dear Charlotte, I would have withered away to nothing from boredom by now."

"That," declared Philip, "we cannot have. Come, let us discuss the sorts of entertainments that might suit you." He offered his arm, and Lucia slid her hand the entire length of it before nestling her fingers in the crook of his elbow.

"How very kind of you, my lord," she purred. Philip laughed softly, bending his head near to hers to reply in a manner that left no doubt of his intentions.

Charlotte turned away as they drifted off, absorbed in each other, her eyes tearing with suppressed laughter. It appeared Lucia had found her muse, at long last. She would have to find a better pianoforte.

"How old is he?" she whispered to Stuart as he drew her away.

"Five-and-twenty," said Stuart with a wicked grin. "He's got five good years left." Charlotte choked, then burst out laughing, clinging to his arm. He laughed with her, reveling in the sound. He would have to make her laugh more, he thought. With a quick glance around to make sure they were unneeded, he whisked her out of the house to the garden, to a bench almost hidden in the sprawling hedge.

He told her many things Terrance had told him, about her father and about his. Some things he left out; he was still trying to absorb them himself. He would have a lifetime to tell her everything, after all.

It was still unbelievable to him, that she would be there every day.

"And he's restored my income," Stuart finished. "So all your worries about marrying a penniless beggar can be put to rest."

"Oh, Stuart." She smiled and shook her head. "And you can keep Oakwood Park now."

He nodded. "Yes. Or we could live at Honeyfield until Susan marries. By then the house at Oakwood may be livable again."

She squeezed his hand. "What relief you must feel, not just about that but about everything."

He looked over the garden. Susan was tossing a stick for Amelia's terrier, actually smiling as the little dog raced in circles around her. Philip and Lucia had followed them and were deep in conversation near the house. "Everyone is safe and happy, and that is a great relief. Even Terrance may find himself more at ease, now he has discovered someone loved him all along. I cannot blame him for being bitter; all his life has been a sacrifice to atone for someone else's sins."

"At least he did not discover it too late."

He turned to her. "And you? Are you comforted to learn your father regretted sending you away?"

She heaved a pensive sigh. "I suppose. It seems his regret came later than it should have, but I shan't dwell on it. What's done is done."

"Which only leaves us to decide what will be done," he said, lifting her into his lap. "When do you wish to be married? Where do you wish to live? And do you think anyone would notice if I kissed you here and now?"

"Damn their eyes if they do." She kissed him, long and sweet, and then rested her head on his shoulder.

"So. Susan has returned, sadder and wiser but unharmed. Your father has realized he misjudged you and treated you unfairly, and your mother will no longer be caught between the two of you. Lucia has a new muse, for five years or so, which means she'll be staying in London to put Marcella Rescati in her place. And I have a priceless Italian treasure that does not rightly belong to me, and enough worthless statuary and paintings to fill a museum, which—sadly enough—are all mine. All in all, an excellent day's work."

"And me," he said. "Don't forget me. I'm slightly less worthless than your statuary now."

"I would never forget you," she said softly, winding her arms around his neck. "I have you to fill my heart."

Author's Note

In painting the fresco of the Battle of Anghiari, Leonardo da Vinci attempted to replicate a technique he had read about in the writings of Pliny. Unfortunately, it was not suitable for use on walls, a point Leonardo either overlooked or ignored, and the paint did simply run down the walls; what little remained of the painting crumbled away within a few years. Eventually the magistrati commissioned Giorgio Vasari to paint the wall, and all that was left of Leonardo's work was a small collection of studies and some copies made by others, most notably *The Battle of the Standard* by Peter Paul Rubens. In 1976 the wall was examined with ultrasound, but no traces of Leonardo's painting were ever found.